TO SEE NO EVIL

Inside the tent, Sharbaraz made a noise. It wasn't a word, nor yet a cry; it wasn't a noise quite like any Abivard had heard. He ducked through the entry flap, even as the camp bed inside went over with a crash.

Sharbaraz was thrashing on the floor, wrestling with something he could see and Abivard could not. Abivard sprang to his aid. Guided by the motions of Sharbaraz's grasping hands, he tried to pull away the King of Kings' foe, even though that foe was invisible to him. But his hands passed through the space between himself and Sharbaraz as if that space held only the empty air his eyes perceived.

The same was manifestly not true for Sharbaraz. He writhed and twisted and kicked and punched, and when his blows landed, they sounded as if they struck flesh.

"By the God," Abivard cried, "what is this madness?"

By Harry Turtledove
Published by Ballantine Books:

The Videssos Cycle:
  THE MISPLACED LEGION
  AN EMPEROR FOR THE LEGION
  THE LEGION OF VIDESSOS
  SWORDS OF THE LEGION

The Tale of Krispos:
  KRISPOS RISING
  KRISPOS OF VIDESSOS
  KRISPOS THE EMPEROR

The Time of Troubles:
  THE STOLEN THRONE

EARTHGRIP
DEPARTURES
THE GUNS OF THE SOUTH

WORLDWAR: IN THE BALANCE
WORLDWAR: TILTING THE BALANCE

THE STOLEN THRONE

Book One of
The Time of Troubles

Harry Turtledove

A Del Rey® Book
BALLANTINE BOOKS • NEW YORK

A Del Rey® Book
Published by Ballantine Books

Library of Congress Catalog Card Number: 95-92018

ISBN 0-345-38047-9

Map by Christine Levis

Manufactured in the United States of America

First Edition: July 1995

10 9 8 7 6 5 4 3 2 1

To the Redlines, father and son.

AUTHOR'S NOTE

The events chronicled in the three books of *The Time of Troubles* begin about 150 years before those described in *The Tale of Krispos* and thus about 650 years before those of *The Videssos Cycle*.

I

FROM THE BATTLEMENTS OF THE STRONGHOLD, ABIVARD LOOKED north across the broad sweep of land his father, Godarz, held in the name of the King of Kings. Out beyond the village that surrounded the stronghold, most of what he saw was sere and brown from high summer; only near the Vek Rud River, and in the gardens nourished by the underground channels called *qanats*, did green defy the blazing sun.

Off to the east, the Videssians, Makuran's longtime foes, gave reverence to the sun as a symbol of their god. To Abivard, the sun was too unreliable for worship, roasting the highland plateau of Makuran in summertime and then all but disappearing during the short, cold days of winter.

He raised his left hand in a gesture of benediction familiar to his folk. In any case, the Videssian god was false. He was as certain of that as of his own name. *The* God had spoken to the Makuraners through the Prophets Four: Narseh, Gimillu, the lady Shivini, and Fraortish, eldest of all.

"Whom are you blessing there, son?" a gruff, raspy voice asked from behind him.

Abivard whirled. "I greet you, Father. I'm sorry; I didn't hear you come up."

"No harm, no harm." Godarz let loose a few syllables of laughter, as if he held only so much and didn't want to use it all up at once. Abivard sometimes thought his father was a mold into which he himself had been pressed not quite hard enough. They had the same long, rectangular faces; the same proud noses; the same dark, hooded eyes under thick brows; the same

1

swarthy skin and black hair; even, these past five years or so, the same full beards.

But Abivard's face still lacked the lines of character the years had etched across Godarz's features. The creases in his cheeks told of laughter and sorrow, the furrows in his forehead of thought. By comparison, Abivard seemed to himself a house not yet lived in to the fullest.

There was one furrow the years had not put in Godarz's face: the scar that seamed his left cheek came from the shamshir of a Khamorth raider. That mark vanished under his beard but, like a *qanat* traced by the greenery above it, a line of white hair showed its track. Abivard envied him that mark, too.

"Whom were you blessing?" Godarz asked again.

"No one in particular, Father," Abivard said. "I thought of the Four, so of course I made their sign."

"Good lad, good lad." Godarz was in the habit of repeating himself. Abivard's mother, Burzoe, and the *dihqan*'s other wives teased him about it all the time. He always took it good-naturedly; once he had cracked, "The lot of you would be less happy if I hadn't cared to repeat my vows."

Abivard said, "If I asked the Four to ask the God to bless any part of this domain in particular, I suppose I should ask his favor for the flocks."

"You couldn't do better." Godarz thumped Abivard fondly on the shoulder. "We'd be poor—thieving nomads take *poor*, son; we'd be *dead*—without 'em."

"I know." Away from the river, away from the *qanats*, the land was too dry to support crops most years. That was true of most of the highland plateau. After the spring rains, though, grass and low shrubs carpeted the hills and valleys. Enough of the hardy plants lived on through the rest of the year to give fodder for sheep and cattle, horses, and camels. From those the *dihqans*—the lesser nobility—and all who depended on them made their livelihoods.

Godarz scratched at the puckered scar; though it was years old, it still sometimes itched. He said, "While you're about your prayers, you might do as I've done and beg the Four to give us another year of peace along the northern frontier. Maybe they'll harken to the two of us together; maybe they will." His expression grew harsh. "Or maybe they won't."

Abivard clicked his tongue between his teeth. "It's as bad as that?"

"Aye, it is," Godarz said. "I was out riding this morning, giv-

ing the new gelding some work, and I met a rider homeward
bound toward Mashiz from the Degird River. The Khamorth are
stirring again, he says."

"A messenger from the King of Kings?" Abivard said. "Why
didn't you invite him to refresh himself at the stronghold?" *Then
I'd have had a chance to talk with him, too, instead of getting
my news secondhand,* he thought.

"I did, son, I did, but he said me nay," Godarz answered.
"Said he grudged the time; he'd stop to rest only at night. The
news for Peroz King of Kings was that urgent, he said, and
when he gave it me, I could but bob my head up and down and
wish him the God's protection on his road."

"Well?" Abivard practically hopped with impatience and excitement. Concern rode his voice, as well; not too many farsangs
east of Godarz's domain, the little Vek Rud bent north and
flowed into the Degird. The frontier and the steppe nomads who
dwelt beyond it were close, close.

"He learned why the tribes are stirring," Godarz said porten-
tously. After another pause that almost drove Abivard mad, the
dihqan went on, "The tribes are stirring because, by the Four,
Videssos is stirring them."

"Here?" Abivard exclaimed. "How could that be?"

Godarz's face went harsh; his scar, normally darker than the
rest of his skin, turned pale: rage. But he held his voice under
tight control. "The Pardrayan plain runs east almost forever.
Videssos could send an embassy across it—not quickly, but it
could. And, by all the signs, it has. The God, for reasons best
known to Himself, has made Videssos rich in gold."

Abivard nodded. His father's treasure horde had more than a
few fine Videssian goldpieces in it. Every nation in the world
took those goldpieces and was glad to have them. The corruption and deviousness of the Empire of Videssos were bywords in
Makuran, but the imperials kept their coinage honest. No matter
which Avtokrator's face graced a coin's obverse, it would be
pure gold, minted at seventy-two to the pound.

Makuran coined mostly in silver. Its arkets were good money,
but money changers always took a premium above their face
value when exchanging them for Videssian gold.

"I see I've no need to draw you a picture in the sand, no need
at all," Godarz went on. "The cowardly men of the east, not
having the kidneys to fight us as warriors against warriors, bribe
the nomads to do their work for them."

"They are no fit warriors, then—they're no better than assassins," Abivard said hotly. "Surely the God will open a pit beneath their feet and drop them into the Void, to be nothing forevermore."

"May it be so." Godarz's left hand twisted in a gesture different from the one Abivard had used: one that condemned the wicked. The *dihqan* added, "Vicious dogs that they are, they know no caste."

Abivard copied the sign his father had used. To his way of thinking, Godarz could have pronounced no curse more deadly. Life in Makuran pivoted on its five castes: the King of Kings and the royal household; the priests and the Seven Clans of the high nobility; the lesser nobles like Godarz—Makuran's backbone, they called themselves; the merchants; and the peasants and herders who made up the bulk of the populace.

The Seven Clans and the *dihqans* fought for the King of Kings, sometimes under his own banner, sometimes under one of the high nobles. Abivard could no more imagine paying someone so he could evade that duty than he could think of taking a knife and cutting off his manhood. He would lose it no more one way than the other.

Well, if the Videssians were hucksters even at war, the nobles of the plateau would surely teach the nomads they had bought where true honor lay. Abivard said as much, loudly.

That brought back his father's smile. Godarz thumped him on the back and said, "When the red banner of war returns from Mashiz, blood of my blood, I think it likely you will ride with me against those who would despoil us."

"Yes," Abivard said, and then again, in a great shout: *"Yes!"* He had trained for war since he was a boy who barely reached Godarz's chest. He had learned to ride, to thrust with the lance, to bear the weight of armor, to wield a scimitar, to wield the bow.

But Makuran had been unwontedly peaceful of late. His lessons remained lessons only. Now at last he would have the chance to apply them against a real foe, and one who needed beating. If the nomads swarmed south over the Degird, as they had a way of doing every generation or two, they would kill, they would steal, and worst of all they would wreck *qanats* so people would go hungry until the underground channels were laboriously repaired.

Godarz's laugh was the small, happy one of a man well pleased with his son. "I can see you want to get into your mail shirt and clap on your helmet this very moment. It's a long way to Mashiz and back—we shan't be riding out tomorrow, or next week, either. Even after the red banner warns of war, it will be a while yet before the army reaches us and we join its ranks."

Abivard shifted restively from foot to foot. "Why doesn't the King of Kings have his palace in Makuran proper, not on the far side of the Dilbat Mountains overlooking the Thousand Cities?"

"Three reasons," Godarz said, sounding like a pedagogue though Abivard had only been venting spleen. "First, we of Makuran are most likely to be loyal to our lord, being of his blood, and hence require less oversight. Second, the land between the Tutub and the Tib, above which Mashiz sits, is full of riches: not just the famous Thousand Cities but also farmlands more fertile than any the plateau boasts. And third, Mashiz is a hundred farsangs closer to Videssos than the plateau, and Videssos is more important to us most times than our northwestern frontier."

"Most times, aye, but not today," Abivard said.

"No, today the Khamorth tribes are stirring, or so it's said," Godarz agreed. "But who set them in motion? Not their own chieftains."

"Videssos," Abivard said.

"Aye, Videssos. We are her great rival, as she is ours. One day, I think, only one of us will be left standing," Godarz said.

"And that one will rule the world," Abivard said. In his mind's eye, he saw the King of Kings' lion banner floating above the Videssian Avtokrator's palace in Videssos the city, saw priests of the Prophets Four praising the God in the High Temple to false Phos.

The setting for the capital of Videssos remained blurry to him, though. He knew the sea surrounded it on three sides, and he had never seen a sea, not even the inland Mylasa Sea into which the Degird River flowed. He pictured a sea as something like one of the salt lakes that dotted the Makuraner plateau, but bigger. Still, his imagination could not quite grasp a body of water too vast to see across.

Godarz smiled. "You're thinking we shall be the one, aren't you? As do I, son, as do I. The God grant it be so."

"Yes," Abivard said. "I was also thinking—if we conquer, Father, I'll see the sea. The sea around Videssos the city, I mean."

"I understood you," Godarz said. "That would be a sight, wouldn't it? I've not seen it, either, you know. But don't expect the day to come in your time, though. Their border has marched with ours for eight hundred years now, since the Tharpiya hill-men ruled Makuran. They've not smashed us yet, nor we them. One day, though—"

The *dihqan* nodded, as if very sure that day would come. Then, with a last grin at his son, he went on down the walkway, his striped caftan flapping around his ankles, every so often bending down to make sure a piece of golden sandstone was securely in place.

Abivard stayed up on the walk a few minutes more, then went down the stairs that led to the stronghold's inner courtyard. The stairs were only a couple of paces wide and had no railing; had a brick shifted under his feet, he could have dashed out his brains on the rock-hard dirt below. The bricks did not shift. Godarz was as careful and thoroughgoing in inspecting as he was with everything else.

Down in the courtyard, the sun beat at Abivard with redoubled force, for it reflected from the walls as well as descending directly. His sandals scuffed up dust as he hurried toward the shaded living quarters.

The stronghold was a rough triangle, taking advantage of the shape of the rocky knob on which it sat. The short wall on the eastern side ran north and south; the other two, which ran toward each other from its bottom and top, were longer and went northwest and southwest, respectively. The living quarters were tucked into the corner of the eastern wall and the one that went northwest. That gave them more shadow than they would have had anywhere else.

Abivard took a long, happy breath as he passed through the iron-faced wooden door—the living quarters, of course, doubled as citadel. The thick stone walls made the quarters much cooler than the blazing oven of the courtyard. They were also much gloomier: the windows, being designed for defense as well as—and ahead of—vision, were mere slits, with heavy shutters that could be slammed together at a moment's notice. Abivard needed a small stretch of time for his eyes to adjust to dimness.

He stepped carefully until they did. The living quarters were a busy place. Along with servants of the stronghold bustling back and forth, he had to be alert for merchants and peasants who, failing to find his father, would press their troubles on him. Hearing those troubles was one of his duties, but not one he felt like facing right now.

He also had to keep an eye out for children on the floor. His two full brothers, Varaz and Frada, were men grown, and his sister Denak had long since retreated to the women's chambers.

But his half brothers ranged in age from Jahiz, who was older than Frada, down to a couple of brats who still sucked at their wet nurses' breasts. Half brothers—and half sisters under the age of twelve—brawled through the place, together with servants' children, shepherd boys, and whomever else they could drag into their games.

When they weren't in hot pursuit of dragons or evil enchanters or Khamorth bandits, they played Makuraners and Videssians. If Videssos had fallen as easily in reality as in their games, the domains of the King of Kings would have stretched east to the legendary Northern Sea centuries ago.

One of his half brothers, an eight-year-old named Parsuash, dodged around Abivard, thwarting another lad who pursued him. "Can't catch me, can't catch me!" Parsuash jeered. "See, I'm in my fortress and you can't catch me."

"Your fortress is going to the kitchens," Abivard said, and walked off. That gave Rodak, his other half brother, the chance to swoop down for the kill. Parsuash screeched in dismay.

In the kitchens, some flatbread just out of the oven lay cooling on its baking pan. Abivard tore off a chunk of it, then stuck slightly scorched fingers into his mouth. He walked over to a bubbling pot, used the piece of flatbread to scoop out some of the contents, and popped it into his mouth.

"Ground lamb balls and pomegranate seeds," he said happily after he swallowed. "I thought that was what I smelled. Father will be pleased—it's one of his favorites."

"And what would you have done had it been something else, son of the *dihqan*?" one of the cooks asked.

"Eaten it anyhow, I expect," Abivard answered. The cook laughed. Abivard went on, "Since it is what it is, though—" He tore off another piece of flatbread, then raided the pot again. The cook laughed louder.

Still chewing, Abivard left the kitchens and went down the hall that led to his own room. Since he was eldest son of Godarz's principal wife, he had finally got one to himself, which led to envious sighs from his brothers and half brothers. To him, privacy seemed a mixed blessing. He enjoyed having a small place to himself, but had been so long without one that sometimes he felt achingly alone and longed for the warm, squabbling companionship he had known before.

Halfway down the hall, his left sandal started flapping against his foot. He peered down and discovered he had lost the bronze buckle that held a strap around his ankle. He looked around and even got down on his hands and knees, but didn't find it.

"It probably fell into the Void," he muttered under his breath. Moving with an awkward half-skating motion, he made it to his doorway, went into his room, and put on a new pair of sandals.

Then he went out again, damaged sandal in hand. One of Godarz' rules—which, to his credit, he scrupulously followed himself—was that anything that broke had to be set right at once. "Let one thing slide and soon two'll be gone, two lead to four, and four—well, there had better not be four, there had better not," he would say.

Had just a bit of leather fallen off the sandal, Abivard could have gotten some from the stables and made his own rough repair. But to replace a buckle, he had to visit the cobbler in the village that surrounded the stronghold.

Out into the heat again, then. The sun smote him like a club. Sweat sprang out on his face, rolled down his back under his baggy garment. He wished he'd had farther to go; he wouldn't have felt foolish about getting on his horse. But if his father had seen him, he would have made sarcastic noises about Abivard's riding in a sedan chair next time, as if he were a high noble, not just a *dihqan*'s son. Abivard walked.

The gate guards pounded the butts of their spears against the hard ground as he went by. He dipped his head to return the salute. Then he left the stronghold and went into the village, an altogether different world.

Homes and shops straggled down to the base of the hill the stronghold topped and even for a little distance out onto the flat land below. Some were of stone, some of mud brick with widely overhanging thatched roofs to protect the walls from winter storms. Set beside the stronghold, they all seemed like toys.

The hill was steep, the streets winding and full of stones; if you tumbled, you were liable to end up at the bottom with a broken leg. Abivard had been navigating through town since he learned to toddle; he was as sure-footed as a mountain sheep.

Merchants cried their wares in the market square: chickpeas, dates, mutton buzzing with flies, utterances of the Prophets Four on parchment amulets—said to be sovereign against disease, both as prevention and cure; Abivard, whose education had included letters but not logic, failed to wonder why the second would be necessary if the first was efficacious. The calls rose from all around: knives, copper pots and clay ones, jewelry of glass beads and copper wire—those with finer stuff came to sell at the stronghold—and a hundred other things besides. The smells were as loud as the shouts.

A fellow was keeping a pot of baked quinces hot over a dung fire. Abivard haggled him down from five coppers to three; Godarz was not a man who let his sons grow up improvident. The quince *was* hot. Abivard quickly found a stick on the ground, poked it through the spicy fruit, and ate happily on his way down to the cobbler's shop.

The cobbler bowed low when Abivard came in; he was not near enough in rank to the *dihqan*'s son to present his cheek for a ceremonial kiss, as a couple of the richer merchants might have done. Abivard returned a precise nod and explained what he required.

"Yes, yes," the cobbler said. "Let me see the good sandal, pray, that I may match the buckle as close as may be."

"I'm afraid I didn't bring it." Abivard felt foolish and annoyed with himself. Though Godarz was back in the stronghold, he felt his father's eye on him. "I'll have to go back and get it."

"Oh, never mind that, your Excellency. Just come here and pick out the one that nearest suits it. They're no two of 'em just alike, anyhow." The cobbler showed him a bowl half full of brass buckles. They jingled as Abivard sorted through them till he found the one he wanted.

The cobbler's fingers deftly fixed it to the sandal. Deft as they were, though, they bore the scars of awl and knife and needle and nail. "No trade is simple," Godarz would say, "though some seem so to simple men." Abivard wondered how much pain the cobbler had gone through to learn his business.

He didn't dicker so hard with the cobbler as he had with the fruit seller. The man's family had been in the village for generations, serving villagers and *dihqans* alike. He deserved his superiors' support.

Sandal repaired, Abivard could have gone straight back to the stronghold to escape the worst of the heat in the living quarters. Instead, he returned to the bazaar in the marketplace and bought himself another quince. He stood there taking little bites of it and doing his best to seem as if he were thinking about the goods offered for sale. What he was really doing was watching the young women who went from this stall to that dealer in search of what they needed.

Women of the merchant and peasant castes lived under fewer restrictions than those of the nobility. Oh, a few wealthy merchants locked their wives and daughters away in emulation of their betters, but most lower-caste women had to go out and about in the world to help feed their families.

Abivard was betrothed to Roshnani, a daughter of Papak, the *dihqan* whose stronghold lay a few farsangs south and west of Godarz'. Their parents having judged the match advantageous, they were bound to each other before either of them reached puberty. Abivard had never seen his fiancée. He wouldn't, not till the day they were wed.

When he got the chance, then, he watched girls—the serving women in the stronghold, the girls in the village square here. When one caught his eye, he imagined Roshnani looked like her. When he spotted one he did not find fair, he hoped his betrothed did not resemble her.

He finished nibbling the quince and licked his fingers. He thought about buying yet another one; that would give him an excuse to hang around in the square awhile longer. But he was sensitive to his own dignity and, whenever he forgot to be, Godarz made sure his memory didn't slip for long.

All the same, he still didn't feel like going back to the stronghold. He snapped his slightly sticky fingers in inspiration. Godarz had given him all kinds of interesting news. Why not find out what old Tanshar the fortune-teller made of his future?

An additional inducement to this course was that Tanshar's house lay alongside the market square. Abivard could see that the old man's shutters were thrown wide open. He could go in, have his fortune read, and keep right on eying the women hereabouts, all without doing anything in the least undignified.

The door to Tanshar's house was on the side opposite the square. Like the shutters, it gaped wide, both to show the fortune-teller was open for business and to give him the benefit of whatever breeze the God chose to send.

One thing Tanshar certainly had not done: he had not used the prophetic gift to get rich. His home was astringently neat and clean, but furnished only with a much-battered low table and a couple of wickerwork chairs. Abivard had the idea that he wouldn't have bothered with those had he not needed to keep his clients comfortable.

Only scattered hairs in Tanshar's beard were still black, giving it the look of snow lightly streaked with soot. A cataract clouded the fortune-teller's left eye. The right one, though, still saw clearly. Tanshar bowed low. "Your presence honors my house, son of the *dihqan*." He waved Abivard to the less disreputable chair, pressed upon him a cup of wine and date cakes sweet with honey and topped by pistachios. Not until Abivard had eaten and drunk did Tanshar ask, "How may I serve you?"

Abivard explained what he had heard from Godarz, then asked, "How shall this news affect my life?"

"Here; let us learn if the God will vouchsafe an answer." Tanshar pulled his own chair close to Abivard's. He pulled up the left sleeve of his caftan, drew off a silver armlet probably worth as much as his house and everything in it put together. He held it out to Abivard. "Take hold of one side whilst I keep a grasp on the other. We shall see whether the Prophets Four grant me a momentary portion of their power."

Busts of the Four Prophets adorned the armlet: young Narseh, his beard barely sprouted; Gimillu the warrior, a strong face seamed with scars; Shivini, who looked like everyone's mother; and Fraortish, eldest of all, his eyes inset with gleaming jet. Though the silver band had just come from Tanshar's arm, it was cool, almost cold, to the touch.

The fortune-teller looked up at the thatched roof of his little cottage. Abivard's gaze followed Tanshar's. All he saw was straw, but he got the odd impression that Tanshar peered straight through the roof and up to the God's home on the far side of the sky.

"Let me see," Tanshar murmured. "May it please you, let me see." His eyes went wide and staring, his body stiffened. Abivard's left hand, the one that held the armlet, tingled as if it had suddenly fallen asleep. He looked down. A little golden light jumped back and forth from one Prophet's image to the next. At last it settled on Fraortish, eldest of all, making his un-blinking jet eyes seem for an instant alive as they stared back at Abivard.

In a rich, powerful voice nothing like his own, Tanshar said, "Son of the *dihqan*, I see a broad field that is not a field, a tower on a hill where honor shall be won and lost, and a silver shield shining across a narrow sea."

The light in the silver Fraortish's eyes faded. Tanshar slumped as he seemed to come back to himself. When Abivard judged the fortune-teller had fully returned to the world of rickety wicker chairs and the astounding range of smells from the ba-zaar, he asked, "What did that mean, what you just told me?"

Maybe Tanshar wasn't all the way back to the real world: his good eye looked as blank as the one that cataract clouded. "I have delivered the prophecy?" he asked, his voice small and un-certain.

"Yes, yes," Abivard said impatiently, repeating himself like his father. He gave Tanshar back the words he had uttered, doing his best to say them just as he had heard them.

The fortune-teller started to lean back in his chair, then thought better as it creaked and rustled under his weight. He took the armlet from Abivard and put it back on his parchment-skinned arm. That seemed to give him strength. Slowly he said, "Son of the *dihqan*, I remember nothing of this, nor did *I* speak to you. Someone—something—used me as an instrument." Despite the bake-oven heat, he shivered. "You will see I am no youth. In all my years of telling what might lay ahead, this has befallen me but twice before."

The little hairs prickled up on Abivard's arms and at the back of his neck. He felt caught up in something vastly bigger than he was. Cautiously he asked, "What happened those two times?"

"One was a skinny caravaneer, back around the time you were born," Tanshar said. "He was skinny because he was hungry. He told me I foresaw for him piles of silver and gems, and today he is rich in Mashiz."

"And the other?" Abivard asked.

For a moment, he didn't think Tanshar would answer. The fortune-teller's expression was directed inward, and he looked old, old. Then he said, "Once I was a lad myself, you know, a lad with a bride about to bear him his firstborn. She, too, asked me to look ahead."

So far as Abivard knew, Tanshar had always lived alone. "What did you see?" he asked, almost whispering.

"Nothing," Tanshar said. "I saw nothing." Again Abivard wondered if he would go on. At last he did: "She died in childbed four days later."

"The God give her peace." The words tasted empty in Abivard's mouth. He set a hand on Tanshar's bony knee. "Once for great good, once for great ill. And now me. What does your foretelling mean?"

"Son of the *dihqan*, I do not know," Tanshar answered. "I can say only that these things lie across your future. When and where and to what effect, I cannot guess and shall not lie to claim I can. You will discover them, or they you, as the God chooses to unwind the substance of the world."

Abivard took out three silver arkets and pressed them into the fortune-teller's hand. Tanshar rang them against one another, then shook his head and gave them back. "Offer these to the God, if that please you, but not to me. I did not speak these words, whether they came through me or not. I cannot accept your coin for them."

"Keep them, please," Abivard said, looking around the clean but barren little house. "To my mind, you stand more in need of them than the God."

But Tanshar again shook his head and refused to take the money. "They are not for me, I tell you. Had I read your future in the ordinary way, gauging what was to come by the motions of the Prophets' armlet between your hand and mine, I should be glad of the fee, for then I had earned it. For this—no."

One of the things Godarz had taught Abivard was to recognize a man's stubbornness and to know when to yield to it. "Let it be as you say, then." Abivard flung the arkets out the window. "Where they go now, and with whom, is in the God's hands."

Tanshar nodded. "That was well done. May the foretelling you heard through me mean only good for you."

"May it be so," Abivard said. When he rose from the chair, he bowed low to Tanshar, as he might have to one of the upper nobility. That seemed to distress the fortune-teller even more than the prophecy that had escaped its usual bounds. "Accept the salute, at least, for the God," Abivard told him, and, reluctantly, he did.

Abivard left the fortune-teller's house. He had thought to linger in the bazaar awhile longer, buying more small things he didn't really need so he could look at, maybe even talk with, the young women there. Not now, though.

He peered out over the sun-scorched land that ran out toward the Vek Rud River. Nothing much grew on it now, not at this season. Did that make it a broad field that was not a field? Prophecy had one problem: how to interpret it.

He turned and looked up the slope of the hill on which the stronghold perched. Was it the tower where honor would be won and lost? It didn't look like a tower to him, but who could judge how the God perceived things?

And what of the sea? Did Tanshar's words mean he would see it one day, as he hoped? Which sea had the fortune-teller meant? Who would shine a silver shield across it?

All questions—no answers. He wondered if he would have been happier with an ordinary foretelling. No, he decided. If nothing else, this surely meant he would be bound up in great events. "I don't want to watch my life slide by while I do nothing but count the days," he said aloud.

For all his father's teaching, he was still young.

* * *

In the days and weeks that followed, Abivard took to looking south and west from the walls. He knew what he was waiting to see. So did Godarz, who teased him about it every so often. But the *dihqan* spent a good deal of time at the corner where the eastern and the south-facing walls met, too.

Abivard felt justified in haunting that corner when he spied the rider approaching the stronghold. The horseman carried something out of the ordinary in his right hand. At first, Abivard saw only the wriggling motion. Then he recognized that a banner was making it. And then he saw the banner was red.

He let out a whoop that made heads turn his way all around the stronghold. "The war banner!" he cried. "The war banner comes forth from Mashiz!"

He didn't know where Godarz had been, but his father stood on the wall beside him in less than a minute. The *dihqan* also peered south. "Aye, that is the war banner, and no mistake," he said. "Let's go down and greet the messenger, shall we? Let's go."

The horseman who carried the token of war was worn and dusty. Godarz greeted him with all the proper courtesies, pressing wine and honey cakes on him before inquiring of his business. That question, though, was but a formality. The crimson banner, limp now that the messenger no longer rode at a fast trot, spoke for itself.

Still, Makuran was built on formality, and, just as Godarz had to ask the question, the messenger had to answer it. He raised the banner so the red silk fluttered again for a moment on its staff, then said, "Peroz King of Kings, having declared it the duty of every man of Makuran entitled to bear arms to band together to punish the Khamorth savages of the steppe for the depredations they have inflicted on his realm and for the connivance with Videssos the great enemy, now commands each high noble and *dihqan* to gather a suitable force to be joined to Peroz King of Kings' own armament, which shall progress toward and across the river Degird for the purpose of administering the aforesaid punishment."

Getting all that out in one breath was hard, thirsty work; when the messenger had finished, he took a long pull at the wine, then let out an even longer—and happier—sigh. Then he drank again.

Ever courteous, Godarz waited till he was comfortable before asking, "When will the armament of the King of Kings—may his years be many and his realm increase—reach the river Degird, pray?"

In effect, he was asking when it would reach the stronghold, which lay only a couple of days' journey south of the frontier. He was also asking—with perfect discretion—how serious the King of Kings was about going on campaign: the slower he and his army traveled, the less they were likely to accomplish.

The messenger answered, "Peroz King of Kings began mustering his forces the day news of the plainsmen's insolence reached him. The red banner began its journey through the land that same day. The army should reach this neighborhood inside the month."

Abivard blinked to hear that. Godarz didn't, but he might as well have. "He is serious," the *dihqan* murmured. "Serious."

The word ran through the courtyard. Men's heads—swarthy, long-faced, bearded: basically cut from the same cloth as Godarz and Abivard—solemnly bobbed up and down. The King of Kings of Makuran had great power, and most often wielded it with ponderousness to match.

"Peroz King of Kings *does* want to punish the steppe nomads," Abivard said. He got more nods for that, from his father among others. Excitement blazed in him. He'd been a boy the last time the King of Kings—it had been Valash then, Peroz's father—campaigned against the Khamorth. He still remembered the glorious look of the army as it had fared north, bright with banners. Godarz had gone with it and come back with a bloody flux, recalling that took some shine off the remembered glory.

But still . . . *This time*, he thought, *I'll ride with them.*

Godarz asked the messenger, "Will you lay over with us tonight? We'll feast you as best we can, for your own sake and for the news you bring. We on the frontier know the danger from the plainsmen; we know it well." One hand went to the scar he bore; a forefinger tracked the white streak in his beard.

"The *dihqan* is gracious," the messenger replied, but he shook his head. "I fear I cannot take advantage of your generosity. I have far to travel yet today; all the domains must hear the proclamation of the King of Kings, and time, you will have gathered, is short."

"So it is," Godarz said. "So it is." He turned to one of the cooks, who stood in the courtyard with everyone else. "Go back to the kitchens, Sakkiz. Fetch pocket bread stuffed with smoked mutton and onions, aye, and a skin of good wine, as well. Let no man say we sent the mouth of the King of Kings away hungry."

"The *dihqan* is gracious," the messenger said, now sincerely rather than out of formal politeness. He had meant what he had said about his journey's being urgent: no sooner had Sakkiz brought him the food and wine than he was on his way again, urging his horse up into a trot. He held the war banner high, so it fluttered with the breeze of his motion.

Abivard had eyes only for the crimson banner until a bend in the road took it behind some of the village houses and out of sight. Then, as if awakening from a dream, he glanced toward his father.

Godarz had been looking at him, too. Abivard had trouble reading the expression on his face. The *dihqan* gestured to him. "Here, step aside with me. We have things to talk about, you and I."

Abivard stepped aside with Godarz. The folk of the stronghold stood back and gave them room to talk privately. Makuraners were a polite folk. Had they been Videssians, they probably would have crowded forward to hear better. So tales from the east said, at any rate. Abivard had never set eyes on a Videssian in his life.

"I suppose you expect to come with me on this campaign," Godarz said. "I suppose you do."

"Yes, Father. You said I would." Abivard gave Godarz an appalled stare. Could his father have been thinking of leaving him behind? How could he hope to hold his head up in the stronghold, in the village, if he was judged not enough of a man to fight to defend the domain?

"I can ill spare you here, son," Godarz said heavily. "The God only knows what would befall this place if one of us, at least, did not have his eyes on it."

Hearing that, Abivard felt his heart drop into his sandals. If his father didn't let him go, he would . . . He didn't know what he would do. He needed a gesture full of grand despair but couldn't think of one. What he felt like doing was bursting into tears, but that would only humiliate him further.

Godarz chuckled at his expression. "No need to look like that. I am taking you along, never fear—what I say I will do, I do. You should get a taste of war while you're still young."

"Thank you, Father!" Now Abivard wanted to caper like a colt. His heart returned to its proper place in his chest and began pounding loudly to remind him it was there. Of itself, his hand made slashing motions through the air, as if he were hacking a steppe nomad out of the saddle.

"The God grant you thank me after we come home once more," Godarz said. "Aye, the God grant that. One reason I want you to go to war, lad, is so you'll see it's not all the glory of which the pandoura players sing. It's a needful business at times, that it is, needful, but maiming and killing are never to be taken lightly, no matter how much they're needed. That's what I want you to see: there's nothing glorious about a man with his guts spilled out on the ground trying to slit his own throat because he hurts too bad to want to go on living."

The image was vivid enough to give Abivard a moment's pause. He knew you could die in battle. When he thought of that, though, he thought of an arrow in the chest, a moment's pain, and then eternity in the loving company of the God. A long, tormented end had never crossed his mind. Even now, he could not make himself believe it, not below the very surface of his mind.

"You think it can't happen," Godarz said, as if reading his thoughts. Abivard didn't answer. His father went on, "I see you think it can't happen. That is one of the reasons I want to take you to war: to show you it can. You'll be a better man for knowing that."

"Better how?" Abivard asked. What could an intimate acquaintance with war and brutality give him that he didn't already have?

"Better because you won't take war lightly," Godarz answered. "Men who don't know it have a way of getting into it too easily, before they think carefully on whether it answers their need. They kill themselves off that way, of course, but they also kill off too many excellent retainers bound to them by kinship and loyalty. When your day here comes, son, I'd not have you be that kind of *dihqan*."

"As you say." Abivard's voice was sober: Godarz's seriousness impressed him. He was a few years past the age when he would think anything his father said wrong, merely because his father said it. His brother Frada and some of his older half brothers were still caught up in that foolishness. Having come through it, Abivard had concluded that his father generally had a good idea of what he was talking about, even if he did repeat himself.

Godarz said, "I don't forget it's your first time, either. I just want you to go into it with your wits about you. Remember your first girl, all these years ago? You weren't the same afterward. You won't be the same after this, either, but it's not as much fun as your first woman, not unless you have a taste for butchery. I don't see that in you, no, I don't."

Abivard didn't see it in himself, either, nor did he look very hard. He remembered how exalted he had felt after he left a bit of silver at a certain widow's house down in the village. If he felt that way after a battle . . . Godarz's last few sentences undermined the lesson he had tried to get across.

Godarz ceremoniously inserted a long bronze key into the lock that held the door to the women's quarters of the stronghold sealed. He turned the key. Nothing happened. He scowled, pulled out the key, glowered at it, and inserted it once more. This time Abivard heard a satisfying click when the *dihqan* turned it. He raised the bar and pushed open the door.

A sigh ran through the men who gathered together at a respectful distance down the hallway. Abivard tried to remember the last time his female relatives and Godarz' secondary wives came forth from their seclusion. It had been years; he knew that.

As was her right, Burzoe led them. Abivard's mother had to be close to Godarz in age, but did not show her years. Her wavy hair remained black, with none of the suspicious sheen that would have pointed to the dyepot. Her face was a little broader than the Makuraner norm, and fairer, through being secluded and seldom getting the chance to go out into the sun kept well-bred women paler than their toiling sisters.

Burzoe walked out into the courtyard with a queen's pride. Behind her, another coin stamped from the same die, came Abivard's sister Denak. She grinned when she saw him, and stuck out her tongue. They had been born hardly more than a year apart, and stayed almost as close as twins until she became a woman and had to withdraw from the eyes of the world.

After Denak came the parade of Godarz's secondary wives and those of their daughters old enough to have gone into seclusion. The last couple of wives were no older than some of the daughters. Had it not been for the set order in which they came forth, Abivard would not have known into which group they fell.

The sun flashed from gold bracelets and rings, from rubies and topazes, as Burzoe raised her right hand to show she was about to speak. Silence at once fell over the courtyard. The *dihqan*'s principal wife rarely appeared in public; she was, after all, a respectable Makuraner matron. But she was also a person of great consequence in the stronghold. Her body might be confined to the women's quarters, but through Godarz her influence extended to every corner of the domain.

"My husband, my sons, their brothers go off now to war," she said. "The army of the King of Kings is nigh; they shall add their strength to his host so he can cross into the plainsmen's country and punish them for the harm they have done us and the greater harm they plan."

Also, Abivard thought, *the sooner we join the King of Kings' army and the sooner that host moves on toward the frontier, the sooner they stop eating our domain out of house and home.* His mother had a glint in her eye that said she was thinking the same thing, but it was not something she could say out loud.

Burzoe went on, "Our clan has won distinction on the field times beyond counting. I know the coming campaign will be yet another such time. I pray to the God that she grant all the sons of this house come home safe."

"May it be so," the women intoned together. To them, the God was a woman; to Abivard and those of his sex, a man.

"Come home safe from the broad field beyond the river," Burzoe said.

"Safe," the women chorused. For a moment, Abivard listened to his mother going on. Then his head whipped around to stare at her. Was it coincidence that she used that phrase to describe the steppe country north of the Degird? Tanshar had seen a broad field in Abivard's future, too, though he had not known where it lay.

"Go swiftly; return with victory," Burzoe said, her voice rising to a shout. Everyone in the courtyard, men and women together, cheered loudly.

Godarz walked over, embraced his principal wife, and kissed her on the lips. Then he hugged Denak and moved down the line of women, hugging and kissing his wives, hugging his daughters.

Abivard and his younger brother Varaz, both of whom would accompany the *dihqan* to the camp of the King of Kings, embraced Burzoe and Denak. So did Frada, though he was sick-jealous of his brothers because Godarz would not let him go fight.

A couple of Abivard's half brothers were also joining the King of Kings' host. They hugged their mothers and sisters, too, as did their siblings who would stay behind in the stronghold. When the *dihqan*'s women showed themselves in public, such greetings were permitted.

"As the wife of your father the *dihqan*, I tell the two of you to fight bravely, to make every warrior in the host admire your courage," Burzoe said to Abivard and Varaz. Her expression lost its sternness. "As your mother, I tell you both that every moment will seem like a year till you come back to me."

"We'll be back with victory, as you told us," Abivard answered. Beside him, Varaz nodded vigorously. His younger brother had something of the look of Burzoe, though his burgeoning beard helped hide that. He was wider through the shoulders than Abivard, a formidable wrestler and archer.

Denak said, "*I'm* wed to no *dihqan*, so I have no special pride to uphold. That means I can tell both of you to make sure you come back, and make sure Father does, too."

She spoke to both her brothers, but her eyes were chiefly on Abivard. He nodded solemnly. Though she had stayed behind the doors of the women's quarters since her courses began, some of the closeness she and Abivard had known as children still remained. He knew she chiefly relied on him to do what she had asked, and resolved not to fail her.

Varaz said, "They work gold well out on the plains. We'll bring back something new for the two of you to wear."

"I have gold," Burzoe said. "Even if I wanted more, I could get it easily enough. Sons, though, sons are few and precious. I would not exchange a one of them for all the gold in the world, let alone on the steppe."

Abivard hugged his mother again, so tightly that she let out a faint squeak. He said, "Have no fear, Mother. When the Khamorth see the armament we have brought against them, they will flee away in terror. More likely than not, our victory will be bloodless."

"May it be so, my son; may it be so," Burzoe said.

"Are you repeating yourself now?" Abivard asked her.

She smiled, looking almost as young as Denak beside her. But then she grew serious again, and time's mark showed in her concern. "War is seldom bloodless; I think you men would esteem its prizes less if they were more easily got. So I say again, take care." She raised her voice to speak to everyone, not just her sons: "Take care!"

As if that had been a signal—and so it may have been—Godarz's youngest and most recently married wife turned and walked slowly into the living quarters of the stronghold on her way back to the women's chambers. Behind her went the next most junior wife, then the next and her oldest daughter.

Denak squeezed Abivard's hands in hers. "It'll be my turn in a moment, mine and Mother's. Come back safe and soon. I love you."

"And I you, eldest sister. Everything will be all right; you'll see." Everyone was making such a fuss about coming home safe and avoiding disaster that he wanted to avert any possible bad omen.

As Denak had said, her turn to withdraw soon came. She and Burzoe walked with great dignity back toward the entrance to the living quarters. Godarz waited for them there, the key to the women's chambers in his right hand.

Burzoe said something to him, then, laughing, stood on tiptoe to brush his lips with hers. The *dihqan* laughed, too, and made as if to pat her on the backside. He stopped well before he completed the motion; had he gone through with it, the stronghold would have buzzed with scandal for weeks. That he even mimed it showed how close to the frontier his holding lay. Closer to Mashiz, manners were said to be more refined.

Denak went into the living quarters. A moment later, smiling still, so did Burzoe. Godarz followed them inside. After a couple of steps, they seemed to disappear into shadow. The doorway looked very dark and empty.

Abivard felt he had put on a bake oven, not his armor. Sweat ran down his face under the chainmail veil that hid his features from the eyes down. A similar mail hood attached to the rear of his tall, conical helmet protected the back of his neck and his shoulders.

And yet, compared to the rest of him, his head was well ventilated: the breeze could blow through the mail there and cool him a little. Under the leather backing for the rest of his armor, he wore cotton batting to keep a sword blow that iron might block from nonetheless breaking his bones.

Mail covered his rib cage, too; below it, two vertical rows of iron splints protected his belly and lower back. From the bottom of the lower splints depended a short mail skirt; his leather sleeves and trousers bore horizontal rings of laminated iron armor. So did his boots. Semicircular iron guards projected from the ends of his armored sleeves toward the backs of his hands; only his palms and fingers were free of armor.

His horse was armored, too, with a long scale-mail trapper open at the front and rear to let its legs move freely. A wrought-iron chamfron protected the animal's face. A ring at the top of the chamfron held several bright red streamers. A similar ring at the crown of his own helmet held others of the same shade.

He carried a stout lance in a boss on the right side of his saddle; a long, straight sword hung from his belt. The strength of Makuran lay in its heavy horse, armored to take punishment until they closed with the foe and gave it in return. Videssians fought mounted, too, but were more often archers than lancers. As for the steppe nomads . . .

"Half the plainsmen's way of fighting lies in running away," he said.

"That's so, but it's from necessity as well as fear," Godarz answered. The *dihqan* was armored much like his son, save that over his mail shirt he wore an iron plate bound to his breast with crisscross leather straps. He went on, "They ride ponies on the far side of the Degird: they haven't fodder enough to raise big horses like ours." He set an affectionate hand on the side of his gelding's neck, just behind the last strap that held the chamfron in place.

"We'll smash them, then, when we come together," Abivard said.

"Aye, if we can make them stand and fight. That's why they generally come to grief when they raid south of the Degird: we concentrate on them and force them to fight on our terms. Out on the steppe, it's not so easy—our army is like one dot of ink on a vast sheet of parchment."

The horses clattered out of the stronghold, Godarz first, then Abivard and Varaz, then their eldest half brother Jahiz, and then two other half brothers of different maternal lineages, Arshak and Uzav. Godarz' domain did not yield enough to support more than half a dozen fully armored riders. That made it a medium-sized fish in the pond that was Makuran.

The King of Kings' encampment had sprung up between the stronghold and the Vek Rud. Pointing to the sudden vast city of canvas and heavy silk, Abivard said, "*That* will be one dot of ink, Father? I cannot believe it."

Among the tents, men boiled like ants on spilled food. Some, maybe most, were warriors; the sun kept glinting off iron down there, although many soldiers, like Abivard and his kin, wore baggy caftans over their mail to keep themselves cooler. But along with the fighting men would be wagon drivers, cooks, merchants, body servants, and likely women as well, to keep Peroz King of Kings and his more prominent warriors happy of nights. More people milled in the camp than Abivard had imagined in Mashiz.

But Godarz laughed and said, "It's different on the far side of the Degird. You'll see, soon enough."

Abivard shook his head, disbelieving. Godarz laughed again. Varaz said, "I'm with you, brother mine. That's not an army; that's a country on the march."

Jahiz said, "Where are the villagers? I expected they'd cheer us on our way." Abivard had expected the same thing, but the narrow lanes were almost deserted. Getting a wave from a toothless old woman with a water jug balanced on her head was not the send-off he'd looked for.

"They have more important things to do than wave good-bye to us," Godarz said. "Everyone who's missing here is sure to be down at the camp, trying to squeeze arkets from the soldiers as if they were taking the seeds from a pomegranate. They won't have another chance at such riches for years to come, and they know it."

He sounded amused and pleased his subjects were making the most of their opportunity. Some *dihqans* would have turned a handsome profit themselves, by squeezing as much of their people's sudden wealth from them as they could. The motto Godarz had repeated until Abivard grew sick of hearing it was, *Take the fleece from the flock, not the hide.*

Down off the stronghold's knob rode Godarz and his five sons. Abivard's heart pounded nervously. All his life he had been something special, first son of the domain's *dihqan*. The nearer he got to the camp, the less that seemed to matter.

Banners marked the pavilions of the *marzbans* of the Seven Clans, who served as division commanders under Peroz King of Kings. Abivard's head went this way and that, searching for the woad-blue flags of Chishpish, in whose division he and his family were mustered. "There!" he exclaimed, pointing.

"Good for you, lad," Godarz said. "You spotted them before any of us. Well, I suppose we'd best go pay our respects to his High and Mightiness, eh?" He urged his horse forward with the pressure of his heels against its barrel.

Behind Abivard, Jahiz let out a half-strangled cough. Abivard was a little scandalized himself, although he had heard his father speak slightingly of the high nobility before. As far as Godarz was concerned, the *dihqans* were the most important caste of Makuran.

The camp sprawled across a vast stretch of ground, with no

order Abivard could see. Spotting Chishpish's banner from afar didn't mean he and his relatives could easily get to it. They had to pick their way around tents pitched at random and through groups of warriors and hangers-on intent on their own destinations.

At last, though, they stood before the entrance of the big silk pavilion. A pair of guards in armor fancier than Godarz's barred their way. "Who comes?" one of them asked as Godarz dismounted and tied his horse to a stake pounded into the rock-hard ground. The fellow spoke with a mincing southern accent, but Abivard would not have cared to have to fight him; he looked tougher than he sounded.

Godarz answered with flowery formality. "I am Godarz son of Abivard, *dihqan* of Vek Rud domain." He pointed back toward the stronghold. "I bring my five sons to kiss the feet of the *marzban* Chishpish, as we shall have the ineffable honor of fighting under his banner."

"If you fight as well as you speak, the *marzban* will be well served," the guard answered. Abivard sat up straight with pride. Godarz waved his hand to acknowledge the compliment, then turned to his sons. At his nod, they also got down from their horses and tethered them. The guard pulled up the tent flap, stuck his head in, and declared, "Godarz *dihqan* of Vek Rud and his sons."

"Let them enter," a voice from within said.

"Enter." The guard and his companion held the flaps apart so Godarz, Abivard, and the rest could easily pass within.

Abivard's first dazed thought was that Chishpish lived with more luxury in the field than Godarz did in his own stronghold. Light folding tables of fragrant sandalwood inlaid with ivory, silver bowls decorated in low relief and piled high with sweetmeats, a richly brocaded carpet that was to Abivard's mind far too fine to set on bare dirt, a small Videssian enamelwork icon of some Phos-worshiping holy man . . . it was as if the high noble had simply packed up his home and brought it with him on campaign.

He should have used the elephant for something more than its ivory, Abivard thought impolitely as he caught sight of his leader. *Riding, for instance.* Chishpish was heavy enough to strain any horse, that was certain. His flesh bulged against the fabric of his caftan, which sparkled with silver threads. His pilos, the bucket-shaped Makuraner headgear, had rings of bright colors broidered round it. He smelled of patchouli; the strong scent made Abivard want to sneeze.

For all his bulk, though, he had manners. He heaved himself to his feet and offered a cheek for Godarz and his sons to kiss. Not all high nobles would have conceded that a *dihqan* and his scions were but a little lower in rank than his own exalted self; Abivard had expected literally to have to kiss the *marzban*'s feet.

"I am sure you will fight bravely for the King of Kings, Godarz of the Vek Rud domain," Chishpish said. "Your sons are . . . ?"

"Abivard, Varaz, Jahiz, Arshak, and Uzav," Godarz answered.

The *marzban* repeated the names without a bobble, which impressed Abivard. The fat man did not look like a warrior—he looked more like two warriors—but he did not sound like a fool. Being Godarz's son, Abivard feared fools above all else.

Outside the tent, a trumpet blew a harsh fanfare. A herald bawled, "Eat dirt before the divine, the good, the pacific, the ancient Peroz, King of Kings, fortunate, pious, beneficent, to whom the God has given great fortune and great empire, giant of giants, formed in the image of the God. Eat dirt, for Peroz comes!" The fanfare blared out again, louder than before. Chishpish's guards flung the tent flap wide.

Abivard went down on his belly on Chishpish's fine carpet, his forehead pressed against the wool. His armor rattled and clanked as he prostrated himself. Around him, his siblings and father also went down into the posture of adoration. So did Chishpish, though his fat face reddened with the effort the sudden exertion cost him.

"Rise," Peroz said. Abivard's heart beat fast as he returned to his feet, not from having to stand while burdened with iron and leather but rather because he had never expected to encounter the King of Kings face to face.

Despite the herald's formal announcement, Peroz was not ancient, was not, in fact, much older than Godarz. His beard was mostly black; his mustaches, waxed stiff, stuck out like the horns of a bull. He wore his hair long, and bound with a fillet in back. His cheeks seemed unnaturally ruddy; after a moment, Abivard realized they were rouged.

"Chishpish of the Seven Clans, present to me these warriors whom I find in your tent," the King of Kings said.

"As your Majesty commands, so shall it be," Chishpish answered. "Here first we have the *dihqan* Godarz of Vek Rud domain, our present home. With him he brings the army his sons—" Again the high noble rattled off Abivard's name and the rest. His memory swallowed as much as his mouth—which, given his girth, was no mean feat.

"You are well equipped, and your sons, also," Peroz told Godarz. "Those are your horses outside the pavilion?" At Godarz's nod, Peroz went on, "Fine animals, as well. Makuran would be stronger if all domains contributed as yours does."

"Your Majesty is generous beyond my deserts," Godarz murmured. Abivard marveled that his father could speak at all; had the King of Kings addressed him, he was sure his tongue would have cloven to the roof of his mouth.

Peroz shook his head. "You are the generous one, offering yourself and your five stalwart sons that the kingdom may flourish. Which is your heir?"

"Abivard here," Godarz said, setting a hand on his eldest's armored shoulder.

"Abivard son of Godarz, look to your father as a symbol of loyalty," Peroz said.

"Aye, your Majesty; I do," Abivard said. He could talk, after all.

"Good," Peroz told him. "The God grant that you never need to put forth a like sacrifice. Should this campaign progress as I plan, that may come true. I aim to go straight at the nomads, force them to battle, and crush them like this." The King of Kings ground one fist against the palm of his other hand.

"May it be so, your Majesty," Abivard said—there, he had spoken twice now! All the same, he remembered what his father had said about the difficulties of fighting the plainsmen on their own ground. The wisdom of the King of Kings was an article of faith among Makuraners; the wisdom of Godarz, Abivard had seen with his own eyes and heard with his own ears.

Peroz turned back to Chishpish, whom he had truly come to see. "Chishpish of the Seven Clans, on you will fall much of the responsibility for bringing the Khatrishers to bay. Is all in readiness in that regard?"

"It is, your Majesty. We shall burn great swaths of steppeland, compelling the nomads either to face us or to lose their pasturage. Thousands of torches await in the wagons."

A torch, a bright one, flared inside Abivard's head. North of the Degird, the Khamorth lived by their flocks and herds. If those animals could not graze, the plainsmen would starve. They would have to fight to prevent that. He glanced over at Godarz. His father was slowly nodding. Abivard nodded, too, his faith in the wisdom of the King of Kings restored.

II

THE BROAD, MUDDY DEGIRD SEPARATED THE FARMS AND STRONG-
holds and towns of Makuran from the barbarians who lived on
the far bank. No permanent bridges spanned the stream; any
King of Kings who proposed erecting one would have had every
dihqan in the northwestern part of the realm rise in revolt
against him. The Khamorth managed to slip across the Degird
too often as things were—no point in giving them a highway.

But the grand army of Peroz King of Kings could not go over
the river by dribs and drabs. Nor could they wait for it to freeze
solid, as the nomads often did. With the barrier of the Degird
stretched out ahead of him, Abivard wondered how Peroz proposed to solve the problem.

Though he had yet to put his knowledge to much use,
Abivard knew how to fight. He had some idea how to go about
besieging a bandit's lair or other stronghold. Past that, his military knowledge stopped.

Over the next few days, it advanced several paces. The baggage train the army carried with it seemed preposterously large
to him—until the engineers who had made the journey from
Mashiz started driving two parallel rows of piles, about forty
feet apart, into the bed of the Degird toward the northern bank.

The upstream piles tilted in the direction of the current; the
downstream ones leaned against it. The engineers linked each
upstream-downstream pair with a crossbeam whose fit the force
of the current only improved as time went by.

Then the engineers ran trestles along each row of piles, from
the south side of the Degird to the north. Across the trestles
went planks, and over the planks poles and bundles of sticks.

27

The army advanced from Makuran onto the plains of Pardraya less than a week after it reached the Degird.

It did not cross the river unobserved. Abivard had watched the Khamorth, tiny as horseflies on the far shore, watching the bridge march toward them. When the engineers got close enough, the plainsmen shot at them. Soldiers advanced down the growing bridge to shoot back and keep the nomads at a distance. The engineers took to carrying big wicker shields. Arrows pierced a few men anyhow, but the bridge and the army advanced regardless.

The hooves of Abivard's horse drummed over the bridge when his turn came to cross. The horse didn't care for that, or for the vibration of the timbers that came up through its feet from the motion of other animals and wagons on the bridge. The beast laid back its ears and tried to rear; Abivard fought it back down.

"So this is Pardraya," he said when he was back on solid ground. "It doesn't look much different from the land by the stronghold."

"No *qanats*," Varaz said beside him. "No cropland at all, come to that."

His younger brother was right. Grass and bushes, yellow-brown from summer heat, stretched ahead as far as the eye could see: that sereness was what had reminded Abivard of home. But he had always thought of the Pardrayan plain as being flat as a griddle. That wasn't so: it had rises and dips just like any other land.

The undulations reminded him of the waves of the sea. That, in turn, reminded him of the prophecy Tanshar had given. But no one could call this sea narrow.

Peroz King of Kings left behind a good-size garrison to protect the bridge, the army's lifeline back to Makuran. As he watched the chosen warriors begin to set up their encampment, Abivard spared them a moment's pity. Poor fellows, they had come all this way only to be denied the chance to help crush the Khamorth.

The main body of the army moved north across the plains. When Abivard turned around for another look at the bridge guards, he found they had disappeared in the great cloud of dust kicked up by thousands of horses and hundreds of wagons. The dust made his eyes water and gritted in every fold of skin he had. When he spat, he spat brown.

He looked up into the sky. The sun, at least, was still visible;

the only clouds were the ones the army made. All the same, he said, "I wish it would rain."

Godarz' hand twisted in a gesture of aversion. "You don't know what you're saying, boy," he exclaimed. "A good downpour and all this turns to porridge, same as it does down by the stronghold. With one rider, it's a bloody nuisance. You try and get an army through it and you'll be weeks on a journey that should take days. Simple rule: dust is bad, mud is worse."

Abashed, Abivard said little after that till the army halted for the evening. He also realized that, if it rained, Peroz's plan to fire the plain would come to naught. Since he couldn't make himself be happy with the weather as it was but knew a change would be worse, he passed a discontented night.

Breakfast was hard rolls, dates preserved in honey, lamb sausage so salty and smoky it made Abivard's tongue want to shrivel up, and bad wine. After Varaz choked down his length of sausage, he made a dreadful face and said to Godarz, "You'd flog the cooks if they fed us like this back at the stronghold."

"I just might," Godarz said. "Aye, I just might." He finished his own sausage, then took a long swig of wine to wash away the taste. "But if we were going on a long journey, I'd flog them if they didn't pack us food like this. All of it will keep almost forever."

"The vermin can't stomach it, either," Abivard said. He meant it for a joke, and his siblings smiled, but Godarz nodded seriously, spoiling his fun.

The *dihqan* and his sons knocked down the tent they had shared, tied its wool panels and poles and their bedding aboard a packhorse, then armed themselves—each helping the others with clumsy catches—and rode north. One long, slow farsang followed another. Abivard's heart leapt once, when he spied a couple of bow-carrying men wearing only leather and mounted on unarmored horses, but they proved to be scouts riding in to report to their commanders.

"We can't all go rattling around in mail, or the Khamorth would ride rings around us and we'd never even know they were there," Godarz said. Abivard chewed on that and decided it made sense. The business of soldiering got more complicated every time he turned around.

The wind, what there was of it, came from the west. A little past noon, smoke and flames sprang up from the steppe, about half a farsang east of the army's line of travel. That was far enough to keep embers and smoke from spooking the warriors' horses, which moved on unconcerned. Trot, canter, walk, trot, canter, walk ... the slowly changing rhythm filled Abivard's body.

As the armament of Peroz King of Kings moved north over the Pardrayan plain, his men set more fires, or rather extended the length of the first one. Every sudden gust gladdened Abivard, for it meant the flames were spreading over more of the nomads' pasturage.

He pointed east. "They can't let us do that for long, or they'll soon start to starve."

"That's the idea," Jahiz said. His handsome face—his mother was famous for her beauty—creased in a leer of anticipation. He reached for his upthrust lance. "Then they have to come to us."

For the rest of that day, though, and most of the following one, the advancing warriors saw no sign of the Khamorth through whose territory they rode. But for the fire that burned alongside them, they might have been alone on the steppe.

Late the next afternoon, the scouts brought in sheep and cattle they had captured north of the main body of the King of Kings' force. Abivard cheered as loud as anyone when he saw the animals. "We won't have to eat that beastly sausage tonight," he said.

"So we won't, so we won't," Godarz said. "But that's not all these captures tell me. They say we're getting very close, very close, I tell you, to the nomads themselves. Their herds are their lives; if we come across the beasts, the men who follow them across the plains must be close by."

Abivard looked this way and that. He saw his relatives, his comrades, the steppe, the fires the men from Makuran had set. Of the nomads there was no sign. Yet they were out there somewhere—probably not far. His father was bound to be right about that. The idea made Abivard uneasy, as if someone were peeking at him through a crack in his door back at the stronghold.

He looked around again, this time concentrating on the thousands of armored men who had come north with him from Makuran, their equally well protected mounts, the clever engineers who had bridged the Degird, and all the other appurtenances of a great and civilized host. Against such might, how could the plainsmen prevail?

When he said that aloud, Godarz let out a wry chuckle. "That's why we come here, son—to find out." Abivard must have looked stricken, for the *dihqan* continued, "Don't take it like that, for that's not how I meant it. I've seen a few armies in my day, aye, just a few, and this one's stronger than all the rest. I don't know how we can lose once the Khamorth decide they have to face us."

That eased Abivard's mind. If his father couldn't see any way for the plainsmen to win, he was willing to believe no such way existed. He said, "The King of Kings, may his years be many and his realm increase, strikes me as a man who will deal a hard blow when the time comes."

"He strikes me the same way," Godarz said. "If the lion banner isn't at the fore when at last we clash with the Khamorth, I'll be greatly surprised. Although I know of him only by repute, I've heard his son Sharbaraz is another of the same sort. He'd be your age, more or less."

"I've not seen his banner here," Abivard said.

"Nor will you," Godarz answered. "Peroz, may his years be long, left him back in Mashiz, as I left Frada back at the stronghold. Our reasons were different, though. I just didn't think Frada quite ready, not quite. Sharbaraz is a man grown, and I expect the King of Kings wants him to keep the eunuchs and nobles in line while Peroz goes off on campaign."

"Surely they'd not take advantage when the King of Kings was away ..." Abivard faltered, very much aware of Godarz' cynical eye on him. He felt himself flush. "All right, maybe they would."

"No maybe to it, son, no maybe at all," Godarz said. "I just thank the God that's not something I have to worry about. I may be master of only a domain, not a realm, but I can rely on the people around me when my back is turned. In more ways than a few, I have the better half of that bargain."

"I think you do, too." Abivard could not imagine his father's servitors going against the *dihqan*'s wishes. He had heard tales of corruption emanating from Mashiz but hadn't believed them. To learn they had some substance was a jolt. He said, "It must be that they're too close to the Videssian border, Father."

"Aye, that may have somewhat to do with it," Godarz allowed. "I suspect they're too close to too much silver, as well. Having the coin you need to do what you must and a bit of what you like is pleasant, as wine can be. But a man who gets a rage for silver is as bad as one with a rage for wine, maybe worse. Aye, maybe worse."

Abivard chewed on that. He decided his father probably had

a point, and admitted as much by nodding before he asked, "When do you think the plainsmen will stand at bay?"

Godarz scratched at his scar while he thought it over. "They won't wait more than another couple of days," he said at last. "They can't, else we'll have burned too much of the plain. Their herds need broad fields on which to graze."

That phrase again! Abivard had heard it twice now since Tanshar gave him his strange prophecy. What it meant, though, he still could not say. He wondered when he would find out.

When two days had passed, Abivard was ready to reckon his father a better fortune-teller than Tanshar. The first Khamorth fighters appeared in front of the Makuraner host the morning after the two of them had spoken. They shot a few arrows that did nothing in particular, then galloped away faster than their armored foes could pursue.

Such archers as the Makuraners had rode out in front of the main force to protect it from the plainsmen's hit-and-run raids. The rest of the warriors shook themselves out into real battle lines rather than the loose order in which they had been traveling before.

Under his veil of iron, Abivard's teeth skinned back in a fierce grin of excitement—at any moment, he might find himself in action. He glanced over at Varaz. He couldn't see much of his brother's face, but Varaz's flashing eyes said he, too, was eager to get in there and fight.

Godarz, on the other hand, just kept riding along at an easy canter. For all the ferocity and passion he displayed, the nearest Khamorth might have been a thousand farsangs away. Abivard decided his father was an old man after all.

A couple of hours later, more plainsmen appeared off the left flank of the army and plied it with arrows. Makuraner horsemen thundered out against them, raising even more dust than the host normally kicked up. They drove the nomads away, then returned to their comrades once more. The whole army raised a cheer for them.

"By the God, I wish the left were our station," Abivard exclaimed. "They have the first glory of the campaign."

"Where?" Godarz asked. "In chasing after the Khamorth? I didn't see them kill any. Before long, the nomads will come back and prick at us some more. That's how warfare works out here on the steppe."

Before long, Godarz's foretelling was again fulfilled. Not only did the Khamorth return to shadow the army's flanks, they began showing themselves in greater numbers, both on the left and at the front. A couple of men were fetched back to the healers' wagons, one limp, the other writhing and shrieking.

Abivard shivered. "The last time I heard a noise like that was when the old cook—what was his name, Father?—spilled the great kettle of soup and scalded himself to death. I was still small; Denak told me she had nightmares about that for years."

"His name was Pishinah, and you're right, he cried most piteously." Godarz lifted his helm off his head to wipe away sweat with a kerchief. He looked worried. "More nomads dogging us than I'd have guessed."

"But that's what we want, isn't it: to make them fight?" Abivard said, puzzled.

"Oh, aye." His father laughed sheepishly. "I get suspicious when the plainsmen give us what we want, even if we are forcing it from them."

"You predicted this, though, just the other day," Abivard protested. "Why are you unhappy now that what you foretold has come true?"

"It's not coming true the way I thought it would," Godarz answered. "I expected we'd force the Khamorth to battle, that they'd be desperate and afraid. Their archers out there don't have the manner of desperate men; they're moving to a plan of their own." He shrugged; his chain mail rattled about him. "Or, of course, maybe I'm just seeing evil spirits behind every bush and under every flat stone."

Jahiz said, "Couldn't the scriers scent out what the nomads intend?"

Godarz spat on the ground. "That for what the scriers can do. If you've lost a ring back at the stronghold, lad, a scrier will help you find it. But when it has to do with fighting, no. For one thing, men's passions make magic unreliable—that's why love philtres work so seldom, by the bye—and war is a hot-blooded business. For another, the plainsmen's shamans are using magic of their own to try to blind us. And for a third, we have to be busy to make sure the demon worshipers don't spy out what *we're* about. War is for iron, son; iron, not magic."

"A good thing, too," Abivard said. "If war were a matter for sorcerers, no one else would have the chance to join in it."

"Is that a good thing?" Godarz said. "I wonder, I do wonder."

"Why did you join the King of Kings' host, then?" Abivard asked him.

"For duty's sake, and because Peroz King of Kings—may his years be many and his realm increase—so bade me," Godarz answered. "Would you have me cast aside my honor and that of our clan?"

"By the God, no," Abivard exclaimed. Though he let it drop there, he wished his father sounded more as if his heart were in the campaign Peroz had undertaken.

At the head of the King of Kings' force, horns screamed the call Abivard had awaited since the crossing of the Degird: *the foe's army in sight.* The Makuraners had been advancing in battle array since the plainsmen began to harass them, but a hum of excitement ran through them all the same. Soon now they would have the chance to punish the Khamorth for the pinpricks they had dared inflict on the King of Kings' men.

Abivard rode to the top of a low swell of ground. Sure enough, there were the nomads, perhaps half a farsang to the north. They had mustered in two groups, a relatively small one in front and a larger one some little distance farther away.

"I think I see their scheme," Godarz said. "They'll try to keep us in play with their advance party while the rest of them spread out and flank us. Won't work—we'll smash the little band before the big one can deploy." He sounded more cheerful than he had before.

"Shouldn't we be at them, Father?" Abivard demanded. Finally seeing the Khamorth there waiting to be assailed made him want to set spurs to his horse and charge on the instant.

But Godarz shook his head. "Too far, as yet. We'd meet them with our animals blown from going so far at the gallop. We'll close to not far out of bowshot and pound home from there."

As if to echo Godarz, Chishpish, who rode not far away, bellowed to the horsemen under his command. "Anyone who goes after the plainsmen before the horns signal shall answer to me personally."

Varaz chuckled. "That's no great threat. He'd never catch up with anyone who disobeyed." And indeed, Chishpish's horse was as heavyset as the *marzban* himself, as it had to be to bear his weight. But Chispish's threat, as every warrior who heard it knew full well, had nothing to do with physical chastisement. With the influence the high noble wielded, he could drop a man's reputation and hope for the future straight into the Void.

Abivard took his lance from its rest and hefted it in his hand. All through the ranks of the Makuraners, those iron-tipped lengths of wood were quivering as if a great wind swept through a forest. Abivard kept the lance upright, to avoid fouling his comrades; he would couch it only at the command.

Closer and closer the King of Kings' host drew to the foe. Peroz's banner fluttered ahead of Abivard; by Makuraner custom, he commanded from the right wing. The harsh war cries of the Khamorth floated faintly to Abivard's ears. He heard them without understanding; though the steppe tongue was cousin to his own, the plainsmen's shouts were so commingled that no separate words emerged from the din.

A horn cried, high and thin. As if with one voice, thousands of Makuraners hurled a battle cry back at the Khamorth: "Peroz!" Abivard yelled his throat raw, the better to terrify the enemy.

When the Makuraners closed nearly to within the range Godarz had specified, the small lead group of plainsmen spurred forward to meet them, screeching like wild things and shooting arrows into the massed armored ranks. A couple of lucky shots emptied saddles; a few more wrung cries of pain from men and horses. Most, as is the way of such things, either missed or were turned by the Makuraners' mail and plate and shields.

Just when Abivard wondered if the Khamorth would be mad enough to rush to close quarters with Peroz' vastly superior army, the nomads wheeled their little steppe ponies in a pretty piece of horsemanship and, almost in single file, galloped back toward their more distant comrades.

"Cowards!" Abivard screamed along with half the Makuraner host. "White-livered wretches, come back and fight!"

Beside him, Godarz said, "What *are* they doing?"

No one answered, for at that moment the horns rang out again, a call for which the whole host had waited: the charge. "Lower—lances!" Chishpish roared. The iron points glittered in the sun as they swung down to the horizontal. Even louder than before, Chishpish cried, "Forward!"

Already the banner of the King of Kings stood straight out from its staff as Peroz and his guards thundered toward the Khamorth. Abivard booted his own horse in the sides with iron-shod heels. Because the gelding was armored itself, it needed such strong signals to grasp what he required of it.

The ground flew by beneath him, slowly at first and then faster, fast enough for the wind of his passage to whip water from his eyes, fast enough for it to seem as if one more stride, one more bound, would propel him into the air in flight. The rumble of thousands, tens of thousands of hooves was like being caught in the middle of a thunderstorm. And thousands, tens of thousands of men charged with Abivard. He knew the great exaltation of being one small part of an enterprise vast and glorious. The God might have set a hand on his shoulder.

Then his horse stepped into a hole.

Maybe a rabbit had made it, maybe a badger. That didn't matter. What came of it did. Abivard felt the gelding stumble at the same instant he heard—amazingly distinct through the din around him—the bone break. Even as the horse screamed and fell, he kicked his feet out of the stirrups and threw himself clear.

He hit the ground with a crash and thud that made him glad for his mail. Even with it, he knew he would be a mass of bruises. His comrades thundered by; one horse sprang clean over him as he lay on the ground. How no one trampled him, he never knew.

He didn't care, either. Tears of mingled pain and frustration rolled down his cheeks. Here was what should have been the great moment of his life, ruined. Unhorsed, how could he close with the enemy and show his mettle? The answer was simple: he couldn't. His father and siblings would have the triumph all to themselves, and what about him? He would be the butt of jokes forever—Abivard, late for the fight.

The last Makuraners rode by, crying the name of the King of Kings. Abivard's horse cried, too, in anguish. He forced himself to his feet, staggered over to the thrashing animal, and cut its throat.

That done, he turned and started walking north—maybe, just maybe, the battle wouldn't be over when he got to it. Perhaps he could take the mount of someone who had fallen, or even ride a Khamorth steppe pony for a while, though it would not be pleased at supporting the weight of him and his armor.

Through swirling dust, he watched the proud banners that marked the front ranks of the Makuraner host. For a moment, he refused to believe his eyes when almost all of them went down at once.

The screams and shrieks of injured men and horses rose to the deaf, unfeeling sky. The men and horses themselves tumbled into the trench the Khamorth had dug across the plain and then cunningly concealed with sticks and dirt and grass. Only at the very center, where the nomads' advance party had withdrawn to their main force, could the Makuraners follow, and then in small numbers. Their foes set on them savagely, wolves tearing at a bear.

Abivard's shout of horror was drowned in the cries that went up from the overthrown Makuraner host. The King of Kings' banner was down. He could not see it anywhere. He moaned, deep in his throat. Nor were the frontmost ranks the only ones to fall in ruin. The warriors behind could not check their mounts in time and crashed into the ditch on top of its first victims.

"Father!" Abivard cried. Godarz was up there, somewhere in the middle of that catastrophe. So were Abivard's brother and half brothers. Clumsily, heavily he began to run in armor designed for fighting from horseback.

Even the Makuraners not caught by the plainsmen's ditch had to halt as best they could, any semblance of order lost. The Khamorth chose that moment to storm round both ends of the trench and begin to surround their foes.

"Not a broad field." Abivard groaned. "A trap!" Too late, the meaning of Tanshar's first vision came clear.

A trap it was. The Makuraners, the momentum of their charge killed, their ranks thrown into confusion, were easy meat for the nomads. At short range, horn-reinforced bows could punch their shafts through mail. Two plainsmen could set on a single armored warrior, assail him from so many directions at once that sooner or later—most often sooner—he had to fall.

Abivard found himself outside the killing zone, one of a handful of Makuraners who were. At first his only thought was to keep on clumping ahead and die with his family and countrymen. Then he saw that riderless horses, mostly Makuraner stock but the occasional steppe pony as well, were getting out through the nomads' cordon.

They'll round them up later, he thought. *For now they reckon the men more important.* Had he been a nomad chieftain, he would have made the same choice.

Seeing the horses made him start to think again, not run blindly toward his doom like a moth flying into a torch flame. He could all but hear Godarz inside his head: *Don't be foolish, boy, don't be foolish. Save what you can.* A mounted demigod would have had a battle on his hands, smashing through the plainsmen to rescue the trapped warriors of Makuran. The chance of one horseless young man in his first fight managing it wasn't worth thinking about.

Abivard tried again to guess—no, to *work out*; Godarz didn't approve of guessing—what the Khamorth chiefs would do once their riders had finished slaughtering the Makuraners. The answer came back quick and clear: they would plunder the baggage train. Not till then would they start scouring the steppe for survivors.

"Which means I'd best get out of here while I can," he said aloud. A riderless horse, a steppe pony, had paused to graze less than a furlong from where he stood. He walked slowly toward it. It looked up, wary, as he approached, but then lowered its head and went back to cropping dry, yellow grass.

In a pouch on his belt he had some dried apricots, treats he had intended to give his gelding after the battle was won. Now the battle was lost, and the gelding, too. He dug out three or four apricots, put them in the palm of his hand, and walked up to the steppe pony.

"Here you are, boy," he said coaxingly; the pony was entire, with stones big for the size of the rest of it. It made a snuffling noise, half suspicion, half interest. Abivard held out his hand. The horse sniffed the apricots, delicately tasted one. It snuffled again, this time sounding pleased, and ate the rest of the fruit.

After that, it let Abivard come around alongside it and did no more than lay back its ears when he mounted it. At his urging, it trotted off toward the south. He found the ride uncomfortable; like a lot of nomads, the Khamorth who had owned it kept his stirrup leathers very short so he could rise in the saddle to use his bow. Bowless, Abivard perforce rode with his legs bent up.

Evidently he wasn't the first or only Makuraner to escape the disaster to the north; when he came up to it, the baggage train was boiling like a stomped anthill. He kept on riding. He had intended to give the alarm: he couldn't have faced himself had he simply fled. But he did not aim to be caught in the new catastrophe sure to come soon.

He could feel by the steppe pony's gait that carrying his armored self was more than it could easily handle. He knew he would have to shed the iron as soon as he could. If the pony foundered before he got back to the Degird, he was a dead man.

Perhaps half an hour later, he looked over his shoulder. A new column of smoke was rising into the sky. The men of Makuran hadn't set this one. The Khamorth were having their revenge.

The one good thing Abivard saw there was that it meant the plainsmen would be too occupied with their looting to comb the plain for fugitives for a while. He wasn't the only Makuraner to have escaped from the overthrow of the King of Kings' host; scattered over the steppe in front, behind, and off to the sides were riders traveling singly or in small groups. Some would be men fleeing from the baggage train; others warriors like Abivard who met with mischance before the trap closed on them; others, perhaps, men who had broken out of the ring of death the no-mads had cast around the Makuraners.

Abivard thought hard about joining one of those small groups of retreating men from Makuran. In the end, he decided to keep clear and go his own way. For one thing, even all the fugitives he saw banded together lacked the numbers to stand up to the swarm of Khamorth who would soon be following. For another, bands traveling together were limited to the speed of their slow-est member. He wanted to get as far away from the disastrous field that was not a field as he could.

Shock still dazed him. He had lost his father and four siblings. Makuran had lost Peroz King of Kings and the flower of its manhood. The twin misfortunes echoed and reechoed inside his head, now one louder, now the other.

"What shall I do?" he moaned. "What will the kingdom do?"

Since he had no idea what the kingdom would do, he ended up concentrating on the first question. The first thing he had to do was get back over the bridge the King of Kings' engineers had thrown across the Degird. If he couldn't do that, he would be too dead to worry about anything thereafter.

If he did get back to the stronghold, he would be *dihqan*. He had known that would happen one day, but had thought *one day* lay years ahead. Now it was on top of him, a weight heavier on his shoulders than that of his armor on the steppe pony he rode.

"Speaking of which," he muttered, and reined in. He swung down off the horse, gave it a chance to graze and blow a little. He couldn't think just of the mad dash for escape, not when he was several days' ride north of the Degird. He had to keep the pony sound for the whole journey, even though every heartbeat he waited made him fidget as if taken by the flux.

He stopped again when he came to a small stream. He let the steppe pony drink, but not too much. It snapped at him when he pulled it away from the water. "Stupid thing," he said, and cuffed it on the muzzle. Horses would drink themselves sick or dead if you let them. They would eat too much, too, but that wasn't going to be a problem, not now.

How best to escape pursuit? At length, Abivard rode south-west, still toward the Degird but not as directly—and out of the line of march by which the host of Peroz King of Kings had ap-proached disaster. Sure as sure, the Khamorth would ride down that line, sweeping away the warriors who had not the wit to avoid it.

By the time evening neared, Abivard no longer saw any of his fellow fugitives. That he took for a good omen: the nomads would not be likely now to spot him while chasing someone else.

When he came to another stream, he decided to stop for the night and let the steppe pony rest till morning. He dismounted, rubbed down the animal with a clump of dry grass for lack of anything better, then tied its reins to the biggest bush—almost a sapling—he could find.

After that, time came to shed his armor. He undid the catches at the side of his coat of mail and splints, and got out of it after unhooking the mail skirt that depended from it. He took off his iron-faced boots, then peeled down his iron-and-leather breeches.

The cuirass, the mail shirt, and the armored trousers he flung into the stream: no point in leaving them on dry land for some plainsman to take back to his tent as spoils. He stripped off the veil and hood from his helmet and threw them away, too. The helmet he kept, and the boots. They were heavy, but he feared he would hurt his feet if he did without them.

"You can stand that much weight, can't you, boy?" he said to the steppe pony. Its ears twitched to show it had heard, but of course it could not understand.

Wanting to keep the animal happy with him, he fed it another apricot from his dwindling supply. He ate one himself; he had had nothing but water since early that morning. Had a lizard skittered by, he would cheerfully have sliced it in two with his sword and eaten both pieces raw. But no lizard came.

Then he thumped his forehead with the heel of his hand and cursed his own foolishness. The steppe pony's saddle had saddlebags hanging from it. In them might be . . . anything. He felt like shouting when he found strips of dried mutton. They were just about as hard as his own teeth and not much tastier, but they would keep him from starving for a while.

All he had on were thin linen drawers. He wished for his surcoat, then laughed. "Might as well wish for the army back while I'm at it," he said. With all that passion that was in him, he did wish for the army back, but he was too much Godarz's son not to know what such wishes were worth.

He passed a chilly, miserable night curled up on the ground like an animal, sword at his side so he could grab it in a hurry. He lost track of how many times he woke up to some tiny noise or a shift in the breeze or for no reason at all. Renewed sleep came harder and harder. At last, between dawn and sunrise, it stayed away for good. He gnawed more dried mutton and began to ride.

That day after the battle, he caught himself weeping again and again. Sometimes he mourned for his family, sometimes for his overthrown monarch and for Makuran at large, sometimes for himself: he felt guilty for living on when all he held dearest had perished.

That's nonsense, son. You have to go on, to set things right as best you can. So vividly did he seem to hear his father's voice that his head whipped around in sudden wild hope that the *dihqan* had somehow survived. But the steppe was empty as far as the eye could see, save for a crow that cawed harshly as it hopped into the air.

"Stupid bird, what are you doing here?" Abivard pointed over his shoulder. "The rich pickings are back that way."

Every so often, he saw rabbits lolloping across the plain. Just looking at them made him hungry, but hunting rabbits with a sword was like trying to knock flies out of the air with a switch, and he had no time to set a snare and linger. Once he spied a fox on a rabbit's heels. He wished the beast more luck than he had had himself.

Though he ate sparingly, he ran out of dried meat halfway through the third day. After that, his belly gnawed at him along with worry. He caught a couple of frogs by the side of a stream, gutted them with his dagger, and ate them raw. His only regret after he finished them was that he had thrown the offal into the water.

He looked for more frogs, or maybe a turtle or an incautious minnow the next time he stopped to water the steppe pony, but caught nothing.

Toward evening on the fourth day after the battle, he reached the Degird. He wanted to strip off his drawers, dive in, and swim across, but knew that, weak and worn as he was, he would probably drown before he reached the southern bank. Nor could he let the horse swim the stream and tow him with it, for it was in no finer fettle than he.

"Have to be the bridge, then," he said; he had talked to himself a lot lately, for lack of any other company. And if the bridge was down, or the Khamorth already across it . . . he tried not to think about such things.

Before night descended, he rode about half a farsang away

from the river. Khamorth searching for fugitives still at large in their country were most likely to ride along the northern bank of the Degird, he reasoned. No point in making things easy for them. If they were already searching along the riverbank, the bridge was sure to be down, too, or in their hands, but he made himself not think about that, either.

Hunger woke him before the sun rose. He mounted the steppe pony, marveling at its stamina. A Makuraner horse could carry more weight, yes, and gallop faster for a little ways, but probably would have broken down on the long, grueling ride south. He had done his best to keep the pony rested but knew his best hadn't been good enough.

He rode into the morning sun, keeping the Degird in sight but not actually riding up to it unless he needed to water his horse or himself. He didn't know how far east he would have to ride to come on the bridge. "Only one way to learn," he said, and booted the pony up into a trot.

The sun climbed higher, burned off the early-morning chill, and grew hot. Abivard started to sweat, but he wasn't as uncomfortable as he might have been. A couple of weeks earlier, he had fared north in like weather armored from head to toe. He still had helm and iron-covered boots, but the drawers in between were far easier on his hide than mail and padding.

Was that the bridge up ahead? He thought he had seen it a couple of times already, only to find himself deceived by mudbanks in the river.

But no, not this time—that was the bridge, with riders in unmistakable Makuraner armor still in place on the Pardrayan plain: a gateway to a murdered dream of conquest. But even if the dream was dead, the bridge might keep Makuraner warriors—"Or at least one," Abivard told himself—alive.

He wrung the best pace he could from the tired steppe pony and waved like a man possessed to the garrison still loyally holding open the way back to freedom. A couple of the Makuraners broke away from their main body and came toward him at the trot, their lances couched and pointing at a spot about a hand's span above his navel. With a shock of fear, he realized they were ready to skewer him. He was, after all, riding a Khamorth horse.

"By the God, no!" he screamed hoarsely. Getting slaughtered by his own countrymen after escaping the nomads seemed a fate too bitterly ironic to bear.

The lances wavered when the riders heard him cry out in their own language. "Who are you, then?" one of them called, his face invisible and so all the more menacing behind his veil of mail.

"Abivard son of Godarz, *dihqan* of Vek Rud domain," Abivard answered, doing his best to sound like the real Makuraner he was rather than a plainsman trying to get across the Degird in disguise.

The two warriors looked at each other. The one who had spoken before asked, "D'you mean he's the *dihqan*, or are you?"

"He is," Abivard said automatically, and then had to correct himself: "He was. He's dead, along with my brother and three half brothers. That leaves me."

"So it does, and on a steppe pony, too," the lancer said, suspicious still. "How'd you stay alive through the fight if all your family perished?" *What sort of coward are you?* lurked under the words.

"My horse stepped in a hole and broke a leg as the charge was beginning," Abivard answered. "So I didn't go into the trench and I didn't get trapped when the cursed nomads sallied forth. I managed to get hold of this horse when it came out of the press, and I've ridden it ever since."

The Makuraners looked at each other again. The one who had been quiet till now said, "It could happen."

"Aye, it could," the other agreed. He turned back to Abivard. "Pass on, then. Makuran will need every man it can lay hands on, and we'd about given up on having any more get here—we were going to burn the bridge to make sure the nomads couldn't use it to swarm over the river."

"I'm surprised you haven't seen them yet," Abivard said.

"Why?" the talkier lancer asked. "When they wrecked the army, they ate the whole leg of mutton, and it filled 'em too full to bother with pan scraps like you."

The homely comparison made sense to Abivard. He nodded and rode on toward the bridge. The other warrior called after him, "Make your horse take it slow and easy as you cross. We've already doused it with rock oil, so it'll be slick as a melon rind. We'll torch it once we've all crossed."

Abivard nodded and waved to show he'd heard. The steppe pony's nostrils flared when it caught the stink of the rock oil; it snorted and shook its head. Abivard urged it on regardless. It stepped carefully through the black, smelly stuff poured onto the northern part of the bridge. In some parts of Makuran, they used rock oil in their lamps instead of butter or tallow. Abivard wondered how they put up with the smell.

About half a furlong in the center of the bridge was bare of the disgusting coating. The southern end, though, the part that touched the blessed soil of Makuran, also had rock oil poured over it.

Abivard halted his mount a few steps into Makuran. He turned around to watch the last of the garrison that had held the bridge come back over it. One final horseman remained on the planks. He carried a flickering torch. After pausing for a moment at the northern edge of the stretch that had no rock oil, the warrior tossed the torch into the stuff. Yellow-red flames and thick black smoke rose from a rapidly spreading fire. The Makuraner wheeled his horse and hurried across the bare patch and then through the oil that coated the southern end of the bridge.

"That was cleverly done," Abivard said. "The parts with the rock oil will burn quickly once flame reaches them, and the stretch in the middle without any made sure the fire wouldn't spread too fast and catch you still on the bridge."

"Just so," the fellow who had thrown the torch answered. "Have you worked with rock oil, then, to see this so quickly?"

Abivard shook his head. "No, never yet, though I thank you for the courteous words." Then his belly overrode everything else. "Sir, might a hungry man beg of you a bit of bread?"

"We haven't much ourself, for we've been feeding hungry men for a couple of days now, and our supply wagons left yesterday afternoon. But still—" He opened a saddle bag, drew out a chunk of flatbread wrapped around cracked bulgur wheat, and handed it to Abivard.

The food was stale, but Abivard didn't care. Only the memory of his father kept him from gulping it down like a starving wolf. He made himself eat slowly, deliberately, as a *dihqan* should, then bowed in the saddle to his benefactor. "I am in your debt, generous sir. If ever you have need, come to the domain of the Vek Rud and it shall be met."

"The God keep you and your domain safe," the warrior answered. The wind shifted and blew acrid, stinking smoke into his face and Abivard's. He coughed and rubbed his eyes with his knuckles. Then, glancing back toward the burning bridge and the Degird River, he added, "The God keep all Makuran safe, for if the nomads come in force, I don't know if we have the men left to save ourselves."

Abivard wanted to argue with him but could not.

* * *

The bridge across the Vek Rud remained intact. When Abivard rode over it, he had food in his belly and a caftan over his dirty, ragged drawers, thanks to the kindness of folk he had met on the road. There ahead, crowning the hillock on which it stood, was the stronghold in which he had grown to manhood ... his stronghold now.

The steppe pony snorted nervously as it picked its way through the village's winding streets; it wasn't used to buildings crowding so close on either side. But it kept going. Abivard, by now, figured it might keep going forever. He had never known a horse with such stamina.

A few people in the village recognized him and called his name. Others asked after his father in a way that said word of the full magnitude of the disaster on the steppe hadn't yet got here. He pretended not to hear those questions. People other than the villagers needed to hear their answers first.

The gates to the stronghold were closed. Someone knew—or feared—something, then. The sentry on the wall above let out a glad cry when he saw Abivard. The gates swung open. He rode in.

Frada stood waiting for him, panting a little—he must have come to the gateway at a dead run. Also panting was a black and tan dog at the heel of Abivard's younger brother. Frada's hands were greasy; maybe he had been feeding the dog scraps when the sentry's cry rang out.

"What became of your armor?" he asked Abivard. "For that matter, what became of your horse? Is the campaign ended so soon? Where are Father and our sibs? Will they come soon? All we have here is fourthhand tales, and I know how Father says they always grow in the telling."

"Not this time," Abivard answered. "All you've heard is true, I daresay, and worse besides. Peroz King of Kings is dead, slain, and most of the army with him—"

He had meant to plow straight ahead, but he couldn't. A low moan went up from the gathering crowd at that first grim sentence. Frada took a step backward, as if he had been slapped in the face. He was young enough to find disaster unimaginable. Whether he had imagined it or not, though, it was here. He did his best to rally, at least enough to ask the next question that had to be asked. "And Father, and Varaz, and Jahiz—"

Abivard cut him off before he named them all. "They charged bravely with the host. The God grant they took some plainsmen into the Void before they died. Had I charged with them, I would have perished, too." He told again what had happened to his horse, and how the accident kept him from falling into the Khamorth trap with the rest of the Makuraner army. He had told the story several times now, often enough to make it feel almost as if he were talking about something that had happened to someone else.

"Then you are *dihqan* of this domain," Frada said slowly. He bowed low to Abivard. He had never done that before, save to Godarz. The salute reminded Abivard of how much had changed in bare days' time.

"Aye, I am the *dihqan*," he said, weariness tugging at him like an insistent child. "Whatever is piled up on the platter while I've been away will have to wait another day or two before I'm ready to look at it, though."

"What's the name of the new King of Kings?" someone called from the middle of the crowd.

"Sharbaraz," Abivard answered. "Peroz King of Kings left him behind in Mashiz to look after affairs while he himself fared forth against the plainsmen. Father said he was reckoned a likely young man."

"The God bless Sharbaraz King of Kings." That phrase rose to the sky too raggedly to be a chorus, but in the space of a few seconds everyone in the courtyard repeated it.

Frada said, "You'll have to tell Mother and the rest of Godarz's wives."

"I know," Abivard said heavily. He had thought about that more than once on the long ride south. Telling Burzoe and the other women would be only the barest beginning of his complications there. Along with the domain, the *dihqan*'s wives passed under his control. They were *his* wives now, save only Burzoe who had borne him.

His thoughts had not been of sensual delights. For one thing, he had been afraid and half starved, a state anything but conducive to lickerish imaginings. For another, he had serious doubts about how well he would manage the women's quarters. Godarz had done pretty well, but Godarz had been older and added his women one at a time instead of inheriting them all at once.

He would worry about such things later. For now, he stuck to small, practical details. "The first thing I'll need to do is find a way into the quarters. Father certainly took the key and—" He stopped in confusion. "No, I'm a ninny. There must be a way in through the kitchens, not so?" So much for practicality.

"Aye, there is," one of the cooks said. "A serving girl can show you. We don't speak of it much, though." Makuraner formality dictated that noble women be separated from the world. Common sense dictated that the world needed to get to them. Common sense prevailed, but formality tried to pretend it didn't.

Abivard scanned the crowd for one of the women who served his mother and Godarz's other wives—no, Godarz's other widows. He pointed to the first one he spied. "Yasna, do you know this way?"

"Yes, lord," Yasna answered. Abivard shook his head like a man bedeviled by gnats. The title was his father's, or rather had been. Now he would have to get used to wearing it.

He followed her into the living quarters, through the kitchens, and into the larder. He had seen the plain door there a hundred times, and always assumed it led into another storage chamber. It didn't. It opened onto a long, narrow, dark hall. At the far end was another door, without a latch on this side but with a grill-work opening so those on the other side could see who came.

Yasna rapped on the door. She stood close by the grille, with Abivard behind her. After a moment, she rapped again. A woman's head obscured the light that came through the opening. "Ah, Yasna," the woman said. "Who is with you?"

"I bring the *dihqan*, lady Ardini," Yasna answered.

Ardini was one of Godarz' most junior wives, younger than Abivard. She let out a squeak, then cried, "The *dihqan* returns? Oh, the God be praised for bringing him home safe!" She unbarred the door and opened it wide.

As the door swung open, Abivard wondered if a man ever came this way and sneaked into the women's quarters. Some nobles kept eunuchs in the quarters to guard against such mishaps. Godarz had never bothered, saying "If you can't trust a woman, a guard will only make her sneaky, not honest."

At Ardini's cry, women came running up the hall. They were crying out, too. But when they recognized Abivard, they gave back in confusion. One of his half sisters said to Ardini, "You said the *dihqan* was here, not his son."

"That's what Yasna told me," Ardini answered sulkily. "Is it a crime that I believed her?"

"She told the truth," Abivard said, "though by the God I wish she'd lied. I am *dihqan* of this domain."

Some of the women stared at him, not understanding what he meant. Others, quicker, gasped and then began to shriek.

The wails spread quickly as the rest realized their loss. Abivard wished he could cover his ears, but would not insult their grief so.

Even as they cried out, some of them eyed him with frank speculation. He could guess what was in their minds: *If I can but intoxicate him with my body, he may make me principal wife.* That meant riches, influence, and the chance to bear a son who would one day command the stronghold and rule Vek Rud domain.

He knew he would have to think of such things . . . but not now. Godarz had often gone to Burzoe for advice. That, from the wily *dihqan*, was recommendation enough for Abivard. He saw Burzoe at the back of the group of women, Denak beside her, and said, "I would have speech with my mother and sister first of all." If Godarz had trusted his principal wife's wits, Abivard respected those of his own sister.

Burzoe said, "Wait. Before you speak with us two, everyone who dwells in the women's quarters needs to hear what passed of our husband and sons who went off to war and who—who returned not." Her voice almost broke at the end; not only had she lost Godarz, but Varaz as well.

Abivard realized she was right. As quickly as he could, he went over the doomed campaign yet another time, taking it a further step from memory into tale. Spako and Mirud, mothers to Jahiz and Uzav, burst into fresh lamentation; Arshak's mother, a woman named Sarduri, was dead.

"And so I, and a few others, had the good fortune to escape the ambush, though I thought my fortune anything but good at the time," Abivard finished. "But the flower of the army fell, and times will be hard henceforward."

"Thank you, son . . . or should I say rather, thank you, lord," Burzoe said when he was done. She bowed deeply to him, as Frada had out in the heat of the courtyard. Holding her voice steady by what had to be force of will alone, she went on, "And now, if it is your pleasure to take counsel with Denak and me, follow and I shall lead you to a suitable chamber."

Godarz's widows and those of his daughters who had come into womanhood stepped back to make room for Abivard as he strode through their ranks. Some of the old *dihqan*'s wives contrived not to step back quite far enough, so that he brushed against them walking by. He noted that without being stirred by it; grief and weariness smothered desire in him.

He looked curiously this way and that as Burzoe and Denak

took him to the room they had in mind: he had not been in the women's quarters since he was little more than a babe. They struck him as lighter and airier than most of the living area in the stronghold, with splendid carpets underfoot and tapestries covering the bare stone of the walls, all products of the patient labor of generations of women who had made their homes here since the stronghold rose in the unremembered past.

"It's—pleasant here," he said.

"You needn't sound so surprised," Burzoe answered with quiet pride. "We are not mewed up here because we are guilty of some crime, but for our honor's sake. Should we live as if this were a prison?"

"Sometimes it has the feel of one," Denak said.

"Only if you let it," Burzoe said; Abivard got the feeling this was a running argument between mother and daughter. Burzoe went on, "No matter where your body stays, your mind can roam the whole domain—wider, if you let it."

"If you are a principal wife, if your husband deigns to listen to you, if you have learned—have been allowed to learn—your letters, then yes, perhaps," Denak said. "Otherwise you sit and gossip and ply your needle and work the loom."

"One thing you do not do, if you are wise, is air petty troubles before the *dihqan*," Burzoe said pointedly. She paused, waving Abivard into a sitting room spread with carpets and strewn with embroidered cushions. "Here we may speak without fear of disturbance."

"No one in Makuran can do anything without fear of disturbance, not today, not for months, maybe not for years," Abivard said. Nevertheless, he went in and folded himself into the tailor's seat on a carpet in the style of the steppes: it showed a great cat springing onto the back of a fleeing stag.

Burzoe and Denak also made themselves comfortable, reclining against big pillows. After a moment, the serving girl Yasna came in with a tray of wine and pistachios, which she set on a low table in front of Abivard. He poured for his mother and sister, offered them the bowl of nuts.

"We should serve you," Burzoe said. "You are the *dihqan*."

"If I am, then let me use my power by doing as I please here," Abivard said.

In spite of the dreadful news he had brought, that made Burzoe smile for a moment. She said, "You are very like your father, do you know that? He could always talk his way around anything he pleased."

"Not anything, not at the end," Abivard said, remembering horses crashing down into the trench the Khamorth had dug and others tumbling over one another as their riders tried desperately to bring them to a halt.

"No, not anything." The smile had already left Burzoe's face. "For the kingdom—is it as bad as that, truly?"

"Truly, Mother," Abivard said. "Only the river stands between us and the plainsmen; we have lost so many that if they do cross, we will be hard-pressed to throw them back to their proper side once more."

"I have to remind myself to think in wider terms than this domain alone," Burzoe said with a shaky laugh. "We have lost so many, I find it hard to take in that the realm at large has suffered equally."

"Believe it," Abivard said. "It is true."

"So." His mother stretched the word into a long hiss. Her eyes were bright with tears, but they remained unshed. "For the sake of the domain, then, I can tell you two things that must be done."

Abivard leaned forward: this was what he had hoped to hear. "They are?"

"First," Burzoe said, "you must send to Papak's domain and ask that your wedding with Roshnani be celebrated as soon as is possible."

"What? Why?" Advice on making a marriage he had not expected.

"Two reasons," his mother said. "Do you know if Papak or any of those who fared forth with him survived the battle on the steppe?"

"I don't know. I would doubt it; few came forth alive. But I know nothing for a fact."

"If the *dihqan* and all his likeliest heirs fell fighting, those who find themselves in charge of the domain will be weak and will be looking round for any props they can find to bolster their hold on it. A strong brother-in-law is not the least of assets. And you will also have a claim on them if Vek Rud domain needs aid against the nomads. Do you see?"

"Mother, I do." Abivard inclined his head to Burzoe. He could admire such subtlety, but knew he was not yet capable of it himself. He said, "That's one reason. What's your other?"

"One that will benefit you more than the domain: when you bring Roshnani here, you can establish her as your principal wife with far less jealousy and hatred than if you were to choose one of Godarz's widows. The women here will understand why, for the sake of the domain, you have chosen someone not of their number. Were you to pick one of them, though, all but that one will think you have made a dreadful blunder and torment you and the lucky one without cease. Believe me, you do not want that. No *dihqan* can hope to accomplish anything with the women's quarters in turmoil."

"If Roshnani seems able to bear the burden, I shall do as you say," Abivard answered.

"She *will* bear the burden, because she must," Burzoe said.

Abivard let that go; his mother, he suspected, assumed all other women had her own strength of will. He said, "You've given me one thing I must do, then. What's the other?"

"What you would expect," Burzoe said. Abivard didn't know what he should expect but did his best not to let his face show that. Maybe it did and maybe it didn't; he couldn't tell. Burzoe went on, "It involves Denak, of course."

"Ah?" Now Abivard couldn't disguise that he was lost.

Burzoe sniffed in exasperation. Denak grinned; she knew what her mother was talking about. "You're not the only one in the family who was betrothed, you know."

"No, I didn't know," Abivard said, though on reflection he should have: a *dihqan*'s eldest daughter by his principal wife was a valuable piece in the game of shifting power the nobles of Makuran played among themselves. He plucked at his beard. "To whom?" Now that *he* was *dihqan*, he would have to keep track of such things for all of Godarz's daughters.

"To Pradtak, eldest son of Urashtu," Denak answered.

"Ah," Abivard said. "Father made a fine match for you, then." Urashtu's domain lay southeast of the one Abivard unexpectedly found himself holding. Not only did it have good grazing land and hot springs that drew the wealthy infirm from all over Makuran, its stronghold perched on Nalgis Crag, an eminence so imposing that it made Vek Rud's castle seem to lie on flatlands by comparison.

Burzoe said, "As much as your match with Roshnani, we should pursue Denak's with Pradtak. If he survived the battle on the steppe, he will be eager to bring it to accomplishment for the same reasons we are; the God grant it be so. But if not, we can begin discussion with whoever now holds that domain."

Abivard looked over at Denak. Marriages were always chancy; family considerations counted for far more than passion. But at least in Pradtak Denak had the hope of a husband about her own age. If he had died in the Khamorth trap, she might find herself pledged to some wizened uncle who now held Nalgis Crag domain only because he had been too old to go out and fight. That seemed a dreadful fate to inflict on his sister.

Denak smiled back at him, but in a way that said, she, too, was worried about such things. She said, "No less than you, I will do what's best for the domain."

"Of course you will, child," Burzoe said; with her, there was no room for doubt. "Now we need solid allies, and marriage is the best way to come by them. It will be well enough. Have I not prospered here, though I never set eyes on Godarz till the day my hands were set in his?"

Prospered, Abivard noted. His mother had said nothing about being happy. If the idea entered her mind at all, it was less important to her than the other.

She went on in similar vein. "This domain shall prosper, too. You have your father's wits, Abivard; I know the God will help you use them as he did, for she loves the folk of Makuran more than those of any other land."

"As you say, Mother," Abivard answered. Not a word had Burzoe said of her outlining the course he was to follow. She had been the ideal *dihqan*'s wife, always ready with ideas but content to let her husband, the public part of the pairing, take credit for them. Now she was doing the same for Abivard.

Maybe she thought to rule the domain as well as advise. With someone other than Godarz her husband, she might already have been doing that for years. Abivard was uncomfortably aware that, for the moment, she had more and better ideas than he did. If Vek Rud domain was to be his in fact as well as name, he would have to acquire wisdom and experience in a hurry.

A corner of his mouth quirked upward. Given the straits in which Makuran found itself, he would have plenty of chances.

III

"A RIDER APPROACHES!" A SENTRY BAWLED FROM THE WALL OF the stronghold.

Down in the courtyard, everyone stopped what he was doing and looked up to see whence that cry had come. *The south-facing wall,* Abivard thought. The tension that knotted his stomach at every warning shout eased a little: Khamorth raiders would not come out of the south.

The sentry said, "He bears a red banner!"

"A messenger from the King of Kings," Abivard said to no one in particular. He walked over to the gate: making a royal messenger wait would have been as great an insult as delaying the King of Kings himself. As he walked, Abivard called for wine and fruit and meats, to show the horseman that everything in the domain was for his sovereign to command.

The lookout had spotted the rider well away from the stronghold, so the servitors had time to take their position behind Abivard with refreshments ready to hand when the fellow came through the gateway. He swung off his horse with a sigh of relief, swigged wine, and ran a wet towel over his face and head to cool down and wash away some of the dust of travel.

"Ahh," he said, a slow sigh of pleasure. "You are gracious to a man long in the saddle. In the name of the God, I thank you."

"The God enjoins us to meet the stranger's needs," Abivard replied. "Were not the Four wanderers themselves, seeking righteousness and truth among men?"

"You speak well; obviously you are as full of sound doctrine as you are of courtesy to your guests," the messenger said, bowing to Abivard. He pulled a sheet of parchment from the pouch on his belt and glanced at it. "You would be—Godarz, *dihqan* of Vek Rud domain?" He spoke as if he doubted his own correctness.

He had reason to doubt, after the catastrophe in Pardraya. Gently Abivard answered, "No, I am Abivard son of Godarz, now *dihqan* of this domain."

The meaning of that was unmistakable. "The God grant your father peace and his companionship," the royal messenger replied. "If I may be permitted an opinion, his domain finds itself in good hands."

It was Abivard's turn to bow. "Thank you for your kindness."

"Not at all." The messenger took another sip of wine. "Because of the ... sudden changes ... we have undergone, I and others like me fare forth from one domain to the next, seeking oaths of allegiance to the new King of Kings, the God bless him and keep him, from nobles old and new alike."

"I would gladly swear allegiance to Sharbaraz son of Peroz, King of Kings of Makuran," Abivard said. "My father always spoke highly of him, and I am sure the kingdom will soon recover its glory under his rule."

Flattery was always more effective with truth stirred into the mix, or so Godarz had taught. Abivard waited for the royal messenger to give forth with more flowery phrases about his kindness or magnanimity or something else the fellow was equally unqualified to judge.

Instead, though, the messenger coughed delicately, as if to show he was willing to pretend he hadn't heard what Abivard said. After a moment he murmured, "Well, Vek Rud domain does lie hard by the frontier. I suppose I should not be surprised I am first to bring here news of the accession of Smerdis King of Kings, may his years be many and his realm increase."

Abivard felt that, instead of standing on solid ground, he found himself above the Void into which the God would cast all those who transgressed against his teaching. He said, "Truly, sir, I had not heard of Smerdis King of Kings. Perhaps you would be good enough to tell me more of him. I trust he is of the true royal line?"

"He is indeed," the messenger replied. "He is sister's son to the late Peroz's grandfather of the same name."

After a bit of thinking, Abivard realized that made Smerdis Peroz's second cousin and Sharbaraz's third: a member of the royal family, yes, but of the royal line? That, however, was not the issue. Abivard knew what the issue was: "Sir, before I speak further on this, I would have you tell me how it passed that Sharbaraz failed to succeed Peroz King of Kings."

"Naturally, I respect your caution in this matter," the messenger said. "The truth, however, is not difficult to set forth: Sharbaraz, feeling himself inadequate to hold the throne because of his youth, ignorance, and inexperience, stepped aside in favor of a man to whom years have given the wisdom Makuran needs in this time of trouble."

That sounded well enough, but if any great-aunt's son had presumed to tell Abivard how to run his domain, he would have sent the fellow packing, or maybe thrown him off the stronghold wall, depending on how importunate he got. And Abivard remembered the praise his father had given to Sharbaraz. If Peroz's son was anywhere near the man Godarz reckoned him to be, he would not tamely yield the throne to anyone, let alone some blueblood who had managed to remain invisible his whole life till now.

And yet Smerdis, by this messenger's account, ruled in Mashiz and reckoned himself entitled to the lion banner of Makuraner royalty. Abivard carefully studied the messenger's regalia. As far as he could tell, the man was genuine. He also knew he did not know and had no way of learning the reasons for everything that happened in Mashiz.

His answer, then, had to be submissive, if cautiously so: "Sir, do you swear by the God that what you have told me of the accession of Smerdis King of Kings is true?"

"By the God I swear it," the messenger answered, his voice deep and solemn, his face open and sincere—but if he lied, he would, had Smerdis a barleycorn of sense, have been chosen to lie well.

"Well, then, so long as your oath shall be shown to be true, I pledge myself the loyal subject of Smerdis King of Kings, and pray the God to grant him the wisdom he will need to rescue Makuran from the troubles ahead," Abivard said. "As you remarked, sir, we are close to the frontier here. We hear news from Mashiz but slowly. But from over the Degird we hear only too clear. With so many of our warriors fallen, the borderlands are going to be ravaged."

"Smerdis King of Kings shall do everything in his power to prevent it," the messenger said. That Abivard was willing to believe. The question was, how much lay in his power? Not as much as had belonged to the King of Kings until Peroz threw away his army, that was certain.

Abivard glanced at the lengthening shadows. "Pass the night here," he told the messenger. "You'll reach no other stronghold before dusk overtakes you, that's certain."

The messenger gauged the shadows, too. He nodded. "Your hospitality leaves me in your debt."

"I am always pleased to serve the servants of the King of Kings." Abivard turned to his retainers and said, "See to the horse of—" He looked at the messenger. "Your name, sir?"

"I am called Ishkuza."

"See to the horse of Ishkuza the messenger of Smerdis King of Kings." That still seemed strange in Abivard's mouth. He wondered if his father had been wrong about Sharbaraz. Vek Rud domain was a long way from Mashiz. "Let us also see to his comfort. I know there's a leg of mutton cooking. We'll unstopper one of our finer jars of wine, as well."

Hospitality and upholding the reputation of his domain came first with Abivard. Not far behind them, though, ran the desire to ply Ishkuza with as much wine as he could drink in the hopes that it would loosen the messenger's tongue and let him learn more about the man who now controlled Makuran's destiny.

Ishkuza filled himself full of mutton and bulgur and flatbread and yogurt sweetened with honey; he drank horn after horn of wine, and praised it with the knowing air of a man who had tasted many vintages in his day. His face flushed. He grew merry and tried to pull a serving woman down onto his lap. When she evaded him, he laughed boisterously, not a bit out of temper.

But for all Abivard's questions—and he asked them freely, for who could blame a man for wanting to find out all he could about his new suzerain?—Ishkuza said remarkably little. He answered what he could on matters of fact. Of opinions or gossip he seemed entirely bereft.

So Abivard learned Smerdis was about sixty, which struck him as elderly but not necessarily doddering. Of course he had served—"with distinction," Ishkuza added, though when speaking of a King of Kings it could have gone without saying—at the courts of Peroz and his predecessor, Valash.

"How did he serve there?" Abivard asked, wondering whether his duties had been purely ceremonial or if he had done some real work.

"For many years, he has overseen the operation of the mint," Ishkuza answered. Abivard nodded: not a post in which a man was liable to win great glory or repute, but not a sinecure, either.

That made him feel a bit better about Smerdis: he had accomplished something in those sixty years, anyhow.

About the character and temperament of the new King of Kings, his messenger said nothing. Abivard accepted that: they were not likely to become a matter of intimate concern to a frontier *dihqan*, at any rate.

He was heartily glad Ishkuza had accepted his provisional oath of allegiance to this Smerdis King of Kings. Perhaps, if Makuran's new ruler had been dealing with the mint for many years, he had developed a calm and judicious temperament, one not like that of the usual noble.

Or, on the other hand, maybe Smerdis had enough troubles of his own to be content with any sort of allegiance he could get. Until Peroz's charger crashed down into the trench, Abivard hadn't imagined a King of Kings could have troubles like any other man. He knew better now.

The longer he thought about it, the likelier the second explanation felt.

A few days after Ishkuza rode out of the stronghold, another messenger rode in. This one brought more unambiguously welcome news: Abivard's request for an early wedding with Roshnani was accepted.

Yet even the sweet came stirred with bitter these days, for the *dihqan* acceding to the request was not Papak but his third son, Okhos. "No," the messenger said sadly, "he never came back from the steppe country, neither he nor his two eldest who rode with him."

"It was much the same with us," Abivard answered. "I lost my father, my full brother, and three half brothers, and only through what I thought to be misfortune did I escape the trap myself." He told how his horse's fall had led to his own survival.

"Truly the God watched over you," Okhos' messenger said. "As I told you, none of those from our stronghold returned; my new master carries but fifteen years."

"In times like these, youth must needs learn young," Abivard said, to which the rider, himself a stolid, middle-age fellow, nodded solemnly. Abivard wondered how much advice Papak's principal wife was putting into Okhos' ear, and how willing to listen to her a fifteen-year-old would be. Some, evidently, or perhaps Okhos had wit enough to see the sense in this offer on his own.

The messenger said, "By your leave, lord, the lady Roshnani and her wedding party will make for your domain the moment I get home. She and they might even have come in my place—gossip I hear says she wanted it so—but it was less than polite to show up at your gate without fair warning."

"Tell Okhos she and hers shall be most welcome, and the sooner the better," Abivard said; he already had preparations in train. He raised a forefinger. "Tell your master also to be certain her escort includes a good many full-armed men. These days they may find worse than brigands on the road."

"I'll give him your words, just as you've spoken them to me," the messenger promised, and repeated them back to show he could.

"Excellent," Abivard said. "May I put one more question to you?" At the fellow's nod, Abivard lowered his voice: "Is she pretty?"

"Lord, if I could tell you one way or the other, I would," the man answered. "But I can't. I never chanced to be in the courtyard when she came out of the women's quarters, so I just don't know. And I can't say I paid much attention back when she was a brat underfoot."

"Very well." Abivard sighed, reached into a pouch he wore on his belt and pulled out two silver arkets. "This for your honesty, at any rate."

The messenger sketched a salute. "You're generous to a man you've never seen. For your sake, I hope she's lovely. Her father and brothers, they aren't—or weren't—" His mouth twisted, "the worst-looking men the God ever made." With that limited reassurance, he rode back toward Papak's—no, Okhos' now—stronghold.

The very next day, another rider came into the stronghold, this one sent out by Pradtak son of Urashtu. After the usual courtesies, the man said, "My master is now *dihqan* of Nalgis Crag domain and is pleased to accept your proposal to link our two holdings through his prompt marriage to your sister Denak."

"In that, you bring me good news," Abivard said, "though I grieve to learn his father has gone into the Void. Did he fare north into Pardraya?"

"He did," Pradtak's man replied. He said no more; after the disastrous end of Peroz' campaign, no more needed to be said.

"And your lord was lucky enough to come home safe?"

Abivard asked. He was eager to learn of others who had survived the fight. Their numbers were not large.

And now Pradtak's messenger shook his head. "No, lord, for he did not go. Much to his chagrin, he broke an arm and an ankle in a fall from his horse during a game of mallet and ball not a week before he was to set out on campaign, and so had to remain at the stronghold. Now we say the God took a hand in preserving him."

"I understand what you mean," Abivard answered. "A fall from a horse kept me from disaster, too." He told his tale again, finishing, "I thought at the time the God had forsaken me, but I learned better all too soon. I wish he had watched over the whole army as he did over me."

"Aye, lord; you speak nothing but truth there." The messenger added, "It would greatly please Pradtak if you were to send your sister to his stronghold as quickly as you might, provided she be escorted well enough to see to her safety on the journey."

"Only one matter shall delay me," Abivard said. Without moving a muscle, Pradtak's man contrived to look unhappy; obviously, as far as he was concerned, no delay could be acceptable. Then Abivard explained: "My own bride will soon be traveling hither. After I am wed to her, I can accompany Denak to Nalgis Crag."

"Ah." The messenger had a mobile face; Abivard watched him concede the exception. "The God grant you and your wife great happiness, as he shall surely do with your sister and my master."

"May it be so," Abivard said. "And, speaking of my sister's happiness, I trust the *dihqan* Pradtak is healing well?" No matter what had been agreed when Denak was a little girl, Abivard did not intend to yoke her to a brooding cripple who might take out on her the resentment for his injuries.

But the messenger made a sign to turn aside evil suggestions. "Lord, by my head, by the God, in half a year no one shall know he was hurt. We have skilled bonesetters in our domain, and they have done their best for Pradtak. Oh, he may end up with the slightest limp, but he shall assuredly be a full and manly man for the ornament he receives from your women's quarters."

"Well enough, then. I shall hold you and him responsible for the truth of what you say." Abivard would have bet the fellow's expressive features would give him away if he lied. But they radiated candor. That reassured him.

Pradtak's man let out a couple of polite coughs, then spoke from behind the palm of his hand. "May I bring word to my lord of the beauty of your sister? I do not wish to see her—I ask nothing improper," he added hastily, "but you understand your word will help ease my master's mind."

Abivard almost burst out laughing; he had asked Okhos' man nearly the identical question. He thought before he answered; a man's word was as precious a gift as he could give. Was Denak beautiful? She was his sister; he did not look on her as he did on other women. But when he had gone into the women's quarters, she had not seemed out of place alongside Godarz' younger widows, who were quite lovely indeed.

"You may tell Pradtak that, in my humble opinion, he will not be disappointed in her appearance," he said at length.

The messenger beamed. "I shall do just as you say, lord. A last question and I depart: when shall we look for your presence to honor us at Nalgis Crag?"

"I expect my bride to reach this stronghold in a week's time, more or less. Add in another week for the wedding and the festivities that go with it, and the better part of another for traveling to your domain with an armed party and a woman. Say, three weeks in all. I shall send out a messenger on a fast horse two days before our wedding party departs, so that we do not take your master by surprise."

"You are thoughtfulness itself." Pradtak's man bowed deeply, then remounted his horse and rode back toward his own domain. Abivard nodded to himself. The position of the domain among its neighbors stood to be strengthened. Whether that would save it against the Khamorth remained to be seen.

Abivard's heart thumped as it had just before Chishpish ordered his warriors to couch their lances. He shook his head and twisted his fingers in a sign to turn aside the evil omen. Disaster had followed close on Chishpish's order; he prayed to the God and the Four to keep the same from happening in his marriage.

Soon now, he thought, peering out into the courtyard from a window close by the fortified door to the living quarters. There stood Okhos, shifting nervously from foot to foot, catching himself at it and stopping, then forgetting and starting to jiggle again.

And I reckoned taking over this domain hard, Abivard thought as he watched Okhos squirm. Not only had he been a man grown when Vek Rud domain landed on his shoulders, he had also been Godarz's chosen heir. But Okhos' beard was only dark

down on his cheeks; he had been just another of Papak's sons
... until Papak and everyone ahead of Okhos in the succession
went off to Pardraya and did not come back. Now, for better or
worse, Okhos had to cope with a *dihqan*'s duties. Despite his
own nervousness, Abivard spared him a moment's sympathy.

Next to Okhos stood the servant of the God, in the yellow
robe that proclaimed his calling. His hair and beard were uncut
and unkempt, to symbolize his devotion to things of the next
world rather than this.

Abivard spared the God's servant only a passing glance. His
gaze returned, as it had all morning long, to the gateway to the
stronghold. There in the shade waited Roshnani. When she came
out into the courtyard, it would also be his own time to advance.

"I wish he'd let me see her," Abivard muttered. Okhos and
the wedding party had arrived the evening before. But the young
dihqan, perhaps because he lacked the experience to know
which customary practices he could safely omit, adhered rigidly
to them all. And so, while Abivard had been able to greet his
bride-to-be—and to learn her voice was pleasant enough—he
still had not looked on her face; she wore a veil that must have
left her nearly blind, and one that defeated all Abivard's efforts
to learn what lay beneath it.

Out in the courtyard, one of Abivard's half brothers began to
beat on a drum. On the fourth slow, deep reverberation,
Roshnani stepped out from the shadows and began to walk
slowly toward her brother and the holy man in yellow.

A younger half brother, Parsuash, gave Abivard a shove. "Go
on," he squeaked. "It's time."

Roshnani's gown was bright as a beacon, orange-red silk twill
decorated with a pattern of ornate, stylized baskets of fruit. Beneath its hem, the upturned toes of her red shoes peeked out.
Her veil, this time, was of the same fabric as the gown, though
not quite so opaque.

Parsuash shoved Abivard again. He took a deep breath and
walked out into the courtyard. As when he had charged into battle, fear and exultation mingled.

When he came up to the people waiting for him, Okhos gave
him a formal bow, which he returned. He bowed also to the servant of the God—who, having a higher master than Smerdis
King of Kings, did not bow back—and last to Roshnani. Okhos
returned that salute for his sister.

The servant of the God said, "In the names of Narseh,
Gimillu, the lady Shivini, and Fraortish eldest of all, we are met

here today to complete and accomplish what was set in motion years ago, the marriage of the *dihqan* Abivard to Roshnani, daughter of Papak the late *dihqan* and sister to the *dihqan* Okhos."

Okhos' face twisted. He looked as if he would have given anything to have Papak standing in his place. Abivard understood that; he longed to have Godarz standing strong behind him. But he was on his own, and so was Okhos.

His glance went over to the filigreed screens that covered the windows of the women's quarters. His mother would be behind one of those screens, his sister behind another. All the rest of Godarz's women—now *his* women—would be watching, too, watching as this stranger from another domain came into their world and likely eclipsed them all in status.

"The God grants his blessings, even in adversity," the holy man went on. "From him, as well as from men and women, springs each new generation, each new life. Is it your will, Abivard son of Godarz, that your betrothal be made into a true marriage this day?"

"It is my will," Abivard said as he had been coached. Not far away, Frada nodded slowly, as if making note of what to expect when his turn before the servant of the God came.

"Is it your will, Okhos son of Papak, that the betrothal of your sister agreed to by your father be made into a true marriage this day?"

"It is my will." Okhos' voice broke as he answered. He scowled and flushed. Abivard wanted to tell him not to worry, that it didn't matter, but the man in the yellow robe was already turning to Roshnani, who also had a say in this affair.

"Is it your will, Roshnani daughter of Papak, that your betrothal be made into a true marriage this day?"

"It is my will," she answered, so low Abivard could hardly hear her. No wonder she was nervous, he thought. He was but adding a new wife to several already in the women's quarters. If she turned out not to suit him, he had but to ignore her. But her whole life changed forever with her leaving the stronghold where she had been born . . . and it was so easy for the change to be catastrophically for the worse.

"In token of your wills, then—" The servant of the God handed Abivard and Roshnani each a date. She then gave hers to Abivard, he his to her. As he ate the one she had given him, he wondered if he would see her face as she put hers into her mouth. But no, she reached under the concealing veil and then again to take out the seed. She handed that seed back to the holy man, as Abivard did with his. The servant of the God said, "I shall plant these seeds side by side, that they may grow together as do the two of you."

Then he took Roshnani's hands and set them between Abivard's. That action completed and formalized the wedding ceremony. Cheers rang out in the courtyard and from some, though not all, the windows in the women's quarters. Frada pelted the new couple with wheat to remind the God to make them fertile.

Now that her hands rested in his, Abivard gained the right to lift Roshnani's veil. He had proved his own word and his faith in her father and brother by marrying her first. With that done, she passed from them to him.

The silk of the veil was slick against his fingers as he raised it. Roshnani tried to smile as he saw her for the first time. She was round-faced, pleasant-looking beneath her tension, with pretty eyes accented by kohl. She had painted a beauty mark on one side of her chin. Her cheeks were rouged—but not as heavily as Peroz's had been, that day in camp.

She was less than he had dreamed of, more than he had feared. As Godarz's son, he was plenty practical enough to make the best of that. "Welcome to Vek Rud domain, wife of mine," he said, smiling back at her. "The God grant you long years of happiness here."

"Thank you, husband of mine," she answered, her voice steadier—maybe she knew how to make the best of things, too. "May she be generous enough to grant you what you have wished me."

Frada threw another handful of wheat over them. Abivard took Roshnani's hand in his once more and led her through the crowd toward the living quarters of the stronghold. Retainers and kin all bowed low as they passed. Abivard paused for a moment as he went inside, to let his eyes adjust to the gloom.

Roshnani looked around curiously at people, wall hangings, and furniture. This was, after all, the first stronghold she had seen other than her own. "You've done well for yourselves here," she observed.

"So we have," Abivard said. "And now the domain has a fine new ornament in it." He smiled at her to show what he meant.

She had been properly brought up; she cast down her eyes with becoming modesty. "You are kind," she whispered. Her tone made Abivard wonder if she was saying what she meant or what she hoped.

"We go this way now," he said, and led her down the corridor that ended at the *dihqan*'s bedchamber. He knew some trepidation in going that way himself. Since he had come home as lord of Vek Rud domain, he had kept on sleeping in the little room that had been his before the army plunged onto the steppe. He had slept alone every night, too, reasoning that he wanted to establish no favorites before Roshnani arrived.

Now, though, everything changed. He would have to occupy the chamber that had been his father's. Not only was its bed longer than the little pallet in his old room, but it had a door that connected to the women's quarters. After much searching, he had found a spare key to the lock on that door glued to the back of a frame that mounted a tapestry.

The outer door to the *dihqan*'s bedchamber had a bar to it. When he shut the door, his siblings and retainers in the hallway behind him cheered and called out ribald advice. The cheers doubled when they heard the bar fall.

Abivard glanced over at Roshnani, who was looking at the bed, on which a serving woman had spread a square of white cotton cloth. She flushed when she noticed him watching her, then said, "By the God I swear I have known no man before, but—" She stopped in confusion.

"One of the things my father told me—" *One of the many useful things my father told me,* Abivard thought "—was that women don't always bleed the first time. If that proves so, there's a little pot of fowl's blood hidden in the chest of drawers, to make appearances proper."

"I think I may be luckier than I dared dream," Roshnani said quietly.

"I hope you go on thinking so," Abivard answered. "Meanwhile, though, whether you end up needing that pot of blood or not, we are here for a reason."

"A reason, yes." Roshnani turned her back on him. The gown had carved bone toggles all the way down. To undo some of them herself, she would have had to be a contortionist. He opened them one by one. His own hands grew less steady the farther he went. In a land where women concealed themselves, removing one from that concealment was intoxicatingly exciting.

Under the gown, Roshnani wore drawers of shimmering silk. She let Abivard slide those to the floor, too, then laughed nervously. "I feel I should cover myself from you, but I know that is not the way of what we do now."

"No," he said, a little hoarsely. Like her face, her body was, if not surpassingly beautiful, then plenty inviting enough. He pulled his caftan over his head, then hastily took off his own drawers. He was a little surprised to find Roshnani looking at him with even more curiosity than he had shown her. After a moment, the surprise vanished. She, after all, knew less of how men were made than he did of women.

He took her hand. It was cold in his. He led her over to the bed, saying "I will do my best not to hurt you, this being your first time."

"Thank you," she answered. "All of Papak's—Okhos', now—women have told me what to expect, but since no two of them say the same thing, my thought is that I shall have to find out for myself."

Even as he was about to draw her down onto the square of cloth, he paused in admiration of her words rather than her body. "Do you know," he told her seriously, "my father would have said the very same thing, and he was the wisest man I ever knew." With that, he began to think she might have the makings of a principal wife after all.

Then they did lie down on the bed, which creaked and rustled under their weight. Abivard knew a certain nervousness himself; till this moment, the only virginity he had disposed of had been his own. Taking his bride's was another matter altogether.

He wondered if she even knew how to kiss. On making the experiment, he discovered she did. She let out a small giggle when their lips separated. "Your beard and mustache tickle," she said.

He had never thought of the act of love as a way to make the acquaintance of someone, but that was what it proved to be. He learned every time he touched her, every time his lips moved from here to there. And merely taking part in the act together joined them in a way nothing else could.

Some little while later came the time when he at last went into her. Her face twisted beneath him as he made his way through the gate no one had opened before. He did his best not to hurt her, but his urgency had its demands, too. He spent in a long, groaning rush of pleasure.

She wriggled a little after he gasped himself to completion. It wasn't a motion associated with arousal; it seemed more like *get off me—you're heavy.* He took his weight on his elbows, then slipped out of her.

He glanced down at himself and at Roshnani. "We won't have any need for the fowl's blood," he said.

She sat up, looking at the little driblet of blood from between her legs that stained the cloth. "So we won't."

"Are you all right?" he asked.

"Yes, I think so," she answered. "It hurt some, but I expected it to, so that wasn't so bad. I'm sure it will be easier next time, easier still the time after that."

"Did you—like it?" he asked hesitantly.

She gave the question serious consideration before she answered. He was getting the idea she generally thought before she spoke. That, to him, was a point in her favor. After a moment she said, "When it doesn't hurt any more, I think it will be pleasant enough, though I still may find your lips and tongue sweeter, as they can touch just the right spot." She looked at him anxiously. "Does that make you angry?"

"Why should a truthful answer make me angry?" Abivard said.

"I knew I shouldn't believe everything I heard in the women's quarters," his new bride answered. "They said a man was apt to be so proud of his prong—"

"Is *that* what they call it?" Abivard broke in, amused.

"Well, yes. Anyhow, they said he was apt to be so proud of it that he'd forget anything else. I'm glad to find they were wrong."

"Men aren't all the same, any more than women are, I suppose," he said. Roshnani nodded. Abivard wondered if she already knew the touch of lips and tongue. Stories said the inhabitants of the women's quarters, especially if their husband was old or infirm or had a great many wives and made love to each only rarely, sometimes sated one another's lust. He couldn't find any way to ask her. He didn't suppose it was properly his concern, anyway.

Roshnani said, "What you say stands to reason, but of men I must say I know little."

"I hope you will end up satisfied with this man, at least." Being young, Abivard was ready for a second round almost at once, but didn't take it from her, not when he had just made her bleed. Tomorrow would be another day. If she was to become his principal wife, he wanted her pleased with him in bed: they were more likely to be in accord thus on the proper running of the domain. Hurting her again wouldn't help that.

He got out of bed, pulled on his caftan, and picked up the bloodstained square of cloth. Roshnani started to put on her silk drawers, then shook her head. "I don't care to soil them," she said, and stepped back into her gown. "Fasten enough of the toggles to make me decent for the showing, will you please?"

Abivard did as she asked, then threw wide the door to the *dihqan*'s chamber. The hallway outside was packed with eagerly—and curiously—waiting people. He held up the cloth with Roshnani's virgin blood on it. Everyone broke into loud cheers, as the proper sealing—or, in this case, unsealing—of a bargain. Roshnani faced the folk of Vek Rud domain with her head held high.

After the ritual showing, Abivard shut the door once more. From the hallway came ribald howls, but he had already decided against that second round. Instead of undoing the silk gown once more, he made sure all its toggles were closed in their proper loops. "We'll have you just as you should be before you go into the women's quarters," he said.

"I thank you for the care you show me." Roshnani looked and sounded as anxious now, in a different way, as she had when he had brought her to bed. And no wonder—she would live with these women for the rest of her days and, a newcomer, find her place among them.

Abivard took the key and used it to unlatch the door that led into the secluded part of the stronghold. Burzoe and Denak waited not far down that hall; he had expected them to be there. Leading Roshnani up to them, he said, "My mother, my sister, I present to you my wife."

The three women embraced one another. Burzoe said, "May you serve this domain as you did your father's. May you give us many fine heirs. May you be happy here." As usual, that came last with her.

"The God grant your wishes, mother of the *dihqan*," Roshnani said softly.

Denak said, "You must tell me everything of your journey here, and of the ceremony, and—" She, too, lowered her voice after a glance at Abivard "—other matters. I, too, am to be wed this season."

Roshnani turned her eyes toward Abivard. "I shall speak of whatever you wish—soon."

He could take a hint. Bowing to his wife, his mother, and his sister in turn, he said, "With your gracious permission, ladies, I shall take my leave. No doubt you will wish to discuss matters with which my merely male ears should not be profaned."

Roshnani, Burzoe, and Denak all laughed in a way that made him retreat even faster than he had planned. *No doubt you will wish to discuss matters with which my merely male ears would be scorched,* he thought. If Roshnani was going to tell Denak about his performance, he didn't want to be anywhere within fifty farsangs when she did it. Fleeing that far was impractical, but he could take himself out of earshot, and he did.

Frada let out a low whistle and pointed ahead to Nalgis Crag and the stronghold that sat atop it. "Will you look there?" he said. "Any army could sit at the bottom of that pile of rock forever, but if it tried to go up—"

"It'd go back down again, and a lot faster, too," Abivard finished for his younger brother. Only one narrow, winding track led up to the stronghold of Nalgis Crag domain; even from a quarter of a farsang away, Abivard could see a dozen places where a handful of determined men could hold up the army Frada had mentioned.

"They have to have a way to get water, too, else the stronghold wouldn't have got the reputation it owns," Frada added, speaking with the tones of an aspiring general.

"I'll be pleased to get inside strong walls again," Abivard said. "I've felt half naked on the road." He gestured at himself. Like all the warriors in Denak's wedding party, he wore a helmet and carried sword and lance, as a proper Makuraner fighting man should. But the rest of his gear, and theirs, was leather hardened with melted wax, the same sort of light protection some of the Khamorth nomads used. The stronghold smiths were beginning to re-create the iron suits lost in the Pardrayan debacle, but even one of them would be awhile in the making.

Frada turned to Denak and said, "How fare you, sister?"

"I revel in being out of the women's quarters," she answered, "but I wish I did not have to travel veiled. I could see so much more of the countryside without this covering for my face."

"Till we got into the territory of Nalgis Crag domain this morning, there wasn't much to see," Abivard said. "Only desert and rocks between our lands and Pradtak's; save for patches of oasis, Makuran is less than fertile."

"When you've done nothing but look out windows these past ten years, even desert seems interesting," Denak said. As she usually did, she tried to look on the bright side of things: "Nalgis Crag stronghold is so high above the rest of the domain, I should have a broad view from the women's quarters."

Abivard had never worried much about the propriety of shutting high-born women away form the world as soon as they became women: it was the custom of his land, and he went along with it. He had not even worried about his sister being closed up in the women's quarters of the stronghold of Vek Rud domain. That had happened when he was scarcely more than a boy himself, and he had grown used to it. But to have her closed up in a women's quarters far away . . . that sent a pang through the core of him.

"I'll miss you, sister of mine," he said seriously.

"And I you," Denak answered. "We can, perhaps, write back and forth; I hope Pradtak won't mind." If Pradtak did mind, that would be the end of the idea, as they both knew. Denak went on, "What point to learning my letters, though, if I'm not allowed to use them?"

Abivard wondered why Godarz had decided to let Denak learn to read and write. Few Makuraner women could; he didn't think Burzoe knew how, for all her cleverness. His best guess was that Godarz, seeing ability, couldn't bear to let it lie fallow no matter how unusual the field. One thing his father had never been was wasteful.

High and thin in the distance, a horn call rang out from Nalgis Crag stronghold: the wedding party had been seen. "Come on!" Abivard shouted. "Let's give them all the swank we can, for the sake of our pride and the name of our domain." He wished the band could have ridden up Nalgis Crag and into the stronghold with armor jingling sweetly around them, but that could not be. At least Pradtak would understand and sympathize: few domains these days faced no such predicament.

The track that led up to the stronghold had been hacked into the side of the crag. As he rode up it, Abivard saw his earlier estimates had been wrong. At fifteen places on the narrow, twisting road, maybe even a score, a few determined men could have held up a host. Stones were heaped every furlong or less to rain down on the heads of attackers and tumble them to their doom.

At the end of the track, Nalgis Crag stronghold was no mean piece of fortcraft in and of itself. If any army somehow fought its way to the top of the crag, those frowning granite walls, cunningly made to hug every bit of high ground, would hold it at bay for a long time.

"Who comes?" a guard standing in the open gateway demanded fiercely, spear ready to bar the new arrivals' path.

"Abivard son of Godarz, *dihqan* of Vek Rud domain," Abivard answered formally. "With me comes my full sister Denak, intended bride of Pradtak son of Urashtu, the great and powerful *dihqan* of Nalgis Crag domain." He had no idea how great and powerful Pradtak was in person, but any *dihqan* who controlled this domain had access to power that would make some *marzbans* jealous.

The guard performed a fancy flourish with the spear. "The God watch over you and your party as you enter Nalgis Crag stronghold, Abivard son of Godarz, and may your sister's union with our *dihqan* prove joyous and fruitful." He stepped aside so the wedding party could go ahead.

Now Abivard had to take the role young Okhos had played at Vek Rud stronghold. He helped Denak dismount; they stood in the shade of the gate while the rest of the wedding party had their horses seen to and took their places among the spectators from Pradtak's domain.

The servant of the God came out and stood waiting in the center of the courtyard, his yellow robe shining bright as the sun that beat down on him. Abivard turned to Denak, helping her off with the mantle that had kept her gown clean. "Are you ready?" he murmured. The veil hid her face, but she nodded. He took her hands—the only part of her visible—and led her toward the holy man.

The sun shimmered from the gown, too. It was a rich blue silk, patterned with back-to-back peacocks that shared a golden, jewel-decked nimbus. Above each pair floated a lily leaf; between pairs stood fancy columns with floral capitals.

"May the God and the Four bless you and keep you," the holy man said as they took their places by him. Abivard's eyes turned to the doorway to the stronghold's living quarters. It opened. Out came Pradtak, one arm in a sling, the other hand clutching a stick to help hold him upright. He took almost all his weight on his right leg. Pain cut through the grim determination on his face every time his left foot touched the ground.

Abivard studied him—was this man worthy of his sister? Pradtak was somewhere close to thirty, of a good height, with regular features and a beard trimmed more closely than most. He had courage, to walk on an ankle that so obviously had yet to heal. At first glance, he seemed suitable, though in his heart Abivard reckoned none but the King of Kings a suitable groom for Denak—and even that would not do, not now, not when a graybeard like Smerdis held the throne of Makuran.

The wedding ceremony began. Pradtak agreed it was his will that he marry Denak. The servant of the God turned to Abivard and said, "Is it your will, Abivard son of Godarz, that the betrothal of your sister agreed to by your father be made into a true marriage this day?"

"It is my will," Abivard declared, as firmly as he could. The servant of the God asked Denak if she also consented to the marriage. She put more voice into her answer than Roshnani had, but not much.

The holy man gave her and Pradtak the ritual dates they ate together in token of union and fertility. Denak handed hers to her new husband; he gave his to her. As Roshnani had, she contrived to eat the fruit without showing Pradtak her face. *Let him wait,* Abivard thought. *I had to.*

The servant of the God took the pits from the dates and put them in a pouch on his belt for later replanting. Then he set Denak's hands between Pradtak's. The folk of Nalgis Crag cheered and threw grain at the newlywed couple.

And then, as he now could with propriety, Pradtak lifted his bride's veil to see what manner of woman his father's bargain with Godarz all those years before had got him. Abivard needed an effort of will not to curl his hands into anxious fists. If Pradtak humiliated his sister . . . he didn't know what he would do, but it would be ugly. For Denak's sake, it would have to be.

But Pradtak smiled. He nodded to Abivard. "I find I am a fortunate man this day, my brother-in-law."

"May you and my sister be fortunate together for many years to come," Abivard answered, returning courtesy for courtesy. Then he said, "Now that we have been joined, my clan and yours, may I take the liberty of asking you one question that has nothing to do with this wedding?"

"A quick one," Pradtak said, his eyes full of Denak.

"Quick indeed; I would not delay you. Just this, then: have you yet sworn loyalty to Smerdis King of Kings?"

That made Pradtak think of something other than the nuptial bed. Cautiously, he answered, "Aye, I have. I found no compelling reason to do otherwise, as Sharbaraz has renounced the throne. And you?"

"The same," Abivard said, "and for the same reasons. Thank you, my brother-in-law."

"As you said, the question was quick," Pradtak said. "Now,

though, with my bride and my ankle, I have two good reasons to want to be off my feet."

"You may lean on me, if it eases you," Denak said. "Am I not to be your support in years to come?"

"You are," Pradtak admitted, "but not in public. This journey I shall make unaided, to feed my own pride. Walk beside me, if you will."

Denak's eyes flicked to Abivard—*maybe for the last time,* he thought with another stab of pain—asking him what she should do. Very slightly, he nodded. Robbing a man of his pride would not do, not on a wedding day, and, if Pradtak had managed to walk out here, he would probably make it back to the living quarters by himself.

So he did, albeit slowly, Denak at his side but not touching him. The crowd in the courtyard that would have surged after the newlyweds perforce came slowly instead, and jammed up at the entrance. Once inside, most of them turned to the left, toward the delicious smells coming from the kitchens. Others followed Pradtak and Denak rightward, toward the *dihqan's* bed-chamber, baying the same sort of advice Abivard had heard not long before.

He went right himself, not out of lubricity but to show he had confidence in Denak and to deal with any difficulties that might arise. Should that square of cloth come out unbloodied, Pradtak could, if it suited him, declare the marriage void. Abivard did not expect that, but duty demanded that he be there in case of problems.

The door to the bedchamber closed. He heard the bar thud into place. After that, all was silent within. Some of the men speculated lewdly on what was going on. Abivard wanted to draw sword on them, but restrained himself: at a wedding, such jokes had their place. As minutes stretched, people got tired of waiting and drifted off toward the food.

Thump! In the bedchamber, someone removed the bar. The door opened. To cheers from the people still in the hallway, Abivard's not softest among them, Pradtak showed off a blood-stained square of cotton. "My brother-in-law indeed," he called to Abivard, removing any possible doubts.

Abivard bowed in return, then made his way to the kitchens, too. Denak would be going into the women's quarters, to emerge but seldom thereafter. It seemed imperfectly fair.

"Is all well?" Frada asked with his mouth full. He had pocket bread stuffed with mutton and pine nuts in one hand, a mug of wine in the other.

"All is well," Abivard said. "Did you expect otherwise?" He waited for Frada to shake his head, then went on, "Let me get some food, too; what you have there looks good. But after we've stayed long enough for politeness' sake, I want to leave for home as soon as we may."

"Why?" Concern etched Frada's face. "Did Pradtak offer offense to you or to our sister?" His hand slipped to the hilt of his sword. "If he did—"

"No, no," Abivard said quickly. "Nothing of the sort. All the same, this stronghold puts me out of spirit. The sooner I see Vek Rud domain once more, the gladder I shall be."

Here and there, Makuran was a spectacularly fertile land. Between here and there, it was desert. Not even lizards skittered across the gravel-strewn path from Pradtak's domain back to Abivard's.

He and his party set out at earliest dawn, to make as much distance as they could before the worst heat of the day. As the sun rose, it painted the hills north and west of Nalgis Crag in shadows of rose and coral, so that several men pointed to them and exclaimed over their loveliness.

But when the sun rose higher and its own rays lost the ruddiness of early morning, the hills revealed their true hues—dun brown and ashen gray. "They might as well be women," Frada said. "Take away their paint and they are beautiful no longer."

Most of the horsemen laughed heartily at that sally. Under other circumstances, Abivard would have joined them. But he was lost in thoughtful silence, wondering how Denak fared not only in Pradtak's arms but also in the women's quarters of the stronghold. For that matter, he wondered how Roshnani was faring back at Vek Rud domain. All had seemed well when he set out with Denak, but who could say what might have happened in the days since?

Frada asked him, "Do you think the smiths will have finished an armor by the time we get back to our stronghold? I know that first suit will be yours—you're *dihqan*, after all. But I'll wear the second."

"Don't be too eager to wear it, even once it's made," Abivard answered. "Had the domain boasted a seventh suit, you likely would have fared with us out onto the steppe, which meant you'd have been unlikely to come home safe again."

Frada only snorted. He didn't believe anything bad could ever happen to him. Abivard hadn't believed that, either, not until he saw the banner of Peroz King of Kings fall into the Khamorth trench. After that, he could not doubt misfortune fell on all, base and royal alike.

Out in the middle of the rocky, waterless plain, in stretches bare even of thorn bushes, a blue, shimmering mirage—a ghost lake, Godarz had always called it—gave the illusion of water in plenty. To make itself even more tantalizing, it kept pace with the travelers as they rode along, never letting them gain a foot on it. A thirsty man who did not know the lake for illusion would surely have perished pursuing it.

"By the God," Abivard said, "if the Khamorth do invade our land, may they seek to drink deep from a ghost lake and follow it to their ruin."

Frada said, "Perhaps they will remain on their own side of the Degird. If they were going to push into Makuran, would they not have done it already?"

"Who can say what's in a nomad's mind?" Abivard answered. "We and the steppe have warred since the days when heroes walked the earth. Now one side wins, now the other." Seldom, though, he thought, had victory been so absolute.

As day dwindled, the riders looked for a halting point. After unspoken consultation with men older and more experienced than himself, Abivard chose the tip of a low hillock that even boasted a few bushes and shrubs to fuel watch fires. He did not need advice in ordering sentries out in a triangle around the camp. Anyone, bandit or nomad, who wanted to surprise him in the darkness would have to work for it.

He never knew whether his precautions had anything to do with the peaceful night that followed, but he had no intention of neglecting them when evening twilight came again. After pancakes fried on a flat griddle and sour wine, the wedding party set out for Vek Rud domain once more.

Several days passed thus, and the stronghold grew ever nearer. Then, about an hour before noon, when Abivard was thinking of laying up for a while until the weather cooled, he spotted a group of men on horseback coming toward him and his followers.

"Not a caravan," Frada said, curiosity in his voice. "They're riding all the horses they have. I wonder what they're doing here." He shaded his eyes with the palm of his hand in hope of seeing better.

"No doubt they're wondering the same of us." Abivard made sure his sword was loose in its scabbard and his lance in its rest on the saddle. The men who approached might have been celebrants like the group he led. Or they might have been bandits, in which case they would sheer off soon: the numbers of the two parties were close to even, and bandits seldom relished odds like those.

Frada peered through heat haze again. "Miserable little horses they're on," he said. "They're no better than that steppe pony you brought back from—" He stopped, his mouth and eyes both opening wide.

Abivard knew what he was thinking; the same idea blazed in his own mind. "Khamorth!" he shouted, loud enough to startle himself. "Form line of battle. By the God, let's see if we can get ourselves a small measure of revenge."

His companions peeled off to either side of the road. They hadn't been trained to fight as a unit, but they knew what they had to do. When Abivard waved them forward, they booted their horses into a trot: no point to an all-out gallop till they drew closer to the foe.

"Stay in line," Abivard urged, eyes on the nomads ahead. They milled about in confusion for a moment, as if surprised at being recognized for what they were. But then they, too, shook themselves out into a fighting line more ragged than that of their Makuraner foes. They came on with as little hesitation as Abivard's men.

"Makuraaan!" Frada shouted. In an instant, the whole wedding party was screaming the war cry. No one, Abivard noted, yelled the name of Smerdis King of Kings. He remained too new on the throne to make much of a symbol for the land he ruled.

The Khamorth shouted, too, harshly. To Abivard, their unintelligible yells seemed like the bellows of wild beasts. Then, almost at the same instant, the nomads reached over their left shoulders for arrows, rose from their short stirrup leathers until they were all but standing, and let fly. Abivard flung up his shield. Buzzing like an angry wasp, an arrow flew past his head. One of his men let out a cry of pain, but no saddles emptied.

"Gallop!" Abivard cried, and spurred his horse forward.

The Khamorth broke off their own advance and fled back the way they had come, shooting arrows over their shoulders. But their aim was poorer that way, and the men pursuing them, though not armored in iron, still had some protection against glancing hits. And because the Makuraners were without their usual heavy mail and horse trappings, their big steeds ran faster than they would have otherwise. They quickly gained ground on the plainsmen.

The nomads realized that, too. They broke into several small groups and raced across the barren plain in different directions.

Abivard and Frada pounded side by side after a couple of Khamorth. One of the nomads yanked out his curved shamshir, but too late. Abivard's lance took him in the back, just below the left shoulder. He had never before felt the soft resistance flesh and bone gave to sharp-pointed iron. The Khamorth threw his arms wide; the sword flew from his hand. He let out a bubbling shriek and crumpled.

Blood gushed from the hole in the nomad's back when Abivard yanked the lance free. The point, which had gone in bright and shiny, came out dripping red, as did the last foot of the shaft. Abivard gulped. Talking about slaughtering Khamorth was all very well, but the harsh reality almost made him lose his breakfast.

"No time to be sick," he told himself aloud, and wheeled his horse to see how Frada was doing against his foe. His younger brother's lance thrust had missed; now he was using the long spear to hold at bay the plainsman he faced. Abivard spurred toward the battling pair. When the Khamorth turned his head to gauge the new threat, Frada punched the lancehead through his throat.

More blood spurted. Its iron stink filled Abivard's nostrils, as at the butchering of a sheep. He looked around to learn how the rest of the Makuraner wedding party fared.

Two big horses were down, and another galloped across the plain with an empty saddle. But the Khamorth had lost six or seven men, and the rest fled wildly from the Makuraners. The little battle hadn't lasted long but, such as it was, it brought victory to Abivard and his followers.

He expected them to burst into wild cheers, the cheers denied them when they had invaded the steppes. That didn't happen. He didn't feel like cheering himself, not now. Just savoring being alive sufficed.

He rode toward a shaggy-bearded man in the sueded leather of Pardraya who lay writhing on the ground. One of the Khamorth's legs twisted at an unnatural angle; both his hands were pressed to hold in his belly, trying without hope of success to keep the red tide of his life from ebbing away. Abivard speared him again, this time in the neck. The nomad thrashed a few times, then quit moving.

"Why did you do that?" Frada asked.

"He wasn't going to live, not with wounds like those," Abivard said, shrugging. "I don't have the stomach to torment him for the sport of it. What else would you have me do but put him out of his pain, then? I pray to the God someone would do the same for me, were I in such straits."

"Put that way, what you say makes sense." Frada sounded surprised even so, especially at the idea of having anything dreadful happen to him in battle. Abivard understood that. Up until a few weeks before, he had felt the same way. Not any more. He knew better now.

The Makuraners reassembled. Some of them dismounted to strip their fallen foes of bows and arrows, curved swords, and ornaments. "Look here," someone called, holding a gold brooch. "This is Makuraner work, surely plunder from the lost battle on the plains."

"Good and fitting that it return to its proper home, then," Abivard said. He looked around, seeing how his own men had come through the fight. Someone had just broken off an arrow and pulled it through Vidarnag's arm; the rag tied around the wound was turning red, but not too fast. Farnbag had a cut on his cheek through which Abivard could see several of his teeth. *Have to sew that up now,* he thought, *or it may be a hole for the rest of his days.* A couple of others had lesser hurts.

And Kambujiya and Dostan were missing. Half a furlong away lay a body with a lance beside it. The Makuraner's helm had fallen off, revealing a shiny bald pate. That was Dostan, then. And there sprawled Kambujiya, over in the other direction.

"The God grant them peace," Abivard said. He made some quick mental calculations. The wedding party was at most two days from Vek Rud domain. The very last part of the ride would be unpleasant, but ... "We'll tie them onto a couple of pack-horses. Let them rest in the soil with their fathers."

"And let the jackals and ravens and buzzards squabble over the remains of the Khamorth," Frada added.

"Aye," Abivard said, "and may they find them sweet." He plucked at his bearded chin in a gesture he had picked up from his father. "Now what we have to find out is whether these plainsmen were on their own or if they're part of a bigger band. If they are ..." He made a sour face. If they were, his assumption that the nomads would stay on their own side of the Degird had to go.

After the corpses of the two slain men had been picked up, the Makuraners started north and west again. Now they rode as if expecting battle at any time and from any direction, with one man a couple of furlongs ahead at point and another the same distance behind the main group to serve as rear guard.

They saw no more plainsmen for the rest of the day. When evening drew near, Abivard looked for a defensible campsite with even more care than he had before. Then he had worried about what might happen. Now he knew it could.

He finally found a steep hillock that might have been crowned with a stronghold had the land around it boasted any water. As he had before, he set out pickets in a triangle around it. He took his own turn at watch, too, replacing Frada for the middle-of-the-night stint.

"All quiet here," his brother reported, yawning. Lowering his voice, Frada added, "I would not say so in front of the men, but I mislike the omen we're bringing home."

"Aye, I had the same thought myself," Abivard answered, also quietly. "A wedding party's supposed to fetch back joy and hope. Instead, we'll hear women wailing when we get home to the stronghold." He spread his hands. "But what choice have we?"

"None I see," Frada said. "But all Makuran has heard too much of women wailing this season."

"Which does not mean we shall not hear more." Abivard slapped his brother on the back. "You fought well. Now go back up by the fire and get some rest."

Frada took a couple of steps, then stopped and turned back. "It's an uglier business than I thought—fighting, I mean. The blood, the stinks, the fear—" He hesitated before that last, as if afraid of being thought unmanly.

"Oh, yes," Abivard said. He couldn't see his brother's face; it was dark, and Frada stood between him and the embers of the fire, with his back to their glow. But he did see Godarz's younger son let his shoulders slump in relief.

Abivard paced back and forth on watch, not to be more vigilant but because he knew he was liable to fall back to sleep if he sat down in one place. But for the faint *scrape-scrape* of his boots on dirt and gravel, the night was eerily quiet. Once, a long way away, a fox yipped. After so much silence, the sound made Abivard start and grab for his sword.

He laughed at his own nerves as he began to pace again. Even to himself, though, the laughter seemed hollow. With the Khamorth loose in Makuran, every traveler who went beyond sight of his own stronghold would run risk of ambush. Some of those who failed to start at imaginary dangers would also fail to start at real ones.

The moon was down. The night was very black, stars glittering like tiny jewels set on velvet. The faint glimmer of what the Makuraners called the God's Robe stretched from horizon to horizon. Abivard never remembered seeing it clearer.

A shooting star flashed across the sky, then another. He whispered a prayer for the souls of Dostan and Kambujiya, carried through the Void on those stars. A third star fell. He couldn't believe it ferried the spirit of a Khamorth to the God. On the other hand, all too likely more Makuraners than his own two companions had fallen to the nomads today.

IV

THE RIDER TOOK FROM HIS BELT A TUBE OF LEATHER BOILED IN WAX to make it impregnable to rain and river water. With a flourish, he undid the stopper and handed Abivard the rolled-up parchment inside. "Here you are, lord."

"Thank you." Abivard gave the fellow half a silver arket; people often cut coins to make change. The horseman bowed in the saddle, dug heels into his mount's sides, and rode away from Vek Rud stronghold.

Abivard unrolled the parchment. He had been sure the letter was from Denak; not only had he recognized the courier from his own trip to Nalgis Crag domain, but no one save his sister was likely to write him in any case. Still, seeing her carefully formed script always made him smile.

" 'To the *dihqan* Abivard his loving sister Denak sends greetings,' " he read, murmuring the words aloud as if to call up her voice. " 'I am gladder than I can say that you came home safe from the fight with the Khamorth. We have not seen any of the barbarians in this domain, and hope we do not. And, as you can see, Pradtak my husband has no objection to your writing to me or to my replying. I think he was surprised to learn I have my letters; I may be the only one in the women's quarters here who does.' "

Abivard frowned when he read that. Being singled out as different wouldn't make life in the women's quarters any easier for Denak. He read on: " 'While caring greatly that his domain should prosper, Pradtak also enjoys the pleasures of the hunt. He still cannot ride, and pines for the day when he will again be able to pursue the wild ass and the gazelle.' "

When he can stop worrying about the domain and go off and have fun, Abivard read between the lines. His father had occasionally had some pointed things to say about *dihqans* who put their own pleasures first. Denak would have heard them, too. Abivard wondered if she was trying to make her new husband see sense.

He looked down at the letter again. " 'Because I read and write, he entrusts me day by day with more of the administration of the domain. Everything here is new to me, and I have more responsibilities than I am used to shouldering, but I try to decide what our father would have done in any given case. So far this seems to work well; the God grant it continue so. I pray to her to keep you well, and eagerly await next word from you.' "

So Father now runs two domains, even if not in the flesh. The thought made Abivard smile. He suspected it would have made Godarz smile, too. From Denak's letter, she was well on the way to becoming Pradtak's right hand, and probably three fingers of the left, as well.

He rolled up the letter again and put it back in its tube. Later he would read it to Burzoe, who no doubt would be proud of what her daughter was accomplishing. He wondered if he should read it to Roshnani. Maybe she would think it obligated her to try to run Vek Rud domain as Denak was taking over at Nalgis Crag. But Abivard was no Pradtak: he had his own ideas about how things should go.

For now, he would put guards out with his herdsmen, to protect them and their flocks from small Khamorth raiding parties. If a whole clan decided to try to settle on his grazing lands, guard detachments wouldn't be enough to hold them at bay, but he kept hoping that wouldn't happen. Of course, none of his hopes had come to much since he crossed into Pardraya.

"Well," he said to no one in particular, "everything that possibly could go wrong has already gone and done it. Things have to get better from here on out."

The cry from the battlements brought Abivard up the stairs at a dead run: "Soldiers! Soldiers under the lion banner of the King of Kings!"

Following a sentry's pointing finger, Abivard saw for himself the approaching detachment. It was bigger than he had expected, a couple of hundred men in bright surcoats over iron armor. If they hit the Khamorth, they could hit them hard. Abivard's heart leaped to see the sign of returning Makuraner might. "Open the gates," he shouted. "Let us make these heroes welcome."

While the gates swung slowly open, Abivard descended to greet the newcomers in person. All the doubts he had had about Smerdis King of Kings vanished like a brief rain shower into the soil of the desert. The new ruler was stretching forth his hand to protect his distant provinces.

Not all the riders could enter the courtyard together. Abivard ordered bread and wine sent to those who had to wait outside the walls. "You are blessed by the God for coming to the frontier in our hour of need," he told the commander of Smerdis' force, a tough-looking veteran with gray mustachios waxed into stiff spikes.

Even from a man who was nothing more than a soldier, he had expected a courteous reply; the folk of Makuran could swap compliments from morning till night. But the commander, instead of praising Abivard's hospitality or the site of his stronghold, suffered an untimely coughing fit. When at last he could speak again, he said, "You would be better advised, magnificent *dihqan*, to address your remarks to my colleague here, the famous Murghab."

Abivard had taken the famous Murghab to be the commander's scribe. He was a desiccated little man in a plain gray-brown caftan who looked uncomfortable on his horse. But if the soldier said he was a person of consequence, Abivard would greet him properly. Bowing low, he said, "How may I serve the splendid servant of Smerdis King of Kings, may his years be many and his lands increase?"

"Your attitude does you credit," Murghab said in a voice like rustling leaves. "I shall speak frankly: Smerdis King of Kings finds himself in need of silver and is levying a special assessment on each domain. We require from you payment of—" He pulled out a sheet of parchment and ran his finger down till he found the line he needed. "—eight thousand five hundred silver arkets, or their equivalent in kind. The assessment is due and payable forthwith."

Now Abivard coughed, or rather choked. He also felt like an idiot. He could not possibly say no, not now, not after he had let so many of the King of Kings' warriors into Vek Rud stronghold. A dozen of them sat their horses between him and the doorway to the living quarters. They watched him with polite but careful attention, too—they were readier for trouble than he had been.

He gathered himself. He had that much silver in his treasury. If Smerdis was going to use it to defend the kingdom, it might even prove money well spent, however much he regretted parting with it. He said, "I hope Smerdis King of Kings is using my silver and what he gets from other *dihqans* to enroll new soldiers in his lists and to hire smiths to make armor and weapons for them."

The famous Murghab said not a word. Puzzled, Abivard looked to the military commander. The officer fidgeted in the saddle, waiting for Murghab to reply, but when he remained mute, the fellow said, "Smerdis King of Kings orders this silver collected so as to pay an enormous sum of tribute to the Khamorth, that they may withdraw over the Degird and stay on their side of the river henceforward."

"What?" Abivard howled, forgetting the disadvantage at which Smerdis' soldiers had him. "That's crazy!"

"So Smerdis King of Kings has ordained; so shall it be," Murghab intoned. "Who are you to question the will of the King of Kings?"

Put that way, Abivard was nobody, and he knew it. Instead of answering Murghab, he turned to the commander. "But don't you see, bold captain, that paying tribute when we're too weak to defend ourselves only invites the plainsmen back to collect a new pile of silver next year, and the year after that?"

"So Smerdis King of Kings has ordained; so shall it be," the officer said tonelessly. Though his words echoed Murghab's, his expression and manner argued he was less than delighted at the policy he had been ordered to uphold.

Murghab said, "The sum heretofore cited is due and payable now. Do not waste time even to scratch your head. Surely you would not wish to be construed as resisting the King of Kings?"

Had Abivard not let the foxes into the henhouse, he would have thought hard about resisting—as well throw his silver down a *qanat* as convey it to the Khamorth. As things were . . . Tasting gall, he said, "Bide here, O famous Murghab." He could not resist putting a sardonic twist on the man's honorific. "I shall bring you what you require, and may Smerdis King of Kings—and the Khamorth—have joy of it."

Godarz had been a methodical man. The silver in the stronghold's treasure room was stored in leather sacks, a thousand arkets to each. Abivard picked up two sacks, one in each hand, and, grunting a little, carried them through the halls and out of the living quarters to the courtyard, where he set them in front of Murghab's horse. He made the same trip three more times.

"Bide here a moment more, famous sir," he said when he had brought out eight thousand arkets. He went back into the treasury. Only three sacks of coins remained there, as well as some empty ones neatly piled to await filling. Abivard took one of those and dumped jingling silver coins into it till it weighed about as much as the sack from which he was taking the money. He sighed; this wasn't how Godarz had intended the sack to be used. He had wanted silver coming in, not going out. But Abivard could do nothing about that, not now. He carried out the half-filled sack and set it with the rest. "This may be twenty or thirty arkets too light, or it may be so much too heavy. Will you be satisfied, or must you have an exact count?"

Murghab pursed his lips. "The order of the King of Kings, may his years be long, calls for eight thousand five hundred, no more, certainly no less. Therefore I am of the opinion that—"

"It suffices, lord," the officer who led the detachment of royal soldiers broke in. "You have cooperated most graciously with our request."

What am I supposed to do, when you're already inside my stronghold? Abivard thought. Nonetheless, the soldier at least adhered to the courtesies Makuraners held dear. Abivard put the best face on extortion he could, saying with a bow, "It is a privilege for any subject to serve the King of Kings in any manner he requires. May I have your name, that I may commend you to him for the manner in which you perform your duties?"

"You honor me beyond my deserts," the soldier replied. Abivard shook his head. He wished he didn't know the famous Murghab's name. He couldn't say that aloud, but had the feeling the officer knew it. The fellow added, "Since you ask, lord, I am Zal."

"Zal," Abivard repeated, locking the name in his memory. He would not forget it. Nor would he forget Murghab, however much he tried. He asked, "May I serve you in any other way?"

"I think we are quits here." Zal sketched a salute to Abivard. At his order, a couple of men dismounted and loaded the silver from Vek Rud domain onto the patient back of a packhorse. Without apparent irony, Zal said, "May the God grant you continued prosperity."

Why? So you can come back and shear me again? Probably for that very reason, Abivard judged. But he could not afford such an outrageous payment again . . . and now he knew better than to open his gates to Smerdis' men. The next time they wanted silver for tribute, the would have to get it from him the hard way.

The *dihqan*'s bedchamber had a window that faced east, giving its occupant the chance to look out over the domain. That window also let in early-morning sunbeams, to ensure that its occupant did not sleep too far into the day. Had the chamber not belonged to *dihqans* long before Godarz's time, Abivard would have guessed that was his father's scheme. Whosever idea it had been, back in the dim days when the stronghold was raised, it still worked.

One of those sunbeams pried his eyelids open. He sat up in bed and stretched. Roshnani was lying with her back to the sun, and so remained asleep. He smiled and set a gentle hand on the curve of her bare hip. His skin, toasted over years by the sun, was several shades darker than hers.

A dihqan's wife should be pale, he thought. *It shows she doesn't have to leave the women's quarters and work like some village woman.* Even after Smerdis' depredations, the domain was not so far gone as that.

Roshnani shifted on the down of the mattress. Abivard jerked his hand away; he hadn't wanted to waken her. But her squirming brought her face into the path of the sunbeam. She tried to twist away, but too late: her eyes came open.

She smiled when she saw Abivard. "Good morning, sun in my window," she said. "Maybe that last one started a boy in me." She set a hand on her belly, just above the midnight triangle between her legs.

"Maybe it did," he answered. "And if it didn't, we could always try again." He made as if to leap at her then and there. It was only play; he'd learned she wasn't in the mood for such things at daybreak. He did let his lips brush across hers. "Who would have thought a marriage where neither of us saw the other till after we were pledged could bring so much happiness with it?"

"I saw you," she corrected him. "Dimly and through the veil, but I did."

"And?" he prompted, probing for a compliment.

"I didn't flee," she answered. He poked her in the ribs. She squeaked and poked him back. He was ticklish, a weakness his father and brothers had exploited without mercy. He grabbed Roshnani to keep her from doing anything so perfidious again.

One thing led to another, and presently he discovered she could be in the mood for an early-morning frolic after all.

Afterward, he said, "I'm greedy for you. I want to call you here again tonight."

"I'd like that, too," she said, running a fingertip down the middle of his chest, "but you might be wiser to choose another."

"Why?" He suspected his frown was closer to a pout. Having a great many lovely women at his disposal was a young man's fantasy. Reality, Abivard had discovered, was less than imagination had led him to believe. Oh, variety every once in a while was enjoyable, but he preferred Roshnani over the wives he had inherited from Godarz.

When he told her as much, she glowed like a freshly lighted lamp. All the same, she said, "You still might be better advised to choose someone else tonight. If you call only for me, I will be hated in the women's quarters—and so shall you."

"Has it come to that?" Abivard asked, alarmed.

"I don't believe so, not yet, but I've heard mutters around corners and from behind closed doors that make me fear such a thing is not far away," Roshnani answered. "Your lady mother might perhaps tell you more. But this I say: better to give up a little happiness now if in the giving you save a great deal later."

The words had the ring of sense Abivard was used to hearing from Burzoe, which to his mind meant Roshnani had the makings of as fine a principal wife as any *dihqan* could hope for.

"Do you know what you are?" he asked her. She shook her head. "A woman in ten thousand," he said. "No, by the God, in a hundred thousand."

That earned him a kiss, but when he tried for more this time, Roshnani pulled away. "You must be able to give your best to whomever you call tonight," she said.

He glowered in mock indignation. "Now you presume to question my manhood?" But since he had a pretty good notion of what he could do in that regard, he made no more than that mild protest—Roshnani was too likely to be right.

When evening came, he summoned Ardini instead of Roshnani. She came to his bedchamber in a silken gown so transparent he could see the two tiny moles she had just below her navel. That excited him, but she had drenched herself in rose water till she smelled stronger than a perfumer's. He almost sent her back to the women's quarters to scrub it off, but desisted: no point in embarrassing her. He regretted that later, for the bedchamber was redolent of roses for the next several days.

Abivard conscientiously summoned each of his wives from the women's quarters in turn. A couple of times, he had to pretend to himself that he was really making love with Roshnani, though he took special pains to make sure those partners never noticed. Thinking of what he did as a duty helped him get through it. He suspected that would have amused Godarz.

The duty done, though, he went back to spending most of his nights with Roshnani. Most of the times he summoned other women were at her urging. Some principal wives, he knew, would have grown arrogant if shown such favor. Roshnani did her best to act as if she were just one of many. That only inclined Abivard to favor her more.

One morning after sleeping alone—he had been drinking wine with Frada and some of his older half brothers, and came to bed too drunk to be much interested in female companionship—he woke with a headache so splitting, he didn't even feel like sitting up. Still flat on his belly, he reached down and blindly groped for his sandals. All he managed to do, though, was push them farther under the bed, beyond the reach of his sweeping arm.

"If I have to call a servant to bend down to get my shoes, everyone will know how bad I feel," he said aloud. Just hearing his own voice hurt, too. But even hung over, Abivard was dutiful. He got out of bed—actually, he came close to falling out of bed—and pulled out first one sandal, then the other.

Suffused in a warm glow of virtue that almost masked his crapulence, he was about to don the captured footgear when his bloodshot gaze fell on something else under the bed, something he didn't remember seeing there before—not that he spent a lot of time looking under the bed: a small, dark-gray, rectangular tablet.

Before he thought much about what he was doing, his hand snaked out and seized the tablet. His eyebrows rose as he pulled it out to where he could get a good look at it: it was heavier than he had expected. "Has to be lead," he said.

The upper side of the tablet was blank and smooth, but his fingers had felt marks on the thing, so he turned it over. Sure enough, the other side had words cut into the soft metal, perhaps with an iron needle. They were, at the moment, upside down.

Abivard turned it over. The words became clear. As he read them, his blood ran cold. *May this tablet and the image I make bind Abivard to me in cords of love. May he waste away from wanting me; may desire cling to him like a leech from the swamps. If he wants me not, may he burn with such pain that he would wish for the Void. But if he should die of desire for me, let him never look on the face of the God. So may it be.*

Moving as if in a bad dream, Abivard broke the curse tablet in two and spat on the pieces. Now his heart pounded as hard as his head. He had heard of women using magic to bind a man to them, but he had never imagined such a thing happening in the women's quarters of Vek Rud stronghold.

"Who?" he whispered. Roshnani? He couldn't believe that— but if she had ensorceled him, he wouldn't believe it, would he? Did she make him so happy because she had magically compelled him to fall in love with her?

It was possible. With cold rationality, he recognized that. He wondered how he would ever trust another woman if it proved to be so. But he also knew it didn't have to be so, not when he had had every one of his wives out of the women's quarters and into his bedchamber in the recent past.

He started to call for Burzoe, but then shook his head. He did not want even his mother to know of the curse tablet. If she let slip an unfortunate word, as even the wisest person, man or woman, might do, chaos would rule the women's quarters, with everyone suspecting everyone else. If he could find any way to prevent that, he would.

Whistling tunelessly between his teeth, he tossed the broken pieces of the tablet onto the down-filled mattress. When he had thrown on a caftan and buckled the sandals whose escape under the bed had led him to find the tablet, he put on his belt and stuck the two chunks of lead in one of the pouches that hung from it.

He was out the door and walking down the hall before he realized he had stopped noticing his headache. *Amazing what fear will do,* he thought. It was not a hangover cure he hoped to use again any time soon.

The normally savory cooking smells wafting through the living quarters only made his stomach churn: terror hadn't cured him after all. He hurried out into the courtyard and then down into the village that lay below the stronghold on its knob.

He knocked at the door of Tanshar the fortune-teller. The old man was as close to being a proper wizard as anyone in the domain—and that thought made Abivard wonder if Tanshar had prepared the curse tablet and whatever image went with it. But he could more easily imagine the sky turning brown and the land blue than Tanshar involving himself in something like this.

Tanshar awkwardly held a crust of bread and a cup of wine in one hand to free the other so he could open the door. His eyes, one clouded, the other clear, widened in surprise when he saw who had disturbed his breakfast. "Lord Abivard," he exclaimed. "Come in, of course; you honor my home. But what brings you to me so early in the day?" Tanshar made it sound more like curiosity than reproach.

Abivard waited till the old man had closed and barred the door behind him before he fished out the broken pieces of the tablet and held them in the palm of his hand so Tanshar could see them. "I found this curse under my bed when I arose this morning," he said in a flat voice.

The fortune-teller reached for them. "May I?" he asked. At Abivard's nod, he took the two flat pieces of lead, put them together, and held them out at arm's length so he could read them. When he was done muttering the words to himself, he clicked his tongue between his teeth several times. "Am I to infer one of your wives left it there, lord?"

"I can't see anyone else wanting to. Can you?"

"It seems unlikely," Tanshar admitted. "What would you now of me, lord? Have you felt yourself under the influence of this spell? Love magic, like that of the battlefield, is often chancy, because passion reduces the effectiveness of sorcery."

"I honestly don't know whether the magic has hold of me or not," Abivard said. "I won't be able to decide that until I learn who put the tablet there." If it was Roshnani, he didn't know what he would do . . . No, he did know, but didn't want to think about it. He forced himself to steadiness. "I know you're a scryer. Can you see who did set that thing under my bed?"

"Lord, I believe I could, but is that truly what you'd have of me?" Tanshar asked. "If I were to look into your bedchamber for the moment in which the tablet was placed there, I would likely find you and the woman who left it in, ah, an intimate moment. Is that your desire?"

"No," Abivard said at once; he was wary of his own privacy, and even more wary of that of the denizens of the women's quarters. He scowled as he thought, then raised a finger. "The tablet speaks of an image. Can you scry out where that image is hidden? That will help tell me who made it."

"The domain is lucky to have a man of your wit at its head," the fortune-teller said. "I shall do as you command."

He set the pieces of the curse tablet down on a stool, then went off into the back room of the little house. He returned a moment later with a water jug and a small, glittering bowl of almost transparent black obsidian. He put the bowl on top of the two pieces of lead and poured it half full of water.

"We must wait until the water grows altogether still," he told Abivard. "Then, without roiling its surface with our breath, we shall look into it together and, unless the God should will otherwise, we shall see what you seek to learn. When the time comes, remember to think on the image whose whereabouts you'd find."

"As you say." Abivard waited as patiently as he could. He glanced down into the bowl. The water there looked calm to him. But scrying was not his business. Tanshar did not presume to tell him how to run the domain, so he would not joggle the fortune-teller's elbow.

When Tanshar was satisfied, he said quietly, "Lay your hand on the edge of the bowl—gently, mind, so as to stir the water as little as you may—and set your thoughts on the God and the Four and what you would learn."

Abivard wondered how he was supposed to keep two different sets of thoughts in his head. He did his best. The obsidian was glassy smooth under his fingertips, but his touch disturbed the glassy smoothness of the water in the bowl. He glanced over at Tanshar. The fortune-teller nodded back; this, evidently, was expected.

When the water settled to stillness again, it showed not the reflection of the ceiling, or of Abivard and Tanshar peering down into it, but a little doll of wool and clay, almost hidden in shadows. Four strings were wrapped around it, at head, neck, heart, and loins. Each was made of four threads of different colors.

"That is a perversion of the reverence due the Four." Tanshar's voice was still low, but full of anger.

Abivard hissed in frustration. He could see the image, yes, but hardly anything else, so he had no idea where in the stronghold—if it was in the stronghold—it rested. But the thought itself was enough to give him a wider view. He saw the image lay enshadowed because it rested behind a chest of drawers in a chamber he recognized as Roshnani's.

He jerked his hand away from the bowl as if it burned his fingers. Instantly the scrying picture vanished from the water, which now gave back the reflections it should have. His own face, he saw without surprise, was twisted into a grimace of anguish.

"The news is bad?" Tanshar asked.

"The news could not be worse," Abivard answered. To think that what he had imagined to be joy was just sorcery! He still could not believe Roshnani capable of defiling him so. But what else was he to think? There lay the doll in her room of the women's quarters. Who else would have hidden it so?

When he said that aloud, Tanshar answered, "Would you not sooner learn than guess? The bowl and the water still await your view, if that be your will."

Almost, Abivard said no. Seeing Roshnani conceal the magic image, he thought, would cost him more pain than he could bear. But he had borne a great deal of pain lately, so down deep he knew that was only cowardice talking. "That is my will," he said harshly. "Let the thing be certain."

"Wait once more for the water to settle," Tanshar said. Abivard waited in grim silence. The fortune-teller nodded at last. Abivard brought his hand to the bowl again, then had to wait for the water to grow calm after his touch.

This time he expected to have to wait before a picture formed. When it did, it showed Roshnani's chamber once more, and Roshnani herself sitting on a stool close by the chest behind which hid the image intended to bind Abivard in the ties of sorcerously induced love. She was bent over some embroidery, her pleasant face intent on the delicate needlework.

Abivard's glance flicked over to Tanshar. The fortune-teller's eyes were closed; he had the delicacy not to gaze upon his *dihqan*'s woman. At the moment, Abivard did not care about that. He peered down into the quiet water, waiting for Roshnani to get up from the stool and conceal the image.

She looked up from the needlework and rose. Abivard forced himself to absolute stillness, lest he disturb the scrying medium. He stared at the simulacrum of his wife, wondering how far into the past Tanshar's magic reached.

Whenever it was, Roshnani did not go over to the chest, though it was but a couple of paces away. Instead, she smilingly greeted another woman who walked into the chamber. The newcomer pointed to the embroidery and said something. To Abivard, of course, her lips moved silently. Whatever her words were, they pleased Roshnani, for her smile got wider.

The other woman spoke again. Roshnani picked up the embroidery from the stool and sat back down. She started to work again, perhaps demonstrating the stitch she had been using. The other woman watched intently for a little while—Abivard wasn't sure time ran at the same rate in the scrying bowl as in the real world—then leaned back against the chest of drawers.

There! Her hand snaked to the rear edge of the chest, opened for an instant, and then was back at her side. Intent on the needlework, Roshnani never noticed.

"By the God," Abivard said softly. He took his hand away from the polished obsidian bowl. The scrying picture vanished as if it had never been.

Tanshar felt the motion of withdrawal and opened his eyes. "Lord, have you that which you require?" he asked.

"I do." Abivard opened the pouch at his belt, took out five silver arkets, and pressed them into Tanshar's hand. The fortune-teller tried to protest, but Abivard overrode him: "For some things I would not spend silver so, not after the way the famous Murghab robbed the domain in the name of the King of Kings. But for this, I reckon the price small, believe me."

"Are you then ensorceled, lord?" Tanshar asked. "If it be so, I don't know if I am strong enough to free you from such a perverse enchantment."

But Abivard laughed and said, "No, I find I am not." He wondered why. Maybe his naturally conceived passion had been too strong for the artificial one to overcome; Tanshar had said love magic was a chancy business.

"I'm pleased to hear it," the fortune-teller said.

"I'm even more pleased to say it." Abivard bowed to Tanshar, then took the broken pieces of the lead tablet and headed up the dusty road to the stronghold. He stopped and stooped every few paces until he had picked up three black pebbles.

Roshnani looked up from her embroidery when Abivard stepped into the doorway. The smile she gave him reminded him of the one he had seen in the scrying bowl not long before. "What brings you here at this hour of the day?" she asked. Her smile grew mischievous as she thought of the obvious answer, then faded when she got a better look at his face. "Not that, surely."

"No, not that." Abivard turned to the serving woman who hovered behind him. "Fetch my lady mother and all my wives to this chamber at once. I know the hour is yet early, but I will have no excuses. Tell them as much."

"Just as you say, lord." The serving woman bobbed her head and hurried away. She knew something was wrong, but not what.

The same held for Roshnani. "What is it, husband of mine?" she asked. Now her voice held worry.

"Just wait," Abivard answered. "I'll tell the tale once for everyone."

Roshnani's chamber quickly grew crowded. Burzoe looked a question at her son as she came in, but he said nothing to her, either. Some of his wives grumbled at being so abruptly summoned from whatever they were doing, others because they had had no chance to gown themselves and apply their cosmetics. Most, though, simply sounded curious. A couple of Avibard's half sisters peered in from the corridor, also wondering what was going on.

Abivard brought the flat of his hand down onto the chest of drawers. The bang cut through the women's chatter and brought all eyes to him. He pulled out the two pieces of the curse tablet, held them high so everyone could see them. Quietly he asked, "Do you know what this is?"

Utter silence answered him, but the women's eyes spoke for them. Yes, they knew. Abivard dropped the pieces of lead onto the chest. They did not ring sweetly when they hit, as silver would have. The sound was flat, sullen.

He pushed a corner of the chest of drawers away from the wall and bent down to scoop up the image that went with the tablet. It was no longer than the last two joints of his middle finger, easy to conceal in the palm of a hand. He held it up, too. Someone—he didn't see who—gasped. Abivard removed the four cords that bound the image. Then he let it fall to the top of the chest. It broke in pieces.

He took out one of the black pebbles. He dropped it not onto the chest but onto the floor: the forms here had to be observed precisely. In a voice with no expression whatever in it, he said, "Ardini, I divorce you."

A sigh ran through the women, like wind through the branches of an almond grove. Ardini jerked as if he had stuck a sword in her. "Me!" she screeched. "I didn't do anything. This is Roshnani's room, not mine. If anyone's been in your bedchamber enough to try bewitching you, lord, she's the one, not me. You never want the rest of us, women who've been here for years. It's not right, it's not natural—"

"In a scrying bowl, I saw you hide the image here," he said, and dropped the second pebble. "Ardini, I divorce you."

"No, it wasn't me. It was somebody else. By the God I swear it. She—"

"Don't make your troubles in the next world worse by swearing a false oath." Formal and emotionless as a soldier making his report, Abivard told exactly what he had seen in the still water.

The women sighed again, all but Ardini. Roshnani said, "Yes, I remember that day. I was working on a bird with the bronze-brown thread."

"No, it's a lie. I didn't do it." Ardini's head twisted back and forth. Like so many people, she had figured out what her scheme's success would bring, but she had never stopped to think what would happen if she failed. Her voice sank to a whisper: "I didn't mean any harm." It might even have been true.

Abivard dropped the third pebble. "Ardini, I divorce you." It was done. With the fall of the third pebble, with the third repetition before witnesses of the formula of divorce, his marriage to her was dissolved. Ardini began to wail. Abivard clenched his jaw tight. Casting loose even a wife who had betrayed him was wrenchingly hard. So far as he knew, Godarz had never had to divorce one of his women, and so had left him no good advice on how to do it. He didn't think there could be any easy way.

"Please—" Ardini cried. She stood alone; all the other women had invisibly contrived to take a step away from her.

"I would be within my rights if I sent you forth from the women's quarters, from this stronghold, from this domain, naked and barefoot," Abivard said. "I will not do that. Take what you wear, take from your chamber whatever you can carry in your two hands, and be gone from here. The God grant we never see each other again."

Burzoe said, "If you let her go back into her chamber, son, send someone with her, to make sure she tries no more magic against you."

"Yes, that would be wise, wouldn't it?" Abivard bowed to his mother. "Would you please do that for me?" Burzoe nodded.

Ardini began screaming curses. Tears ran down her face, cutting through paint like streams of rainwater over dusty ground. "You cast me out at your peril," she cried.

"I keep you here at my peril," Abivard answered. "Go now and take what you would, or I will send you away as law and custom allow."

He thought that would shut Ardini up, and it did. She cared more for herself than anything else. Still weeping, she left Roshnani's room, Burzoe with her to keep her from working mischief.

Roshnani waited until the other wives, several of them loudly proclaiming undying loyalty to Abivard, had left her chamber. While they, Abivard's half sisters, and the serving women exclaimed in the hallway over the scandal, she told him, "Husband, I thank you for not thinking I set that image when you saw it. I know something of scrying; sometimes I can even make it work myself—"

"Can you?" Abivard said, interested. So much he still did not know about this young woman who had become his wife . . .

"Yes, though far from always. In any case, I know you would first have looked to find the image. When you saw it behind that chest, it would have been easy for you to look no farther and cast me out with the three black pebbles."

Abivard did not tell her how close he had come to doing just that. She thought better of him because he hadn't, and that was what he wanted. He said, "Tanshar—the town fortune-teller and scryer—said love magic was never sure to work, because it depended on passion. And my passion seems to have turned long since away from Ardini."

Roshnani cast down her eyes at that, but her face glowed. "I'm very glad it has," she said quietly.

"So am I." Abivard sighed. "And by now, I think Ardini has had enough time to gather whatever she would, so I shall have the delightful task of escorting her out of the women's quarters and the stronghold and ordering her out of the domain. By the God, I wish she could have been content here."

"Beware lest she try to stab you or some such," Roshnani said.

"She wouldn't—" Abivard stopped. He would never have done anything so foolish. But Ardini might indeed think that, with her life ruined, she had nothing to lose. "I'll be careful," he promised Roshnani.

The women parted before him as he strode down the hall to Ardini's chamber. She looked up from the bulging knapsack she had filled. She wasn't crying any more; such hatred filled her face that Abivard almost made a sign to avert the evil eye. He covered his brief alarm with brusqueness, jerking a thumb toward the doorway that led out of the women's quarters.

Muttering under her breath, Ardini walked up the hall toward the bedchamber where she had left the lead tablet. Abivard thanked the God it was the last time she would ever go there. He did his best not to listen to whatever she was saying, for fear he would have to take formal notice of it.

All the same, he watched her while he relocked the door, letting his fingers do the work without help from his eyes: he wanted to make sure she placed no other curses in the chamber. She stood in the middle of the room for a moment, then spat at the bed. "You're not a quarter the man your father was," she hissed.

That stung. He wanted to hit her. Only the thought that she was deliberately baiting him made him hold back—he didn't care to do anything she wanted him to. As mildly as he could, he answered, "Praising my father will not gain you my forgiveness." The deliberate misunderstanding made Ardini snarl. Even so, it didn't satisfy Abivard; when he flung open the outer door to the bedchamber, he let it slam against the wall with a loud crash.

A servant in the hallway spun round in startlement. "Lord, you frightened me there," he said, smiling. "You—" He broke off when he saw Ardini beside Abivard. That was a bigger surprise, and one that could not be met with a few glib words. "Is all well, lord?"

"No," Abivard said. "I have pronounced divorcement against this woman, for she used sorcery to try to bind me to her. I cast her forth from the women's quarters, from the stronghold, from the domain."

The servant stared. He nodded jerkily, then retreated almost at a dead run. *He'll have gossip to drink wine on for the next fortnight,* Abivard thought. He turned to Ardini. "Come along, you."

Out to the doorway of the living quarters they went, and out through the courtyard. People stopped and gaped, then tried to pretend they had done no such thing. At the gateway, Ardini fell to her knees and clasped Abivard around the thighs. "Let me stay!" she wailed. "By the God, I swear to love you forever."

He shook his head and freed himself as gently as he could. "You are already forsworn, thanks to your magic," he said. "Get up; go. May you find a life of peace somewhere far from here."

She hissed a filthy curse at him as she rose, then stalked off down the steeply sloping road. He made a mental note to send word to all the villages in the domain that she had been divorced and expelled. He wondered where she would go; back to her family's stronghold, he supposed. He realized he did not even know who her father was. *Have to ask my mother,* he thought. What Burzoe did not know about the *dihqan*'s women wasn't worth knowing.

Abivard sighed, wondering how much trouble the lying tales Ardini was sure to tell would cause him. He resolved to save the tablet, the fragments of the image, and the multicolored cords that had been tied around it, to prove he had indeed been sorcerously beset. Then he sighed again. Nothing ever seemed simple. He wished for once it was.

" 'To the *dihqan* Abivard his loving sister Denak sends greetings.' " Abivard smiled as he began the latest letter from Denak. Though he read it with his own voice, he could hear hers, too, and see the way her face would screw up in concentration as she dipped pen into jar of ink before committing words to parchment.

The letter went on, " 'I rejoice that you escaped the wicked magic aimed your way, and grieve for the scandal to your women's quarters. When you wrote of it to me, I confess I guessed Ardini's name before I saw it on the parchment. I know she expected to be named your principal wife—though as far as I know she had no reason save her pride and ambition for that expectation—and did not take well to the affection that flowered between you and Roshnani even in the brief time I was there after your wedding.' "

Abivard nodded slowly to himself. Ardini was young and lovely and, as Denak had said, ambitious. She had thought that was plenty of reason for him to make her his chief wife. Unfortunately for her, he had had other things in mind.

" 'I am well, and entrusted with ever greater management of this domain's affairs,' " Denak wrote. " 'Pradtak says he reckons me as useful as a Videssian steward, and by the work he gives me, I believe it. Yet our lady mother could do as much, even without the advantage of her letters. Parni, one of the women in the quarters, is with child. I hope I may soon be, as well.' "

"I hope you are, too, sister of mine," Abivard murmured. Indignation grew in him—how could Pradtak prefer this Parni, whoever she was, to Denak? Abivard laughed at himself, knowing he was being foolish. Starting a child was as much a matter of luck as anything else. Roshnani, for instance, was not pregnant, either, though not from lack of enthusiastic effort on his part.

All the same, he worried. If Parni gave Pradtak a son, presumably his first since becoming *dihqan*, she was liable to rise in his estimation and Denak to fall. That would not be good.

He read on: " 'My lord husband continues to recover from the bones he broke this summer. He no longer wears his arm in a sling, and can use it for most things, though it still lacks the strength of the other. He walks now with but a single stick, and can make several paces at a time without any aid whatever. He is also eager to return to horseback; he is in the habit of complaining how much he misses his games of mallet and ball, even if without them he would never have been hurt.'

" 'Meanwhile,' " Denak wrote, " 'aside from the pleasures of the women's quarters, he consoles himself with some scheme or other that he has not yet seen fit to impart to me—or to anyone, for if he had, word of it would surely have reached me through the serving women or his other wives. As I daresay you will have seen for yourself, the women's quarters hear gossip sometimes even before it is spoken.' "

"Isn't that the truth?" Abivard said aloud. He wondered what Pradtak was up to that even his principal wife couldn't know. Something foolish, was his guess: if it hadn't been, Pradtak would have let Denak in on it. Abivard hid nothing from Roshnani. How could he, if she was to give him all her aid in administering Vek Rud domain? Maybe Pradtak didn't see things that way; maybe Pradtak really was a fool.

Denak finished, " 'I look forward to your next letter; the God grant it may hold better news than Khamorth raiders and a wife who could not be trusted. Every time I see your familiar hand, I return to the stronghold where I grew up. I am well enough here, but the place and its people are not those I knew so long and so well. I rely on you to keep them green in my heart. Remember always your loving sister.' "

Down in the village, a carpenter was making Abivard a frame of pigeonholes, twenty by twenty, so it would have in all four hundred openings. After he had stored that many letters from Denak, he supposed he could have the man turn out another frame. He rolled up the letter, retied it with the ribbon that had held it closed, and went off to set it in the drawer that served for such things until the pigeonhole frame was done.

No sooner had he taken care of that than a shout from the wall brought him out of the living quarters in a hurry: "A band of riders off in the distance, making for the flocks northwest of us!"

He sprinted for the stables. So did every other warrior who had heard the lookout's cry. He had taken to leaving his helmet and shield there. No time for more armor, not now. He clapped the helm on his head, snatched up his lance, and hurried for the stall where stable boys were saddling his horse. As soon as they had cinched the last strap tight, he set a foot in the stirrup and swung up into the saddle.

In the next stall over, Frada mounted at almost the same instant. Abivard grinned at him and said, "We have it easy. From what Father used to say, his grandsire remembered the days before we learned from the nomads to use stirrups."

"How'd great-grandfather stay on his horse, then?" Frada asked.

"Not very well, is my guess." Abivard looked round the stables. More and more men were horsed, enough to make bandits or nomads or whoever the riders proved to be think twice about running off his sheep and cattle. He raised his voice to cut through the din: "Let's go get back what's ours. The shout will be 'Godarz!' "

"Godarz!" the Makuraners yelled, loud enough to make his head ring. He used the pressure of his knees and the reins to urge his gelding out of the stall, out of the stable, and out of the stronghold.

Going down the knob atop which sat Vek Rud domain, he had to keep the pace slow, lest his horse stumble on the slope. But when he got to the flatlands, he urged the animal ahead at a trot he could kick up into a gallop whenever he found the need.

Behind him, someone shouted, "There they are, the cursed carrion eaters!"

There they were indeed, not far from the Vek Rud River, cutting out half a flock of sheep. "They're Khamorth—'ware archery," Abivard called as he got close enough to recognize the robbers. He wondered what had happened to the shepherd and the men guarding the flock with him. Nothing good, he feared.

"Godaaarz!" The war cry rang out again. This time the Khamorth heard it. All at once they stopped being thieves and turned back into warriors. To Abivard, their moves had an eerie familiarity. After a moment, he realized they were fighting like the band that had attacked the wedding party on the way back from Nalgis Crag domain.

Instead of making him afraid, that sparked a sudden burst of confidence. "We beat the plainsmen once before," he yelled. "We can beat them again." Only when the words had passed his lips did he remember that the nomads had beaten his countrymen, too, and far more disastrously than his retainers had hurt them.

The horsemen who galloped alongside him seemed to have

forgotten that, too. They screamed like men possessed by demons. He had a decent number of archers with him today, too; he wouldn't have to come to close quarters to hurt the Khamorth.

The nomads started shooting at very long range. Abivard managed a scorn-filled laugh when an arrow kicked up dust a few yards away from his horse's hooves. "They think they can frighten us off with their bows," he said. "Will we let them?"

"No!" his men cried. Bowstrings thrummed to either side of him. One nomad's steppe pony slewed sideways and crashed to the ground. The Makuraners' shouts redoubled.

Then a shriek of pain cut through the war cries. Just to Abivard's left, a man slid off his galloping horse. He hit the ground limp as a sack of meal and did not move again. Now the plainsmen yelled in triumph.

With a deliberate effort of will, Abivard made himself not think about that. The Khamorth ahead grew from dots to dolls to men in what felt like a single heartbeat. He picked out a nomad, couched his lance, and bored in for the kill.

The Khamorth did not stick around to be stuck. In a fine bit of horsemanship, he made his animal wheel through a turn tighter than any Abivard would have imagined possible. As he galloped away, he shot back over his shoulder.

Abivard flung up his shield. The arrow ticked off its bronze-faced rim and tumbled away harmlessly. He knew a moment's relief, but only a moment's: the Khamorth shot again and again. He was not the finest archer the God had ever made, and shooting from a pounding horse at a moving target was anything but easy, anyhow. On the other hand, though, Abivard's horse was faster than his, which meant the range kept shortening.

"Aii!" Fire kissed the edge of Abivard's right leg. He looked down and saw he was bleeding. The shaft wasn't stuck in his leg; it had sliced his outer calf and flown on. Had he been wearing the lamellar armor the smiths were just now finishing, he might have escaped unwounded. No such luck, though.

Seeing he was about to be ridden down, the Khamorth drew his shamshir and slashed at Abivard's lance in the hope of chopping off its head. That did the nomad no good; the lancehead was joined to the shaft by a long iron ferrule. Abivard felt the blow in his shoulder but pressed on regardless.

At the last moment, the plainsman hacked at the lancehead again. He turned it enough to keep it from his own flesh, but it drove deep into the barrel of his horse. Appalled, Abivard yanked it back. The horse screamed louder and more piercingly—and with better reason—than Ardini ever had.

The Khamorth snarled a curse. His face, twisted in a grimace of hate, would stay in Abivard's memory forever: unkempt beard with threads of gray running through it, wide mouth shouting something perhaps a quarter comprehensible—two front teeth missing, a third black—beaky nose with a scar on the bridge, red-tracked eyes, lines on the forehead accented by ground-in smoke. The two men were close enough together that Abivard found himself trapped in the reek of ancient stale sweat and sour milk that hovered round the plainsman like a stinking cloud.

The steppe pony galloped wildly for perhaps a hundred yards, blood splashing the dry, dusty ground from the wound Abivard had made. Then, like a waterlogged ship at last slipping beneath the waves, it went down, slowly and gently enough for its rider to slip off and try to run.

The plainsman was slow and clumsy—his boots were not made for hard use on the ground. He had hung onto his bow; he had just wheeled around and was reaching for an arrow when Abivard's lance took him in the middle of the chest. The nomad grunted. The cry his horse let out had been much worse. A new stench joined the rest as the fellow folded up on himself.

Abivard jerked the lance free. He had to twist the head to clear it; it grated against the Khamorth's ribs as it came out. On the shaft, the plainsman's blood mingled with that of his horse. The new stains almost completely covered the older marks, now browned, where Abivard had first blooded the lance a few weeks before.

As in that first clash, he found that when he was engaged he could pay no attention to how the fight as a whole was going. When he looked around to get his bearings, he saw that most of the Khamorth had broken away and were galloping north for all they were worth.

Abivard and his men pounded after the nomads. The steppe ponies' hooves drummed on the timbers of the new bridge that spanned the Vek Rud. Three or four nomads reined in on the far side of the river and waited with nocked arrows for the Makuraners to try to force a passage.

"Hold!" Abivard flung up his hand. Shooting down the bridge at men and horses who had to come straight toward them, the Khamorth could have taken a fearful toll, maybe even turned defeat into triumph.

"But they were running away," Frada protested.

"They're not running now," Abivard said. "Take a good look at them, brother. What do they want us to do? If you were a Khamorth chieftain on the other side of that river, what would you hope those stupid Makuraners on your tail would do?"

Frada was also Godarz's son: Confront him with an idea and he would worry it like a dog shaking a rat. "I expect I'd hope they threw themselves at me," he said.

"I expect the same thing," Abivard answered. "That's why we're going to stay right here until the plainsmen ride away. Then—" He scowled, but saw no help for it. "Then I'm going to burn that bridge."

Frada stared at him. "But it's stood since our great-grandfather's day, maybe longer."

"I know. Losing it will cost us commerce, too. But with the Khamorth loose in the realm, if I leave it whole I might as well paint 'ROB ME' in big letters on the outside of the stronghold wall." Abivard's laugh rang bitter. "See how the great tribute Smerdis King of Kings paid to the Khamorth is keeping them on their own side of the Degird."

"Aye, that thought had already crossed my mind. How much did the famous Murghab squeeze from us?"

"Eighty-five hundred mortal arkets," Abivard answered. "Years of patient saving gone in a day. And for what? For the nomads to fatten their coffers at the same time as they batten on our lands."

Frada pointed back to the downed ponies and plainsmen dotting the plain to the south. "They paid a price, too."

"They should," Abivard said. "They were trying to take what's ours. But we paid our heavy price at Smerdis' command and got nothing in return for it. Smerdis' messenger said Sharbaraz renounced the throne because he didn't have the experience he needed to rule. If this is what experience bought us, then I wouldn't mind a raw hand on the reins, by the God."

The farther he went there, the softer his voice got: he realized he was speaking treason, or at least lese majesty. But Frada nodded vigorously. "How could we do worse?"

Instead of cheering Abivard, that made him thoughtful. "The hurtful part is, we likely *could* do worse: every tribe on the steppe swarming down over the Degird, for instance, to try to take this land out of the realm forever. That was everyone's worst nightmare after Peroz King of Kings fell." The proud lion banner crashing into the trench—that dreadful image would stay with Abivard if he lived to be a hundred.

"Maybe we could at that," Frada said. "But the way things are is plenty bad enough. These little fights will drain us of men, too."

"Yes," Abivard said. Along with the plainsmen, three of his own followers were down, one lying still, the other two thrashing and crying their pain to the unheeding sky. *Maybe they'll heal*, he thought, and then, *Yes, but maybe they won't*. He made a fist and brought it down on his thigh. "You know, brother of mine, I wonder how bad things are elsewhere in the realm. What would Okhos say, for instance, if I wrote him and asked?"

"Does he have his letters?" Frada said.

"I don't know," Abivard admitted. He brightened. "Roshnani can tell me. Come to that, she's been after me to teach her to read and write. I think my getting letters from Denak showed her I didn't mind women learning such things."

"Are you teaching her?" Frada sounded as if Abivard had been talking not about letters but of some exotic, not quite reputable vice.

Abivard nodded anyhow. "Yes, and she seems to have the head for it. Father would have done the same, I'm certain; he let Denak learn, after all."

"So he did," Frada said thoughtfully. He, too, nodded. Even more than was true for Abivard, he used what Godarz would have done as a touchstone for right behavior.

Seeing that their foes would not obligingly impale themselves, the Khamorth rode north. The Makuraners moved over the field, finishing off wounded Khamorth, capturing steppe ponies, and doing their best to round up the scattered flock. That done and the wounded men hastily bandaged and splinted and tied onto horses, they headed back toward the stronghold. The skirmish with the plainsmen was, by every conventional sense of the word, a victory. But it had cost Abivard at least one man and maybe as many as three, and he doubted it had done anything to keep the Khamorth from raiding his lands again. He let his men cheer, but he didn't feel victorious.

"Aye, my brother has his letters, or he learned them, at any rate," Roshnani said. "How much use he has given them since the tutor left the stronghold, I could not say."

"Only one way to find out," Abivard said. "I'll write him and see what sort of answer I get. Just to be on the safe side, though,

I'll have my rider memorize the message, too, to make sure it's understood. And I'll write to Pradtak, as well. I know he reads, for Denak remarked he was surprised to find out she could do likewise."

"Will you write the letters here in your bedchamber?" Roshnani said. "I want to watch you shape each word and see if I can figure out what it says."

"I know I have pen and ink here. Let's see if I can find a couple of scraps of parchment, too." Abivard kept a pot of ink and a reed pen in a drawer in a little chest by the bed, along with knives, a few coins, little strips of leather, and other oddments. He found himself rummaging through that drawer at least once a day; you never could tell when some piece of what looked like junk would come in handy.

He grunted in satisfaction when he came across a sheet of parchment as big as his hand. He used one of the knives to cut it neatly in half; each of the two pieces he made was plenty big enough for the notes he wanted to send.

He pulled the stopper from the ink pot and set it on the bedside chest. He put the first scrap of parchment on top of the chest, too, then inked his pen, leaned forward, and began to write. Roshnani sat beside him on the bed, so close that her breast brushed against his side. He ignored the pleasant distraction as best he could. *Plenty of time for sport later,* he told himself sternly. *Business now.*

Because he was not sure how well Okhos read, and because Roshnani was just learning letters herself, he took special pains to make his writing neater than the scrawl he usually turned out. "Okhos!" Roshnani exclaimed. "That's my brother's name you just wrote." A moment later she added, "And there's yours!" She almost bounced with excitement.

"You're right both times," he said, slipping his free arm around her waist. She leaned even closer; the scent of her hair filled his nostrils. He needed all his will to keep his mind on the letter. When he was done, he waited for the ink to dry, then handed it to her. "Can you read it?"

She did, one word at a time, more slowly than he had written it. When at last she had finished, she was sweating with effort but proud. "I understood it all," she said. "You want to know how much Smerdis took from Okhos to pay off the Khamorth and how badly they've raided his domain since."

"That's exactly right. You're doing very well," Abivard said. "I'm proud of you." To show how proud he was, he put both arms around her and kissed her. Whether by chance or by design—*whose?* he wondered later—she overbalanced and lay back on the bed. The letter to Pradtak got written rather later than he had planned.

Roshnani read that one aloud, too. Abivard paid less attention to her reading than he might have; neither of them had bothered dressing again, and this afternoon he was thinking about a second round. Roshnani, though, concentrated on what she was doing despite being bare. She said, "Except for the names, you used just the same words in this letter as in the one to Okhos. Why did you do that?"

"Hmm?" he said. Roshnani let out an irritated sniff and repeated herself. He thought about it for a moment, then answered, "Writing's not the easiest thing in the world for me, either. If the same words would serve me twice, I don't have to trouble myself thinking up new ones the second time around."

She considered that in her usual deliberate way. "Fair enough, I suppose," she said at last. "Okhos and Pradtak aren't likely to compare letters and discover you haven't been perfectly original."

"Original?" Abivard rolled his eyes. "If I'd known you'd turn critic when I taught you your letters, I might not have done it." She snorted. He said, "And I know something else that's just as good the second time as the first, even if done just the same way."

Roshnani still cast down her eyes as she had the day she first came to Vek Rud stronghold, but now more in play than in earnest. "Whatever might that be?" she asked, as if they were not naked together on the big bed.

Eventually the letters were sealed and dispatched. Okhos' reply came back in a bit more than a week. " 'To the *dihqan* Abivard the *dihqan* Okhos his brother-in-law sends greetings,' " Abivard read, first with Frada peering over his shoulder and then, later, in the bedchamber with Roshnani. To Roshnani, he added, "See? He writes well enough after all." Okhos' hand was square and careful, perhaps not practiced but clear enough.

"Go on. What does he say?" Roshnani asked.

" 'Yes, my brother-in-law, we have also been beset, both by Smerdis' men and the nomads. We lost five thousand arkets to the one, and sheep and cattle, horses and men to the other. We have hurt the nomads, too, but what good does it do to bat away one grain of sand when the wind lifts up the whole desert? We go on fighting as best we can. The God give you victory in your war, too.' "

"Is that all?" Roshnani asked when he paused to take a breath.

"No, there's one thing more," he said. " 'Say to my sister who is your wife that her brother thinks of her often.' "

Roshnani smiled. "I shall write him a letter in return. Don't you think that will surprise him?"

"I'm sure it will," Abivard said. He wondered whether Okhos would be merely surprised or scandalized to boot. Well, if he was scandalized, that would be his own hard luck. It wasn't as if Abivard let his women wander around out of their quarters like a Videssian or allowed them something else that truly merited condemnation.

He had to wait longer for his reply from Pradtak. Not only did his letter to Denak's husband have a longer journey than the one to Okhos, but Pradtak also took his time before replying. Most of a month went by before a rider from Nalgis Crag domain rode up to the stronghold.

Abivard tipped the man half an arket for his travels. He might not have done so before the battle on the steppes, but any trip by a lone man was dangerous these days. Abivard knew that only too well—travel by a lone armed bands wasn't necessarily safe, either.

He opened the leather message tube and unrolled the parchment on which Pradtak had written his reply. After the polite formula of greeting, his brother-in-law's letter was but one sentence long: *I am loyal in all ways to Smerdis King of Kings.*

"Well, who ever said you weren't?" Abivard asked aloud, as if Pradtak were there to answer him.

"Lord?" the rider asked.

"Never mind." Abivard scratched his head, wondering why on earth his brother-in-law thought he suspected him.

V

"Now, THIS IS MORE LIKE IT," ABIVARD SAID TO THE TIRED-looking man who swung down off his horse in the courtyard to Vek Rud stronghold. "No letter at all from Nalgis Crag domain for almost a month, and now two in the space of a week."

"Glad you're pleased, lord," the messenger said. Instead of a caftan, he wore leather trousers and a sheepskin jacket: winter hadn't started, but the air said it was coming. The man went on, "This one is from the lady your sister. That's what the serving woman who gave it to me said, anyhow. I've not read it myself, for it was sealed before it ever went into my tube here."

"Was it?" Abivard said; Denak hadn't bothered with such things before. He gave the rider a silver arket. "You deserve special thanks for getting it here to me safe, then, for you couldn't have told me what it said, had anything happened to it."

"You're kind to me, lord, but if anything had happened to that letter, likely something worse would have happened to me, if you know what I mean." The messenger from Nalgis Crag domain sketched a salute, then rode out of the stronghold to start his journey home.

The seal Denak had used was Pradtak's: a mounted lancer hunting a boar. Abivard broke it with his thumbnail, curious to find out what his sister hadn't wanted anyone to see. As usual, he read her words aloud: " 'To the *dihqan* Abivard his loving sister Denak sends greetings.' " Her next sentence brought him up short. " 'It were wiser if you read what follows away from anyone who might overhear.' "

"I wonder what *that's* in aid of?" he muttered. But Denak had always struck him as having good sense, so he rolled up the

107

parchment and carried it into the *dihqan*'s bedchamber. *No one to listen to me here,* he thought. Then he glanced through the grillwork opening in the door that led to the women's quarters. He saw no one.

Satisfied, he unrolled the letter and began to read again. Denak wrote, " 'Pradtak my husband recently walled off the chamber next to mine, which is close by the entrance to the women's quarters here, and had a separate doorway made for it alone. I wondered what his purpose was, but he spoke evasively when I asked him. This, I must confess, irked me no little.' "

Abivard did not blame his sister for her pique. The likeliest explanation he could find for Pradtak's behavior was installing another woman in the special room, though why he wouldn't simply admit her to the women's quarters baffled Abivard.

He read on. " 'My temper vanished but my curiosity grew when, after I heard through the wall that the chamber was inhabited, I also heard it was inhabited by a man. Pradtak, I assure you, is not inclined to seek his pleasures in that direction.' "

"Well, what is he doing, then, putting a man into the women's quarters, even if the fellow is walled away from his wives?" Abivard asked, as if the letter would up and tell him and save him the trouble of reading further.

It didn't, of course. His eyes dropped back down to the parchment. " 'With my door closed, I called quietly out my window,' " Denak wrote, " 'not certain if the masons had sealed away the one in the adjacent room. I found they had not. The man in there was more than willing to give me his name. I now give it to you, and you will understand my caution with this letter: he is Sharbaraz son of Peroz and, he claims, rightful King of Kings of Makuran.' "

Abivard stared at that for most of a minute before he read on. If Sharbaraz had renounced the throne of his own free will, as Smerdis King of Kings claimed, why mure him up in a secret cell like a criminal awaiting the headsman's chopper? The only answer that came to him was stark in its simplicity: *Smerdis lies.*

Denak's next sentence might have been an echo of that thought: " 'The first meal Sharbaraz ate after word of his father's overthrow reached Mashiz must have had a sleeping potion sprinkled over it, for when he awoke he found himself in a dark little room somewhere in the palace, with a knife to his throat and a written renunciation of the throne before him. Not wishing to perish on the spot, he signed it.' "

Someone let out a tuneless whistle. After a moment, Abivard

realized it was himself. He had wondered that a young man of whom his father had expected so much should tamely yield the rule to an elder of no particular accomplishment. Now he learned Sharbaraz had not yielded tamely.

The letter went on, " 'Smerdis sent Sharbaraz here for safe-keeping: Nalgis Crag stronghold is without a doubt the strongest fortress in all Makuran. The usurper pays Pradtak well to keep his rival beyond hope of escape or rescue. You may not be surprised to learn I read your latest letter to my husband; I grieve to hear how the Khamorth ravage my homeland in spite of the great tribute Smerdis handed over to them to stay north of the Degird. This tells me he whose fundament now befouls the throne has no notion of what the kingdom requires.' "

"It told me the same thing," Abivard said, as if Denak were there to hear him.

He had almost finished the letter. His sister wrote, " 'I do not think any army has a hope of rescuing Sharbaraz from the outside. But he may perhaps be spirited out of the fortress. I shall bend every effort toward finding out how that might be done. Since the area in front of Sharbaraz's cell remains formally within the women's quarters, and since I am trusted with affairs here, I may be able to see for myself exactly how he is guarded.' "

"Be careful," Abivard whispered, again as if Denak stood close by.

" 'I shall take every precaution I can think of,' " Denak wrote—*she might be answering me,* Abivard thought. " 'Be circumspect when you reply to this letter. Pradtak has not formed the habit of reading what you write to me, but any mistake here would mean disaster—for me, for Sharbaraz King of Kings, and, I think, for Makuran. May the God bless you and hold you in her arms.' "

Abivard started to put the letter with the others he'd had from Denak, but changed his mind almost at once. Some of his servitors could read, and this was a note they must not see. He hid it behind the wall hanging to whose frame Godarz had glued the spare key to the women's quarters.

That done, Abivard paced round the bedchamber as if he were a lion in a cage. *What to do?* echoed and reechoed in his mind, like the beat of a distant drum. *What to do?*

Suddenly he stood still. "As of this moment, I owe Smerdis miscalled King of Kings no allegiance," he declared as the realization crystallized within him. He had sworn loyalty to Smerdis on condition that Makuran's overlord had spoken truth about how he had come to power. Now that his words were shown to be lies, they held no more power over Abivard.

That, however, did not answer the question of what to do next. Even if all the *dihqans* and *marzbans* renounced Smerdis' suzerainty and marched on Nalgis Crag stronghold, they would be hard-pressed to take it—and would surely cause Sharbaraz to be killed to keep them from uniting behind him.

Then he thought of Tanshar's prophecy: a tower on a hill where honor was to be won and lost. Nalgis Crag stronghold was indeed a tower on a hill, and with the rightful King of Kings penned up there, plenty of honor waited to be won. But how would it be lost as well? That worried Abivard.

The trouble with prophecy, he thought as he read through Denak's letter again, was that what it foretold, while true, had a way of going unrecognized till it was past and could be seen, as it were, from behind. He wouldn't know if this was what Tanshar had predicted until after the honor was won and lost, if it was. Even then, he might not be sure.

"I have to talk with someone about this," he said; he sensed he needed another set of wits to look at the problem Denak had posed from a different angle. He started to call Frada, but hesitated. His brother was young, and too liable not to keep a secret. Word of Sharbaraz' imprisonment getting out could doom Peroz's son as readily as an army invading Nalgis Crag domain.

For the thousandth time, Abivard wished he could hash things out with Godarz. But if his father were alive, Peroz would probably still live, too, with Sharbaraz his accepted heir and Smerdis a functionary whose ambition, if he had had any before Peroz died, would be well concealed.

Abivard snapped his fingers. "I am a fool," he said. "This is an affair of the women's quarters, so who would know better what to do about it than the women here?"

He hesitated again before he went to Burzoe and Roshnani, wondering if they could keep so great a matter to themselves. Women's-quarter gossip was notorious all through Makuran. If a maidservant heard of this, she would surely spread word through the whole stronghold. But Burzoe had been Godarz's right hand for many years, something she couldn't have done without holding secrets close, and Roshnani did not seem one to talk out of turn. Abivard nodded, his mind made up.

He took the key and let himself into the women's quarters. He would have summoned his mother and principal wife to the bedchamber, but that struck him as more likely to alert others to something out of the ordinary.

Roshnani was embroidering in her chamber, much as she had been when Ardini hid the magical image behind her chest of drawers. She looked up from the work when Abivard tapped lightly on the open door. "My husband," she said, smiling. "What brings you here in the middle of the day?" The smile got wider, suggesting that she had her suspicions.

"No, not that," Abivard said, smiling, too. "That will have to wait for another time. Meanwhile, where's my lady mother? Something's come up on which I need your thoughts, and hers, as well."

"Do you want to talk here?" Roshnani asked. At his nod, she set aside the cloth on which she had been working. "I'll fetch her. I won't be but a moment." She hurried down the hall.

She was as good as her word. When she came back with Burzoe, Abivard shut the door to Roshnani's chamber. His mother raised an eyebrow at that. "What sort of secret has such earthshaking importance?" she asked, her tone doubting that any could.

Despite the closed door, Abivard answered in what was little more than a whisper. He summarized Denak's letter in three or four quick sentences, then finished, "What I want to do is find some way to rescue the rightful King of Kings. Not only is Smerdis forsworn, but his rule brings Makuran only more troubles."

Burzoe's eyes flicked to the door. "I owe you an apology, son," she said, speaking as quietly as Abivard had. "You were right—this is a secret that must not spread."

"Will Sharbaraz truly be better for Makuran than Smerdis is?" Roshnani asked.

"He could scarcely be worse," Abivard said. But that was not an answer, not really. He added, "My father thought he would make an able successor to Peroz, and his judgment in such things was usually good."

"That's so," Burzoe said. "Godarz spoke well of Sharbaraz several times in my hearing. And we paid Smerdis eighty-five hundred arkets at as near sword's point as makes no difference, and for what? He said he would spend them to keep the nomads from crossing the Degird, and we see how well he kept that promise. If Denak can rescue Sharbaraz, I think she should— and we must help all we can."

"But *can* she rescue him?" Abivard asked. "The two of you

know more of the workings of a women's quarters than I could ever learn. That's why I brought this to you."

"It will depend on how Pradtak has rearranged things to make a cell there," Burzoe answered. "My guess is that he will have installed a guard—a man, whether his or Smerdis'—in front of Sharbaraz's cell, and walled off part of the corridor to keep the lustful fellow from sporting among the women. If Denak can get to the corridor in front of the cell, she may indeed accomplish something. If not, I know not what advice to give you: matters become more difficult."

"Perhaps she can offer to serve Sharbaraz—cook for him, or something of that sort," Roshnani said. "He may be a prisoner, but he is still of royal blood. And Smerdis, you said, is old. What if he dies tomorrow? Most likely, Sharbaraz gets his crown back—and he will remember, one way or the other, how Pradtak treated him at Nalgis Crag stronghold."

"A thought," Abivard agreed. "If Pradtak's principal wife were to wait upon him, Sharbaraz might see his captivity as honorable. Or so Denak could present the matter to Pradtak, at any rate."

"You are not without wit, child," Burzoe said to Roshnani, at which the younger woman blushed bright red. Pretending not to notice, Burzoe turned to Abivard. "The scheme has some merit. Much depends on how tightly Pradtak is used to controlling his women's quarters. If no man save he is ever allowed to see his wives' faces, he will not grant this to Denak. If on the other hand he learned an easier way from his father Urashtu, our chance for success looks better."

"Worth a try, anyway." Abivard bowed to his mother and his principal wife. "Thank you for your wisdom. Whatever we do, we have to keep it secret. No word of this can get out, or we are ruined before we begin."

Roshnani and Burzoe looked at each other. Abivard watched amusement pass between them, and something else—something hidden in the way women had of hiding things from men. It made him feel perhaps seven years old again, in spite of his inches, his strength, and his thick black beard.

In a voice dry as the desert beyond the stronghold, Burzoe said, "See to it that you keep the secret as well as we. You may count on it that no one in the women's quarters will learn from us the reason you came here today."

Roshnani nodded. "Women love to spill secrets that do not

truly matter—but then, so do men. And men, I think, are more likely to betray those that do."

Abivard hadn't thought about that. He shrugged, unsure if it was true or not. Then he opened the door and headed down the corridor that led out of the women's quarters.

Behind him, Burzoe's voice rose to a screech. "Wretch of a daughter-in-law, you bring embarrassment on us all when my son the *dihqan* notices how uneven the stitches of your embroidery are."

"They are no such thing," Roshnani retorted, just as hotly. "If you'd taught Abivard to recognize good work, he'd know it when he saw it."

The two women shouted even louder, both at once so Abivard couldn't understand a word they said. He almost ran back to Roshnani's chamber to break up the fight. Then he realized his principal wife and his mother were staging a quarrel based on something that would have given him a plausible reason for visiting them. The women's quarters might buzz with gossip for days, but it would be the right kind of gossip. He wanted to bow back toward the women in admiration, but that might have given away the game.

No one in the women's quarters came running to watch the fight. No one, as Abivard saw, affected to give it any special notice. But no one paid heed to what she was supposed to be doing, either. *Misdirection,* Abivard thought, *not concealment*: something worth remembering on the battlefield, too.

He went back to his bedchamber, locked the door that led into the women's quarters, and put the key into one of the pouches he wore on his belt. He flopped down onto the bed and thought hard.

"I can't even write back and tell Denak what to do, not in so many words," he muttered. "If Pradtak—if anyone—happens to set eyes on the letter, everything goes up in smoke."

Circumspection was not his strength. By Makuraner standards, he was blunt and straightforward. But Godarz had always said a man should be able to put his hand to anything. Like a lot of good advice, it sounded easier than it was liable to prove.

He thought awhile longer, then took out pen and parchment and began to write, a few careful words at a time: *To Denak her loving brother the* dihqan *Abivard sends greetings. The news of which you write is, as always, fascinating, and gives me much to think about.*

Abivard snorted when he reread that. "By the God, nothing

but truth there!" he exclaimed. He bent to his work again. Without his noticing, the tip of his tongue stuck out of one corner of his mouth, as it had in boyhood days when a scribe first taught him his letters.

He went on, *If you can help your neighbor, the God will surely smile upon you for your kindness. Perhaps he will look gladly on you if you make the approach.*

To someone who did not know what Abivard was talking about, that "he" would refer back to the God. Abivard hoped Denak would understand it meant Pradtak. He glowered at the parchment. Writing in code was hard work.

I am sure that, because of the bad temper your neighbor has shown to those placed over her, someone needs to keep an eye on her every minute. Perhaps you will be able to make friends with that woman or eunuch—however Pradtak sees fit to order his women's quarters—and so have a chance to improve your neighbor's nature.

He read that over. Denak should have no trouble following it. Most people who read it probably would not catch on. But if it fell into Pradtak's hands, the game was up. Abivard chewed on his lower lip. Denak had said her husband was not in the habit of reading the letters he sent them. Pradtak certainly didn't read her answers, or she would not have been able to write as frankly as she did. But he was liable to say something like "The gate guards tell me a letter came from your brother today. Show it to me, why don't you?" How could she say no?

To keep her from having to, Abivard got out another sheet of parchment and wrote a cheery letter about doings at Vek Rud stronghold that said never a word about imprisoned royalty. If Pradtak wanted to know what was in Abivard's mind—and keeping Sharbaraz prisoner in Nalgis Crag domain was liable to make him anxious even if he hadn't been before—Denak could show him the image of an empty-headed fellow full of chatter and not much else.

Abivard sighed as he put both sheets into a leather travel tube. Life would have been simpler—and perhaps more pleasant—if he could have lived the life he wore like a mask in that second letter.

He sighed again. "If the God had wanted life to be simple, he wouldn't have put Makuran next to the Khamorth—or to Videssos," he murmured, and set the stopper in the tube.

* * *

Tanshar opened the door, then blinked in surprise and bowed low. "Lord, you do me great honor by visiting my humble home," he said, stepping aside so Abivard could come in.

As always, the fortune-teller's dwelling was astringently neat—and almost bare of furnishings. Abivard took a few pistachios from the bowl Tanshar proffered but held the shells in his hand rather than tossing them onto the rammed earth on the floor. In some houses, they would have been invisible; here, they would have seemed a profanation.

Tanshar solved his dilemma by fetching in another, smaller bowl. As Abivard dropped the shells into it, the fortune-teller asked, "And how may I serve my lord the *dihqan* today?"

Abivard hesitated before beginning. Spreading the secret Denak had passed to him made him nervous. But if Denak was to get Sharbaraz free of Nalgis Crag stronghold, she would probably need magical aid: it stood a better chance of helping than an army, at any rate, or so Abivard judged. Cautiously he said, "What I tell you must spread to no one—no one, do you understand?"

"Aye, lord." In a wintry way, Tanshar looked amused. "And to whom would I be likely to retail it? To my numerous retainers?" He waved a hand, as if to conjure up servitors from empty air and bare walls. "To the townsfolk in the market square? That you might more easily believe, but if I gossiped like any old wife, who would trust me with his affairs?"

"Mock if you like," Abivard said. "The matter is important enough that I must remind you."

"Say on, lord," Tanshar said. "You've made me curious, if nothing else."

Even that worried Abivard; as he knew, Tanshar had ways of learning things not available to ordinary men. But he said, "Hear me, then, and judge for yourself." He told Tanshar what he'd learned from Denak.

The fortune-teller's eyes widened, both the good one and the one clouded by cataract. "The rightful King of Kings?" he murmured. "Truly, lord, I crave your pardon, for care here is indeed of the essence. You intend to free this man?"

"If it happens, Denak will have more to do with it than I," Abivard answered. The irony of that struck him like a blow. The men of Makuran shut away their women to keep power in their own hands, and now the fate of the realm would rest in the hands of a woman. He shook his head—nothing he could do about it but help his sister any way he could.

Tanshar nodded. "Aye, that makes sense; so it does. Your sister's husband—did you say his name was Pradtak?—would hardly give you the chance to storm his women's quarters with warriors, now would he?"

"It's not likely," Abivard said, which won him a slow smile from Tanshar. He went on, "Seems to me magic might manage more than men. That's why I've come to you: to see how you can help. Suppose I were to take you along with me on a visit to Nalgis Crag domain one of these days—"

"When would that be, lord?" Tanshar asked.

"Right now, the time lies in the hands of the God," Abivard said. "Much will depend on what—if anything—Denak can do from within. But if that proves possible, will you ride with me?"

"Gladly, lord—usurping the throne is surely an act of wickedness," Tanshar said. "How I can help, though, I do not yet clearly see."

"Nor I," Abivard said. "I came here now so we could look together for the best way." They talked quietly for the next couple of hours. By the time Abivard headed up to the stronghold again, he had the beginnings of a plan.

Winter was another invader from the Pardrayan steppe. Though more regular in its incursions into Makuran than the nomads, it was hardly less to be feared. Snowstorms spread white over fields and plains. Herdsmen went out to tend their flocks in thick sheepskin coats that reached to their ankles. Some would freeze to death on bad nights anyhow. Abivard knew that—it happened every winter.

Smoke rose black from the stronghold, as if it had fallen in war. Makuran was not a land rich in timber; the woodchoppers had traveled far to lay in enough to get through the season. Abivard asked the God for mild days and got another blizzard. He did his best to shrug it off; prayers over weather were hardly ever answered.

What he could not shrug off was that winter also slowed travel to a crawl. He had sent his letter off to Denak, hoping the weather would hold long enough for him to get a quick reply. It didn't. He wanted to gnash his teeth.

Whenever one clear day followed another, he hoped it meant a lull long enough for a horseman to race from Nalgis Crag stronghold to Vek Rud domain. Whenever snow flew again afterward, he told himself he should have known better.

The horseman from Pradtak's domain reached Vek Rud

stronghold a few days after the winter solstice, in the middle of the worst storm of the year. Children had been making snowmen in the stronghold courtyard and in the streets of the town below the walls. When the rider reached the gate, so much white clung to his coat and fur cap that he looked like a snowman himself, a snowman astride a snow horse.

Abivard ordered the half-frozen horse seen to, then put the rider in front of a blazing fire with a mug of hot spiced wine in his hand and a steaming bowl of mutton stew on a little round table beside him. "You were daft to travel," Abivard said, "but I'm glad you did."

"Wasn't so bad, lord *dihqan*," the man answered between avid swigs from the mug.

"No? Then why are your teeth still chattering?"

"Didn't say it was *warm* out there, mind you," the fellow answered. "But the serving woman who gave me the letter from the lady your sister said she wanted it to reach you as soon as might be, so I thought I'd try the journey. Here you are, lord *dihqan*." With a flourish, he presented a leather letter tube.

"I thank you." Abivard set the tube down on the stone floor beside him and reached into his belt pouch for a couple of silver arkets with which to reward the rider. Then he took a pull at his own wine; though he hadn't been on a horse in the snow, the inside of the stronghold was chilly, too.

"You're generous, lord *dihqan*." The man from Nalgis Crag domain stowed the silver in a pouch of his own. When he saw Abivard was making no move to unstopper the tube, he asked, "Aren't you going to read the letter now that it's here?"

"Alas, I should not, not here." Abivard had expected that question and trotted out the answer he had prepared: "Were I to read it in another man's hearing, it would be as if I exposed Pradtak's wife to another man's sight. With him generous enough to allow Denak my sister to correspond with me, I would not violate the privacy of his women's quarters."

"Ah." The messenger respectfully lowered his head. "You observe the usages with great care and watch over my lord's honor as if it were your own."

"I try my best." Abivard fought hard to hold his face stiff. Here he and Denak were plotting how to spirit a man out of Pradtak's women's quarters, and Pradtak's man reckoned them paragons of Makuraner virtue. That was what he had hoped the fellow would do, but he hadn't expected to be praised for it.

The man yawned. "Your pardon, lord," he said. "I fear I am not yet ready to head back to Nalgis Crag stronghold at once."

"I'm not surprised," Abivard answered. "Neither is your horse. Rest here as long as you like. We'll give you a room and a brazier and thick wool blankets."

"And maybe a wench to warm me under them?" the messenger said.

"If you find one willing, of course," Abivard said. "I'm not in the habit of making the serving women here sleep with men not of their choosing."

"Hmm." The rider looked as if he would grumble if he dared. Then he got to his feet. "In that case, lord, I shall have to see what I can do. The kitchens are that way?" At Abivard's nod, he swaggered off. Whatever his luck might prove, he didn't lack for confidence.

Abivard went in the other direction, toward his own bedchamber. As soon as he had barred the door behind him, he undid the stopper and took out Denak's letter. It was sealed, as the last one had been. He used his thumbnail to break the wax, unrolled the parchment, and began to read.

Even in the bedchamber, he kept his voice to a whisper. He wondered if one day, thanks to all this secrecy, he would be able to read without making any sound. That might prove useful.

After the usual greetings, Denak wrote, " 'In the matter of Sharbaraz, I have done as you suggested. Much the same thought came to me before your latest letter, in fact. Pradtak has not objected. I do not know whether he thinks he is hedging his bets by letting me serve the rightful King of Kings, but if he does, he is mistaken; Sharbaraz seems to me a man who forgets neither friend nor foe.' "

"Good!" Abivard exclaimed, as if his sister were in the room with him. Feeling foolish, he returned to the letter.

" 'Though Pradtak was willing to permit me to pass into the new hall that now holds Sharbaraz's cell—so long as I come and go when no one save he is in the bedchamber—the guards who came here with Sharbaraz have proved harder to persuade. They are Smerdis' men, not Pradtak's, and what the *dihqan* thinks matters little to them.' "

They would be, Abivard thought. He had hoped Smerdis would not have solidly loyal men behind him—he was, after all, a usurper. But if he did have any men who valued him above all others, standing watch on his rivals was the sensible place to put them. Too bad—he would have made matters much simpler if only he had been dumber.

Denak went on, " 'I have, however, used every tool to persuade them—they are three in all, and watch in turn, one day, one evening, one dead of night—that their lives in Vek Rud stronghold will be happier if they let me do as Pradtak thinks best.' "

Abivard nodded vigorously. His sister was clever. A stronghold where everyone hated you, where your bread was moldy and your wine more nearly vinegar, could quickly come to seem like prison, even to a guard.

" 'I pray to the God that my efforts here will be crowned with success,' " Denak wrote. " 'Even if she grant that prayer, though, I do not see how I can hope to flee the stronghold with Sharbaraz. If you have thoughts on that score, do let me know of them. I add, by the way, that you were wise to enclose the harmless sheet with the earlier letter you sent—I was able to show it to Pradtak without his being any the wiser that more important words came also in the tube. May your wisdom find a like way around this present difficulty.' "

Abivard went to the window. Clouds scudded across the sky, gray and ragged as freshly sheared wool. "When the weather clears—if the weather clears—I think I shall have to pay my brother-in-law a visit," he said.

"Who comes to Nalgis Crag stronghold?" The cry arose as Abivard was still a couple of furlongs before the stronghold itself.

He gave his name, then added, "Your lord should be expecting me; I wrote to say I was coming."

"Aye, you're a welcome guest here, Lord Abivard, and, as you say, looked for," the sentry answered. "Who's the old man with you, and what's his station? We'll guest him properly, as his rank warrants."

"My physician's name is Tanshar. He'll stay with me."

"However it pleases you, lord," the sentry said. "But did you think we have no healers here in Nalgis Crag domain? We're not Khamorth here, by the God." He sounded indignant.

"Tanshar has looked after me since I was a babe." Abivard spoke the lie with the ease of endless rehearsal on the road from Vek Rud stronghold. "I don't care to trust myself to anyone else."

The sentry yielded, repeating, "However it pleases you, of course. Come ahead. The gate is open."

Abivard urged his horse forward. Tanshar rode behind him on the narrow track up to the gateway. Situated as it was, Nalgis

Crag stronghold could afford to leave the gate open almost all the time—a threatening army could not approach unobserved. In fact, a threatening army could hardly approach at all. Not for the first time, Abivard wished his own stronghold were as secure.

Pradtak came out of the living quarters to greet him in the courtyard. The *dihqan* of Nalgis Crag domain still walked with the help of a stick and was liable to limp for the rest of his life, but he moved far more easily than he had on the day of Denak's wedding.

"Fine to see you again, my brother-in-law," he said, advancing with his hand outstretched. He looked from Abivard to Tanshar to the pair of packhorses the latter led. "I would have expected you to come with more men, especially with the barbarians loose in the land."

"We managed," Abivard said with a shrug. "I didn't care to detach many men from keeping the nomads off our flocks and *qanats*. Let me present to you my physician Tanshar."

"Lord Pradtak," Tanshar said politely, bowing in the saddle.

Pradtak nodded back, then returned his attention to his social equal, asking Abivard "What ails you, that you need to bring a physician with you as you travel?"

"I have biting pains here—" Abivard ran his hand along the right side of his belly. "—as well as a troublesome flux of the bowels. Tanshar's potions and the hot fomentations he prepares while we camp give me enough relief to stay in the saddle."

"However it pleases you," Pradtak said; Abivard wondered if the sentry had borrowed the phrase from his master. The *dihqan* of Nalgis Crag domain went on, "Come in, refresh yourselves. Then, Abivard, you can speak to me more of the reasons for your visit. Do not misunderstand me, you are most welcome, only your letter was—you will forgive me?—rather vague."

"I forgive you most willingly," Abivard said as he walked with Pradtak toward the stronghold's living quarters, "for I intended to be vague. Some things should not be set down on parchment in so many words, lest the wrong eyes light on them. I would not have said even as much as I did, were I not sure of your loyalty to Smerdis King of Kings, may his years be many and his realm increase."

Pradtak looked sharply at him and more sharply at Tanshar. "Should you say even so much, when we do not discuss this matter in privacy?"

"What do you mean?" Abivard said. Then his eyes followed Pradtak's to Tanshar. "Oh, the physician?" He laughed loud, long, and a little foolishly. "He is a valued counselor, and has been since my grandfather's day. Godarz my father even admitted him to the women's quarters to treat his wives and daughters, Denak among them. I'd sooner distrust the moon than Tanshar."

"Again I pray your forgiveness, but my father Urashtu sometimes wondered if Godarz was not too liberal for his own good," Pradtak said. "I speak not to offend, merely to inform. And I must remind you I know this Tanshar not at all, only what you say of him. This makes me hesitant to rest on him the same trust you do."

Well it might, since I've been filling your ears with lies, Abivard thought. To Pradtak, however, he presented the picture of affronted dignity. Setting a hand on Tanshar's shoulder, he said, "Let us return to Vek Rud domain, my friend. If Pradtak cannot trust you, I see I cannot trust him." He took a couple of steps toward the stables, as if to reclaim his horse.

Tanshar had rehearsed, too. "But what of the news you bear for Denak, lord?" he cried. "Your lady mother's heart will surely break if you come home without delivering it."

"I don't care, not a fig," Abivard said, drawing himself up to his full height. "I will not stand by and let you be impugned. It reflects badly on me."

Pradtak stared from one of them to the other. *He's hooked,* Abivard thought, though he kept his face cold and haughty. "Perhaps I was hasty—" Pradtak began.

"Perhaps you were." Abivard took another step or two stableward.

"Wait," Pradtak said. "If you rely on this man so, he must deserve it. I apologize for any insult I may have accidentally given."

"The *dihqan* is gracious," Tanshar murmured.

Abivard let himself be persuaded by his retainer's acquiescence. "Since Tanshar feels no insult, none could have been given," he said, but kept his tone grudging. "And the matter, as I say, is of some importance. Very well, Pradtak, I overlook it; it never happened."

Pradtak still seemed pained. "I do not object to your seeing your sister, so long as I remain in the chamber, as well. A woman's close kin may view her without impropriety even after she has passed into the women's quarters of another man. But the physician—"

"Is a physician, and old, and blind in one eye," Abivard said firmly. "And he has seen Denak before. Do you believe he intends to fall on her and ravish her? Too, he would be the better choice to pass on some of what my lady mother said to me. The shock to my sister will perhaps be less, hearing it from someone outside the family."

"However it pleases you." Pradtak sounded sullen, but he yielded. "Since you have come so far, your words must be important—and, from the dire hints you keep dropping, I am about to perish of curiosity. Tell me at once what you can, don't even pause to scratch your head."

"My throat is dry," Abivard said. "Even in winter, much of the road between my domain and yours is but a dusty track."

Pradtak twisted the head of his stick back and forth in his hand. Hospitality came first; so decreed custom binding as iron. And so, however much he fidgeted, he had to lead Abivard and Tanshar into the kitchens and do his best to make small talk while they drank wine and munched on pocket bread stuffed with grapes and onions and crumbly white cheese and chunks of mutton sprinkled with ground cardamom seeds. Whatever might be said against him, he set an excellent table.

At last Abivard said, "Perhaps you would be gracious enough to have more of this fine red wine brought to your chamber, lord *dihqan*, so we can wet our lips further while we discuss the concerns that brought us here."

"Of course, lord *dihqan*," Pradtak said with ill-concealed eagerness. "If you and your distinguished retainer will be so kind as to follow me—" He used a hand to help push himself upright from the table, but walked several steps before he remembered, almost as an afterthought, to let the tip of his stick touch the floor. As Denak had said, he was mending.

"You walk quite well," Abivard said. "Can you also ride these days?"

"Aye, and you have no idea how glad I am of it," Pradtak said; he, on the other hand, had no idea how glad Abivard was of it. Pradtak went on, "These past few weeks, I've been hunting a great deal to try to make up for all the time I lost while I was lamed."

"No man may do that." Tanshar's somber tones might have come from a servant of the God.

Pradtak looked at him with more respect than he had shown before. "I fear you are right, but I try nonetheless." To Abivard, with the air of a man making a concession, he added, "He has wisdom."

"So he does." Abivard hoped he didn't sound surprised. It wasn't that he reckoned Tanshar foolish; he wouldn't have brought him along if he had. But he hadn't expected the village fortune-teller to act so convincingly a role far above his true station. That made him wonder if Tanshar's station should perhaps be raised.

Before he had time to do more than note the thought, Pradtak said, "Let's take these discussions where we can pursue them more privately, as you yourself suggested." He tapped his stick impatiently on the stone floor.

"I am your servant." Abivard got up and followed him, Tanshar close behind as usual.

Abivard had been down the hall to Pradtak's bedchamber on Denak's wedding day, but then, of course, he had stopped short of the door. Now Pradtak unlocked it and held it open with his own hands, waving for his guests to precede him. "Go in, go in," he said. As soon as Abivard and Tanshar were inside, he barred the door behind them. "Now—"

But Abivard wasn't quite ready to start talking yet. He looked around in some curiosity: this was the first *dihqan*'s bedchamber he had seen outside Vek Rud stronghold. In most regards, it was much like his own—a bed, a chest of drawers ornamented by some exceptionally fine cups, a little table. But, as Denak had said, it now had two doorways side by side in the far wall, one of them plainly of recent construction.

He pointed to them and pasted a leer on his face. "What's this? Do you put your pretty wives behind one door and the rest behind the other? How d'you keep 'em from quarreling?"

Pradtak blushed like a maiden brought to her wedding bed. "No. One of the doors leads to the apartment of a, ah, special guest."

"The bar is on this side," Tanshar noted.

"And what concern of yours is that?" Pradtak asked.

"Oh, none whatever, lord," the fortune-teller said cheerfully. "This is your domain, and you hold it as you think best. My mouth but said what my eyes—my good eye, anyhow—chanced to see."

Pradtak opened his own mouth, perhaps to warn Tanshar to watch his words more closely, but he shut it again without speaking and contented himself with a sharp, short nod. Into the silence, Abivard said, "Brother-in-law, could I trouble you for more wine? What I have to say comes so hard that I fear I need the grape to force my tongue to shape the words."

"However it pleases you," Pradtak said, but with a look that warned the matter was not as it pleased *him*. He limped back to the outer door and bawled for a servant. The fellow quickly returned with a jar big enough to get half a dozen men drunk. He dipped some up into the fine porcelain cups, then bobbed his head and vanished. Pradtak tossed back his own wine, then folded his arms across his chest. "Enough suspense," he growled. "Tell me at once of what you have been hinting at since you arrived here."

Abivard glanced at both inner doors. He lowered his voice; he did not want anyone behind either of them to hear. "I have word of a dangerous plot against Smerdis King of Kings, may his years be long and his realm increase. So many are involved in it that I fear the King of Kings may find himself in desperate straits if those of us who remain loyal to him do not do everything in our power to uphold him."

"I feared as much," Pradtak said heavily. "When you sent me that letter complaining of the payment his men had taken from you, I also feared you were part of the plot, seeking to draw me in: that is why I replied as I did. But Denak persuaded me you could not be disloyal."

"Good," Abivard said from the bottom of his heart: even before she had learned what Pradtak was up to, his sister had kept an eye out for the welfare of Vek Rud domain. He went on, "We received many complaints from those who had trouble giving to the treasury officials what Smerdis King of Kings demanded of them."

"I'd wager one of them was from your other new brother-in-law," Pradtak said. He was, in his way, shrewd. "He's but a lad, isn't he, not one to know the duties *dihqans* owe their sovereign."

"Many of the names would surprise you," Abivard answered. "Much of the northwest may rise with the coming of spring. Because you so plainly told me you were loyal to Smerdis King of Kings, I knew you would help me devise how best to stand against the rebels should they move."

"You did right to come to me," Pradtak said. "I have some small connection with the court of the King of Kings, and I—" He broke off. However much he wanted to brag, he had wit enough to realize that would be unwise. With hardly a pause, he went on, "Well, never mind. I am glad you came here, so we—"

He broke off again, this time because someone rapped on the door that led from the women's quarters. He stumped over to it, peered through the grillwork to see who was on the other side, then unbarred the door. Denak came through, carrying a silver tray.

"I crave your pardon, husband of mine," she began. "I did not know—" She brightened. "Abivard! And Doctor Tanshar with you."

Pradtak chuckled. "You mean word they were here had not reached you? I find that hard to believe. Be it as it may, though, I would have summoned you soon in any case, for your brother and the physician have news from your mother they say you must hear."

"From my mother? What could it be?" Denak said. Abivard was appalled at the way she looked. She seemed to have aged five years, maybe ten, in the few months she had dwelt at Nalgis Crag stronghold. Harsh lines bracketed either side of her mouth; dark circles lay under her eyes. Abivard wanted to shake Pradtak to force from him what he had done to her to have worked such a harsh change.

Pradtak said, "Why don't you take supper there in to our— guest? Then you can return free of your burden and learn this portentous news."

"However it pleases you," Denak answered—the phrase seemed to run all through Nalgis Crag domain.

Tanshar raised an eyebrow. "A guest splendid enough to be served by the *dihqan*'s wife? Surely he deserves wine, then, to go with his supper." He picked up a cup from the chest of drawers, carried it over to the wine jar, and filled it.

"I thank you, good doctor, but two men wait behind that portal," Denak said.

"Then let them both have wine," Tanshar said grandly, and poured out another cupful. He set it on the tray as if he were a *dihqan* himself, tapping it once or twice with a forefinger as if to show how special it was.

Denak looked to Pradtak, who shrugged. He unbarred the newly built door. Denak passed through it. Pradtak shut it again behind her.

"More wine for you, as well, generous lord?" Tanshar plucked the cup from Pradtak's hand, now acting the conjurer instead of the noble. He gave it back to the *dihqan* full to the brim.

Pradtak sipped the wine. Abivard glanced to Tanshar, who nodded slightly. Abivard raised his cup in a toast. "The God grant that we put an end to all conspiracies against the King of

Kings, may his years be many and his realm increase." He drained the wine still in his cup. Tanshar, also, emptied his. And Pradtak followed his guests by drinking his cup dry, too.

He smacked his lips, frowning a little. "I hope that jar's not going bad," he said. He swayed on his feet. His mouth came open in an enormous yawn. "What's happening to me?" he asked in a blurry voice. His eyes rolled up in his head. He slid, boneless, to the floor. The lovely cup slipped from his hand and shattered. Abivard felt bad about that.

He turned to Tanshar and bowed with deep respect. "What was in that sleeping draft of yours, anyhow?" he asked.

"Elixir of the poppy, henbane, some other things I'd rather not name," Tanshar answered. "It took but a few drops in a cup. All I had to do was get between Pradtak and the wine so he wouldn't see me drug his share—and the one for the guard in there." He spoke in a near whisper as he pointed to the doorway through which Denak had gone.

Abivard slid his sword out of its sheath. If Denak had given the wrong cup to Sharbaraz's guard, or if the fellow hadn't drunk it straight off, he was going to have a fight on his hands. Fear ran through him—if by some horrid mischance she had given the drugged wine to Sharbaraz, all the careful planning they had done would fall straight into the Void.

He walked over to the door, unbarred it, and sprang into the hallway, ready to cut down the guard before the fellow could draw his own blade. To his vast relief, the man slumped against the wall, snoring. Another door at the end of the short hallway was barred on the outside. Abivard opened it. Out came Denak, and with her a broad-shouldered man a few years older than Abivard.

"Your Majesty," Abivard said. He started to go down on his belly.

"No time for that, not now," Sharbaraz snapped. His eyes flashed with excitement at getting out of his prison. "Unless I escape this stronghold, I'm no one's majesty. We'll deal with ceremony when we can."

He hurried past the drugged guard and out into Pradtak's bed-chamber. Denak paused for a moment in the hallway. She kicked the guard in the belly, as hard as she could. He grunted and twisted but did not wake. Abivard stared at her. She glared back. "I'd do it to all three of them if I could—I'd do worse," she said, and burst into tears.

"Come," Tanshar said urgently. "We haven't time to waste, as

his Majesty reminded us." Abivard went into the bedchamber.
Denak followed him, still sobbing. When Tanshar saw her tears,
he exclaimed, "My lady, you must be brave now. If they see you
weeping, we fail."

"I—know." Denak bit her lip. She wiped her eyes on the brocaded silk of her robe, shuddered, and at last nodded to Tanshar.
"Do what you must. I will not give away the illusion."

"Good," Tanshar said. Things were still moving too fast for
Abivard to follow all that was going on, and they did not slow
down. Tanshar beckoned to Sharbaraz. "Your Majesty, I need
your aid now. Take Pradtak's hands in yours."

"As you say." Sharbaraz bent by the unconscious *dihqan*.
Tanshar sprinkled both men with reddish powder—"Ground
bloodstone," he explained—and began to chant. Abivard knew
the sorcery was possible—any hope of escape from Nalgis Crag
stronghold would have been impossible without it—but seeing it
performed still raised awe in him. Before his eyes, Sharbaraz
took on Pradtak's semblance, clothes and all, and the other way
round.

When the change was complete, Abivard and Sharbaraz-who-
seemed-Pradtak dragged the changed Pradtak into the cell that
had held Sharbaraz, then barred the door. Tanshar said to Denak,
"Now, my lady, to give you the appearance of the guard here,
and then we're away."

Her eyes grew so wide, white showed all around her pupils.
"I knew it would come to that, but how can I bear it?" she said.
"Will I also see myself in his guise?"

"Lady, you will not." Sharbaraz held out a hand, looked at
it. "To my own eyes, I remain myself." He sounded like
Pradtak, though.

"That is the way of it," Tanshar agreed. "Your own essence
remains undisturbed, and to you the change will be invisible."

Denak nodded jerkily. "I will do it, then, but must I touch
him?"

Tanshar shook his head. "The ritual here is rather different,
for the two of you will not exchange appearances; rather, you
will borrow his. Stand there close by him, if you would."

Even that seemed more than Denak wanted, but she obeyed.
Tanshar set a crystal disk between her and the guard; when he
let go of it, it hung in the air by itself. He chanted again, to a
different rhythm this time, and invoked the name of the Prophet
Shivini, the lady, again and again. The crystal glowed for per-

haps half a minute. When it faded, there might have been two
guards, identical twins, in the hallway.

"Let me get away from him," Denak said, and her voice came
out a man's harsh rasp.

Abivard closed the outer door to the hallway on the unconscious guard and barred it, again from the outside. He was grinning from ear to ear; things had gone better than he had dared
hope. "Won't they be confused?" he said happily. "Not only will
they *be* confused, in fact, they'll *stay* confused for—how long
will the spells of seeming last, Tanshar?"

"A few days, if no magic is brought to bear against them."
Tanshar sounded exhausted. "If a sorcerer should challenge
them, though, he'll pierce them as an embroidery needle pierces
silk. All the more reason to get away as fast as we can."

"Oh, I don't know," Sharbaraz said with Pradtak's voice.
"When the *dihqan* stops looking like me and becomes himself
again, they may still think him me, and using sorcery to try to
escape. A lovely coil you've wound." He laughed with the joy
of a man who has not laughed in a long time. "But the wise
Tanshar is right—we should not test the magic overmuch." He
trotted toward the outer door to the bedchamber.

"Your Majesty, uh, husband of mine for the moment—
remember, you limp," Denak said. "Forget that and you may yet
give the game away."

Sharbaraz bowed. "Lady, you are right," he said, though
Denak's semblance was anything but ladylike. "I shall remember." He snatched up Pradtak's stick from where it lay on the
floor and gave a convincing impression of a man with a bad ankle. "And now—away."

Sharbaraz made sure to close the newly installed bar outside
Pradtak's bedchamber. Abivard nodded approvingly: now that
the bedchamber was in effect the outer portion of the women's
quarters, no *dihqan* would leave it open, lest the women somehow depart without his knowledge.

"Where now?" Sharbaraz asked in a low voice as the bar
thudded home.

"The stables," Abivard answered, just as quietly. "Here, walk
beside me and make as if you're leading me and not the other
way round. Tanshar, Denak, you come behind: You're our retainers, after all."

Pradtak's household accepted the escaping fugitives as what
they seemed. Once reminded, Sharbaraz kept up his limp quite
well. He gave friendly greetings to Pradtak's kinsfolk and retain-

ers; if he didn't address any of them by name, that was no flaw in a brief conversation—and he made sure all the conversations were brief.

At the stables, though, one of the grooms seeing to Abivard's horses looked up in surprise. "You seldom come here without bow and spear for the chase, lord," he said. "You are riding to hunt, not so?"

Abivard froze, cursing himself for a fool. All that careful planning, to be undone by a moment's carelessness! But Sharbaraz said calmly, "No, we're for the village of Gayy, east of here. Lord Abivard was asking about the *qanat* network there because it stretches so far from the Hyuja River, and he was hoping to do the same along the Vek Rud. My thought was that showing him would be easier than talking at him. What say you?"

"Me?" The groom looked startled, then grinned. "Lord, of making *qanats* I know nothing, so I have little to say." He looked to Abivard. "You'll want your animal and your councilor's resaddled, then?"

"Yes, and we'll take the packhorses, as well," Abivard answered, vastly relieved Sharbaraz's wits were quicker than his own, and also vastly impressed at Sharbaraz' intimate knowledge of Pradtak's domain. He went on, "I may want to spend the night at, uh, Gayy and look over the *qanats* some more in the morning."

"The town has a sarai, lord," the groom said in mild reproof. Abivard folded his arms across his chest. The groom looked an appeal to the man he thought to be Pradtak.

"However it pleases him," Sharbaraz said, just as Pradtak would have. Abivard had all he could do to keep from laughing.

The groom nodded in resignation and turned to Denak. "You'll be one of the gentlemen who rode in at night a ways back. I'm sorry, sir, but I've not seen you much since, and I've forgotten which of those horses was yours." He pointed down to three stalls at the end of the stable.

Before Denak could answer—or panic and not answer—Sharbaraz came to the rescue again. "It was the bay gelding with the scar on his flank, not so?"

"Yes, lord," Denak said in her sorcerously assumed man's voice.

The groom sent Sharbaraz a glance full of admiration. "Lord, no one will ever say you haven't an eye for horses." Sharbaraz made the image of Pradtak preen.

The horse that had belonged to Smerdis' man snorted a little when Denak mounted it. So did Pradtak's horse when Sharbaraz climbed aboard. The horses knew, even if men were fooled. Sharbaraz easily calmed his animal. Denak had more trouble; the only riding she had done since she became a woman was on her wedding journey to Nalgis Crag stronghold. But she managed, and the four riders started down the steep, winding trail to the bottom of Nalgis Crag.

"By the God, I think we've done it," Abivard breathed as the flat ground drew near. He called ahead to Sharbaraz, who as Pradtak was leading the procession. "Lord, uh, your Majesty, how did you come to know so much about the village of Gayy and its *qanats*? I'd not wager an arket that the real Pradtak could say as much of them."

"My father set me to studying the realm and its domains before my beard first sprouted, so I would come to know Makuran before I ruled it," Sharbaraz answered. His chuckle had more than a little edge to it. "I got to know Nalgis Crag domain, or its stronghold, better than I cared to."

"*My* father was right," Abivard said. "You will make a fine King of Kings for Makuran."

"Your father—he would be Godarz of Vek Rud domain?" Sharbaraz said, and answered himself: "Yes, of course, for you are Denak's brother. Godarz perished on the steppe with the rest of the host?"

"He did, your Majesty, with my brother and three half brothers."

Sharbaraz shook his head. "A victory in Pardraya would have been glorious. A loss like the one we suffered . . . better the campaign had never begun. But with a choice of strike or wait, my father always preferred to strike."

His horse reached the flat land then. He kicked the animal up into a fast, ground-eating trot. His companions imitated him: The farther from Nalgis Crag stronghold they got, the safer they would be.

Abivard said, "The confusion should be lovely back at the stronghold. When Pradtak wakes up in your shape, he'll insist he's himself, and the guards will just laugh at him. They'll say he's gone off to Gayy. And even when he does get his own appearance back, they'll think that's a trick, as you said."

"The only real problem will be that I won't return to the women's quarters," Denak said. "And the folk at the stronghold won't truly notice I'm missing for some time. Who pays any real attention to women, anyhow?" Her voice was deep and strange now, but the same old bitterness rode it.

Sharbaraz said, "Lady, a blind man would note your bravery, on a battlefield where no man would ever be likely to find himself. Do not make yourself less than you are, I pray you."

"How can I make myself less than nothing?" she said. When Abivard protested that, she turned her head away and would not speak further. He did not press her, but wondered what had passed at Nalgis Crag stronghold to make her hate herself so. His left hand, the one not holding the reins, curled into a fist. If he had thought Pradtak was abusing her, he would have served her husband as she had the guard who disgraced himself by helping to confine the rightful King of Kings.

The pale winter sun scurried toward the horizon. The weather, though cold, stayed clear. When the riders came to an almond grove not far from the edge of Pradtak's irrigated land, Abivard said, "Let's camp here. We'll have fuel for a fine fire."

When no one argued with him, he reined in, tethered his horse, and began scouring the ground for fallen branches and twigs. Sharbaraz joined him, saying "The God grant we don't have to damage the trees themselves. We should be able to glean enough to keep them intact."

Behind the two young men, Denak said to Tanshar, "Take your seeming off me this instant."

"My lady, truly I would sooner wait," Tanshar answered hesitantly. "Our safety might still ride on your keeping the guardsman's face."

"I would rather die than keep it." Denak began to cry again. Tanshar's magic transmuted her sobs into the deep moaning of a man in anguish.

Abivard dumped a load of wood on the ground and dug in a pocket of his belt pouch for flint and steel. Tanshar sent him a look of appeal and asked, "Lord, what is your will? Shall I remove the enchantment?"

"If my sister hates it so, perhaps you had better," Abivard answered. "Why she should hate it—"

"She has reason, I assure you." Sharbaraz dropped more twigs and branches on top of the load Abivard had gathered.

His support, instead of cheering Denak, only made her cry harder than ever. Abivard looked up from the slow business of getting a fire going and nodded to Tanshar. The fortune-teller took out the crystal disk he had used to give Denak the appearance of Sharbaraz's guard. Again he suspended it in the air be-

tween them. This time his chant was different from before.
Where the disk had briefly glowed, now it seemed to suck up
darkness from the gathering night. When that darkness left it,
Denak was herself again.

Abivard walked over to her and put his arms around her. "It's
gone," he said. "You're you, no one else, just as you should be."

She shuddered under his touch, then twisted away. "I'll never
be just as I should be, don't you understand?" she cried. "I left
what I should be behind forever at Nalgis Crag stronghold."

"What, being Pradtak's wife?" Abivard said scornfully. "The
cursed traitor doesn't deserve you."

"That's so," Sharbaraz agreed.

He started to say something more, but Denak cut him off with
a sharp chopping motion of her right hand. "What you say of
Pradtak is true, but not to the point. I left more than marriage
behind in that stronghold. I lost my honor there, as well."

"Aiding the King of Kings against those who wrongfully imprisoned him is no dishonor," Abivard said. "You . . ." His voice
trailed away as at last he found a reason why Denak might have
kicked Sharbaraz' guard while he was unconscious, why don-
ning his image was almost more than she could bear. He stared
at her. "Did he . . . ? Did they . . . ?" He couldn't go on.

"He did. They all did," she answered bleakly. "It was the
price they took from me for letting me in to serve the rightful
King of Kings. They cared nothing that I had Pradtak's permission; they were Smerdis' men, they said. And if I spoke a word
of it to anyone, Sharbaraz would be dead in his cell one day. I
knew, as you did, that he was Makuran's only hope, and so—I
yielded myself to them."

"It's done. It's over." The words came flat and empty from
Abivard's mouth. It might be done, but it would never be over.
He felt sick inside. No matter why Denak had done what she
did, how was he supposed to look at her after knowing of it?

She understood that, too. Shaking her head, she said, "All the
way along the track down Nalgis Crag, I kept wishing I had the
courage to throw myself over a cliff. Without my honor, what
am I?"

Abivard found no answer. Nor did Tanshar, who sat by the
fire, slumped and numb with fatigue. Nor did Sharbaraz, not at
first; he got down on hands and knees and scratched in the dirt
for several minutes. At last, with a grunt of triumph, he rose
once more and showed what he held in his hands: three black
pebbles.

"As rightful King of Kings, I have certain powers beyond those of ordinary men," he declared. He threw one of the black pebbles down onto the ground from which he'd grubbed it. "Denak, I divorce you from Pradtak." He repeated the formula twice more, making the divorce complete.

Denak remained disheartened. "I know you mean that kindly, your Majesty, but it does nothing for me. No doubt Pradtak, too, will cast the pebbles against me when he eventually gets free of your shape and your cell. But what good does it do me?"

"Lady, not even the King of Kings has the power—though some have claimed it—to ask the hand of a woman wed to another man," Sharbaraz said. "Thus I needed to free you from that union."

"But . . . your Majesty!" Denak's words stumbled out one and two at a time. "You—of all people—know how I . . . threw away my honor in the hall in front of your cell."

Sharbaraz shook his head. "I know you won great honor there, giving without concern for yourself that I, that Makuran, might go on. If you know nothing else of me, know I always aid those who aid me and punish those who do me wrong. When I sit on the throne in Mashiz once more, you shall sit beside me as my principal wife. By the God and the Four I swear it."

Abivard was never sure whether he or Denak first went down into a prostration before Sharbaraz. His sister was sobbing still, but with a different note now, as if, against all expectation, the sacrifice and humiliation she had endured might have been of some worth after all.

"Honor lost is honor won," Sharbaraz said. "Rise, Denak, and you, Abivard. We have much to do before I return to my proper place in Mashiz."

"Aye, your Majesty." As Abivard got back to his feet, he glanced over at Tanshar, who was taking bread and dates from the saddlebag of a packhorse. The fortune-teller's second prophecy echoed within him: honor won and honor lost in a tall tower. He had seen that, sure enough, and more of each than Abivard had imagined.

Where, he wondered, would he find that flash of light across a narrow sea? And what would it bring with it?

VI

GODARZ HAD TAUGHT ABIVARD MANY THINGS: HOW TO RIDE, HOW to rule a domain, how to think of next year instead of tomorrow. One thing he had not taught him was how to be a rebel. Abivard didn't think Godarz had ever dreamed—or had nightmares—of opposing Vek Rud domain to the power of the King of Kings in Mashiz.

Whatever he did, then, he had to do on his own, without his father's advice and warnings echoing in the back of his mind. He missed them. He had grown used to the idea that Godarz had an answer for everything and, could he but find it, all would be well. In the game he played now, that was not so.

Nor could he simply sit idle and let Sharbaraz bear the whole burden of the war against Smerdis. Not only would that have been unseemly for the King of Kings' brother-in-law—for Sharbaraz had kept his promise and wed Denak as soon as he came into Vek Rud stronghold—but Abivard knew most of the frontier *dihqans* better than his sovereign did.

"Old news," Sharbaraz complained one evening, munching bulgur wheat with pine nuts and mutton drenched in a sauce of yogurt and crushed mint leaves. "I know the domains, and I know of the lords they had before our army went into Pardraya, but how many of those lords still live? One here, one there. Mostly, though, it's their sons and grandsons and nephews who carry on for them, men whose ways I never studied. Whereas you—"

"Aye, I've hunted with some of them and played mallet and ball against others at festivals and the like, but I can't claim to know them well. Most of my dealings with them have been after I made my way back from Pardraya."

"Those are the important dealings, now," Sharbaraz said. "If we cannot bring the northwest to my banner, you might as well have left me mured up in Nalgis Crag stronghold, for that would prove Smerdis, curse him through the Void, will be the sure winner in our struggle."

Abivard rose from the bench in the kitchen and paced back and forth. "If we wrote out the lists of opposing forces on parchment, ours would be much smaller and weaker than Smerdis' even if all the northwestern *dihqans* went over to you," he said. "How do we go about overcoming that advantage?"

"If all the forces loyal to Smerdis today stay loyal to him, we're doomed," Sharbaraz answered. "I don't believe they will. I think most of them are with him because they believe I gave up the throne of my own free will. When they learn that isn't so, they'll flock to my banner."

They had better, Abivard thought. *Otherwise we'll see how bitter a death Smerdis can devise for us.* That, however, was not the sort of notion he could share with the man he reckoned his sovereign.

Sharbaraz looked up at him. Nothing about his dress proclaimed him King of Kings: he wore one of Abivard's woolen caftans, a good enough garment but hardly a royal robe. A bit of yogurt was stuck in his beard, just below one corner of his mouth. But when he spoke, confidence rang in his voice like a horn call: "When you rescued me from Pradtak's stronghold, you didn't stop to reckon up the cost or what would come afterward—you simply did what was right. We'll go on that way, and the God will surely smile on us."

"May it be so, your Majesty," Abivard answered.

"It *shall* be so," Sharbaraz said fiercely, slamming a fist down on the stone table in front of him. As they had before, his words set Abivard afire inside, made him want to leap onto his horse and charge down on Mashiz, sweeping everything before him by sheer force of will.

But however much he wanted to do that, the part of him that was Godarz's heritage warned him it would not be so easy. Peroz had charged down on the Khamorth—and look what it got him.

Frada came in then. One of the cooks handed him a pocket bread filled with the same mutton-and-bulgur mixture Abivard and Sharbaraz were eating. "Your Majesty," he murmured as he sat down beside Sharbaraz. His tone lay somewhere between admiration and hero worship; he had never expected to sit at meat with the King of Kings.

When he glanced toward Abivard, though, resentment congealed on his face. Abivard hadn't told him of the plan to rescue Sharbaraz; Abivard hadn't told anyone who did not absolutely have to know. He could see Frada wishing he had been along, too.

Sharbaraz also saw that. He said to Frada, "Secrets must be kept. You shall yet have the chance to show off your courage before me."

Frada preened like a peacock. Had he had tail feathers, he would have fanned them out in dazzling display. As things were, he had to be content with puffing out his chest, throwing back his head, and, in Abivard's opinion, looking very foolish.

But perhaps Frada wasn't so foolish after all. No less than Abivard, he was now brother-in-law to the rightful King of Kings. When Sharbaraz regained his capital, both Godarz's sons—and their younger half brothers, too—would be great men in Makuran. That hadn't fully occurred to Abivard till then.

For the moment, though, Frada was just his little brother. "Get out of here," he said, "before you stroll into the oven from not looking where you're going." The gesture Frada returned was emphatically not one of benediction, but he departed, chewing noisily.

Sharbaraz chuckled. "The two of you get on well," he said. His voice was wistful. "I grew up distrusting all my brothers, and they me."

"That happens in a fair number of domains, I've heard," Abivard said. "I can see how it would be worse in Mashiz, with the whole realm as a prize for the one who manages to inherit."

"Just so," Sharbaraz said. "When word came of my father's fall, I looked for one of my brothers to try to cast me down from the throne." He laughed a laugh full of self-mockery. "And so I paid no heed to my doddering cousin the mintmaster—and paid the price for that. I'd be paying it yet, without your sister and you."

Abivard dipped his head. Songs said a monarch's gratitude was like lowlands snow on a warm spring day, but he didn't think Sharbaraz typical of the breed. With luck, the rightful King of Kings would remain a man among men even after he gained the throne.

"How do you and your brothers keep from quarreling?" Sharbaraz asked.

"Oh, we quarrel—like pups in a litter," Abivard answered. "But Father never let us turn it to feuds and knives in the back. 'The domain is bigger than any one of you, and big enough for all of you,' he'd say, and clout us now and again to make sure the lesson got through."

"My father used to say much the same thing." Sharbaraz shook his head. "He couldn't quite make us believe it. I wish he had."

"What do you suppose Smerdis will do when he learns of your escape?" Abivard thought it a good time to change the subject. "What would you do, were you in Mashiz and he a rebel in the provinces?"

"Were I on my throne, I would attack any rebel with as strong a force as I could mount, to make sure his men won no battles against forces too weak to do a proper job of rooting them out. That would only give them courage, the last thing I'd want rebel troops to have."

"Our thoughts travel the same track," Abivard said, nodding. "The next question is, does Smerdis think the same way we do?"

Sharbaraz stopped with a bite halfway to his mouth. "By the God, Abivard, I have more reason to bless the day I met you than that it was also the day I gained my freedom and claimed your sister as my bride. Do you know, that notion never occurred to me. I assumed Smerdis would set out from Mashiz with his whole host directly he heard I'd escaped, because I would have done as much in his place. But it may not be so."

"You must have known him at your father's court." Abivard thanked his father for drilling into him that there was commonly more than one way to look at a situation. "What feel do you have for the way he'll act? I've only met him, so to speak, when his men took my money to pay it to the Khamorth. From that, he doesn't strike me as a world-bestriding hero."

"I never reckoned him one, that's certain," Sharbaraz said, "but then, I hardly had him in my mind at all till he stole my throne from me. He was just a gray man with a gray beard, hardly worth noticing even when he spoke, and he didn't speak much. Who would have guessed such ambition hid behind that blank mask?"

"Maybe he didn't know it was there himself till he got the chance to let it out," Abivard said.

"That could be so." With the dainty manners of the royal court, Sharbaraz dabbed at his mouth with a square of cloth—a towel rather than a proper napkin, but as close as Vek Rud domain could come. When Abivard wiped his mouth, he used his sleeve. Setting the towel aside, Sharbaraz went on, "One thing is sure, though: he'll soon learn I'm loose, and then we'll find out what sort of man he is."

The rider from Nalgis Crag domain looked nervous as he waited for Abivard to approach. "Lord," he said, sooner than he should have, "I beg you to remember I am but a messenger here, bearing the words and intentions of Pradtak my *dihqan*. They are not my words or intentions, and I would not have you blame me for them."

"However it pleases you," Abivard said. The rider let out a long, smoky breath of relief, then gave Abivard a sharp look. Abivard carefully kept his own face innocent. He twisted his left hand in a gesture of benediction. "I pledge by the God that no harm will come to you because of the message you bring."

"You are gracious, lord. Pradtak bade me deliver these first of all." The rider unsealed a message tube. Instead of a letter, he let three black pebbles fall into the palm of his other hand. "These are the very pebbles he dropped before witnesses to pronounce divorcement from his former wife the lady Denak, your sister."

Abivard burst out laughing. Pradtak's messenger went from apprehensive to shocked in the space of a heartbeat. Whatever reaction he had expected—fury, most likely, or perhaps dismay—that wasn't it. Abivard said, "You may return the pebbles to your lord with my compliments. Tell him he's too late, that divorcement's already been pronounced."

"Lord, I do not understand," the messenger said carefully. "By custom and law both, you have not the power to end the marriage of your sister to my lord Pradtak."

"True," Abivard admitted. "But the King of Kings, may his years be many and his realm increase, does have that power."

"Smerdis King of Kings has not—" the rider began.

Abivard broke in. "Ah, but Sharbaraz King of Kings, son of Peroz and true ruler of Makuran, *has*."

"*Sharbaraz* King of Kings?" Pradtak's rider stared like a sturgeon netted out of the Vek Rud River. "Every man knows Sharbaraz renounced the throne."

"Evidently not everyone knows the renunciation was forced from him at knifepoint, and that he was locked away in Nalgis Crag stronghold for safekeeping," Abivard said. The rider's eyes got even wider. With relish, Abivard went on, "And not everyone knows my sister and I rescued him out of Nalgis Crag stronghold, and set your precious lord in the cell that had been his. How long did Pradtak take to get his own face back, anyhow?"

The messenger sputtered for close to a minute before he finally managed, "Lord, I know nothing of this. I am but a small man, and it is dangerous for such to meddle in the affairs of those stronger than they. I have here also a letter from my lord Pradtak for you." He handed Abivard another leather tube.

As Abivard opened it, he said, "You may not be powerful, but you must know whether your lord looked like himself or someone else for a while, eh?"

"I am not required to speak of this to you," the man said.

"So you're not." Abivard took out the scrap of parchment and unrolled it. The message was, if nothing else, to the point: *War to the knife*. Abivard showed it to the messenger. "You can tell Pradtak for me that the knife cuts both ways. If he chooses to support a usurper in place of the proper King of Kings, he'll find himself on the wrong end of it."

"I shall deliver your words, just as you say them," the rider answered.

"Do that. Think about them on the way back to Nalgis Crag stronghold, too. When you get there, tell your friends what's happened—and why. Some of them, I'd wager, will know what befell Pradtak when we rescued Sharbaraz. Before you go, though, take bread and wine and sit by the fire. Whatever Pradtak says, I'm not at war with you."

But the messenger shook his head. "No, lord, that wouldn't be right; I'm loyal to my own *dihqan*, I am, and I wouldn't make myself the guest of a man I'm liable to be fighting before long. I do thank you, though; you're generous to offer." He made small smacking noises, as if chewing on what Abivard had told him. His face was thoughtful.

"I wish your *dihqan* had shown the same loyalty to his rightful lord as you do to him," Abivard said. "Go in peace, if you feel you must. Maybe when you hear the whole story you'll change your mind. Maybe some of your friends will, too, when they learn it all."

Pradtak's rider did not answer. But as he turned his horse to start the journey back to Nalgis Crag domain, he sketched a salute. Abivard returned it. He had hopes that Pradtak had done his own cause more harm than good with those three pebbles and the accompanying letter of defiance. Let his men learn how he had betrayed Peroz's son, and Nalgis Crag stronghold, no matter how invulnerable to outside assault, might yet quake beneath his fundament.

The smithy was dark and sooty, lit mostly by the leaping redgold flames of the furnace. It smelled of woodsmoke and hot iron and sweat. Ganzak the smith was the mightiest wrestler of Vek Rud domain; he had a chest and shoulders like a bull's, and his arms, worked constantly with blows of the heavy hammer, were thick as some men's legs.

"Lord, Majesty, you honor my hearth by your visit," he said when Abivard and Sharbaraz came in one wintry morning.

"Your fire's as welcome as your company," Abivard answered with a grin to show he was joking. Yet, as with many jests, his held a grain of truth. While snow lay in the stronghold's courtyard, Ganzak labored bare-chested, and heat as well as exertion left his skin wet and gleaming, almost as if oiled, in the firelight.

"How fares my armor?" Sharbaraz asked him. The rightful King of Kings was not one to waste time on anything when his vital interests were concerned. He went on, "The sooner I have it, the sooner I feel myself fully a man and a warrior again—and I aim to take the field as soon as I may."

"Majesty, I've told you before I do all I can, but armor, especially chain, is slow work," Ganzak said. "Splints are simple— just long, thin plates hammered out and punched at each end for attachment. But ring mail—"

Abivard had played through this discussion with the smith before. But Sharbaraz, being a scion of the royal family, had not learned much about how armor was made; perhaps his study of the domains and their leaders had kept him from paying much attention to such seemingly smaller matters. He said, "What's the trouble? You make the rings, you fit them together into mail, you fasten the mail to the leather backing, and there's your suit."

Ganzak exhaled through his nose. Had someone of less than Sharbaraz's exalted status spoken to him so, he might have given a more vehement reply, probably capped by chasing the luckless fellow out of the smithy with hammer upraised. As it was, he used what Abivard thought commendable restraint: "Your Majesty, it's not so simple. What are the rings made of?"

"Wire, of course," Sharbaraz said. "Iron wire, if that's what you mean."

"Iron wire it is," Ganzak agreed. "The best iron I can make, too. But wire doesn't grow on trees like pistachio nuts. By the

God, I wish it did, but since it doesn't, I have to make it, too. That means I have to cut thin strips from a plate of iron, which is what I was doing when you and my lord the *dihqan* came in."

He pointed to several he had set aside. "Here they are. They're still not wire yet, you see—they're just strips of iron. To turn 'em into wire, I have to hammer 'em out thin and round."

Sharbaraz said, "I believe I may have spoken too soon."

But Ganzak, by then, was in full spate and not to be headed off by mere apology. "Then once I have the wire, I have to turn it into rings. They're all supposed to be the same size, right? So what I do is, I wrap the wire around this dowel here—" He showed Sharbaraz the wooden cylinder. "—and then cut 'em, one at a time. Then I have to pound the ends of each one flat and rivet 'em together to make rings, one at a time again. 'Course, they have to be linked to each other before I put the rivets in, on account of you can't put 'em together after they're finished rings. None of this stuff is quick, begging your pardon, Majesty."

"No, I see it wouldn't be. Forgive me, Ganzak; I spoke out of turn." Sharbaraz sounded humbler than a King of Kings usually had occasion to be. "Another lesson learned: know what something involves before you criticize."

Abivard said, "I've seen mail with every other row of rings punched from plate rather than turned out the way you describe. Wouldn't that be faster to make?"

"Aye, it is." Ganzak spat into the fire. "But that's what I give you for it. You can't link those punched rings one to another, only to the proper ones in the rows above and below 'em. That means the mail isn't near as strong for the same weight of metal. You want his Majesty to go to war in cheap, shoddy armor, find yourself another smith." He folded massive arms across even more massive chest.

Defeated, Abivard said, "When do you think this next armor will be finished?"

The smith considered. "Three weeks, lord, give or take a little."

"It will have to do," Sharbaraz said with a sigh. "In truth, I don't expect to be attacked before then, but I grudge every day without mail. I feel naked as a newborn babe."

"It's not so bad as that, your Majesty," Abivard said. "Hosts of warriors go and fight in leather. The Khamorth make a habit of it, their horses being smaller and less able to bear weight than ours, and I fought against them so while Ganzak was still at work on my suit of iron."

"No doubt," Sharbaraz said. "Necessity knows few laws, as you among others showed in freeing me from Nalgis Crag stronghold. But did you not reckon yourself a hero once more, not just a warrior, when the ring mail jingled sweetly on your shoulders?"

"I don't know about that," Abivard said. "I did reckon myself less likely to get killed, which is plenty to hearten a man in a fight."

"Lord, when I hear you talk plain sense, I can see your father standing there in your place," Ganzak said.

"I wish he were," Abivard answered quietly. Even so, he glowed with pride at the compliment.

Sharbaraz said, "At my father's court, I learned as much of war from minstrels as from soldiers. Good to have close by me someone who has seen it and speaks plainly of what it requires. Doing one's duty and staying alive through it, though not something to inspire songs, also has its place. Another lesson." He nodded, as if to impress it on his memory.

Abivard nodded, too. Sharbaraz was always learning. Abivard thought well of that: the very nature of his office was liable to make the King of Kings sure he already knew everything, for who dared tell him he did not?

Something else occurred to Abivard. Suppose one day Sharbaraz went wrong? As the King of Kings had said, he stood close by now. But how was he to tell Sharbaraz he was mistaken? He had no idea.

In the stronghold, Sharbaraz took for his own the chamber Abivard had used while Godarz still lived; Frada relinquished it with good grace. It lay down the hall from the *dihqan's* bedchamber; that convenience was a point in its favor.

Denak had returned to the women's quarters of Vek Rud stronghold when she, Abivard, Sharbaraz, and Tanshar came back to the domain. True to his vow, Sharbaraz had wed her as soon as a servant of the God could be brought to the stronghold. But though she was his wife, the women's quarters were not his. Had he gone in there to claim her whenever he sought her company, he would have created great scandal even though he was King of Kings.

The way round the seeming impasse created scandal, too, but not great scandal. The outer door to the *dihqan's* bedchamber became the effective boundary to the women's quarters—*just as it had at Nalgis Crag stronghold,* Abivard thought, and kept the thought to himself. Sharbaraz did not go inside. Abivard brought Denak to him there, and he escorted her to the room he was using. For her, that room was also part of the women's quarters.

So far, well and good. The trouble lay in the stretch of hall between the *dihqan*'s bedchamber and Sharbaraz' room. No one in the stronghold was willing to consider a hallway part of the women's quarters, but nobody could see how Denak was supposed to join her husband without traversing it, either. Tongues wagged.

"Maybe Tanshar could magic me from my room to Sharbaraz's," Denak said one evening as Abivard walked her toward the controversial hall.

"I don't think so," he said doubtfully. "I just thank the God his strength sufficed for the uses to which we put it."

"Brother of mine, I meant that for a joke." Denak poked him in the ribs, which made him hop in the air. "It was the only answer I could think of that might stop the gossip about how we have to do things."

"Oh." Abivard tried it on for size. He decided to laugh. "It's good to have you back here."

"It's good to be back," she answered, turning serious again. "After what happened in Pradtak's women's quarters—" Her face twisted. "I wish I could have killed that guard. I wish I could have killed all three of them, a finger's breadth at a time. Escaping that place is not enough, but it will have to do."

He started to put an arm around her, but stopped with the gesture barely begun. She didn't want anyone but Sharbaraz touching her these days. Abivard wished she had killed the guard—all the guards—too, as slowly as she liked. He would have helped, and smiled as he did it.

She said, "In truth, it's just as well Tanshar can't sorcerously flick me about from chamber to chamber. No matter what others may say, walking down that stretch of hall makes me feel free, as if I had the run of the whole stronghold the way I did when I was a girl. Funny what twenty or thirty feet of stone floor and blank walls can do, isn't it?"

"I was thinking the same thing," Abivard said. "Do you know, Roshnani and some of my other wives are jealous of you?"

"I'm not surprised," Denak said as Abivard opened the inner door to the bedchamber for her to pass through. "To those with no freedom, even a tiny bit must look like a lot."

"Hmm." Abivard closed the door that led into the women's

quarters, locked it, and walked with Denak to the outer door of the bedchamber. Sharbaraz stood waiting just outside. Abivard bowed to him. "Your Majesty, I bring you your wife."

Sharbaraz bowed in turn, first to Abivard and then to Denak. He held out his arm to her. "My lady, if you will come with me?" She crossed the threshold. Abivard turned away so that, formally speaking, he had not seen her walking down that much-too-public hall. Then he laughed at himself, and at the way he did his best to pretend custom hadn't been violated when he knew full well it had. He wondered whether custom wasn't more nearly the ruler of Makuran than the King of Kings was.

That evening, he brought Roshnani to the bedchamber. She looked wistfully toward the outer door. "I wish I could go through there, too," she said. "The women's quarters are bearable when you know everyone stays in them alike. When one can go farther—" She paused, perhaps swallowing some of what she had intended to say. "It's hard," she finished.

"I am sorry it troubles you," Abivard said. "I don't know what to do about it, though. I can't throw away untold years of tradition on a whim. Tradition didn't count on a King of Kings' having to take refuge in a back-country stronghold, or on his marrying the *dihqan*'s sister."

"I know that," Roshnani said. "And please understand I do not hold Denak's luck against her. We get on famously; we might have been born sisters. I just wish my stretch of the world were wider, too. All I've seen of the world since I became a woman is two women's quarters and the land between the stronghold where I grew up and this one. It's not enough."

"You might have been born sisters with Denak," he agreed. "She's been saying much the same thing for as long as I can remember. I hadn't heard it from you till now."

"I didn't have any reason to think about it till now," she said, which made Abivard remember what Denak had said about a little freedom seeming a lot. Roshnani went on, "Does it anger you that I speak so? Few men, from what little I know, give their wives even so much rein." She looked anxiously at Abivard.

"It's all right," he said. "Smerdis, I'm sure, would have locked up Sharbaraz's thoughts along with—or ahead of—his body, if only he could. I don't see the sense in that. If you don't say what you think, how am I supposed to find out? I may not always think you're right—and even if I do, I may not be able to do anything about it—but I want to know."

Like the sun emerging and then going back behind the clouds, Roshnani's frown chased a quick smile off her face. She said, "If you think I'm right, why can't you do anything about it?"

He spread his hands. "We'll have nobles aplenty coming here to Vek Rud stronghold, sounding out Sharbaraz to see whether they should side with him or with Smerdis. Do you think he'd do his cause much good if he said he wanted all their wives and daughters out of the women's quarters? I don't think he does want that, but even if he did, saying so would cost him half his support, likely more."

"Not among the women," Roshnani said stubbornly.

"But the women aren't lancers."

Roshnani bit her lip. "Dreadful when a question of what's right and wrong collides with a question of what works well in the world."

"My father would have said that if it doesn't work well in the world, whether it's right or wrong doesn't matter. When Tanshar and I went to Pradtak's, I kept from having to talk too much too soon just by claiming hospitality. Pradtak had to serve me food and wine then, whether he wanted to or not. The women's quarters are the same way: because they're part of the way things have always been done, they won't disappear tomorrow even if Sharbaraz orders that they should."

Abivard watched Roshnani chew on that. By her expression, she didn't care for the flavor. "Maybe not," she admitted reluctantly. "But what about this, then: will you begin to ease the rules of the women's quarters after Sharbaraz wins the war and the assembled nobles of Makuran aren't all peering straight at your—our—stronghold?"

He started to answer, but stopped before any words crossed his lips. He had expected his logic to convince Roshnani—and so it had. But instead of convincing her he was right, it had just convinced her to accept delay in getting what she still wanted. It was, he thought uncomfortably, a very womanly way of arguing—she had conceded his point and turned it against him in the same breath.

So how was he supposed to reply? Every heartbeat he hesitated gave her more hope—and made his dashing that hope harder. At last he said, "I suppose we can try it; that probably won't make the world come to an end."

"If it doesn't work out, you can always go back to the old ways," she said encouragingly.

"That's rubbish, and you know it," he said. "Just as easy to put together the pieces of a butchered mutton carcass and say it's a live sheep again."

"Yes, I do know it," Roshnani admitted. "I was hoping you didn't."

"Devious wench."

"Of course," she said. "Caged away in the women's quarters as I am, what can I be but devious?" She stuck out her tongue at him, but quickly grew serious again. "Even knowing that you'll change the old way, you'd still let me—let us—out now and again?"

Abivard felt Godarz looking over his shoulder. He almost turned around to see what expression his father wore. His best guess was sardonic amusement at the predicament in which his son had landed himself. Break custom or make Roshnani—and his other wives when she was through with them—furious at him? Sighing, he said, "Yes, I suppose we can see how it goes."

Roshnani squeaked, jumped in the air, threw her arms around his neck, and kissed him. He would have called what happened next a molestation if he hadn't enjoyed it so much. Later, the watchful, thoughtful part of him wondered if he had been bribed. One of the nice things about Roshnani was that he could tease her with such without angering her.

"No," she answered. "You just made me very happy, that's all."

He looked at her. "I should make you happy more often."

"Well, why don't you?" she asked mischievously.

He flopped on the bed like a dead fish. "If I did it too often, I'm not sure I'd live through it." When she reached out to tickle him, he quickly added, "On the other hand, it might be interesting to find out."

"Royal soldiers!" a rider bawled as he drove his worn horse up the steep streets of the town toward Vek Rud stronghold. "Royal soldiers, riding this way!"

Ice that had nothing to do with winter ran up Abivard's back when he heard that cry. In one way, he had been expecting it since the moment he managed to get Sharbaraz out of Nalgis Crag stronghold. In another, though, as with battle or with women, all the anticipation in the world wasn't worth a copper when set against reality.

As soon as the horseman rode into the courtyard, Abivard shouted, "Shut the gates!" The men in charge of them hurried to obey. The iron-fronted timbers clanged as they closed. A great bar, thick as a man's leg, thudded down behind them. "How many?" Abivard asked the rider.

"Twenty or thirty, maybe, lord," the fellow answered. "Wasn't any huge host, that much I'll say."

"Do you think a huge host follows?" Abivard persisted.

The rider gave him an exasperated glare. "Lord, begging your pardon, but how should I know? If I'd been fool enough to hang around to try and find out, odds are the buggers would have spotted me."

Abivard sighed. "You're right, of course. Go into the kitchens and grab yourself some bread and wine. Then get your bow out of its case and take your place on the wall with the rest of us."

"Aye, lord." The horseman hurried away. Abivard went up the stairs two at a time as he climbed to the walkway atop the wall and peered south. The day was cloudy and gloomy, with enough snow pattering down to ruin visibility. He muttered under his breath. Smerdis' men weren't coming quickly. After the news his retainer had shouted, he craved action.

Sharbaraz came up on the wall beside him. "I heard the alarm raised," the rightful King of Kings said. "What's toward?"

"We're about to have visitors," Abivard answered. "Just when or how many I can't say, but they're not the welcome sort."

"We knew this would happen," Sharbaraz said, biting his lip. "But Smerdis is moving faster than we thought, curse him. I hadn't looked to be penned in this stronghold before I had an army of my own strong enough to oppose the usurper."

"Yes." Abivard's voice was distracted. He pointed. "Do you think that's them, or is it only a flock?"

Sharbaraz squinted as he looked down along Abivard's outstretched arm. "Your eyes must be better than mine. No, wait, I see what you're pointing at. Those aren't cattle or sheep, I fear. Those are horsemen."

"I think so, too." Abivard would have been surer on a sunny day, with light sparking off lanceheads and horse trappings and chainmail. But the purposeful way the distant specks kept moving north told him all he needed to know.

"There aren't that many of them," Sharbaraz said after a bit.

"No. The rider who brought word said it was a small band," Abivard said. "Seems he was right." He looked toward the approaching troop. "I don't see any more behind them, either."

"Nor I." Sharbaraz sounded indignant, as if he thought Smerdis wasn't playing the game by the rules. "What can he hope to do by sending a boy—no, an unweaned babe—in place of a man?"

"If I knew, I would tell you," Abivard answered. "We'll find out within the half hour, though, I expect."

The royal soldier reined in at the base of the knob atop which Vek Rud stronghold perched. Some of the folk who lived in the town on the knob had fled up to the stronghold before Abivard ordered the gates closed. The rest did their best to pretend they were invisible.

One warrior rode up toward the stronghold with a white-washed shield upraised as a sign of truce. He called in a loud voice, "Is it true Sharbaraz son of Peroz has taken up residence here?"

Abivard recognized the voice a moment before he recognized the face. "None of your affair, Zal," he called back. "Whether the answer is yea or nay, d'you think I'd let you in here again after the way you used me the last time you saw the courtyard?"

Zal's grin was wide and unashamed. "I just followed the orders I was given. But I think I have a token that will buy my way in."

"Do you? I'll believe that when I see it."

"Good thing the weather is so cold," Zal remarked as he reached back to open a saddlebag. "Otherwise this would stink a lot worse than it does." The comment made no sense to Abivard until the royal officer held up by the hair a severed head that, as he had said, was less than perfectly fresh but that had until recently without a doubt adorned the shoulders of the famous Murghab.

Gulping a little, Abivard said, "You're trying to convince me you're for Sharbaraz, not against him?"

Beside him, Sharbaraz whispered, "Whose head is that?"

"It belonged to Smerdis' tax collector, the one who extorted eighty-five hundred arkets from me as tribute for the Khamorth," Abivard whispered back. He raised his voice and called to Zal, "How say you?"

"Of course I'm for his Majesty," Zal cried. "I served Smerdis just as you did, thinking Sharbaraz had truly given up the throne. Then my men and I ran into a courier who had word from Nalgis Crag that his Majesty—his genuine Majesty, I mean—had escaped from imprisonment. That put a whole new light on things. I got rid of the courier and then I got rid of this thing—" He held Murghab's head a little higher. "—but I saved enough to maybe convince you I'm no assassin in the night."

"You ran into a courier, you say?" Abivard answered. "If that's so, you've taken your own sweet time getting here."

Zal shook his graying head. "Not so, youngster. I was a long way south, heading back toward Mashiz myself, when the fellow caught up with me. My best guess is that Smerdis Pimp of Pimps still hasn't heard the real King of Kings is loose."

Abivard and Sharbaraz looked at each other. If that was so . . . "It can't last forever," Abivard said.

"No," Sharbaraz agreed. "But the God would turn his back on us in disgust if we didn't make the best use of it we could."

"Are you two going to spend the whole day blathering up there?" Zal demanded impatiently. "Or will you open up so I can come in and we can talk without lowing at one another like cattle on the plains?"

"Open the gates," Abivard called to the men who served them. To Zal he said, "Come ahead—but you alone, for the time being. I still remember what happened the last time you got men in my stronghold."

"I wish I could give you back your silver, but this thing—" Zal raised Murghab's head. "—had already sent it on to the treasury. Only way for you to get repaid now is to fight and win that treasury for yourself."

He rode through the gates as they opened. Archers on the wall and in the courtyard covered him. Abivard shifted nervously from foot to foot. The soldiers down at the bottom of the knob were all cased in iron, and so were their horses; the King of Kings—even if he was now Pimp of Pimps, as Zal had called him—could afford to keep a great host of smiths busy turning iron strips into wire and wire into rings. If they galloped up for all they were worth, they might get in before the gates slammed, and if they got in, no telling how much damage they would do.

"Your Majesty, it were wiser for you to stay on the wall or on the stairs higher than a lance can reach," Abivard said.

"Wiser some ways, maybe, but not others." Without another word, Sharbaraz hurried down the stairway. He had said—and Abivard had seen, to his and Makuran's dismay—that his father Peroz had tended to strike first and ask questions later. By that standard, Sharbaraz was very much his father's son.

Zal swung down from his horse; though far from young, he was still smooth and limber. Careless of the slush in the courtyard, and of his coat and the armor under it, he went down onto his belly before Sharbaraz, knocking his forehead against the cobblestones.

"Get up, man," Sharbaraz told him. "You're Zal son of Sintrawk, one of the senior guard captains out of Mashiz?"

"Aye, that's me, Majesty." Zal sounded impressed and surprised that Sharbaraz should know of him. Abivard was also impressed, but less surprised. He had already seen Sharbaraz's mastery of detail.

Sharbaraz said, "When word I live does get out, how many other officers will also rally to my call?"

"A good number, Majesty, a good number." Zal went on, "The God willing, enough so all you'll have to do about Smerdis is hunt him down and lop off his head as I did with the famous Murghab. Only trouble is, I don't know whether the God will be *that* willing."

"Always an interesting question, isn't it?" Sharbaraz turned to Abivard. "This is your stronghold, lord *dihqan*; I would not presume to order you in its administration. But do you judge that Zal's men may safely be admitted here?"

The turn had offered Sharbaraz's back to Zal. At first, that alarmed Abivard: it struck him as a foolish chance to take. Then he realized Sharbaraz had done it on purpose. That left him no less alarmed, but he admired the nerve of the rightful King of Kings. Zal made no move to snatch out the sword or dagger that hung from his belt.

Seeing him pass that test, Abivard said, "Very well, Majesty." He asked Zal, "Would you sooner summon them yourself, or shall I do it?"

"Let me," Zal said. "They're less likely to think it's some kind of trap that way. In fact, given how far off they are, why don't I just ride back to them and let them know all's well?"

Abivard felt a whole new set of qualms: what was to keep Zal and his heavily armored fighters from heading back to Mashiz? Hunting them down would not be easy. He shook his head—if he had to reach that far for worries, they weren't worth the reach. He nodded to Zal. The guard captain got back onto his horse and headed down the knob.

Abivard glanced over to Sharbaraz. The rightful King of Kings was not as calm as he looked; he fidgeted most unregally. That made Abivard nervous again, too. He wanted to say something like *This was your idea,* but he couldn't, not to his sovereign.

Zal was too far away for anyone in the stronghold to hear what he said to his men. The cheer the squadron raised, though, rang sweet in Abivard's ears. He felt himself grinning like a fool. A broad, relieved smile stretched over Sharbaraz's face, too. "We got away with it," he said.

"Looks that way," Abivard agreed, doing his best to sound casual.

The horsemen rode up through the town, singing loudly and discordantly. Abivard needed a little while to recognize the tune: a song in praise of the King of Kings. Sharbaraz pumped an excited fist in the air. "The truth brings men to my side," he exclaimed, and Abivard nodded.

"Here comes someone else," Frada said, pointing out toward the southwest.

"I see him," Abivard answered. "If Smerdis chose to hit us now, he'd bag most of the *dihqans* from the northwestern part of the realm."

"If Smerdis chose to hit us now, his army would desert," his younger brother said confidently. "How could it be otherwise? Now that everyone knows he's but a usurper—and now that the rightful King of Kings is free—who could want to fight for him? He'll be cowering in the palace at Mashiz, waiting for Sharbaraz to come and put him out of his misery."

"The God grant that you're right." Though he didn't want to detail them before Frada, Abivard had his doubts. The last time he had been sure something would work perfectly, he had been riding north with Peroz to settle the Khamorth once and for all. That had indeed worked . . . but not the way Peroz intended.

"Who comes?" one of the men at the gate called to the approaching noble and his retinue.

"Digor son of Nadina, *dihqan* of Azarmidukht Hills domain," came the reply.

"Welcome to Vek Rud domain, Digor of the Azarmidukht Hills," the guard replied. "Know that Sharbaraz King of Kings has declared Vek Rud stronghold a truce ground. No matter that you be at feud with your neighbor; if you meet him here, you meet him as a friend. So Sharbaraz has ordered; so shall it be."

"So shall it be," Digor echoed. Abivard couldn't tell whether the order angered him; he kept his voice quiet and his face composed. Unlike a lot of the nobles gathering here, he was neither unusually young nor unusually old. Either he hadn't gone onto the Pardrayan steppe or he had come away safe again.

Abivard took out a scrap of parchment, a jar of ink, and a reed pen. He inked the pen, lined through Digor's name, and replaced the writing paraphernalia. Frada smiled. "Our father would have approved," he said.

"What, that I'm keeping a list?" Abivard smiled, too, then pointed down to the mass of men who milled about in the courtyard. "I'd never manage to have all of them straight without it."

"It took Sharbaraz's summons to bring them all here," Frada said, "and it's taking Sharbaraz's truce call to keep 'em from yanking out swords and going at one another. Some of the feuds here go back to the days of the Prophets Four."

"I know," Abivard said. "I'd hoped, with so many new men heading domains, some of them could have been forgotten, but it doesn't look that way. As long as they hate Smerdis worse than their neighbors, we should do well enough."

"I hope you're right," Frada said. "How many more nobles do we expect to come?"

"Three, I think." Abivard consulted his parchment. "Yes, three, that's right."

"I don't think his Majesty is in the mood to wait for them much longer." Frada pointed back to the living quarters, where Sharbaraz stared from a window. He had been pacing restlessly for the past three days, ever since the northwestern *dihqans* started flooding into Vek Rud domain in response to his summons.

"Just as well, too," Abivard answered. "They're eating us out of house and home, and who knows how long they'll keep honoring the truce here? One knife comes out and everyone will remember all the blood feuds—and drag us into them. Our line has mostly stayed clear of such, but a murder or two on the grounds of Vek Rud stronghold would be plenty to keep our great-grandchildren watching their neighbors out of the corner of the eye."

"You're right about that," Frada said. "Getting into a feud is easy. Getting out of one again—" He shook his head.

Sharbaraz evidently chose that moment to decide he would wait no more for the few remaining sluggards. He came out of the living quarters and strode through the crowd in the courtyard toward the speaking platform Abivard's carpenters had built for him. He had on no gorgeous robe like the one Peroz had worn even on campaign, just a plain caftan of heavy wool and a conical helm with a spray of feathers for a crest. Even so, he drew men's notice as a lodestone draws chunks of iron. The aimless milling in the courtyard became purposeful as the assembled nobles turned toward the platform to hear what he would say.

Abivard and Frada hurried down from their place atop the wall. By the time they began jockeying for a place from which to listen to the rightful King of Kings, they would have had to commit an assault, or rather several, to get a good one. Abivard did not bother. Unlike the rest of the *dihqans*, he had had the pleasure of Sharbaraz's company for some weeks, so he already had a good notion of what the rightful King of Kings was likely to say.

Sharbaraz drew his sword and waved it overhead. "My friends!" he cried. "Are we going to stay enslaved to the Khamorth on the one hand and on the other to the bloodsucking worm in Mashiz who drains us dry to make the nomads fat? *Are* we?"

"No!" The roar from the crowd echoed and reechoed off the stronghold's stone walls, filling the courtyard with tumult. Abivard felt his ears assailed from every direction.

"Are we going to let some wizened clerk defile with his stinking backside the seat that properly belongs to true men?" Sharbaraz shouted. "Or shall we take back what's ours and teach a lesson that will leave would-be traitors and usurpers shivering and sniveling a thousand years from now?"

"Aye!" This time the roar was louder.

Sharbaraz said, "By now you've no doubt heard how the usurper stole the throne—drugs in my supper. And you've likely had him rob you, saying he'd pay the Khamorth to stay on their own side of the Degird. Tell me, lords, have the cursed plainsmen stayed on their side of the Degird?"

"No!" Now it wasn't a roar, but a harsh cry of anger. Few along the border had not suffered from the nomads' raids.

Warming to his theme now that he had stirred his listeners, Sharbaraz went on, "So, lords, my friends, will you leave on the throne this wretch who stole it by treachery and who lies with every breath he takes, whose own officers began to desert him the moment his lies became clear?"

"No!" the crowd cried once more.

Before Sharbaraz could go on, Zal shouted to everybody, "And I'm not the only one who'll flee him as if he were the plague, now that the truth comes out. What honest man could wish to serve a liar?"

"None!" the assembled *dihqans* yelled, again with that note of fury baying in their voices. When a noble of Makuran gave his word, a man was supposed to be able to rely on it. How much more did that apply to the King of Kings?

"So what say you, lords?" Sharbaraz asked. "Do we ride south when the weather turns fine? We'll sweep all before us, ride into Mashiz in triumph, and set Makuran back on its proper course. I'll not deny, we shan't be able to deal at once with the Khamorth as they deserve, but we can keep them out of our land. And, by the God, once I'm on the throne we can settle scores with Videssos. If the easterners, may the God pitch them into the Void, hadn't incited the nomads against us, our brave warriors, my bold father, would yet live. Are you with me, then, in taking vengeance against the Empire and its false god?"

"Aye!" Abivard yelled as loudly as he could. Settling Videssos' arrogance had ranked high with his father. If Sharbaraz chose to lead that way, he would follow.

By the cries that rose around him, most of the *dihqans* felt as he did. The Khamorth were close, but to any man of Makuran, Videssos was *the* enemy. The nomads' confederacies scattered like pomegranate seeds when the fruit was stamped underfoot, now dangerous, now harmless. Videssos endured.

Sharbaraz plunged into the crowd. Men swarmed toward him, to pound him on the back, clasp his hand, pledge loyalty forever, and boast of the mincemeat they would make of any of Smerdis' men misguided enough to stand against them.

Caught up in the moment, Abivard and Frada pushed through the nobles toward the rightful King of Kings along with everyone else. Working as a team, they made good progress. "You know, we're foolish to be doing this," Frada said after an exchange of elbows with some noble from a hundred farsangs west of Vek Rud domain. "The King of Kings has been here a long time, and he'll stay longer still."

"True, but what of afterward?" Abivard said. "When the war is won, he'll go live in Mashiz and never leave save to go on campaign, and we'll likely end up back here."

"That doesn't have to be so, not when he's wed to our sister," Frada said. "We have his ear on account of that; we could make our own place at the capital."

Abivard grunted dubiously. "What would become of the domain, then? The king's favor—any king's favor, be he ever so good—waxes and wanes like the moon. Land goes on forever, and this land is ours."

Frada laughed out loud. "I listen to you, and it's as if Father were still here to sound like a sage."

"Ha!" Abivard said, pleased at the compliment and worried he couldn't live up to it. Whatever other reply he might have made turned into a hissed exclamation of pain when a *dihqan* with a beard braided into three strands stomped on his foot and shoved him aside. Frada caught the fellow with an elbow in the belly that folded him up like a fan. The two brothers grinned at each other.

Only a few nobles stood between them and Sharbaraz. Around the rightful King of Kings, moving at all was hard, for those who had already spoken with him were trying to get away, while those who still wanted to gain his ear pushed in at them. A couple of *dihqans* squeezed out between Abivard and Frada—and incidentally almost knocked over the fellow who had trampled Abivard's instep—letting them gain another couple of steps toward their sovereign.

Men came at Sharbaraz from all directions. Just standing before him did not mean you could speak with him, for *dihqans* also shouted at him from behind and both sides. He kept turning his head and twisting about like a man playing mallet and ball—wary lest an opponent clout him, not the ball, with his mallet.

When Abivard caught his eye at last, Sharbaraz threw his arms wide, as if to encompass the whole packed courtyard. "They're mine!" he cried. "We'll sweep Smerdis Pimp of Pimps—" He had zestfully stolen Zal's mocking title for his rival. "—out of Mashiz like a servant woman getting the dust from a storeroom. Once that's done, we'll turn on Videssos and—"

"Duck, your Majesty!" Abivard and Frada cried together. Sharbaraz might not have seen battle, but he had a warrior's reflexes. Without gaping or asking questions, he started to throw himself flat. That saved his life. The knife the man behind him wielded cut his robe and scored a bleeding line across his shoulder, but did not slide between his ribs to find his heart.

"The God curse you, curse your house, straight to the Void," the *dihqan* cried, drawing back his arm for another stab. The fellow beside him, horror on his face, seized it before he could bring it forward again. Abivard and Frada both leapt on the would-be assassin and wrestled him to the ground.

He fought like a man possessed, even after the nobles forced the knife from his hand. Only the weight of men on top of him finally made him quit by crushing the air from his lungs. Since most of those men were on top of Abivard, too, he struggled for every breath he took.

"Haul him up," Sharbaraz said when the *dihqan* was subdued. One at a time, the nobles who had piled onto him got off.

Abivard and Frada clutched him and yanked him to his feet. When he started to try to break free, someone hit him in the pit of the stomach. That made him double up and cost him the wind he had just regained.

Sharbaraz had his right hand clapped to his left shoulder. Blood stained his robe and trickled out between his fingers. But the wound was at the top of the shoulder, and his left arm and hand worked; he had that hand clenched into a tight fist against the pain. Abivard dared hope the wound less than serious.

The rightful King of Kings stared at his attacker. "What did I do to you, Prypat, to deserve your knife in my back?" Even after narrowly escaping death, he remembered his assailant's name.

Prypat's face twisted. "Why shouldn't I kill you?" he said in hitching gasps. "Thanks to your cursed sire, my own father, my grandfather, all my elder brothers are ravens' fodder and wolves' meat, their gear plunder for the plainsmen. Every man here holds blood debt against you, did he but have the wit to see it."

Sharbaraz shook his head, then grimaced; the motion must have hurt. "Not so," he replied, as if arguing in court rather than passing judgment on the man who had tried to murder him. "My father acted as he thought best for Makuran. No man is perfect; the God holds that for himself. But the campaign did not fail through malice, nor did the King of Kings murder your kin. I grieve that they fell; I grieve that so many from all the realm fell. But my house incurred no blood debt on account of it."

"Lie all you like—my kin still lie dead," Prypat said.

"And you'll join them," someone cried to him. The *dihqans* snarled like angry dogs. Fear wasn't the least part of that, Abivard judged. Here they had come to Vek Rud stronghold to join Sharbaraz against Smerdis. Had Prypat killed Sharbaraz, the revolt against Mashiz would have died with him; none of the northwestern men had the force of character to make a King of Kings. But when Smerdis learned they had assembled here, he would have taken vengeance just the same. No wonder they were so ready to condemn Prypat out of hand.

Sharbaraz asked him, "Have you any reason I shouldn't order your head stricken off?" That in itself was a mercy. Anyone who tried to slay the King of Kings was liable to death with as much pain and ingenuity as his torturers could devise. But here as everywhere else, Sharbaraz was straightforward, direct, averse to wasting time.

Prypat tried to spit on him, then knelt and bent his head. "I die proud, for I sought to restore my clan's pride."

"Knifing a man in the back is nothing to be proud of." Blood still welled between Sharbaraz's fingers. He raised his voice to call to the nobles: "Who carries a heavy sword?"

Abivard did, but he hesitated, not eager to speak up. Killing a man in battle was one thing, killing him in cold blood—even if he was passionately eager to die—another. While Abivard tried to nerve himself, Zal beat him to it. "I do, your Majesty, and practice using it for justice, as well."

"Strike, then," Sharbaraz said. So did Prypat, at the same time. That seemed to nonplus the rightful King of Kings, but he took his right hand off his wound for a moment to beckon Zal forward. Prypat waited without moving as the officer came up, drew the sword, swung it up with both hands on the hilt, and brought it down. The stroke was clean; Prypat's head sprang from his shoulders. His body convulsed. Blood fountained over the cobbles for the few seconds his heart needed to realize he was dead.

"Dispose of the carrion, if you please," Sharbaraz said to Abivard. He swayed where he stood.

Abivard rushed to support him. "Here, come with me, Majesty," he said, guiding Sharbaraz back toward the living quarters. "We'd best learn how badly you're hurt."

Servants exclaimed in dismay when they saw what had happened. At Abivard's barked orders, they arranged pillows in the hallway just inside the entrance. "Let's lay you down, Majesty," Abivard said to Sharbaraz, who half squatted, half toppled down onto the cushions.

Without Abivard's asking for them, a serving woman fetched him a bowl of water and some rags. He made the tear in Sharbaraz's robe bigger so he could get a good look at the wound. Sharbaraz tried to twist his neck and look down the side of his face so he could see it, too. He succeeded only in making himself hurt worse. "How is it?" he asked Abivard, his voice shaky now that he didn't have to keep up a front for the assembled *dihqans*.

"Not as bad as I thought," Abivard answered. "It's long, aye, but not deep. And it's bled freely, so it's less likely to fester." He turned and, as he had hoped, found the serving woman hovering behind him. He told her, "Fetch me the wound paint—you know the one I mean." She nodded and hurried away.

"Will it hurt?" Sharbaraz asked, anxious as a boy with a barked shin.

"Not too much, Majesty, I hope," Abivard answered. "It's wine and honey and fine-ground myrrh. After I put it on, I'll cover the wound with grease and bandage you up. You should be all right if you don't try to do too much with that arm for the next few days." *I hope,* he added to himself. In spite of medicines, you never could tell what would happen when a man got hurt.

The serving woman returned, handing Abivard a small pot. As he worked the stopper free, she said, "Lord, the lady your sister—your Majesty's wife," she added, working up the nerve to speak to Sharbaraz, "wants to know what befell and how the King of Kings fares."

"Tell her I'm fine," Sharbaraz said at once.

"Word travels fast. Tell her he got cut but I think he'll be fine," Abivard said, a qualified endorsement. He upended the pot above Sharbaraz' shoulder. The medicine slowly poured out. Sharbaraz hissed when it touched the wound. "Bring me some lard before you go speak with Denak," Abivard told the serving woman. Again, she rushed to obey.

When Abivard had treated the cut to his satisfaction, he put a bandage pad on top of it and tied the pad in place with a rag that went around Sharbaraz' shoulder and armpit. The rightful King of Kings sighed to have the ordeal done, then said, "I find myself in your debt yet again."

"Nonsense, your Majesty." Abivard poured a cupful of red wine. "Drink this. The magicians say it builds blood, being like blood itself."

"I've heard that myself. I don't know whether it's true, but I'll gladly drink the wine any which way." Sharbaraz fit action to word. "By the God, that's better going down my throat than splashed on my shoulder." He thrust the cup back at Abivard. "I think I may have lost enough to need more building."

As Abivard poured again, the serving woman returned once more and said, "Your Majesty, lord, may it please the both of you, the lady Denak says she wants to see you as soon as may be—and if that's not soonest, she'll come out to do it."

Sharbaraz looked at Abivard. They both knew Denak was capable of doing just that, and both knew the scandal it would create among the *dihqans* would not help the rightful King of Kings' cause. Sharbaraz said, "Lady, tell my wife I shall see her directly in my chamber."

The serving woman beamed at being treated as if of noble blood. She trotted out of the kitchens yet again. Sharbaraz set his jaw and got to his feet. "Here, your Majesty, lean on me," Abivard said. "You don't want to start yourself bleeding hard again by trying to do too much."

"I suppose not," Sharbaraz said, although he didn't sound quite sure. But he put his right arm on Abivard's shoulder and let the *dihqan* take a good deal of his weight as they made their way down the halls of the living quarters to the chamber he was using as his own.

"Wait here," Abivard said when they reached it. "I'll be back with Denak fast as I can." Sharbaraz nodded and sank onto the bed with a groan he did his best to stifle. In spite of the fortifying wine, he looked very pale.

Denak stood impatiently tapping her foot at the door between Abivard's bedchamber and the women's quarters. "Took you long enough," she said when Abivard opened that door. "No talking around it now—how is he?"

"Wounded," Abivard answered. "He can still use the arm. If he heals properly, he should be fine but for the scar."

Denak searched his face. "You wouldn't lie to me? No, you wouldn't, not when I'll see for myself as fast as we can walk there—and would you walk a little faster, please?" In spite of her brittle tone, something eased in her step, in the set of her shoulders, with every step she took. As much to herself as to Abivard, she went on, "Life wouldn't be worth living without him."

Abivard didn't answer. Again, he wanted to take his sister in his arms and hold her to try to make her feel better, but Denak went hard as stone if anyone save Sharbaraz, man or woman, tried to embrace her. Without Sharbaraz's quick thinking, she would have reckoned her honor altogether lost and, without her honor, Abivard didn't think she cared to live. He thanked the God that she had been able to piece together as much of her life as she had.

When she saw Sharbaraz flat on the bed, his face the color of parchment, she gasped and swayed before visibly gathering herself. "What happened?" she demanded of him. "I've already heard three different tales."

"I don't doubt that." Sharbaraz managed a smile that was less than half grimace. "One of the *dihqans* decided I was to blame for what his clan suffered out on the steppe and reckoned to avenge himself on me. He had courage; I've never seen nor heard of a man's dying better after he failed."

His detached attitude won him no points from Denak. "He might have murdered you, and you're talking about how brave he was? It's a good thing he's dead. If he'd done what he set out to do—" Her voice all but broke. "I don't know what I would have done."

Sharbaraz sat up on the bed. Abivard would have pushed him back down, but Denak beat him to it. The ease with which he flattened out again told of the wound he had suffered. Still, his second attempt at a smile came closer to the genuine article than the first one had. He said, "I can afford to be generous, since I'm alive. If I were dead and he still lived, I'd be less forgiving."

Denak stared at him, then let out a strangled snort. "Now I begin to believe you'll get better. No dying man could make such foolish jokes."

"Thank you, my dear." Sharbaraz sounded a bit stronger, but he didn't try to rise again. He went on, "Your brother here put me in his debt three more times: by shouting a warning, by helping to wrestle the knifeman to the ground, and for his excellent doctoring. If I do pull through, it will be because of him."

"Your Majesty is too kind," Abivard murmured.

"No, he's not," Denak said. "If you acted the proper hero, the world should know of it. The *dihqans* will take word back to their domains, but we ought to put a minstrel to singing your praises, too."

"Do you know what Father would say if he heard you talking of such things?" Abivard said, flushing. "First he'd laugh till he cried, then he'd paddle your backside for having the crust to even think of paying a minstrel to praise me for something it was my duty to do."

Invoking Godarz usually ended an argument as effectively as slamming a door. This time, though, Denak shook her head. "Father was a fine *dihqan*, Abivard, none better, but he never involved himself in the affairs of the realm as a whole. You've gone from being an ordinary *dihqan* like him to a man close to the throne. You rescued Sharbaraz and you became his brother-in-law, all in the space of a day. When he takes back his throne, you think some *dihqans* and most *marzbans* won't resent you for an upstart? The more you show you deserve your place at his right hand, the likelier you are to keep it. Nothing wrong with praising the courage you really did show to help you build your fame."

Denak set hands on hips and looked defiance at Abivard. Before he could reply, Sharbaraz said, "She's right. The court works like the women's quarters, though it may be worse. What you are is not nearly so important as what people think you are, and what people think the King of Kings thinks you are."

Godarz had said things like that, most often with a sardonic gleam in his eye. Abivard had never expected to have to worry about them. Now he was hearing them from his sister, and in a position where he had to pay attention to her even if—and partly because—she was a woman. He remembered the talk he'd had with Frada not long before Prypat tried to knife Sharbaraz. He might want to ignore the intrigues of Mashiz, but they would not ignore him.

Sharbaraz said, "Brother-in-law of mine, one thing has to happen before you start worrying about such things."

"What's that?" Abivard asked.

"We have to win."

VII

Spring painted the fields around Vek Rud stronghold with a green that, while it wouldn't last long, was lovely to look at for the time being. So Abivard found it most years, at any rate. Not now. Turning to Frada, he said, "By the God, I'll be glad when we ride south tomorrow. Another forthnight of feeding the fighters and their horses and our storehouses would be empty. Our own folk will need food, too, especially if the harvest isn't a good one."

"Aye." Frada took a couple of paces along the walkway, kicking at the stone under his feet. "I wish I were coming with you when you ride. All I ever do, it seems, is get left behind."

"Don't complain about that," Abivard said sharply. "If you hadn't been left behind last summer, odds are you wouldn't be alive to whine about it now. We've been over this ground a thousand times. I have to ride with Sharbaraz, and that means you have to stay here and protect the domain from whatever comes against it, be that Smerdis' men, or Pradtak's, or the Khamorth."

Frada still looked mutinous. "At the start of winter, you were saying land was most important because it lasted. If that's so, you ought to stay here to watch the land while I go out and fight."

"I hadn't thought through the politics then," Abivard said, reluctant to admit Denak had played a big part in making him change his mind. "Smerdis will know by now the part I played in freeing Sharbaraz from Nalgis Crag stronghold. For better or worse, I rise and fall with the rightful King of Kings. If I'm not at his side, people will say it's because I'm afraid. I can't have that."

"How can anyone say you're afraid of anything when they're probably singing that new song about you in Videssos by now?"

Abivard's ears got hot. "The song's about you, too," he said feebly.

"No, it's not. My name's in it a time or three, but it's *about* you." Much to Abivard's relief, Frada didn't sound jealous. Such things would have torn apart some clans, but Godarz had made jealousy among his sons a sin to rank with blasphemy. Frada went on, "It'll be your way, of course. How can I deny you know more about what's best than I do? I just wish I could shove a lance into Smerdis myself."

"When we ride against Videssos, you'll have your chance," Abivard said. Frada nodded. Everyone would ride against Makuran's great enemy.

"Look—Sharbaraz has come out," Frada said, sticking an elbow into Abivard's ribs. "You'd better go down into the courtyard with him; you know as well as I do that Mother will pitch a fit if the ceremony doesn't come off perfectly."

"Right you are." Abivard went down the stone stairs and took his place alongside the rightful King of Kings. The last time the women of Vek Rud stronghold had come forth from their quarters was the summer before, when he had stood with his father and brother and half brothers; of them all, only he had got home alive. And now his mother and sister and half sisters and wives had to wish him good fortune as he set out on another campaign. A woman's life was anything but easy.

The door to the living quarters opened. Denak and Burzoe came out together, as they had before. This time, though, Denak preceded her mother as they walked toward the waiting men: as principal wife to the King of Kings, she held higher ceremonial rank than anyone merely of Vek Rud domain.

She nodded to Abivard, then passed him to take her place by Sharbaraz. Burzoe stood in front of Abivard. Her face, which had seemed calm at first glance, showed deep and abiding anger when he looked more closely. He scratched his head; could his mother be offended because Denak took precedence over her? It seemed out of character.

Behind Burzoe came Roshnani. Like Burzoe's, her face appeared calm until Abivard got a good look at it. Where his mother hid anger, though, his principal wife was trying to conceal—mirth? Excitement? He couldn't quite tell, and wondered what new convulsion had shaken the women's quarters to set Burzoe at odds with Denak—and with Roshnani, too, he saw, for his mother's fury plainly included both of them. Not wanting to borrow trouble, he didn't ask. He might find out, or the trouble might blow over without his ever learning what had gone wrong. He hoped it would.

Whatever it was, the rest of his wives and his young half sisters didn't look to know anything about it. They stared and chattered quietly among themselves, enjoying the chance to see something wider than the halls of the women's quarters. For them, this was a pleasant outing, nothing more.

Burzoe turned toward Denak. Her lips tightened slightly as she did so; maybe she *was* angry her daughter had usurped her place at the head of the ceremony. Abivard clicked his tongue between his teeth; he hadn't thought her so petty.

Denak said, "We are met here today to bid our men safety and good fortune as they travel off to war." Burzoe stirred but did not speak. Fury seemed to radiate from her in waves; had it been heat, Ganzak might have set her in the smithy in place of his furnace. Denak went on, "We shall surely triumph, for the God stretches forth her arms to protect those whose cause is just, as ours is."

A stir of applause ran through the men and women who listened to her. Abivard joined it, though he was not so convinced by what she said as he would have been before the previous summer. How had the God protected those who followed Peroz into Pardraya? The short answer was *none too well*.

Denak took a step back, beckoned to Burzoe. With exquisite grace, her mother prostrated herself before Sharbaraz. "The God keep you safe, Majesty," she said, and rose. She embraced Abivard. "The God watch over you, as she did before."

Words, gestures—all unexceptionable. What lay behind them ... Abivard wished he could disrupt the ceremony to inquire of Burzoe. But custom inhibited him no less than it had Pradtak back at Nalgis Crag stronghold.

In her turn, Burzoe stepped back and nodded to Roshnani. Polite as usual, Roshnani nodded back, but her gaze went to Denak. Their eyes met. Suddenly scenting conspiracy, Abivard wondered what his sister and principal wife had cooked up between them. Whatever it was, his mother didn't like it.

As Burzoe had, Roshnani gave the King of Kings his ceremonial due and wished him good fortune. Then she hugged Abivard, tighter than decorum called for. He didn't mind—on the contrary. She said, "The God keep you safe from all danger."

"What I'll think about most is coming home to you," he answered. For some reason, that seemed to startle his principal wife, but she managed a smile in return.

Abivard walked down the line of waiting women, accepting the best wishes of his other wives and half sisters. If the God listened to a tenth of their prayers, he would live forever and be richer than three Kings of Kings rolled together.

His youngest half sister started back toward the living quarters. The procession that had emerged withdrew in reverse order, those who had come out first going in last. Soon Burzoe's turn came. She let out a scornful sniff and, her back stiff with pride, stalked away toward the open door of the living quarters.

Roshnani and Denak still stood in the courtyard.

Abivard needed perhaps longer than he should have to realize they didn't intend to go back to the women's quarters. "What are you doing?" His voice came out a foolish squeak.

Roshnani and Denak looked at each other again. Sure enough, the two of them had come up with a plot together. Denak spoke for them both. "My brother, my husband—" She turned to Sharbaraz. "—we are going to come with you."

"What, to fight? Are you mad?" Sharbaraz said.

"No, not to fight, Majesty, may it please you," Roshnani answered. "We would fight for you, the God knows, but we have not the skill and training to do it well; we would be more liability than asset. But every army has its baggage train. The minstrels are not in the habit of singing of it—it lacks glamour, when set beside those whose only duty is to go into battle—but they say enough for us to know it exists, and know an army would starve or run out of arrows without one. And we know one more wagon, a wagon bearing the two of us, would not slow the host, nor endanger your cause."

The rightful King of Kings gaped. He hadn't expected reasoning as careful as that of a courtier who'd had a tutor from Videssos, but then he hadn't truly made Roshnani's acquaintance till this moment. He started to say something, then stopped and sent Abivard a look of appeal.

"It's against all custom," Abivard said, the best argument he could come up with on the spur of the moment. To himself, he added, *It's also getting ahead of the promise I made you of more freedom to move around after the war with Smerdis was over.* He couldn't say that aloud, because he didn't want to admit he had made the promise. He did add, "No wonder Mother is furious at the two of you." If anyone embodied Makuraner propriety, Burzoe was that woman.

Roshnani bore up under the charge with equanimity; Burzoe was but her mother-in-law, to be respected, yes, but not the guardian of proper behavior since childhood. The accusation hit Denak harder, but she was the one who answered: "It was against propriety for Smerdis to steal the throne from him to whom it rightfully belongs. It was against custom for me, a woman, to set his rescue in motion." She looked down at the ground. Of necessity, she had done other things that went against custom, too, things that ate at her still despite the honor Sharbaraz had shown her. She did not speak of them in public, but the people among whom the argument centered knew what they were.

Sharbaraz said, "What possible good could the two of you bring that would outweigh not only setting custom aside but also setting men aside to protect you when the fighting starts?" When the King of Kings retreated from absolute rejection, Abivard knew the war was lost.

But it still had to be played out. "You value our counsel when we are in a stronghold," Roshnani said. "Do we suddenly lose our wits when we're in the field? Abivard planned with both Denak and me—aye, and with his mother, too—before he left to set your Majesty free."

"Having the two of you along would scandalize the *dihqans* who back me," Sharbaraz said.

"I already told Roshnani as much," Abivard agreed.

"Enough to make them head back to their domains?" Denak said. "Enough to make them go over to Smerdis? Do you really believe that?" Her tone said she didn't, not for a moment. It also said she didn't think Sharbaraz did, either. She might not have known him long, but she had come to know him well.

"What would you say if I forbid it?" he asked.

Had he simply forbid it, that would have been that. Making it a hypothetical question was to Abivard another sign he would yield. It probably was for Denak, too, but she gave no hint of that, saying in a meek voice most unlike the one she usually used, "I would obey your Majesty, of course."

"A likely story," Sharbaraz said; he had come to know Denak, too. He turned to Abivard. "Well, brother-in-law of mine, what shall we do with 'em?"

"You're asking *me*?" Abivard said, appalled. "As far as I'm concerned, we can give them both gilded corselets and style 'em generals. My guess is that they'd do a better job than three quarters of the men you might name."

"My guess is that you're right." Sharbaraz shook his head. "My father would pitch a fit at this—he took only tarts on campaign, and not many of them—but my father is dead. I'm going to say aye to your sister, Abivard. What will you say to your wife?"

If you want to be stern and stodgy, go ahead, he seemed to mean. Abivard knew he couldn't get away with it, not if he wanted peace in the women's quarters ever again. He chose the most graceful surrender he could find: "Where you lead, Majesty, I shall follow."

Roshnani's face lit up like the summer sun at noon. "Thank you," she said quietly. "A chance at seeing the world tempts me to do something most publicly indecorous to show how grateful I am."

"You and Denak have already been indecorous enough for any three dozen women I could think of," Abivard growled in his severest tones. His principal wife and sister hung their heads and looked abashed. Why not? They had won what they wanted.

Abivard started to scold them some more, but then got to wondering whether something publicly indecorous might not be privately enjoyable. That distracted him enough that the scolding never got delivered.

In the saddle and southbound . . . Abivard rode joyfully toward civil war. The rightful King of Kings rode at his side, on a horse from his stables. A good copy of the lion banner of Makuran floated at the fore of Sharbaraz's host.

Warriors rode by clan, each man most comfortable with comrades from the same domain. Abivard worried about how well they would fight as a unit, but reflected that Peroz' army, which had ridden forth against the Khamorth, was no more tightly organized, which meant Smerdis' troops weren't likely to be, either.

When he remarked on that, Sharbaraz said, "No, I don't expect them to be. If we were riding against Videssians, I'd worry about how loose-jointed our arrangements are, but they won't hurt us against our own countrymen."

"How are the Videssians different?" Abivard asked. "I've heard endless tales of them, but no two the same."

"My guess is that that's because of how different they are,"

Sharbaraz answered seriously. "They care nothing for clans when they fight, but go here and there in big blocks to the sound of their officers' horns and drums. They might as well be so many cups on the rim of a water wheel or some other piece of machinery. They take discipline better than our men, that's certain."

"Why don't they sweep everything before them, then?" Abivard asked; the picture Sharbaraz had painted was an intimidating one.

"Two main reasons," the rightful King of Kings answered. "First, they prefer the bow to the lance, which means a strong charge into their midst will often scatter 'em. And second and more important, they may have discipline, but they don't have our fire. They fight as if to win points in a game, not for the sake of it, and often they'll yield or flee where we might go on and win."

Abivard filed the lore away in his mind. He was building himself a picture of the foes he had never seen, against the day when Makuran's internal strife ended and Sharbaraz would begin to settle scores. Much of the Empire of Videssos bordered the sea. Abivard wondered if he would meet the third part of Tanshar's prophecy there.

No way to know that but to await the day. He glanced back toward the baggage train, where Tanshar rode with several other fortune-tellers and wizards their lords had brought with the warriors. Abivard wondered if the men could ward the army against the more polished magicians Smerdis might gather from Mashiz. He was glad to have Tanshar along; every familiar face was welcome.

Also traveling with the baggage train was a wagon that carried not wheat or smoked mutton or hay for the horses or arrows neatly tied in sheaves of twenty to fit into quivers and bowcases but his sister, his principal wife, and a couple of serving women from Vek Rud stronghold. He had nothing but misgivings about the venture, but hoped it would turn out well—or not too disastrously.

For the time being, the horses were not eating much of the fodder the army had brought along for them. In spring, even the dun land between oases and rivers took on a coat of green. Soon the sun would bake it dry again, but the animals could graze and nibble while it lasted.

That was as well, for Sharbaraz's host swelled with every new domain it approached. Horsemen flocked to his banner, calling down curses on Smerdis' usurping gray head. When yet another such contingent rode in, Abivard exclaimed to Sharbaraz, "Majesty, this is no campaign, just a triumphal procession."

"Good," Sharbaraz answered. "We threw away too many lives against the plainsmen last summer; we can't afford to squander more in civil war, lest winning prove near as costly as losing. We still need to protect ourselves from our foes and take vengeance on them. In fact, I've even sent a rider on ahead to Smerdis to tell him I'll spare his worthless life if he gives up the throne without a fight."

Abivard weighed that, nodding. "I think you did well. He never showed ambition till the once, and you'd watch him so close, he'd never get another chance."

"Wouldn't I?" Sharbaraz said. "He couldn't sit his arse down in the backhouse without an eye on him."

But before Sharbaraz formally heard from his rival for the throne, he got his answer another way. Off to the east, the snow-capped peaks of the Dilbat Mountains showed the way southward; the army would have to skirt them and then come back up on the far side of the range to approach Mashiz. Already the weather was noticeably hotter than Abivard would have expected so early in the season.

A scout came galloping back toward the main body of Sharbaraz's host, shouting "There's trooopers up ahead looking for a fight. They shot enough arrows at me to make a good-size tree; the God's own mercy I wasn't pincushioned."

"Looking for a fight, are they?" Sharbaraz said grimly. "I think we shall oblige them."

Horns blared; drums thudded. From what Sharbaraz had said to Abivard, that would have been plenty to move units of a Videssian army as if they were pieces going from square to square on a gameboard. Abivard wished his countrymen were as smooth. Zal and his squadron of ironclad professionals came forward front and center, to form the spearhead of the force. Despite martial music and endless shouts both from their own *dihqans* and from the officers Sharbaraz had appointed, most of the rest of the warriors, at least to Abivard's jaundiced eye, did more milling about than forming.

But by the time he saw dust ahead, the host had shaken itself out into a battle line of sorts. Zal shouted frantically at anyone who would listen. The only trouble was, next to nobody listened. A raw army with raw officers wouldn't win battles by discipline and maneuver. Courage and fury and numbers would have to do instead.

Okhos rode by, his fuzz-bearded face alight with excitement. He drew his sword and flourished it to Abivard; he almost cut off the ear of the man next to him, but never noticed. Roshnani's younger brother said, "We'll slaughter them all and wade in their blood!"

Minstrels sang such verses when they wandered from stronghold to stronghold, hoping to cadge a night's supper on the strength of their songs. Grown men who knew war smiled at them and enjoyed the poetry without taking it seriously. Trouble was, Okhos wasn't a grown man; he had fewer summers behind him than Frada. Minstrels' verses were all he knew of the battlefield, or had been until the Khamorth started raiding his domain.

Then Abivard stopped worrying about how his brother-in-law would fare and started worrying about himself. On across the flat ground came Smerdis' army, growing closer faster than Abivard would have thought possible. At their fore flew the lion banner of Makuran. Beside Abivard, Sharbaraz murmured, "The curse of civil war: both sides bearing the same emblem."

"Aye," Abivard said, though that was more philosophical than he felt like being with battle fast approaching. "Well, if they don't see for themselves that they picked the wrong man to follow, we'll have to show them." The oncoming troops seemed resolute enough. Abivard filled his lungs and shouted defiance at them: "Sharbaraaaz!"

In an instant, the whole host took up the cry. It drowned in a cacophony of hatred whatever signals officers and musicians were trying to give. At last the nobles of the northwest and their retainers had a chance to come to grips with the man who had not only stolen the throne but stolen their money and given it to the barbarians who had killed their kin—without keeping those barbarians off their lands afterward as promised.

Inevitably, an answering cry came back: "Smerdis!" As inevitably, it sounded effete and puny to Abivard, who was less than an unbiased witness. He wondered how men could still lay their lives on the line for a ruler who had proved himself both thief and liar.

However they managed it, support Smerdis they did. Arrows began to fly; lanceheads came down in a glittering wave. Abivard picked a fellow in the opposite line as a target and spurred his horse into a full gallop. "Sharbaraz!" he yelled again.

The two armies collided with a great metallic clangor. Abivard's charge missed its man; he had swerved aside to fight someone else. A lance glanced off Abivard's shield. He felt the impact all the way up to his shoulder. Had the hit been squarer, it might have unhorsed him.

A lancer's main weapon was the force he could put behind his blow from the weight and speed of his charging horse. With that momentum spent after the first impact, the battle turned into a melee, with riders stabbing with lances, slashing with swords, and trying to use their horses to throw their foes' mounts—and their foes—off balance for easy destruction.

Sharbaraz fought in the middle of the press, laying about him with the broken stub of a lance. He clouted an enemy in the side of the head. The fellow was wearing a helm, but the blow stunned him even so. Sharbaraz hit him again, this time full in the face. Dripping blood, he slid out of the saddle, to be trampled if he still lived after those two blows. Sharbaraz shouted in triumph.

Abivard tried to fight his way toward his sovereign. If the rightful King of Kings went down, the battle, even if a victory, would still prove a final defeat. He had tried to talk Sharbaraz out of fighting in the front ranks—as well tell the moon not to go from new to full and back again as to have him listen.

An armored warrior who shouted "Smerdis!" got between Abivard and the King of Kings. The soldier must have lost his lance or had it break to pieces too small to be useful, for he hacked at the shaft of Abivard's lance with his sword. Sparks flew as the blade belled against the strip of iron that armored the shaft against such misfortune.

Abivard drew back the lance and thrust with it. The enemy ducked and cut at it again. By then they were almost breast to breast. Abivard tried to smash the fellow in the face with the spiked boss to his shield. A moment later he counted himself lucky not to get similarly smashed.

He and Smerdis' follower cursed and strained and struggled until someone—Abivard never knew who—slashed the other fellow's horse. When it screamed and reared, Abivard speared its rider. He screamed, too, and went on screaming after Abivard yanked out the lance. His cry of agony was all but lost among many others—and cries of triumph, and of hatred—that dinned over the battlefield.

"I wonder how this fight is going," Abivard muttered. He was too busy trying to stay alive to have much feel for the course of the action as a whole. Had he advanced since his charge ended, or had he and Sharbaraz's men given ground? He couldn't tell. Just getting back up with the rightful King of Kings seemed hard enough at the moment.

When he finally made it to the King of Kings' side, Sharbaraz shouted at him: "How fare we?"

"I hoped you knew," Abivard answered in some dismay.

Sharbaraz grimaced. "This isn't as easy as we hoped it would be. They aren't falling all over themselves to desert, are they?"

"What did you say, Majesty?" Abivard hadn't heard all of that; he had been busy fending off one of Smerdis' lancers. Only when the fellow sullenly drew back could he pay attention once more.

"Never mind," Sharbaraz told him. By now, the King of Kings' lance was long gone; his sword had blood on the blade. For one of the rare times since Abivard had known him, he looked unsure what to do next. The stubborn resistance Smerdis' men were putting up seemed to baffle him.

Then, just as he was starting to give orders for another push against the foe, wild, panic-filled shouts ripped through the left wing of Smerdis' army. Some men were crying "Treason!" but more yelled "Sharbaraz!" They turned on the warriors still loyal to Smerdis and attacked them along with Sharbaraz' soldiers.

With its left in chaos, Smerdis' army quickly unraveled. Men at the center and right, seeing their position turned, either threw down their weapons and surrendered or wheeled in flight. Here and there, stubborn rearguard bands threw themselves away to help their comrades escape.

"Press them!" Sharbaraz cried. "Don't let them get away." Now that striking hard had been rewarded, he was back in his element, urging on his warriors to make their victory as complete as they could.

For all his urging, though, a good part of Smerdis' army broke free and fled south. His own force had fought too hard through the morning to make the grinding pursuit that might have destroyed the enemy for good and all.

At last, he seemed to realize that and broke off the chase. "If I order them to do something they can't, next time they may not listen to me when I tell them to do something they can," he explained to Abivard.

"We did have a solid victory there," Abivard answered.

"It's not what I wanted," Sharbaraz said. "I had in mind to smash the usurper's men so thoroughly no one would think of standing against me after this. Just a victory isn't enough." Then he moderated his tone. "But it will have to do, and it's ever so much better than getting beat."

"Isn't that the truth?" Abivard said.

Sharbaraz said, "I want to question some of the men we caught who fought so hard against us: I want to learn how Smerdis managed to keep them loyal after they learned I hadn't given up my throne of my own free will. The sooner I find out, the sooner I can do something about it."

"Aye," Abivard said, but his voice was abstracted; he had only half heard the rightful King of Kings. He was looking over the field and discovering for the first time the hideous flotsam and jetsam a large battle leaves behind. He had not seen the aftermath of the fight on the Pardrayan steppe; he had fled to keep from becoming part of it. The other fights in which he had joined were only skirmishes. What came after them was like this in kind, but not in degree. The magnitude of suffering spread out over a farsang of ground appalled him.

Men with holes in them or faces hacked away or hands severed or entrails spilled lay in ungraceful death amid pools of blood already going from scarlet to black, with flies buzzing around them and ravens spiraling down from the sky to peck at their blindly staring eyes and other dainties. The battlefield smelled something like a slaughterhouse, something like a latrine.

The crumpled shapes of dead horses cropped up here and there amid the human wreckage. Abivard pitied them more than the soldiers; they hadn't had any idea why they died.

But worse than the killed, men or beasts, were the wounded. Hurt horses screamed with the terrible sopranos of women in agony. Men groaned and howled and cursed and wailed and wept and bled and tried to bandage themselves and begged for aid or their mothers or death or all three at once and crawled toward other men whom they hoped would help them. And other men, or jackals who walked on two legs, wandered over the field looking for whatever they could carry away and making sure that none of those they robbed would live to avenge themselves.

Still others, to their credit, did what they could for the injured, stitching, bandaging, and setting broken bones. A couple of the village wizards had healing among their talents. They could treat wounds that would have proved fatal save for their aid, but at terrible cost to themselves. One of them, his hands covered with the blood of a man he had just brought back from the brink of death, got up from the ground where he had knelt, took a couple of steps toward another wounded warrior, and pitched forward onto his face in a faint.

"Looking at this, I wish we hadn't brought our wives," Abivard said. "Even if they don't picture us among the fallen, they'll never be easy in their minds about the chances of war."

Sharbaraz looked back toward the baggage train, which lay well to the rear of the acutal fighting. That distance seemed to ease his mind. "It will be all right," he said. "They can't have seen too much." Abivard hoped he was right.

The prisoner wore only ragged linen drawers. One of Sharbaraz's followers who had started the day in boiled leather—or perhaps in just his caftan—now had a fine suit of mail from the royal armories. The captured warrior held a dirty rag around a cut on his arm. He looked tired and frightened, his eyes enormous in a long, dark face.

Realizing who Sharbaraz was frightened him even more. Before the guards who had manhandled him into Sharbaraz' presence could cast him down to the ground, he prostrated himself of his own accord. "May your years be long and your realm increase, Majesty," he choked out.

Sharbaraz turned to Abivard. "He says that now," the rightful King of Kings observed. "This morning, though, he'd cheerfully have speared me out of the saddle."

"Amazing what a change a few hours can bring," Abivard agreed.

The prisoner ground his face into the dust. "Majesty, forgive!" he wailed.

"Why should I?" Sharbaraz growled. "Once you knew I'd not abandoned my throne of my own free will, how could you have the brass to fight against me?"

"Forgive!" the prisoner said. "Majesty, I am a poor man, and ignorant, and I know nothing save what my officers tell me. They said—I give you their very words, by the God I swear it— they said you had indeed given up the throne of your own accord, and then wickedly changed your mind, like a woman who says 'I want my red shoes. No, my blue ones.' They said you could not go back on an oath you swore, that the God would not smile on Makuran if you seized the rule. Now, of course, I see this is not so, truly I do." He dared raise his face a couple of inches to peer anxiously at Sharbaraz.

"Take him away, back with the others," Sharbaraz told the guards. They hauled the prisoner to his feet and dragged him off. The rightful King of Kings let out a long, weary sigh and turned to Abivard. "Another one."

"Another one," Abivard echoed. "We've heard—what?—six now? They all sing the same song."

"So they do." Sharbaraz paced back and forth, kicking up dirt. "Smerdis, may he drop into the Void this instant, is more clever than I gave him credit for. This tale of my renouncing my oath of abdication may be a lie from top to bottom, but it gives those who believe it a reason to fight for him and against me. I thought his forces would crumble at the first touch, like salt sculptures in the rain, but it may prove harder than that."

"Aye," Abivard said mournfully. "If that one band hadn't gone over to you, we might still be fighting—or we might have lost."

"This had crossed my mind," Sharbaraz admitted, adding a moment later, "however much I wish it hadn't." He sighed again. "I want pocket bread filled with raisins and cheese and onions, and I want a great huge cup of wine. Then I'll show myself to Denak, so she'll know I came through alive and well. But what I want most is a good night's sleep. I've never been so worn in my life; it must be the terror slowly leaking out of me."

"Your Majesty, those all strike me as excellent choices," Abivard said, "though I'd sooner have sausage than raisins with my onions and cheese."

"We may just be able to grant you so much leeway," Sharbaraz said. Both men laughed.

Roshnani said, "Almost I wish I'd stayed back at the stronghold. What war truly is doesn't look much like what the minstrels sing of." Her eyes, which looked larger than they were in the dim lamplight of Abivard's tent, filled with horror at what she had seen and heard. "So much anguish—"

I told you so, bubbled up in Abivard's mind. He left the words unsaid. They would have done no good in any case. He couldn't keep his principal wife from seeing what she had seen now that she was here, and he couldn't send her back to Vek Rud domain. Godarz would have said something like, *Now that you've mounted the horse, you'd better ride it.*

Since he couldn't twit her, he said, "I'm glad your brother only took a couple of small cuts. He'll be fine, I'm sure."

"Yes, so am I," Roshnani said, relief in her voice. "He was so proud of himself when he came back to see me yesterday after the battle, and he looked as if he'd enjoyed himself in the fighting." She shook her head. "I can't say I understand that."

"He's young yet," Abivard said. "I thought I'd surely live forever, right up till the moment things went wrong on the steppe last year."

Roshnani reached out to set a hand on his arm. "Women always know things can go wrong. We wonder sometimes at the folly of men."

"Looking back, I wonder at some of our folly, too," Abivard said. "Thinking Smerdis' men would give up or go over to us without much fight, for instance. The war will be harder than we reckoned on when we set out from the stronghold."

"That's not what I meant," Roshnani said in some exasperation. "The whole idea ... Oh, what's the use? I just have to hope we win the fight and that you and Okhos and Sharbaraz come through it safe."

"Of course we will," Abivard said stoutly. The groans of the wounded that pierced the wool tent cloth like arrows piercing flesh turned his reassurances to the pious hopes they were.

Roshnani didn't say that, not with words. She was not one who sought to get her way by nagging her husband until he finally yielded. Abivard's will was as well warded against nagging as Nalgis Crag stronghold against siege. But something—he could not have said precisely what—changed in her face. Perhaps her eyes slipped from his for a moment at a particularly poignant cry of pain. If they did, he didn't notice, not with the top of his mind. But he did come to know he had done nothing to allay her fears.

He was irked to hear how defensive he sounded as he continued, "Any which way, what we stand to gain is worth the risk. Or would you sooner live under Smerdis and see all our arkets flow across the Degird to the nomads?"

"Of course not," she said at once; she was a *dihqan*'s daughter. Now he recognized the expression she wore: calculation, the same sort he would have used in deciding if he wanted to pay a horsetrader's price for a four-year-old gelding. "If the three of you live and we win, then you're right. But if any of you falls, or if we lose, then you're not. And since you and Sharbaraz and Okhos are all right at the fore—"

"Would you have us hang back?" Abivard demanded, flicked on his pride.

"For my sake, for your own sake, indeed I would," Roshnani answered. Then she sighed. "If you did, though, that would make the army lose spirit, which would in turn make you likelier to be hurt. Finding the right thing to do isn't always easy."

"We chased that rabbit round the bush when we were talking about how—or if—you'd be able to come out of the women's quarters." Abivard laughed. "After a while, you quit chasing— you jumped over the bush and squashed poor bunny flat, or how else did you and Denak get to come along with the host?"

Roshnani laughed, too. "You take it with better will than I thought you would. Most men, I think, would still be angry at me."

"What's the point to that?" Abivard said. "It's done, you've won, and now I try to make the best I can of it, just as I did when I came back from the steppe last summer."

"Hmm," Roshnani said. "I don't think I fancy being compared to the Khamorth. And you didn't lose a battle to me, because you'd already said you were giving up the war."

"I should hope so," Abivard said. "You and Denak outgeneraled me as neatly as the plainsmen bested Peroz."

"And what of it?" Roshnani asked. "Has the army gone to pieces because of it? Has one *dihqan*, even one warrior with no armor, no bow, and a spavined nag, gone over to Smerdis because Denak and I are here? Have we turned the campaign into a disaster for Sharbaraz?"

"No and no and no," Abivard admitted. "We might have done better with the two of you commanding our right and left wings. I don't think the officers we had out there distinguished themselves."

He waited for Roshnani to use the opening he had given her to tax him about the iniquities and inequities of the women's quarters and to get him to admit how unjust they were. She did nothing of the kind, but asked instead about how the wounded were faring. Only later did he stop to think that, if her arguments sprang to life in his mind without her having to say a word, she had already won a big part of the battle.

The farther south and east Sharbaraz' army advanced, the more Abivard had the feeling he was not in the Makuran he had always known. The new recruits who rallied to Sharbaraz's banner spoke with what he thought of as a lazy accent, wore caftans that struck his eye as gaudy, and irked him further by seeming to look down on the men who had originally favored the rightful King of Kings as frontier bumpkins. That caused fights, and led to the sudden demise of a couple of newcomers.

But when Abivard complained about the southerners' pretensions, Sharbaraz laughed at him. "If you think these folk different, my friend, wait till you make the acquaintance of those who dwell between the Tutub and the Tib, in the river plain called the land of the Thousand Cities."

"Oh, but they aren't Makuraners at all," Abivard said, "just our subjects."

Sharbaraz raised an eyebrow. "So it may seem to a man whose domain lies along the Degird. But Mashiz, remember, looks out over the Land of the Thousand Cities. The people who live down in the plain are not of our kind, true, but they help make the realm what it is. Many of our clerks and record keepers come from among them. Without such, we'd never know who owed what from one year to the next."

Abivard made a noise that said he was less than impressed. Had anyone but his sovereign extolled the virtues of such bureaucrats, he would have been a good deal cruder in his response.

Perhaps sensing that, Sharbaraz added, "They also give us useful infantry. You'll not have seen that, because they're of no use against the steppe nomads, so Kings of Kings don't take them up onto the plateau of Makuran proper. But they're numerous, they make good garrison troops, and they've given decent service against Videssos."

"For that I would forgive them quite a lot," Abivard said.

"Aye, it does make a difference," Sharbaraz agreed. "But I'll be less fond of them if they give decent service against me."

"Why would they do that?" Abivard asked. "You're the proper King of Kings. What on earth would make them want to fight for Smerdis and not for you?"

"If they believe the lie about my renouncing my renunciation, that might do it," Sharbaraz answered. "Or Smerdis might just promise more privileges and fewer taxes for the land of the Thousand Cities. That might be enough by itself. They've been under Makuran a long time, because we're better warriors, but they aren't truly *of* Makuran. Most of the time, that doesn't matter. Every once in a while, it jumps up and bites a King of Kings in the arse."

"What do we do about it?" Abivard knew he sounded worried. He had learned about some of what Sharbaraz had mentioned, but till this moment dust had lain thick over what he had studied. Now he saw it really mattered.

Sharbaraz reached out and set a hand on his shoulder. "I didn't mean to put you in a tizzy. I've sent men on to the valleys of the Tutub and the Tib. I can match whatever promises Smerdis makes, however much I'd rather not. And infantry is only so much good against horsemen. Men afoot move slowly. Often they don't get to where they're needed—and even if they do, you can usually find a way around them."

"I suppose so. I know about as much of the art of fighting against infantry as I do of the usages of Videssos' false priests."

"No, you wouldn't have the need, not growing up where you did." Sharbaraz chewed on his mustache. "By the God, I don't want the war against Smerdis to drag on and on. If the northwest frontier stays bare too long, the nomads *will* swarm across in force, and driving them back over the Degird will mean we can't give the Empire the time and attention it deserves."

Abivard didn't reply right away. It wasn't that he disagreed with anything Sharbaraz had said. But his concern with nomads over the border had little to do with what that would mean for the grand strategy of Makuran. He worried about what would happen to his domain: to the flocks and the folk who tended them, to the *qanats* and the farmers who used their waters to grow grain and nuts and vegetables, and most of all to Vek Rud stronghold and his brother and mother and wives, his half brothers and half sisters. Strongholds rarely fell to nomads—up in the northwest they were made strong not least to hold out the Khamorth—but it had happened. Being a worrier by nature, Abivard had no trouble imagining the worst.

Sharbaraz gave a squeeze with that hand on his shoulder. "Don't fret so, brother-in-law of mine. Frada strikes me as able and more than able. Vek Rud domain will still be yours when you go home wreathed in victory."

"You ease my mind," Abivard said, which was true. To him, Frada had seldom been more than a little brother, sometimes a pest, rarely anyone to take seriously. That had changed some after Frada's whiskers sprouted, and more after Abivard came back from the Pardrayan steppe. Still, hearing the rightful King of Kings praise his younger brother made him glow with pride.

But going home wreathed in victory? First there was Smerdis to beat, and then the Khamorth, and after them Videssos. And after Videssos had at last been punished as it deserved, who could say what new foes would have arisen, perhaps in the uttermost west, perhaps on the plains once more?

"Majesty," Abivard said with a laugh that sounded shaky even to him, "with so much fighting yet to do, only the God knows when I'll ever see home again."

"So long as we keep winning, you shall one day," Sharbaraz answered, with which Abivard had to be content.

He was doing his best not to think about the consequences of defeat when scouts came riding in with word of an army approaching from the south. Horns blared. Sharbaraz's forces, aided by officers who now had one battle's worth of experience more than they had enjoyed before, began the complicated business of shifting from line of march into line of battle.

Sharbaraz said, "If the usurper and his lackeys will not tamely yield, I shall have to rout them out. With comrades like you, Abivard, I know we'll succeed."

Such talk warmed Abivard—for a moment. After that, he was too busy to stay warm. His first automatic glance was toward the rear, to make sure the baggage train kept out of harm's way . . . and kept Roshnani and Denak safe with it. That taken care of, he started shouting orders of his own. One thing he had seen was that Sharbaraz did not care for close companions who were nothing but companions: the rightful King of Kings expected his followers to be able to lead, as well.

As he helped position Sharbaraz's riders, Abivard also scanned the southern skyline for the cloud of dust that would announce the coming of Smerdis' warriors. Soon enough—too soon to suit him—he spied it, a little farther east than he had expected from what the scouts said. That gave him an idea.

He had to wait for Sharbaraz to stop barking orders of his own. When he gained his sovereign's ear, he pointed and said, "Suppose we position a band behind that high ground? By the direction from which the enemy approaches, they may not spot our men till too late."

Sharbaraz considered, working his jaws as he chewed on the notion as if it were so much flatbread. Then, with the abrupt decision that marked him, he nodded. "Let it be as you say. Take a regiment and wait there for the right moment. Two long horn calls and one short will be your signal."

"You want *me* to lead the regiment?" To his dismay, Abivard's voice rose in a startled squeak.

"Why not?" Sharbaraz answered impatiently. "The idea's yours, and it's a good one. You deserve the credit if it succeeds.

And if you fought at my right hand in the last battle, you can lead a regiment on your own in this one."

Abivard gulped. The most men he had directly commanded at any one time was the couple of dozen he had led against Khamorth raiders not long before he found out Pradtak was holding Sharbaraz captive. But to say that would be to lose face before the King of Kings. "Majesty, I'll do my best," he managed, and went off to gather his men.

Some of the officers he ordered to shift position gave him distinctly jaundiced looks. They were professionals who had left Smerdis' force for Sharbaraz's. As far as they were concerned, what was he but a frontier *dihqan* of uncertain but dubious quality? The answer to that, however, was that he was also the King of Kings' brother-in-law. So, however dubious they looked, they obeyed.

"We wait for the signal," Abivard told the troopers as he led them into the ambush position. "Then we burst out and take the usurper's men in flank. Why, the whole battle could turn on us."

The horsemen buzzed excitedly. Unlike their skeptical captains, they seemed eager to follow Abivard. Of course, a lot of them came out of northwestern domains, too. Those men weren't polished professionals; they were here because their *dihqans*—and they themselves—wanted to overthrow Smerdis and restore Sharbaraz to his rightful place. Did enthusiasm count for more than professionalism? Abivard hoped so.

He had taken his contingent well behind the low swell of ground he had spotted, the better to conceal it from Smerdis' advancing men. The only problem was, that also meant Abivard and his followers couldn't see the first stages of the fighting. He hadn't worried about that till it was too late to do anything about it without giving away his position.

He hoped sound would do what sight could not: show him how the battle was going. But that proved less easy to gauge than he had expected. He could tell by the racket where the fighting was heaviest, but not who had the advantage at any given spot. He shifted nervously in the saddle until his horse caught his unease and began snorting and pawing at the ground.

The men he led were just as anxious as the animal. "Let us go, Lord Abivard," one of them called. "Hurl us against the usurper!"

Others echoed that, but Abivard shook his head. "We wait for the signal," he repeated, thinking, *Or until I'm sure the battle's swung against us.* That would be time to do what he could. For the warriors, though, he added, "If we move too soon, we give away the advantage of the ambush."

He hoped that would hold them. They twitched every time a horn sounded—and so did he. Sooner or later, they would burst from cover no matter what he did to hold them back. He felt worthless—Sharbaraz would see he wasn't suited to command after all.

Blaaart. Blaaart. Blart. A shiver ran through Abivard. Now the waiting regiment could move, and he would still seem to be in control of it. "Forward!" he shouted. "We'll show Smerdis the proper punishment for trying to steal the throne. The cry is—"

"Sharbaraz!" burst from a thousand throats. Abivard dug his heels into his horse's sides. The beast squealed, half with rage at him and half with relief at being allowed to run at last. It went from walk to trot to gallop as fast as any animal Abivard had ever ridden. Even so, he was hard pressed to stay at the head of the regiment.

"Sharbaraz!" the riders cried again as they burst from concealment. Abivard stared, quickly sizing up the battle. On this wing, Smerdis' men had driven Sharbaraz back a couple of furlongs. Abivard couched his lance and thundered at the enemy.

It worked, he thought exultantly. Startled faces turned to stare at him in dismay while shouts of alarm rang out among Smerdis' followers. He had only moments in which to savor them. Then he speared from the saddle a soldier who had managed to turn only halfway toward him. That struck him as less than fair but most effective.

Sharbaraz's backers shouted, too, with fresh spirit. Abivard and his men rolled up the left wing of Smerdis' army. Its commander had savvy to spare; he pulled men from the center and right to stem the rout before everything was swept away. But a fight that had looked like a victory for the usurper suddenly turned into another stinging defeat.

Smerdis' host had trumpeters, too. Abivard recognized the call they blew: retreat. He screamed in delight: "Pursue! Pursue!" The shout rang through not only the regiment he led but from the rest of Sharbaraz' army, as well. Just as retreat made Smerdis' men lose heart, victory enspirited Sharbaraz's soldiers. They pressed the enemy hard, doing their best to keep him from re-forming his ranks.

The warrior who had urged Abivard to loose the regiment before the signal happened to ride close to him now. The fellow had a cut on his forehead from which blood spilled down over his face, but his grin was enormous. "Lord Abivard, you were right and I was wrong and I'm man enough to admit it," he declared. "We've smashed them to kindling—kindling, I tell you."

Another soldier, this one with more gray than black in his beard, caught Abivard's eye. "Lord, you'd better cherish that," he said. "You'll count the times your men own that you were smarter than them on the thumbs of one hand—and that's if you're lucky, mind."

"You're likely right, friend," Abivard said. Some of Smerdis' men staged a counorcharge to buy their comrades time to get away. The fierce fighting that followed swept Abivard away from the cynical graybeard.

"To the Void with the renunciate! Smerdis King of Kings!" a lancer shouted as his mount pounded toward Abivard. Abivard dug heels into his own horse; the last thing he wanted was to receive an attack with no momentum of his own. He got his shield up just before they slammed together.

The enemy lance shattered on the shield. His own held, but Smerdis' horseman deflected it with his shield so it did him no harm. That left them at close quarters. Faster than Abivard had expected him to be, his foe hit him in the side of the head with the stump of his lance.

His iron helm kept his skull from caving in, but his head suddenly knew what a piece of iron caught between hammer and anvil felt like. His sight blurred; staying on his horse became all he could do. He noticed he didn't have his own lance any more but had no idea where he had dropped it.

The next thing he fully remembered was a tired, thin, worried-looking man holding a candle a couple of fingers'-breadths away from one eye. The fellow moved it to the other eye, then let out a long, wheezing breath. "The pupils are of different sizes," he said to someone—Abivard turned his head and saw Sharbaraz. "He's taken a blow to the head."

"That I have," Abivard said, all at once aware of a headache like a thousand years of hangovers all boiled down into a thick, sludgy gelatin of pain. That made him sad; he hadn't even had the fun of getting drunk. "Did we hold the victory? I lost track there after I got clouted." He found himself yawning.

"Majesty, he needs rest," the worried-looking man said; Abivard realized he was a physician.

"I know; I've seen cases like his," the King of Kings answered. To Abivard he said, "Aye, we won; we drive them still.

I'm going to have Kakia here take you back to the wagon your wife and sister share; they'll be the best ones to nurse you for the next few days."

"Days?" Abivard tried to sound indignant. Instead, he sounded—and felt—sick. He gulped, trying to keep down what was in his belly. The ground swayed beneath his feet as if it had turned to sea.

Kakia put Abivard's arm over his own shoulder. "Lord, it's nothing to be ashamed of. You may not bleed, but you're wounded as sure as if you were cut. With your brains rattled around inside your skull like lentils in a gourd, you need some time to come back to yourself."

Abivard wanted to argue, but felt too weak and woozy. He let the physician guide him back toward the baggage train. The serving women who had accompanied Roshnani and Denak exclaimed in dismay when Kakia brought him to the wagon in which they traveled.

"I'm all right," he insisted, though the gong chiming in his head tolled out *Liar* with every beat of his heart.

"Should the God grant, which I think likely in this case, the lord will be right again in three or four days," Kakia said, which set off a fresh paroxysm of weeping from the women. With the curious disconnection the blow to the head had caused, Abivard wondered how they would have carried on had the physician told them he wouldn't be all right. Even louder, he suspected. They were quite loud enough as it was.

Climbing the steps up into the wagon took every bit of balance and strength he had left. Still twittering like upset birds, the women took charge of him and led him into the little cubicle Roshnani used as her own.

She started to smile when he walked—or rather staggered—in, but the expression congealed on her face like stiffening tallow when she saw the state he was in. "What happened?" she whispered.

"I got hit in the side of the head," he said; he was getting tired of explaining. "I'm—kind of addled, and they say I'm supposed to rest until I'm more myself. A day or two." If he told that to Roshnani, maybe he would believe it, too.

"What were you doing?" Roshnani demanded as he sank down to the mat on which she was sitting.

Even in his battered state, that struck him as a foolish question. "Fighting," he said.

She went on as if he hadn't spoken: "You could have been

killed. Here, you just lie quiet; I'll take care of you. Would you like some wine?"

He started to shake his head but thought better of it, contenting himself with a simple, "No. I'm queasy. If I drink anything right now, I'll probably spew it up." *And if I try to heave right now, I'm sure the top of my head will fall off.* He rather wished it would.

"Here." Roshnani opened a little chest, took out a small pot, and undid the stopper. In a tone that brooked no argument, she said, "If you won't take wine, drink this. I don't think you'll give it back, and it will do you good."

Abivard was too woozy to quarrel. He gulped down whatever the little jar held, though he made a face at the strong, medicinal taste. After a while, the ache in his head faded from unbearable to merely painful. He yawned; the stuff had made him sleepier than he already was, too. "That's done some good," he admitted. "What was it?"

"You'll not be angry at the answer?" Roshnani asked.

"No," he said, puzzled. "Why should I be?"

Even in the dim light of the cubicle, he saw Roshnani flush. "Because it's a potion women sometimes take for painful courses," she answered. "It has poppy juice in it, and I thought that might ease you. But men, from all I've heard, have a way of being touchy about having to do with women's things."

"That's so." Abivard raised a languid hand, then let it fall on Roshnani's outstretched arm. "There. You may, if you like, consider that I've beaten you for your presumption."

She stared at him, then dissolved in giggles. Drugged and groggy though he was, Abivard knew the joke didn't rate such laughter. Maybe, he thought, relief had something to do with it.

Just then Denak came into the cubicle, stooping to get through the low entranceway. She looked from Roshnani to Abivard and back again. "Well!" she said. "Things can't be too bad, if I walk in on a scene like this."

"Things could be better," Abivard said. "If they were, one of Smerdis' rotten treacherous men wouldn't have tried using my head for a bell to see if he liked the tone. But if they were worse, he'd have smashed it like a dropped pot, so who am I to complain?" He yawned again; staying awake was becoming an enormous effort.

"The servants say the physician who brought him here thinks he'll get better," Roshnani said to Denak, as if Abivard were either already unconscious or part of the furniture. "But he'll need a few days' rest."

"This is the place for it," Denak said, an edge of wormwood in her voice. "It's as if we brought the women's quarters with us when we left Vek Rud stronghold. A women's quarters on four wheels—who would have imagined that? But we're just as caged here as we were back there."

"I didn't expect much different," Roshnani said; she was more patient, less impetuous than her sister-in-law. "That we are allowed out is the victory, and everything else will flow from it. Some years from now, many women will be free to move about as they please, and nobody will recall the terms we had to accept to get the avalanche rolling."

"The avalanche rolled over me," Abivard said.

"Two foolish jokes now—your brains can't be altogether smashed," Roshnani said.

Thus put in his place, Abivard listened to Denak say, "By the God, it's not right. We've escaped the women's quarters, and so we should also escape the strictures the quarters put on us. What point to leaving if we still dare not show our faces outside the wagon unless summoned to our husbands' tents?"

Roshnani surely made some reply, but Abivard never found out what it was; between them, the knock on the head and the poppy juice in the medicine she had given him sent him sliding down into sleep. The next time he opened his eyes, the inside of the cubicle was dark but for a single flickering lamp. The lamp oil had an odd odor; he couldn't remember where he had smelled it in the past. He fell asleep again before the memory surfaced.

When he woke the next morning, he needed a minute or so to figure out where he was; the shifting of the wagon as it rattled along and his pounding, muzzy head conspired to make him wonder whether he was getting up in the middle of an earthquake after a long night of drinking.

Then Roshnani sat up on the pallet by his. "How's the spot where you got hit?" she asked.

Memory returned. He gingerly set a finger to his temple. "Sore," he reported.

She nodded. "You have a great bruise there, I think, though your hair hides most of it. You're lucky the usurper's man didn't smash your skull."

"So I am." Abivard touched the side of his head again and winced. "He didn't miss by much, I don't think." Roshnani blew out the lamp. This time, Abivard recognized the smell. "It's burning that what-do-they-call-it? Rock oil, that's it. Peroz's engineers used it to fire the bridge over the Degird after the few stragglers came back from Pardraya. They said the southern folk put it in their lamps."

"I don't like it—it smells nasty," Roshnani said. "But we ran low on lighting oil, and one of the servants bought a jar of it. It does serve lamps well enough, I suppose, but I can't imagine that it would ever be good for anything else."

The serving women fixed Abivard a special breakfast: tongue, brains, and cow's foot, spiced hot with pepper. His head still ached, but his appetite had recovered; he didn't feel he was likely to puke up anything he put in his stomach. All the same, Roshnani wouldn't let him get up for any reason save to use the pot.

Sharbaraz came to see him around midmorning. "The God give you good day, Majesty," Abivard said. "As you see, I've already prostrated myself for you."

The rightful King of Kings chuckled. "You're healing, I'd say," he remarked, unconsciously echoing Roshnani. "I'm glad." Sentiment out of the way, he reminded Abivard he was Peroz' son with a blunt, "To business, then. The usurper's army has made good its withdrawal. We still have some horsemen shadowing us, but they can't interfere as we advance."

"Good news," Abivard said. "Nothing to keep us from getting south of the Dilbat Mountains and then turning north and east to move on Mashiz, eh?"

"On the surface, no," Sharbaraz said. "But what we ran into yesterday troubles me, and not a little, either. Aye, we won the fight, but not the way I'd hoped. Not a man, not a company, went over to us. We had to beat them, and when we did, they either fell back or, if they were cut off, surrendered. Not one of them turned on the others who back Smerdis."

"That is worrying." Abivard could feel he was slower and stupider than he should have been, which left him angry: Sharbaraz needed the best advice he could give. After a moment, he went on, "Seems to me the only thing we can do is press ahead, all the same. We can't very well give up just because things aren't as easy as we thought they'd be."

"I agree," Sharbaraz said. "As long as we keep winning, Smerdis falls sooner or later." He pounded a fist against his thigh, once, twice, three times. "But I was so sure the usurper would go down to ignominious defeat as soon as it was known I lived and hadn't abdicated on my own."

"One of the things my father always said was that the longer you lived, the more complicated life looked," Abivard said. "He said only boys and holy men were ever certain; men who had to live in the world got the idea it was bigger and more complicated than they could imagine."

"I think I've told you my father praised your father's good sense," Sharbaraz said. "The more I listen to Godarz through you, the more I think my father knew whereof he spoke."

"Your Majesty is gracious to my father's memory," Abivard said, warmed by the praise and wishing Godarz were there to hear it. "What do you plan to do next? Keep on with the straight-ahead drive toward the capital?"

"Aye, what else?" The rightful King of Kings frowned. "I know it's not subtle, but we have no other good choices. Smerdis has already had one army wrecked and another beaten; he'll hesitate to hazard a third. With luck, we'll be able to closely approach Mashiz before he tries fighting us head-on again. We win that fight and the city is ours—and if Smerdis wants to flee to Nalgis Crag stronghold, say, he'll learn we have the patience to starve him out." His eyes glowed with anticipation.

In the space of a few minutes, Sharbaraz had gone from gloom about the way Smerdis' backers declined to go over to him to excitement at the prospect of starving his rival into submission. Abivard wished he could lose his depressions as readily. But he, like Godarz before him, seemed a man who went through life without sinking deep into the valleys or climbing high on the peaks.

He said, "First things first, Majesty. Once we have Mashiz, assuming we don't bag Smerdis with it, then we can worry about hunting him down. Otherwise we're riding our horses before we bridle and saddle them." He laughed ruefully. "I have to say I'm just as well pleased we're not storming the capital tomorrow. I'd not be much use to you, even on a horse already bridled and saddled."

"You let yourself mend," Sharbaraz said, as if giving an order to some recalcitrant underling. "Thank the God we won't be doing much in the way of fighting till you're ready to play your proper part once more. You set me straight very smartly there when I let enthusiasm push me like a leaf on the breeze."

"Your Majesty is kind." Abivard was pleased with Sharbaraz.

As long as the rightful King of Kings could recognize when he was letting his passion of the moment—whatever it might be—run away with him, he would do well. The question was, how long would that last after he won his civil war?

Sharbaraz reached out and touched him on the shoulder—gently, so as not to jostle his poor battered head. "I have to go off and see to the army. I expect I'll be back this evening, to visit you and Denak both. Rest easy till then."

"Your Majesty, what choice have I?" Abivard said. "Even if I wanted to be out and doing, Roshnani would flatten me should I try to get up without her leave. Men usually keep their wives shup up in women's quarters, but here she has me trapped."

Sharbaraz laughed loud and long at that, as if it hadn't been true. He ducked out of the cubicle; Abivard listened to him getting onto his horse and riding away. He was already shouting orders, as if he had forgotten all about the man he had just visited. Rationally, Abivard knew that wasn't so, but it irked him anyhow.

As a proper Makuraner wife should, Roshnani had stayed out of sight while another man visited her husband. She returned to the cubicle as soon as Sharbaraz was gone. "So I've trapped you here, have I?" she said.

"You were listening."

"How could I help it, when only curtains separate one part of the wagon from the next?" Looking innocent and mischievous at the same time, she pulled shut the curtain that opened onto the cubicle. "So you're trapped here, are you?" she repeated, and knelt beside him. "Trapped and flat on your back, are you?"

"What are you doing?" Abivard squawked as she hiked up his caftan. She didn't answer, not in words; her long black hair spilled over his belly and thighs. He did his best to rise to the occasion, and his best proved quite good enough.

VIII

WHERE SOUTHERN MAKURAN WAS A DESERT, IT WAS BARER THAN the wasteland around Vek Rud domain. Where it was fertile, it was far richer. "We tax the land here at twice the rate we use in the northwest," Sharbaraz said to Abivard, "and even then, some of the ministers think we are too lenient."

"Crops are very fine here," Abivard admitted. "What are the winters like?"

"You've driven the nail home," Sharbaraz said, nodding. "I'd read of winters on the steppe and close to it, but never lived through one till I was sent to Nalgis Crag stronghold and then went on to yours even closer to the frontier. Here they grow things the year around; they get snow only about one winter in two."

Remembering blizzards and snowdrifts and hail and ice three months of every year and sometimes four or five, Abivard laughed at that. He couldn't make up his mind whether to find it unnatural or one of the most wonderful things he had ever heard.

Before he decided, a scout rode back toward Sharbaraz. Saluting, the fellow said, "Majesty, a party of riders is approaching under shield of truce."

"Let them come to me," Sharbaraz said at once. "Tell them that if they're conveying Smerdis' surrender, I'll be happy to accept it." The scout laughed, wheeled his horse, and booted the animal up to a gallop as he went off to escort the newcomers to the rightful King of Kings. Sharbaraz turned back to Abivard and chuckled ruefully. "I'd be happy to accept Smerdis' surrender, aye, but I don't think I'm going to get it."

A few minutes later, a whole squadron of scouts came back with Smerdis' delegation. Without being ordered to do so, they placed themselves between Sharbaraz and Smerdis' men—no assassinations here. The scout who had announced the coming of the truce party said, "Majesty, here are the usurper's dogs." Scorn harshened his voice.

A couple of Smerdis' followers stirred restlessly on their horses, but none of them spoke. Sharbaraz did. Pointing to one of their number, he said, "Ah, Inshushinak, so you've taken the old man's silver, have you?"

Inshushinak was hardly in the first bloom of youth himself; he was fat and gray-bearded and sat his horse as if he hadn't ridden one in a long time. He nodded to Sharbaraz and said, "Son of Peroz, his Majesty Smerdis King of Kings—"

He got no farther than that. Some of Sharbaraz's scouts reached for their swords, while others swung down lances. One of them growled, "Show proper respect for the King of Kings, curse you."

Sharbaraz raised a hand. "Let him speak as he will. He comes under shield of truce; the God hates those who violate it. I shall remember, but then I already remember he has chosen to follow the man who stole my throne. Say on, Inshushinak."

That did not make Inshushinak look much happier, but he rallied and resumed: "Son of Peroz, his Majesty Smerdis King of Kings, may his years be many and his realm increase, bade me come with these my followers—" He waved to the half-dozen men who rode with him: three soldiers, a couple of bureaucrats, and a skinny little fellow who could have been anything at all, "—to seek to compose the differences that lie between you and him."

"Inshushinak was my father's treasury minister," Sharbaraz murmured to Abivard. "Once Smerdis' superior; now, it seems, his servant." He raised his voice and addressed the delegation from Mashiz. "You may go back to the capital and tell my cousin that if he casts aside the throne and recovers all the arkets he squandered on the Khamorth and agrees to be confined for the rest of his days as he confined me, I may perhaps consider granting him his worthless life. Otherwise—"

"Son of Peroz, Smerdis King of Kings did not send me to you in token of surrender." Inshushinak looked as if he wished Smerdis had not sent him to Sharbaraz at all, but went on, "Would you care to hear the terms he proposes?"

"Not very much." But Sharbaraz relented: "Since you came to deliver them, you may as well."

"You are gracious." Even Inshushinak's years at court could not make that sound sincere. "In the interest of sparing the realm the torment of civil war, Smerdis King of Kings will confer upon you the title of King of the Northwest and will concede you autonomous rule there, subject to your paying him an annual sum to be determined by negotiation."

"Smerdis is generous," Sharbaraz said, and for a moment Inshushinak brightened. But Peroz' son continued, "How kind of him to concede to me a small piece of what I already hold, and to be willing to negotiate the sum I pay for the privilege. Since I can take all the realm, though, I shall not rest content to be given a part."

One of the soldierly men with Inshushinak said, "Be not so sure, son of Peroz. In most wars, unlike the one that overthrew your father last year, a single battle does not decide a campaign."

Sharbaraz bit his lip in anger but held his voice steady as he replied, "My best guess as to why you failed to go with my father, Hakhamanish, is that he reckoned you more a loss than a gain in the field. I'm not even angry at you for choosing Smerdis' side; measured against a real general, you're apter to hurt the usurper's cause than help it."

Hakhamanish's face went darker yet with angry blood. Abivard said, "Well struck, Majesty."

Inshushinak said, "Peroz's son, am I to infer from this that you reject the gracious offer of Smerdis King of Kings?"

"You need not infer it," Sharbaraz said. "I openly proclaim it. I give you leave to take my words back to Smerdis. Be wary of dining with him, though, lest you wake in a place you least expect." He paused. "And one more thing—if you fear to deliver my message out of worry over what he may do to you for reporting what I say, simply tell him I'll be in Mashiz soon enough, to give him the answer in person."

"Son of Peroz, arrogance will be your downfall, as it was your father's," Hakhamanish said. "You shall never approach Mashiz, much less reach it."

Inshushinak scowled at the officer. So did the nondescript little man, who, on any crowded street, would have become invisible as readily as a color-shifting gecko going yellow-brown when set on a slab of sandstone. Hakhamanish might have been on the point of saying more, but instead jerked hard at his horse's reins, made the unhappy animal rear and wheel, and rode away without so much as a farewell. The rest of Smerdis' party imitated his unceremonious departure, although Inshushinak rode off quite sedately: if his horse, an elderly gelding, had reared, no doubt he would have gone off over its tail.

Sharbaraz' eyes narrowed as he stared after Smerdis' backers. "They are more confident than they have any business being," he said to Abivard. "Smerdis, the God curse him, still thinks he can win this war, and he has no business thinking so, not on the way it's gone so far."

"Which means he knows, or thinks he knows, something we don't," Abivard said. "Majesty, might it not be wise to follow this embassy and see if they're part of whatever he plans? Follow them at a discreet distance, of course."

"Not a bad thought." Sharbaraz rubbed his chin, then called to a couple of scouts and gave the orders, adding, "One of you report back to me at nightfall to tell me where they've camped and whether anyone's met with them. The other should watch them through the night as best he can."

The horsemen saluted and rode out after Inshushinak and his companions. Abivard said, "Mind you, Majesty, I don't expect they'll find out anything in particular, but—"

"Better to send them and learn nothing than not send them and not learn something we should have," Sharbaraz said. "I wouldn't think of arguing with you."

The army rode on. Off in the distance, the sun shimmered from a saltpan. A little closer, the illusion of water danced in the air. That happened up by the Vek Rud, too, though not so often. If you believed the water was really there and went after it, you could easily end up dying of thirst.

Evening came. Camp straggled over what seemed to Abivard like a farsang and a half. Had Smerdis had an army in the neighborhood, it could have struck Sharbaraz's scattered forces a deadly blow. The encampment of the grand army Peroz had led into Pardraya had been no better organized. Abivard wondered if something could be done about that.

Before he had the chance to think seriously about it, he all but bumped into Sharbaraz as the rightful King of Kings came back from a walk round the camp to make sure everything was running smoothly. "What word from the scouts, Majesty?" he asked. "Are Smerdis' henchmen planning to transform the lot of us into camels?"

Sharbaraz laughed, but quickly grew sober once more. "Do

you know, brother-in-law of mine, I can't tell you, because that scout never came in."

Abivard glanced to the east. A fat moon, just past full, was climbing over the horizon and spilling pale-yellow light over the barren landscape. "Hard to lose the army, don't you think?"

The smile altogether vanished from Sharbaraz' face. "It is, wouldn't you say? Do you suppose Smerdis' men waylaid them?"

"Smerdis' men didn't look well mounted," Abivard demurred. "And if your scouts can't get away from the likes of the men we saw there, we've got the wrong people doing the job."

"You're right about that," Sharbaraz said. "But what does it leave? Accident? Possible, I suppose, but not very likely. As you say, scouts had better have a pretty good idea of what they're doing and how to get around."

"Magic, maybe." Abivard had meant it half as a joke, but the word seemed to hang in the air. He said, "Maybe we'd better not take any chances with magic, Majesty. Smerdis might well have sent out his men to see if he could buy you and, and if that failed—"

"—he'd turn a wizard loose on me," Sharbaraz finished. "Aye, that makes sense, and it fits the character—or rather, lack of character—Smerdis has shown all through his misbegotten, misnamed reign. What do we do to foil him?" He answered his own question: "We send out men to track down the embassy's camp, see what's going on there, and break it up if it's what we fear." He raised his voice and bawled for the scouts.

"Finding Smerdis' folk won't be easy, especially not at night," Abivard said. "And who knows how long the wizard—if there is a wizard—has been busy? You're going to need magical protection, just to keep you safe." He went out of Sharbaraz's tent, grabbed a man by the arm, and said, "D'you know where Tanshar the fortune-teller and the rest of those skilled in sorcery pitch their tents? Usually they're all close together, off to one side of the stores wagons."

"Aye, lord," the fellow answered. "I went to one of 'em—not Tanshar, I forget what his name was—the other night, and he looked at my palm and told me a big reward was coming my way soon."

"Get Tanshar and the rest of them back here to the King of Kings' tent as fast as you can and that fortune-teller's word will come true," Abivard said. The soldier blinked, scratched his head, then suddenly left at a dead run. He might have needed a moment to figure out what Abivard meant, but he wasted no time once he got it.

Abivard stared up at the moon. When you keep looking at it, he thought, it seemed to stand still in the sky—and if the moon didn't move, how could time pass? But the racket of the camp went right on, with a sudden addition when a troop of scouts resaddled and mounted their horses and rode off into the moonlight.

Inside the tent, Sharbaraz made a noise. It wasn't a word, nor yet a cry; it wasn't a noise quite like any Abivard had heard. He ducked back through the entry flap. As he straightened up, the camp bed in the tent, no finer than that which belonged to any other officer, went over with a crash.

Sharbaraz thrashed on the floor, wrestling with something he could see and Abivard could not. Abivard sprang to his aid. Guided by the motions of Sharbaraz's grasping hands, he tried to pull away the King of Kings' foe, even though that foe was invisible to him.

But his hands passed through the space between himself and Sharbaraz as if that space held only the empty air his eyes perceived. The same was manifestly not true for Sharbaraz. He writhed and twisted and kicked and punched, and when his blows landed, they sounded as if they struck flesh.

"By the God," Abivard cried, "what is this madness?"

When he spoke the God's name, he heard a groan that did not spring from his lips or Sharbaraz's, as if it pained the invisible attacker. That did not stop the thing, whatever it was, from keeping up its assault on Sharbaraz. It started to choke him; struggling like a madman, the rightful King of Kings tore its—hands?—from his throat.

"By the God," Abivard said again. This time he noted no effect, maybe because he was deliberately using the God's name as a weapon rather than invoking his deity out of need. Watching the King of Kings fight for his life and being unable to aid him brought back the dreadful helplessness Abivard had known when, afoot, he had watched Peroz and the flower of the Makuraner army tumble into the trench the Khamorth had dug.

"Lord Abivard? Your Majesty?"

Never had Abivard been so glad to hear an old man's quavering voice. "In here, Tanshar, and quickly!" he cried.

Tanshar burst into the King of Kings' tent, panting from having hurried from his own resting place. The fortune-teller stared at the spectacle of Sharbaraz struggling for his life against a foe imperceptible to others. He burst out with the same ejaculation Abivard had used, the same any Makuraner would have used: "By the God!"

Where the attacker had groaned when Abivard called on the God, he screamed now, as if beaten with red-hot pokers. He still grappled with Sharbaraz, but now, as they rolled over and over, the King of Kings was on top as often as his assailant.

Tanshar wasted no time with another invocation of the God. Instead, he snatched a vial of powder from the pouch he wore on his belt and sprinkled it over both Sharbaraz and whatever he was fighting with. No, not whatever—the powder let Abivard make out the faint outline of a naked, heavily muscled man.

"Strike!" Tanshar cried. "What you can see, you can slay."

Abivard jerked his sword from its scabbard and slashed at the still-misty figure Sharbaraz was fighting. This time he understood why the would-be assassin cried out with pain; the blood the fellow shed was plainly visible. He cut again and again; Sharbaraz got a grip on his opponent's throat. They knew they had slain their foe when, all at once, his body became fully visible to Abivard for the first time.

Sharbaraz stared down at the blood-splashed face of the man who had tried to assassinate him. Turning to Abivard, he said, "Wasn't he one of the warriors who rode with Inshushinak?"

"Majesty, I couldn't say for certain," Abivard answered. "A mail veil doesn't show much of a man's face—and besides, I paid most attention to the men who were talking. But if you say it, I wouldn't presume to disagree."

"You'd better not—I'm the King of Kings." Sharbaraz's laugh was shaky. He felt at his neck. "The wretch was strong as a bear; I must be bruised. I never saw him, either, till he seized me by the throat."

"Nor I, Majesty." Abivard's face went hot with shame. "He must have walked past me and into your tent while I was outside sending for Tanshar here."

Sharbaraz shook his head, then winced; his neck *was* sore. "Don't blame yourself. Magic defeated your vigilance—how can you be expected to see through a mage's charm? Besides, what you say doesn't have to be true. For all we know, he could have been lurking here, pretending to be a piece of air like any other, until you went outside and he found the chance to strike."

"It could be so," Abivard agreed gratefully. "As long as he lived, only Tanshar's magic powder let me see him and fight him."

The fortune-teller's laugh ran raucous in the tent. "Your Majesty, lord, I used no magic powder, for I had none. That was just finely ground salt for my meat, nothing more."

Abivard stared. "Then how did we defeat the spell from Smerdis' sorcerer?"

"I have no idea whether you defeated the spell," Tanshar answered. "You defeated the man on whom it lay, and that sufficed."

"But—" Abivard struggled to put his thought into words. "When I called on the God, and then again when you did, this whoreson was plainly hurt. How do you explain that, if not by magic?"

"That probably was magic," Tanshar said. "When we called on the God, we disturbed the link—the evil link, evidently—through which Smerdis' mage controlled the sorcery he had set in motion. Perhaps we deformed the nature of the spell: not enough to destroy its effectiveness, but enough to cause this fellow pain as the mage regained or retained his power. I am but guessing, you must understand, for such magic is far beyond my power."

"Yet you helped defeat it, just as, against all odds, you helped me get free from Nalgis Crag stronghold," Sharbaraz said. "I think you give yourself too little credit. I shall not make the same mistake. When Mashiz is mine once more, you have but to name your reward."

"Majesty, you cannot give me back thirty years, nor yet the sight in this eye," Tanshar said, raising a finger to point at the one a cataract had dimmed. "I have no great needs, and I've seen enough years go by that I have no great desires, either."

"I wonder whether I should pity you or be bitterly jealous," Sharbaraz observed. "Have it as you will, then, but know that my ear is yours should you ever find any service I can perform for you."

Tanshar bowed. "Your Majesty is generous beyond my deserts. For now, if you will but grant me leave to return to my tent—" The fortune-teller waited for Sharbaraz to nod, then bowed again and slipped out into the night.

When he was gone, Sharbaraz abandoned some of the brave front he had kept up. Prodding the body of his assailant with one foot, he said, "Pour me some wine, brother-in-law of mine, if you'd be so kind. This son of a thousand fathers came far too close to killing me."

"Aye, Majesty." A jar and some cups sat on a folding table

that somehow had not gone over during the fight. Abivard poured two cups full, handed one to the rightful King of Kings. The other he held high in salute. "To your safety."

"A good toast, and one I'll gladly drink to." Sharbaraz raised the cup to his lips. He winced when he swallowed. "That hurts. This cursed murderer—" He prodded the body again, "—was strong as a mule, and I think his hands were as hard as Ganzak the smith's."

Abivard had his doubts about that but held most of them from his reply: "The metal Ganzak pounds is harder than your neck."

"Can't argue with that." Sharbaraz drank again, more cautiously this time, but winced again anyhow. Wheezing a little, he said, "That's three times you've saved me now. But for you, Smerdis would be sitting comfortably on the throne, and I—I expect I'd be heading toward madness, locked up inside Nalgis Crag stronghold."

"To serve the King of Kings is an honor," Abivard said.

"You've earned honor, that's certain." Sharbaraz emptied the cup and held it out to Abivard. "Fill it up again, and drain your own so you can fill that, too. By the God, I've earned the right to drink deep tonight even if it sets my throat on fire, and I don't care to do it by myself."

"Let me drag this carrion out first." Abivard seized the assassin by the feet and hauled him out of the King of Kings' tent. The camp had quieted for the night; no one exclaimed at the sight of a corpse. Returning, Abivard said, "We can leave him there for the dogs and the crows to eat."

"A fine notion. Now pour me that wine, if you please."

The two of them were on their fourth or fifth cups—since Abivard was having trouble keeping track, probably their fifth—when riders came pounding into the camp. "Majesty! Majesty!" The cry rose above the thunder of hoofbeats and probably woke a good many men who had already gone to sleep.

Sharbaraz reached for his sword. "Have to—defend myself—if those aren't my scouts coming back." His speech was thick. Abivard suspected he would be more dangerous to himself with that blade than to any foes. He yanked out his own sword. He had already slain one would-be killer with it tonight. Why not another? The wine that made his movements slow and fumbling eloquently put forward its opinion.

Side by side, the King of Kings and Abivard went out to meet the approaching horsemen. In the moonlight, Abivard recognized the officer who had reported the arrival of Smerdis' embassy. The man saw Sharbaraz. "Majesty," he exclaimed, "we've rid you of a scorpion's nest of traitors."

Sharbaraz and Abivard exchanged glances. "That's—*hic!*—wonderful," the rightful King of Kings said. "Tell me at once what happened." To Abivard he whispered, "He'd better tell me at once; I have to piss fit to burst."

The scout, luckily, didn't hear that. He said, "We rode out until we found the camp where that Inshushinak, the God drop him into the Void, had paused with his henchmen for the night. Outside the camp, at a distance where they could watch and not be seen, we also found the two men you sent to keep an eye on the embassy."

"Why didn't one of them report back here as ordered?" Sharbaraz demanded.

A scout broke in. "Majesty, they was frozen stiff."

"Near enough," the officer agreed. "They were warm and breathing, but otherwise they might as well have been turned to stone. One of the men Inshushinak had with him, he must have been a wizard."

"We found that out for ourselves, as a matter of fact," Sharbaraz said dryly. "But this is your tale; pray go on with it."

"Aye, Majesty," the scout leader answered, curiosity in his voice. "Well, when we got a good look at what the son of a serpent had done to poor Tyardut and Andegan, we were so angry we couldn't even see. We got back on our horses and charged straight for the camp. Some of us probably feared the wizard would do to us what he'd done to our friends, but not a man hung back, and that's a fact."

"Whether you know it or not, charging with rage in your hearts likely was the best thing you could have done," Abivard said. "Sorcery won't bite on a man who's full of passion; that's why love magic and battle magic are such chancy things." He knew he was giving back Tanshar's words, but if Tanshar didn't understand how sorcery worked, who did?

"However that may be, lord," the scout said. "Anyhow, we came down on the camp like wolves jumping on an antelope they've cut out of the herd. Nothing alive there now, just carrion. We had a couple of men hurt, neither one bad, it looks like. And hear this, too—when we started back, we found the scouts had come back to life. Killing that wizard must have broken the spell that held them."

Sharbaraz sighed. "Now Smerdis will curse me for having slain an embassy. And do you know what, brother-in-law of mine? I shan't lose a moment's sleep over it, not when he tried to slay me by sorcery under cover of that embassy."

"Majesty, the only thing concerning me there is that, while you know what you say is true, the rest of the realm may not know it," Abivard said.

Sharbaraz waved scornfully to show how little he cared for what the rest of the realm knew or didn't know. "Soon enough all Makuran will be mine. Then it will know what I wish it to know."

The peaks of the Dilbat Mountains petered out into low, rolling foothills after Sharbaraz's army rode south for another few days. Getting through the mountains then was no longer a matter of forcing a narrow, heavily defended pass but simply heading east and then turning north.

Abivard found the change disconcerting the very first day. "I'm used to watching the sun rise out of the mountains, not set behind them," he said.

"I've seen both," Sharbaraz said. "One's the same as the other, as far as I'm concerned. What I want to see is Mashiz." Restless hunger stalked along his voice.

"How long till we reach it?" Abivard asked. He wanted to see Mashiz, too, not just because entering the capital would mean victory but also because he was curious about what a real city was like. Some of the towns that sheltered under strongholds in the south of Makuran were a good deal larger and busier than the one in his own domain, but basically of the same type. He wanted to find out how different Mashiz would be.

"Ten or twelve days from here," Sharbaraz answered. "That's if we do nothing but ride, mind you. I expect we'll see some fighting, though. If Smerdis doesn't throw everything he has at me now, he loses."

"May he lose any which way," Abivard said, to which the King of Kings nodded. Neither of them spoke as much of Smerdis' men deserting as they had when the campaign was new and their enthusiasm unchallenged. Abivard had concluded that most of the men who followed Smerdis were going to keep right on following him. If Sharbaraz was to win, he would have to do it with the forces that had begun the fight on his side. That didn't make it impossible, but it didn't make things any easier, either.

"As long as we keep winning, we're fine," Sharbaraz said. Maybe he was trying not to think about the desertions that hadn't happened, too. Once his army left the northwest, he had stopped sweeping in whole strongholdsful of recruits. If he ousted Smerdis with what he had, Abivard expected the whole realm to acknowledge him as its ruler. If he didn't . . . Abivard tried not to think about that.

Three days after Sharbaraz's host turned north, they met another of Smerdis' armies. This time the scouts were laughing as they came back to bring the news to Sharbaraz. "Smerdis must be running out of horses, Majesty," one of them said, "for half his men are foot soldiers, maybe more."

"The men of the Thousand Cities," Abivard said.

Sharbaraz nodded. "Aye, no doubt. We'll smash straight through them and scatter them like chaff; one such lesson and they'll know better than to fight for the usurper ever again."

Peroz's son indeed, Abivard thought. Aloud he said, "Wouldn't we be wiser to try to flank them out of their position? We can move faster than they, and if we hit them while they're trying to shift to keep up with us, we stand a better chance of striking the deadly blow you want."

But the rightful King of Kings shook his head and waved to the east, saying, "That's still desert out there; we aren't yet up to the Tutub and the Tib. We'd have a hard time keeping ourselves in fodder for the animals and water for them and us both. Besides, I don't want to be seen as sidestepping Smerdis. I want to show the realm my men are bolder and fiercer than his."

"I hope that's so, Majesty," Abivard said, as close to direct criticism as he dared come. Sharbaraz glared at him, then shouted for Zal and his other captains and began giving orders for the direct assault. No one contradicted him or showed any misgivings.

At the end, he turned to Abivard and said, "Will you do us the honor of accompanying the attack?"

"Certainly, Majesty. May the God grant you success, and may he know I wish it for you," Abivard said. However much he tried to ignore it, Sharbaraz's sardonic question stung. He did not think his sovereign was making the right choice, but how was he supposed to tell that to Sharbaraz when he would not listen? He found no way. All that was left, then, was to go forward and hope the rightful King of Kings was right.

Martial music ordered the men into line of battle. Word that they were facing infantry raced up and down the line. They seemed confident, even contemptuous. "We'll squash 'em flat for you, lord," one of the horsemen said, and all the troopers around him nodded. Abivard's worries eased. Confidence counted a great deal in war. If the soldiers thought they couldn't be beaten, maybe they couldn't.

Smerdis' men came into sight. As the scout had said, they were infantry and cavalry both, the horse on the flanks, the foot in the center. Abivard shouted Sharbaraz's name. The war cry rose from the whole army. Smerdis' soldiers shouted back. A great din rose to the blue sky.

Horns belled the charge. Abivard swung down his lance and spurred his horse. The pound of the beast's hooves, and of all those around him, filled him like a quicker, stronger pulse. The enemy horsemen moved forward from their position on the wings to engage Sharbaraz' riders.

Smerdis' infantry held its ground. As Abivard drew nearer, he saw it sheltered behind a barricade of thorny brush. Through thundering hoofbeats, through the clamor of war cries, the clear, pure note of reed whistles rang out. Abivard scowled under his mail visor; that was no signal he knew. But it meant something to the infantry. In an instant, arrows filled the air, one flight, then another and another. They whistled, too, loud enough to drown out the call that had set them flying. Graceful as birds, they curved high into the sky—then fell on the charging horsemen.

Sharbaraz had archers, too, and they shot back at the foot soldiers, but not with so many arrows so steadily discharged. Men and horses crumpled, and when they fell they fouled others just behind them. The attack faltered.

An arrow slammed into Abivard's upraised shield and stood, thrumming. A palm's breath to one side and it would have pierced his leg instead. The brush barricade was very close now. His horse pushed against it. The animal's body was armored, but the thorns on the brush still tore the tender skin of its legs. It hesitated, whinnying in protest.

Abivard kicked it in the ribs with his boots, inflicting worse pain to force it to obey his will. "Forward, the God curse you!" he yelled. The horse pushed forward, but hesitantly. Abivard got a good look at the foot soldiers on the far side of the barrier: dark, stocky men in leather jerkins, their long, black hair bound in a club at the nape of their necks. Some of them shouted insults in harshly accented Makuraner, others yelled what did not sound like pleasantries in their own guttural language. And all of them kept shooting arrows. Along with the quivers on their backs, they had others at their feet.

Had the brush been stiffened with stakes, it would have made a worse obstacle. As it was, the barrier broke here and there, letting trickles of Sharbaraz's men in among the enemy. They worked a fearful slaughter; but for their bows, the foot soldiers had only knives and clubs to defend themselves.

Abivard thrust his lance over the brush at an archer at the same instant the archer let fly at him. Maybe the two men frightened each other, for they both missed. They stared across the brush, the archer's face tired and worried, Abivard's hidden from the eyes down by chainmail. They both nodded, if not with joint respect, then at least with recognition of their joint humanity. By unspoken common consent, they chose other foes after that.

Pressure from behind forced Abivard's horse forward against the thorns, no matter how little it cared to go. Branches scraped at the beast's armored sides and at the iron rings that protected Abivard's legs. Then he, too, was through the barricade, and a knot of Sharbaraz's warriors right behind him. Shouts of triumph rang in his ears, and cries of fear and dismay from Smerdis' infantry.

Some of the foot soldiers, recklessly brave, rushed toward the horses and tried to pull their riders from the saddle. Most of them were speared before they got close. Panic spread through the archers. Many threw away their bows to run the faster.

But they could not outrun horsemen. Abivard struck with his lance till it shivered; by then it was scarlet almost to the grip. He took out his sword and cut down more of the fleeing foe.

He never looked back on that part of the battle with pride—it always struck him afterward as more like murder than war. With their center broken, the cavalrymen Smerdis' generals had posted on either wing also had to give way, lest they be cut off and defeated in detail. The chase went on until nightfall forced Sharbaraz to break it off.

Abivard's stomach twisted as he rode back over the field. His horse had to pick its way carefully to keep from stepping on the bodies of fallen foot soldiers. Every few yards it would tread on one despite all its care, and snort in alarm as the corpse shifted under its hooves.

Then Abivard passed the broken barrier and saw what the archers had done to his own companions. He had pitied the hapless infantrymen as he had speared and hacked at them and afterward as he saw their bodies sprawled in death. Now he realized they were soldiers, too, in their own fashion. They had hurt Sharbaraz's followers worse than Smerdis' cavalry had managed in either of the earlier two fights.

He looked around for the banner of the rightful King of Kings. The fading light made it hard to spot, but when he found it he rode toward it. Sharbaraz had dismounted from his horse; he held out his arm for the physician Kakia's ministrations.

"You're wounded, Majesty!" Abivard exclaimed.

"An arrow, through my armor and through the meat," Sharbaraz answered. He shrugged, then winced, wishing he hadn't. He tried to make the best of it. "Not too bad. Your sister needn't worry that I need replacing."

Having done his utmost to make light of an injury of his own not long before, Abivard turned to Kakia for confirmation. The physician said, "His Majesty was fortunate in that the arrow pierced the biceps of the upper arm, and again in that the point came out the other side, so we did not have to draw it or force it through, causing him further pain. If the wound does not fester, it should heal well."

"And you'll make sure it doesn't fester, won't you?" Sharbaraz said.

"I have a decoction for that very purpose, yes," Kakia answered, taking a stoppered vial from a pouch on his belt. "Here we have verdigris and litharge, alum, pitch, and resin, stirred into a mixture of vinegar and oil. If your Majesty will undertake to hold the wounded member still—"

Sharbaraz tried valiantly to obey, but when Kakia poured the murky brownish lotion into the wound he hissed like red-hot iron with water poured into it. "By the God, you've set fire to my arm," he cried, biting his lip.

"No, Majesty, or if so but a small fire now to prevent the greater and more deadly fire of corruption later."

"That brew will prevent anything," Sharbaraz said feelingly as Kakia bandaged the arm. "Copper and lead and alum and pitch and resin—if I drank it instead of having it inflicted on me as you did, I'd be poisoned for certain."

"No doubt you would, Majesty, but the same holds true for many nostrums intended to go onto the body rather than within it," Kakia replied with some asperity. "For that matter, your caftan belongs around you, but would you swallow it chopped up with cucumbers? To everything its proper place and application."

With his arm paining him not only from the wound but also from the physician's treatment of it, Sharbaraz was not inclined to be philosophical. He turned to Abivard and said, "Well, brother-in-law of mine, you seem to have come through this fight with your brains unscrambled, for which I envy you."

"Aye, I was luckier this time. The day is ours." Abivard looked around at the grisly aftermath of battle. "Ours, aye, but dearly bought."

Sharbaraz suddenly looked exhausted as well as hurt. His skin stretched tight over his bones; Abivard was easily able to imagine how he would look as an old man—if he lived to grow old, which was never a good bet, most especially for a claimant to the throne of Makuran engaged in bruising civil war.

"Each fight is tougher," the rightful King of Kings said wearily. "I thought Smerdis' backers would collapse after the first battle, but they've given me two tougher ones since. How his officers keep their men in line I could not say—but they do. We'll have to fight again before we reach Mashiz, and if Smerdis is stronger then than now ..." He didn't go on; he plainly didn't want to go on.

"You didn't expect him to offer battle till just in front of the capital." No sooner had he spoken than Abivard wished he could have his words back—no point to reminding Sharbaraz of past errors he couldn't correct now.

But Sharbaraz did not get angry; he only nodded. "My graybeard cousin has proved himself a man of more parts than I'd guessed, the God curse his thieving soul. It won't save him, but it makes our task harder."

Again Abivard envied the King of Kings for being able to haul himself out of swamps of gloom, apparently by sheer force of will. He asked, "How many more foot soldiers do you suppose he can bring against us? They hurt us worse than I would have dreamed such troops could."

"And I," Sharbaraz agreed. "Well, there's a lesson learned—I can't charge straight at archers with any sort of protection, not unless I want more of a butcher's bill than I fancy paying." He curled the hand on his wounded arm into a fist; Abivard was glad to see he could do that. "I hope the lesson wasn't too dearly bought."

"Aye," Abivard said. "Much will depend on the spirit of the men. If they decide this is another victory on our way to Mashiz, all will be well. We have to worry that they don't see it as a setback."

"Too true—if you think you're beaten, you probably are."

Sharbaraz looked bleak. "I thought Smerdis would reckon himself beaten by now."

"Well, Majesty, if he doesn't, we'll just have to convince him," Abivard said, and hoped he sounded optimistic.

The land of the Thousand Cities was a revelation to Abivard. The land of his own domain wasn't rich enough to support one city, let alone a thousand. But in the river valleys, large towns squatted on little hillocks raised above the flat, muddy terrain.

When Abivard asked how those hillocks came to rise in the flatlands, Sharbaraz chuckled and said, "It's the cities' fault." Seeing that Abivard didn't follow, he explained: "Those cities have been there a long, long time, and they've been throwing out their rubbish just as long. When the street gets too much higher than your door, you knock down your house. It's not stone, only mud brick. Then you build a new one at the level the street has risen to. Do that for hundreds of years and pretty soon you're sitting on a hill."

From then on, Abivard looked at the hillocks in a whole new way: as pieces of time made visible. The idea awed him. The hill on which Vek Rud stronghold perched was purely natural—dig down a foot anywhere and you hit rock. That people could make their own hills had never occurred to him.

"Why shouldn't they?" Roshnani said when he spoke of that in her cubicle one evening. Her voice turned tart. "From all I've seen, this land is nothing but mud. Pile mud up and let it dry and you have a hill."

"Hmm," he said; his principal wife had a point, and one that diminished his wonder at what the dwellers in the Land of the Thousand Cities had done. He wasn't sure he wanted that wonder diminished: man-made hills seemed much more impressive than heaps of mud. "It takes a *lot* of mud to make one of those hills."

"As I said, there's a lot of mud here." Roshnani might have been sweet-natured, but she was also as tenacious in argument as a badger. Abivard changed the subject, tacitly conceding the skirmish to her.

Along with the mud went abundant moisture; irrigation canals spread the waters of the Tutub and the Tib over the plain between and alongside them. *Qanats* would have wasted less, but you couldn't drive *qanats* through mud, either.

Wherever it was watered, the plain grew abundantly: grain, dates, onions, melons, beans, and more. Farmers worked their fields wearing only cloths round their loins and straw hats against the pounding sun. Sweltering in his armor, Abivard most sincerely envied them. A few yards past the far ends of the canal, the land turned gray and dusty and held only thorn bushes, if those.

The folk of the Thousand Cities fled into their towns and took shelter behind their walls as Sharbaraz' army drew near. "How are we supposed to get them out?" Abivard asked at an officers' council.

"We don't," Zal answered. "If we besiege every one of these towns, we'll stay in the land of the Thousand Cities forever and we won't get to Mashiz. We just pass 'em by: take what we need from the fields and keep moving."

"They won't love us for that," Abivard observed.

"They don't love us now," Zal said, which, though cynical, was also undoubtedly true.

Abivard looked an appeal to Sharbaraz. "Zal is right," Sharbaraz said. "If we win the war with Smerdis, we'll hold the allegiance of the land of the Thousand Cities. And if we don't—what difference will it make?" He laughed bitterly. "So we take what we need."

Ten days after the battle with the archers Smerdis had mustered against them, Sharbaraz' men turned west again, away from the valleys of the Tutub and the Tib and toward the Dilbat Mountains once more. Ahead lay Mashiz.

Also ahead, and closer, lay the army Smerdis had gathered to hold his rival out of the capital. Smoke from its cook fires smudged the sky as Sharbaraz' forces drew near.

"He's making us come to him," the rightful King of Kings said as his own army encamped for the night. "There's only one broad, straight route into Mashiz. Caravans and such have other choices, but a handful of men can block those passes. I'll send scouts out to check, but I don't think Smerdis would have left them open for us."

"Can his men sally from any of them?" Abivard asked.

Zal did not sound happy when he answered: "It could happen, lord; we have a harder time keeping him away than he does us. But he hasn't shown much in the way of fighting push or trying to do more than one thing at a time with his armies up to now. Odds are good—not great, but good—things will go on that way."

"Since the odds of my ever being free to fight this war were long indeed, I am content and more than content with good odds," Sharbaraz declared. "The chief question ahead of us remains how best to win the main battle. There once more, I fear, we have little choice but to go straight at the foe."

He said *I fear*; the top of his mind still vividly remembered the tough fight when his men had attacked Smerdis' archers head-on. But, despite his words, he sounded eager to go toe to toe with the enemy. Like his father before him, he had as his chief notion of strategy closing with whatever enemies opposed him and pounding them to pieces.

That worried Abivard, but he had to keep silent: he did not know the lay of the land in front of Mashiz and so could not offer an opinion on how best to fight there. Zal had served at the capital. The tough, gray-bearded officer said, "Aye, if they're going to stay there and wait for us, we don't have much choice but to try and hammer 'em out. If we try to outwait them, make them come down and attack us, it's just a gamble on where disease breaks out first, and since the water coming out of the Dilbats is cleaner than what we're drinking, it's a gamble we'd likely lose."

"Onward, then," Sharbaraz said with decision. "Once the capital is in our hands, all the realm will come to see who properly belongs at its head."

"Onward," his captains echoed, Abivard among them. As Zal had said, all other choices looked worse—and one more victory would give Sharbaraz Mashiz and all of Makuran. Viewed thus, chances looked good enough to bet on.

Mashiz! Till he had rescued Sharbaraz, Abivard had never imagined seeing the capital of the realm. He had been born on the frontier and expected to live out his life and die there. But now, tiny in the distance but still plain, his eyes picked out the spreading gray mass of the palace of the King of Kings, and not far from it the great shrine to the God: in all the world, only the High Temple in Videssos the city was said to be a match for it.

Seeing the wonders of Mashiz, though, was not the same as entering the city in triumph. Between those wonders and Abivard stood Smerdis' army in a position its leaders had chosen for making a stand. The closer Abivard got to that position, the more his stomach griped him, the more misgiving grew in his mind. By the look of things, no army made up of mere mortals was going to force its way through Smerdis' host. Yet the effort had to be made.

Horns blared. "Forward the archers!" officers cried. Heavy

horse, usually the cream of a Makuraner force, could not play its normal role today, for Smerdis' captains, perhaps learning from their failure in the recent battle to the south, had posted unmounted bowmen behind a barrier of stones and dirt and timber. What the lancers could not reach, they could not overwhelm.

And so the horse archers, men wearing leather rather than costly mail and splint armor, rode ahead of the lancers to try to drive Smerdis' infantry back from its sheltering barricade. Shafts flew in both directions. Men and horses screamed as they were pierced. Mounted detachments brought fresh sheaves of arrows from the supply wagons to help the horsemen keep shooting.

Smerdis' barricade did not quite cover the entire width of the approach to Mashiz. The usurper's heavy cavalry waited at either wing. When Sharbaraz's archers were well involved in their duel with the foot soldiers, Smerdis' lancers thundered forth.

In that narrow space, the mounted archers could not stand against the charge of their ironclad foes. Some were speared out of the saddle; more fell back in confusion. But Sharbaraz had been waiting for that. "Forward the lancers!" he cried, a command echoed by his officers and the martial musicians in the army.

At last, the chance to fight, Abivard thought, with something between eagerness and dread. He swung down his lance, booting his horse in the side. The foe he struck never saw him coming; his lance went in just below the fellow's right shoulder. The luckless warrior gave a bubbling scream when Abivard jerked out the lancehead. Blood poured from the wound and from his nose and mouth as he slumped over his horse's neck.

The melee in front of the barricade became general. Smerdis' archers kept shooting into the milling crowd of warriors even though some of them were on their side. All of Smerdis' horsemen and horses in the fight were armored in iron, while many of Sharbaraz's were not, so their arrows remained more likely to hurt foe than friend.

Abivard was in the thick of the melee. "Sharbaraz!" he shouted again and again. Riders on both sides cried out the name of the King of Kings they favored; in such a mixed-up fight, that was the only way to tell Smerdis' backers from those who followed Sharbaraz.

A man yelling "Smerdis!" cut at Abivard. He took the blow on his shield, then returned it. Iron sparked against iron as their swords clanged against each other. They traded strokes until the tide of battle swept them apart.

Little by little, Smerdis' cavalry gave ground, retreating back toward either end of the barricade that sheltered the archers. Some of Sharbaraz' riders raised a cheer. Abivard yelled, too, until he took a good look around the field. Driving those horsemen back meant nothing. As long as the barrier kept Sharbaraz' men from breaking through and advancing on Mashiz, victory remained out of reach.

Sharbaraz's mounted archers went back to trading shafts with Smerdis' foot soldiers. That wouldn't do what needed doing if the battle went on for the next week. As long as those archers held their ground behind the barrier, Sharbaraz's men couldn't get close enough to tear it down. That was what had to happen for victory, but Abivard didn't see how it could.

Sharbaraz had another idea. Pointing to the left of the barrier, he cried, "We'll force our way through there—we have more lancers than Smerdis can throw against us. Then we can take those cursed bowmen in flank instead of banging our heads against their wall."

Horns and yelling officers slowly began to position Sharbaraz's army for the charge he had in mind. Abivard didn't know if it would work, but it held more promise than anything he had come up with himself. He swung almost out of the saddle to grab an unbroken lance that had fallen from someone's hands.

Smerdis' horsemen gathered themselves to withstand the assault. Before the charge was signaled, though, the horns on the right wing of Sharbaraz's host rang out in confused discord. Shouts of dismay and fear rose with the alarmed horn calls. "What's gone wrong now?" Abivard cried, twisting his head to see.

All at once, he understood why Smerdis' army had seemed so light in cavalry. It *was* light in cavalry, for the usurper's generals had divided it, sending part of the force to emerge from one of the narrow canyons and take Sharbaraz's men in the flank, much as Abivard had done against Smerdis' troops earlier in the civil war.

The results were much the same here, too. The right wing of Sharbaraz's army crumpled. Even Zal, who commanded there, could do little to stem the collapse. And with their enemy in disarray, Smerdis' men, who had been about to receive a charge, made one instead. They shouted with fresh confidence and fury.

Sharbaraz also shouted. Fury filled his voice, but not confidence. "Fall back!" he ordered, sounding as if he hated the words. "Fall back and regroup. Rally, by the God, rally! The day may yet be ours."

His men did not give way to panic or despair. Most of them were raw troops who had gone from victory to victory; Abivard had wondered how they would face defeat if ever it came. The answer was what he had hoped but hadn't dared expect—they kept fighting hard.

But fighting hard was not enough. With their line broken on the right, under simultaneous attack from flank and front, they had to retreat and keep retreating so they would not have whole bands of men cut off and captured or slain. After a while, retreat took on a momentum of its own.

Smerdis' men did not push the pursuit as hard as they might have. What point? They had the victory they had needed. Sharbaraz would not parade into Mashiz: Sharbaraz would not go into Mashiz at all, not now. And as soon as word of that spread through Makuran, many who had been sitting on the fence between the two rival Kings of Kings would decide in favor of the man who held the capital.

Three farsangs east of the battlefield, Sharbaraz ordered his men to halt for the night. The bulk of the army, or what was left of it, obeyed, but a flow of men, less than a flood but more than a trickle, kept on streaming east and south. "The first ticks dropping off the horse that fed 'em," Abivard said bitterly.

"Bad choice of metaphor," Sharbaraz answered with the air of someone criticizing a bard's work. "Ticks leave a horse when it's dead, and we still have life in us."

"Aye, Majesty," Abivard said. Inside, though, he wondered how much of Sharbaraz' defiance consisted of keeping up a brave front, maybe more for himself than for anyone else. A lot of it, he feared. A rebel needed win after win until power was his. Now the rightful King of Kings had to be wondering how to rally his men and turn his right to the throne into real possession of it.

"We'll renew the assault in the morning," Sharbaraz said, "making sure this time that we've covered the mouths to all the passes."

"Aye, Majesty," Abivard repeated dutifully, but he didn't believe it, not for a moment. Fraortish eldest of all, the most fiery of the Prophets Four, couldn't have rallied the army to a renewed assault if he had promised the God would come through the Void and fight alongside Sharbaraz's men.

Even Sharbaraz seemed to sense his words rang hollow.

"Well, we'll see what seems best when morning comes," he said.

Abivard trudged wearily back to the baggage train. He breathed a silent prayer of thanks that Smerdis' men hadn't pressed the pursuit; if they had, they might have overrun the train and captured the wagon that carried Roshnani and Denak.

His principal wife and sister exclaimed in delight and relief when he went up into the wagon, and then again when he told them Sharbaraz remained hale. "But what happens next?" Roshnani asked. "With the way to Mashiz blocked, what do we do?"

"His Majesty spoke of a new attack tomorrow," Abivard said. Roshnani rolled her eyes and then tried to pretend she hadn't. Even Denak, who supported Sharbaraz as automatically as she breathed, didn't say anything to that. If Denak didn't believe the attack would come off, it was surely foredoomed.

Roshnani called to one of the serving women, who fetched Abivard a mug of wine. He drained it, sprawled out on the carpet in Roshnani's cubicle to relax for a moment, and fell asleep before he realized it.

Attack came the next morning, but Sharbaraz's men did not launch it. Perhaps emboldened by their victory, Smerdis' cavalry, some archers, the rest lancers, followed their foes through the night and struck just as dawn was breaking. Sharbaraz's followers outnumbered them. It did not help. They were demoralized from losing the day before and disorganized from camping hastily after a retreat they had not expected to have to make.

Some of them fought well; others broke and fled as soon as the first arrows hissed down among them. The army as a whole held its own till about midmorning. After that, men began falling back again in spite of desperate shouts from Sharbaraz and their officers. Scenting victory, Smerdis' men kept up the pressure, attacking wherever they saw weakness.

By the end of the day, Sharbaraz's army had returned to the land of the Thousand Cities, the floodplain of the Tutub and the Tib. The rightful King of Kings looked stunned, as if he had never imagined such a disaster overfalling him. Abivard hadn't imagined it, either, so he suspected he looked stunned, too.

"I don't think I can rally them straightaway," Sharbaraz said gloomily. "Best perhaps to fall back to country where the nobles and people back us with whole hearts, there to rebuild our strength to fight again another day."

Fall back to the northwest, he meant: essentially what Smerdis had offered him before the sorcerous attack, and what he had rejected with a sneer then. But at that point of the civil war, he had been winning battles and Smerdis losing. After a couple of losses of his own, he must have thought keeping some of the flock better than losing it all.

"Aye, Majesty, perhaps that would be for the best," Abivard said. Sharbaraz was right; the army he led had lost heart, and Smerdis' no doubt gained a corresponding amount. Under such circumstances, inviting battle also invited disaster. And, while a return to the northwest would seem like exile to the rightful King of Kings, to Abivard it would be going home. He wondered how his brother—and his domain—fared. He had heard not a word since he set out on campaign.

The next morning, Sharbaraz ordered his men to turn south, to skirt the Dilbat Mountains again so they could head north and west into territory friendlier to his cause than the Land of the Thousand Cities. Smerdis' men dogged their trail, not in such numbers as to invite attack, but always lurking, watching, reporting every movement back to their superiors.

Sharbaraz' soldiers had not ridden more than a farsang when they found canals broken open to spill out their water and flood the plain, making the way impassable. On the far side, more of Smerdis' soldiers sat their horses, watching with evident pleasure the discomfiture of their foes.

Abivard shook his fist at them. "Where now, Majesty?" he asked. "They've blocked the way homeward."

"I know." Sharbaraz looked as hunted as Abivard felt. "Here in the valleys of the Tutub and the Tib, we're like flies trying to get out of a spider's web. And the spider can push us to any piece of the web he likes before strolling over and sinking his fangs into the withered husk of our army."

"There's a pleasant picture." Abivard's stomach churned. "Have we any way to start moving by our own will rather than Smerdis'?"

"Perhaps if we strike north and get over one or two of the major canals before they can break the banks and open the sluices. The thing could be done; bridges of boats span the more important waterways."

The army tried. When they got to the canal Sharbaraz had wanted to cross, they found the boats drawn up on the far bank. More of Smerdis' men were strung out along the far bank, too, waiting to see if Sharbaraz would try to force a crossing. They quickly found the canal was too deep to ford.

Sharbaraz sighed. "We'd be asking to get massacred if I had the men swim across, with or without their horses. We can't go south, we can't go north, there's an army behind us to keep us from turning back to the west . . . even if the men would obey."

Sharbaraz thought in terms of strategy, Abivard in the more homely things he had had to worry about back at the domain. "They're herding us," he said.

"Aye, they are, and drop me into the Void if I can see what to do about it, either," Sharbaraz said. "I can't reach Smerdis' traitors there—" He pointed north across the canal. "—or to the south, and if I do make the army turn against the turncoats between us and Mashiz, they won't even deign to accept battle; I can see that already. They'll just fall back and open more canals to hold us up. They can wreck them faster than we can fix them."

"I fear you're right, Majesty," Abivard said. "We've already crossed the headwaters of the Tib. What happens if they force us across the Tutub, as well? What's on the far side of the Land of the Thousand Cities?"

"Scrub country, near desert, and then Videssos." Sharbaraz spat. "Nothing I want to visit, I assure you."

But in spite of what Sharbaraz wanted, the army had to keep moving east. They could not stay in one place more than a couple of days at a time; after that, they began to run low on food and fodder both. Smerdis' men and the canals they had opened blocked the way in other directions. The folk of the Thousand Cities shut themselves up behind their walls and would not treat with Sharbaraz.

"I might as well be leading Videssians," he fumed. "I'd pay the locals well, with money and later with exemptions, to aid me in setting the canals aright and free us up to maneuver . . . but they will not hear me."

Okhos chanced to be riding close to Sharbaraz when the rightful King of Kings loosed that blast. He said, "Majesty, when you sit on your throne as you should, surely you will take such vengeance on them as to make the bards sing and miscreants shudder a thousand years from now."

"Oh, a few city governors will find themselves short a head come the day—no doubt about that," Sharbaraz told Roshnani's brother. "But past that, what point to vengeance? Kill the peasants and craftsmen and where do the realm's taxes come from?"

Okhos stared; he was still new at running a domain, let alone the realm of Makuran. After a moment he asked, "Do taxes count for more than honor?"

"Sometimes," Sharbaraz answered, which made Okhos' eyes get wider. The rightful King of Kings went on, "Besides, the peasants and craftsmen are but obeying the command of their governors. How can I fault them for that when I would expect it of them were those governors mine? Massacre strikes me as wasteful. I'll have revenge, aye, but measured revenge."

Okhos considered that as he would have a lesson from a tutor. At last he said, "Your Majesty is wise."

"My Majesty is bloody tired," Sharbaraz said. "And if I were so wise, I'd be sitting in Mashiz right now, instead of slogging through the Land of the Thousand Cities." A bug landed on his cheek. He slapped at himself, but it flew away before his hand landed. "They ought to call these river valleys the land of the Ten Million Flies. It seems to have more of them than anything else."

"Oh, I don't know, Majesty," Abivard said. "In my humble opinion, it breeds more mosquitoes still." He scratched at a welt on his arm.

Sharbaraz snorted. His laugh was grim but a laugh, one of the few Abivard had heard from him since things went wrong in front of Mashiz. "Brother-in-law of mine, I admit it: you may be right."

Taking advantage of his sovereign's relatively good humor, Abivard said, "May I speak, Majesty?" At Sharbaraz's nod, he went on, "You may be wise to show yourself moderate in more things than vengeance on the Land of the Thousand Cities. Throwing an army headlong into battle cost your father everything and has badly hurt you as well."

The scowl he got from the rightful King of Kings neither surprised nor upset him; how often did Sharbaraz hear criticism? After a long pause, though, Sharbaraz slowly nodded. "Again, you may be right. I aim to do my foe as much harm as I can, as quickly as I can. That I sometimes do myself harm as well—how could I deny it?" His wave encompassed the hot floodplain across which his unhappy army perforce traveled.

Try as he would, he found no opportunity to break free of the network of flooded canals, hostile cities, and enemy forces that hemmed him in. Smerdis, by all appearances, cared nothing for the impetuous charge if he could get results without it. Hardly shooting an arrow, his men drove Sharbaraz's riders ever farther east.

"We'll be at the Tutub soon," Sharbaraz raged. "What then? Does he think we'll drown ourselves in it for his convenience?"

"I'm sure he wishes we would; that would be easiest for him," Abivard answered. "He makes war like a man who used to head the mint: he spends nothing more than he has to. That cheese-paring cost him west of the Dilbat Mountains, but it serves him well here."

Sharbaraz swore at him and rode off in a fury. Abivard wondered what would happen when they came to the Tutub. He was ready to bet the river would be too wide and deep and swift to ford. If Smerdis' men backed their foes against it, Sharbaraz would have no choice but to throw his army at that part of Smerdis' that looked to be most nearly accessible. Abivard didn't expect victory in such an effort, but he would follow without hesitation the man he had chosen as his sovereign. What were the odds Sharbaraz would have escaped from Nalgis Crag stronghold? If he had managed that, anything might happen.

The thought consoled Abivard until he realized how spiderweb-thin was the line that ran from *might* to *would*.

Pushed on, unable to make a stand because their worst enemies were hunger and broken canals rather than archers and lancers, Sharbaraz' men reached the Tutub three days later. Abivard fully expected to have to form up for a last stand of desperate battle. After backing Sharbaraz, he was not dead keen on falling into Smerdis' hands in any case.

He wished Roshnani and Denak hadn't persuaded Sharbaraz and him to let them accompany the campaign. Back at Vek Rud stronghold, they would have been safe enough, no matter what happened to their husbands. Here—

But, to his surprise, scouts who rode up and down the river came back with word that a bridge of boats still stretched across it. "We'll go over," Sharbaraz said at once. "On the far side of the Tutub, we'll be able to move as we please, less harassed by the troops who dog us."

Abivard's horse did not like the way the planks laid across the boats shifted under its feet. It snorted and sidestepped and did its best not to go forward until he booted it in the ribs hard enough to gain its undivided attention.

The far side of the Tutub seemed much like the near one. But as soon as Sharbaraz's army had crossed, Smerdis' men rode up and set fire to the bridge of boats. The rising smoke made

Abivard wonder, too late, how many boats were left on the east bank of the river to aid Sharbaraz's army in returning to the fray. He didn't know, but he had the feeling the answer would be none.

IX

"We can't cross back and we can't stay here long," Abivard said to Roshnani that evening as the unhappy army made camp. "That leaves us little choice."

"If we had a choice, which would be better?" she asked.

"Even if we had a choice, neither would be much good," Abivard answered. "Back on the western side of the Tutub, we'd face all the problems that led to our getting trapped here in the first place. And even if we had all the livestock and grain and fruit in the world at our fingertips here, so what? Being King of Kings for the land east of the Tutub is like being Mobedhan-mobhed for the Khamorth. Not enough of them worship the God to make them need a chief servant for him, and this land is about enough to rate a *dihqan*, but not a sovereign."

"You will have seen more of it than I, since I'm closed up here in this wagon," Roshnani said. Denak would have sounded furious at that; Roshnani just stated it matter-of-factly, to let Abivard draw what conclusions from it he would. She went on, "Your point is well made. Both choices you named seem evil. What if we went east, then?"

Abivard shook his head, a gesture full of patience, love, and the desire to be as gentle with her naïveté as he could. "East of here is scrub country, about as bad as the land between oases back in the northwest. It's no place for us to stay and regather our strength. And east of that lies—Videssos."

He spoke the name with a shudder; to him, as to any Makuraner warrior, Videssos was and could only be the enemy. But Roshnani pounced on it like a cat leaping after a mouse that appeared from a hole it hadn't noticed: "Why don't we fare into

218

Videssos, then? Their Avtokrator—do I rightly remember his name as Likinios?—could hardly do worse by us than Smerdis Pimp of Pimps, could he?" She brought out the contemptuous soldierly title with a fine curl of her lip.

Abivard opened his mouth to begin an automatic condemnation of the idea, but stopped with it unuttered. Put that way, it could not be dismissed out of hand. What he did say was "I don't see much point in throwing myself on a Videssian's mercy when he's not likely to treat me any better than Smerdis would, either."

Once she got a notion, Roshnani was not one to abandon it before she had taken it as far as it would go. She said, "Why wouldn't he treat Sharbaraz better? Likinios is a King of Kings, too, of sorts. Does he take kindly to having a cousin steal a throne that ought to belong to a son? If he does, one fine day he may find a cousin stealing his own throne."

"That's—" Abivard started to say it was foolish and ridiculous, but it wasn't. If Smerdis had the gall to usurp the throne, why shouldn't a Videssian do likewise? By all accounts, Videssians were knavish and thieving by nature. If one of their Emperors left a throne lying around vacant, somebody to whom it didn't properly belong would try to abscond with it. "That's . . . not a bad idea," he finished in tones of wonder.

"My thought was simple: what have we to lose by going into Videssos?" Roshnani said.

While Abivard looked for an answer there, something else occurred to him: the third piece of Tanshar's prophecy. "Where am I likelier to find a narrow stretch of sea than in Videssos?" he said.

Roshnani's eyes got wide. "I hadn't thought of that," she said. "If the prophecy itself is urging us eastward—"

Denak stuck her head through the cloth curtain that screened off Roshnani's cubicle. She nodded to her brother, then said, "Eastward? How can we think of going eastward? Not only would we be fleeing, but there's nothing in that direction but scrub and desert, anyhow."

"There's also Videssos, beyond the scrub," Roshnani answered, which made Denak's eyes widen in turn. Speaking alternate sentences, almost like characters out of a traveling play about one of the Prophets Four, she and Abivard explained their reasons for wanting to take refuge in the Empire and seek aid from the Avtokrator.

When they had finished, Denak stared from one of them to

the other. "I thought we were in a box," she said. "So did Sharbaraz. So, no doubt, did Smerdis—he has to be looking forward to finishing us off at his leisure. But if a box doesn't have to stay a box, if we can break down one of the sides and escape in a way no one imagined—"

Abivard raised a warning hand. "We have no guarantees if we try this," he reminded his sister. "The Videssians may prove as wicked and treacherous as the tales say they are, or they may take us for enemies and attack no matter what we do to show them we're friends. Or, for that matter, some of the men here may prefer Smerdis' mercy to what they think they'll find in Videssos. We'll lose more than a handful to desertion, I fear."

Roshnani laughed. "Here we are, reckoning up the good points and the bad to this move when we have not the power to order it."

Abivard took a deep breath. "Here I am, to say that having women along on this campaign may prove its salvation. I tell you now, I never would have thought of using Videssos for refuge if I lived to be a thousand. If it succeeds, the credit goes to Roshnani."

"Thank you, my husband," Roshnani said quietly, and cast down her eyes to the carpeted floor of the wagon as if she were an ordinary, deferential Makuraner wife who had never imagined setting foot outside the women's quarters of her stronghold.

"Thank you, Abivard," Denak said, "for being open enough to see that and honest enough to say it."

He shrugged. "Father always relied on Mother's wisdom—oh, not out in the open, but he made no great secret of it, either. And wasn't it you who said that if a woman's counsel was worth something back at the stronghold, it would be worth something on campaign, too?"

"I said it, yes," Denak answered. "Whether anyone listened to me is another matter. One of the things I found with Pradtak is that men often don't."

"Judging all men by Pradtak, I suspect, is like judging all women by Ardini," Abivard said, which made Denak frown angrily and Roshnani, after a moment's hesitation, nod. He went on, "Do you expect Sharbaraz to, ah, attend you this evening?"

Still frowning, Denak said, "No, not really. He's come here less often since things went wrong. He'd sooner brood than try to make himself feel better."

"You're probably right." Abivard got to his feet; the top of his head brushed the canvas canopy of the wagon. "I'll go and take the idea to him, then. If he says no and I can't get him to change his mind, I'll send him hither. I hope you won't think less of me for saying wives have ways to persuade a man that brothers-in-law can't use."

"Think less of you? No," Denak said. "But I wish you'd not reminded me of things I did that I'd sooner forget."

"I'm sorry," Abivard said, and left in a hurry.

Sharbaraz's tent had guards round it now, and one of the army's sorcerers stood watch outside. Abivard doubted the need for that; now that Smerdis was winning the war by ordinary means, why would he bother with sorcery? The sentries saluted as he came up to the tent.

Inside, Sharbaraz sat on his camp bed, his head in his hands. "What word, brother-in-law of mine?" he asked dully. By his demeanor, he cared nothing for the answer.

But Abivard gave him a word he had not looked for: "Videssos."

"What of Videssos?" Now Sharbaraz showed interest, if no enthusiasm. "Has Likinios decided to cast his lot with Smerdis and join in crushing me? He would be wise if he did; Smerdis won't trouble Videssos for as long as he lives."

"You misunderstand, Majesty," Abivard said, and went on to explain Roshnani's idea. The longer he talked, the more animated Sharbaraz' features became; by the time he was through, the rightful King of Kings seemed more nearly himself than he had at any time since his army was forced across the Tutub.

"It might work; by the God, it just might," he said at last. "As you say, it will cost us men who refuse to follow. It will cost more than that, too; without a doubt, any aid we get from Likinios will have a price attached to it. But even so—"

"Aye, even so," Abivard said. Then he added, "I barely knew the Avtokrator's name before we set out on this campaign. I still know next to nothing about him. Has he sons of his own? If he wants to make sure the throne passes to one of them, he may be more inclined to take your side."

"He has four," Sharbaraz answered. "For a Videssian, that's a good number—they take but one wife apiece. He's been fighting a war with Kubrat, up north and east of Videssos the city. I daresay that's why he tried to set the Khamorth against us: to keep us from invading his western provinces while he was busy on the other frontier."

"It worked," Abivard said sorrowfully.

The rightful King of Kings snorted. "Yes, didn't it just?" He bowed very low to Abivard. "I would violate custom if I told the lady Roshnani how much in her debt I am. Therefore I rely on you to pass on to her my gratitude. I shall also convey the same message to your sister." He headed toward the tent flap, plainly intending to go out.

"You mean to visit her now?" Abivard asked.

"Indeed I do," Sharbaraz said, and vanished into the night. Abivard left the royal tent a moment later. He did not head back toward the wagon from which he had just come. But if Sharbaraz was going to call on Denak when he had stayed away since things began going wrong, that was a powerful argument that hope—among other things—had revived in him.

Sharbaraz' army, or the two thirds or so of it that was left, descended on the oasis like a pack of wolves tearing to bits a single chicken. With water, a small ring of fields, and a grove of date palms, the place was ideal for caravans crossing the badlands between Makuran and Videssos. Sharbaraz's men ate everything in sight, and he had to post armed guards around the water hole to keep them from fouling it.

When they rode out again two days later, men and beasts refreshed and water skins all filled, Abivard said, "We'd war with the Videssians more often, I think, if we could get at them more easily."

"Most armies, theirs and ours both, go by way of Vaspurakan," Sharbaraz answered. "The passes through the mountains there are the best invasion routes. But with things going against us, we couldn't hope to get there and get through and still have an army left when we were done."

"I wonder what the Videssians will think when we show up on their border," Abivard said. "Maybe that we've started our own invasion." His smile held no humor. "One day—but not yet."

Abivard looked around. Even battered as it was from desertion and defeat, Sharbaraz's army numbered several thousand. If they threw themselves headlong against the Videssians and took them by surprise, they could do a good deal of damage before they were overwhelmed. But, as he had said, that was not the plan ... for now. If they were to regain Makuran, they needed Videssos' help.

Sharbaraz peered eastward. "If the charts and the guides don't lie, one more oasis, two days' ride from here, then a couple of more days of scrub, and then Serrhes—a different Empire, a different world."

"Do you speak Videssian, Majesty?" Abivard asked. He could follow the Khamorth dialects after a fashion, but they were cousins to his own language. Of Videssian he knew nothing.

But Sharbaraz rattled off several sentences in a smooth, purring tongue that rather reminded Abivard of wine gurgling out of a jar: glug, glug, glug. To his relief, the rightful King of Kings dropped back into Makuraner. "I was tutored in it, aye; my father thought it something I needed to know. A fair number of nobles and merchants speak it, especially in the east and south of the realm. Some of the Videssian grandees know Makuraner, too."

"That's a relief," Abivard said. "I was afraid I'd be the same as a deaf-mute all the time we were there."

"No, you'll manage," Sharbaraz told him. "And Videssian isn't that hard to pick up, though some of the sounds are hard for us to pronounce." He lisped and hissed to show what he meant, then went on, "But Videssians can't say *sh*, so it evens out. The language is very good for putting across delicate shades of meaning. I don't know whether that's because they use it so much to quarrel about the exact nature of their god Phos, or whether they quarrel the way they do because Videssian lets them. Which came first, the sheep or the lamb?"

"I don't know," Abivard answered. "I wasn't cut out to be a wise man; whenever I start thinking about complicated things, my wits seize up like a water wheel clogged with mud."

Sharbaraz laughed. "Most of the time, simple is better," he agreed. "If things were simple, I'd have taken my father's throne and that would have been that. But things aren't simple that way, and so we have to face the complications of Videssos."

Abivard pointed to a cloud of dust ahead, just at the edge of visibility. "We may have to face them sooner than we expected. What's that?"

"I don't know," Sharbaraz said in a hollow voice, "but it looks like an army to me." He slammed a fist down on his armored thigh. "How could they have learned we were coming? We can't put up much of a fight against a foe that's ready for us, not now."

Scouts were already riding forward to take the measure of the new threat. After a few minutes, one of them came galloping back toward the main body of the army. Abivard was shocked to see him laughing fit to burst.

Sharbaraz saw that, too, and purpled in fury. "Have you gone mad?" he shouted at the scout. "They're going to beat us like carpets, and you laugh?"

"Majesty, I crave your pardon," the scout said, but he didn't stop laughing. Tears of mirth cut clean tracks through the dust and grime on his cheeks. "That's no army up ahead, Majesty, just a big herd of wild asses raising a cloud, same as if they were cavalry."

Sharbaraz gaped, then laughed himself, a high, shrill cackle that seemed made up of concentrated essence of relief. "Asses, you say? By the God, they made asses out of us."

"Let's make them pay for their presumption," Abivard exclaimed. "They're fresh meat, after all, and we haven't seen much of that for a while. Hunting them would be fitting punishment for frightening us out of our wits."

"So ordered!" Sharbaraz said. Archers pounded after the animals, which fled across the scrubby ground. Watching the asses gallop away in terror made Abivard wish all foes could be so easily overcome.

Abivard was never quite sure just when the army crossed into Videssian territory: one stretch of arid landscape looked much like another. When the soldiers came to a village, though, all possible doubt disappeared: along with the scattered stone houses stood a larger building with a wooden spire topped by a gilded dome—a temple to Phos, the Videssian god of good.

The people had disappeared along with the doubt; dust trails in the distance showed the direction in which they had fled. "Nice to know we still look like a conquering army to someone," Abivard remarked.

Zal, who was riding close by, clicked his tongue between his teeth a couple of times. "This from the trusting young lord who let the tax collector into his stronghold without even checking how sharp his fangs were? Going off to war has coarsened you, lad." He grinned to show he meant no harm by the words.

"You're probably right," Abivard answered. "Once you watch your hopes bounce up and down a few times, you're not as sure things will all turn out for the best as you used to be."

"Isn't that the truth?" Zal said. "It's too cursed bad, but it's so."

From then on, Sharbaraz ordered the scouts to carry shields of truce so the Videssians would learn as quickly as might be that he had come as a supplicant, not an invader. That forethought soon proved its worth. Early the next morning, a scout came back not with the report of a herd of wild asses, but with a Videssian officer in tow.

Like a lot of Sharbaraz's men, Abivard stared curiously at the first Videssian he had ever seen. The fellow was mounted on a medium-good horse, with a medium-good mailshirt worn above leather trousers. He had a bow ready to grab, a quiver on his back, and a curved sword at his belt.

His helmet was halfway between the standard Makuraner cone pattern and a smooth round dome. No veil or iron links descended from it, so Abivard got a good look at his features. His skin was slightly paler than that of most Makuraners, his nose on the thin side, and his face nearly triangular, sloping down from a wide forehead to a chin of almost feminine delicacy. A fringe of beard outlined that chin and his jaw.

"Do you speak my language?" Sharbaraz asked in Makuraner.

"Aye, a bit," the Videssian answered. "Few on this frontier don't." He used Makuraner well enough, though his accent sometimes made him hard to understand. One of his eyebrows—so thin and smoothly curved that Abivard wondered if he plucked it into shape—rose. "But I ought to be the one asking the questions. For starters, who are you and what are you doing in my country with an army tagging along?" His quick, scornful glance up and down the line of riders said he saw better-looking armies every day of the week, and sometimes twice a day. He added, "Which side of your civil war were you on?"

"I am Sharbaraz, rightful King of Kings of Makuran, and I was on my own side," Sharbaraz proclaimed. Abivard had the satisfaction of watching the Videssian's mouth drop open like a toad's when it snapped at a fly. Sharbaraz went on, "I have come to Videssos to seek the Avtokrator Likinios' aid in restoring me to the throne that is properly mine. Surely he will understand the importance of preserving unbroken the legitimate line of succession."

The Videssian stayed silent for most of a minute before he replied. Later, when Abivard came to understand that Videssians rarely kept quiet for any reason, he would have a deeper appreciation of the depth of shock that conveyed. At last the fellow managed to put words together: "Uh, Lord Sarbaraz—"

As Sharbaraz had said, Videssians couldn't make the *sh* sound. But the officer's accent was not what offended Abivard.

"Say 'your Majesty,' as you would for your own Emperor," he growled.

"Your Majesty," the Videssian said at once. "Your Majesty, I'm not the man to treat with you; the lord with the great and good mind knows that's so." His laugh came rueful. "I'm not the man to stop you, either. When the villagers rode into Serrhes screaming that all the soldiers in the world were heading that way, the *epoptes*—the city governor, you'd say—figured a pack of desert bandits had got bold; he sent me out to deal with them. I have fifty men back there, no more."

"Who will treat with me, then?" Sharbaraz asked. "Is this *epoptes* of yours a man of sufficient rank to discuss matters of state?"

"No," the Videssian said, then added, "your Majesty. But I hear tell Likinios' eldest son is traveling through the westlands, keeping things on an even keel here while the Avtokrator, Phos bless him, campaigns against the heathens of Kubrat. Hosios will be able to deal with you."

"Indeed." Sharbaraz regally inclined his head. "Will he come to the town of Serrhes? If so, when?"

"Drop me in the ice if I know," the officer said, apparently an oath but not one Abivard recognized. "If he wasn't planning to come there in his progress, though, I expect he'll change his mind when old Kalamos—sorry, your Majesty, that's the city governor—sends a letter off to wherever he is now, telling him you've come into the Empire."

"I suspect you may be right," Sharbaraz said. He and the Videssian soldier both laughed at the understatement.

Serrhes struck Abivard as being halfway between a stronghold town and a real city. The whole perimeter was fortified, with a wall higher and thicker than Vek Rud stronghold boasted. Inside, on the highest ground in the place, stood a massive citadel where warriors could retreat in case the outer wall was breached.

"Pretty strong fortress to stick out in the middle of nowhere," he remarked to Sharbaraz.

The rightful King of Kings chuckled. "The only reason the Videssians would site a fortress here is to protect their land from us." Abivard thought about that, then nodded. Belonging to a people who could inspire such precautions made him proud.

By the smooth way in which the *epoptes* took over the provisioning of Sharbaraz's men, he might have had Makuraner armies dropping in for a visit every other month. Some of the grain came from the storerooms in the cellar of the citadel; soon pack animals were fetching more from farther east. The spring that made the town possible at all was barely adequate for the sudden influx. Videssian guards made sure no one took more than his fair share. They were stern but, Abivard had to admit, just.

Hosios arrived a bit more than two weeks after Sharbaraz's shrunken host came to Serrhes. The *epoptes*, a plump little man, went about his town in a transport of nervousness: if the protocol for the meeting between the Avtokrator's eldest son and the claimant to the title of King of Kings of Makuran broke down, the blame would all land on him, for both primary parties to the meeting were of rank too exalted for any to stick to them. Had Abivard been wearing Kalamos' boots, he would have been nervous, too.

As a matter of fact, he *was* nervous, and for reasons related to those of the city governor. Coming to Videssos had been Roshnani's idea, which he had sold to Sharbaraz; if it did not bring the results for which he had hoped, Sharbaraz would remember. Of course, if it didn't bring those results, Sharbaraz would not be powerful enough to make his displeasure felt.

The ceremony the *epoptes* devised was as elaborately formal as a wedding. Hosios rode out from the city, accompanied by Kalamos and a ceremonial guard of twenty men. At the same time, Sharbaraz advanced from the tent city that had sprung up outside Serrhes, along with Abivard and twenty men of his own.

"Ah," Sharbaraz murmured as the Avtokrator's eldest son drew near, "he wears the red boots. Do you see, Abivard?"

"I see they *are* red," Abivard answered. "Does that mean something special?"

Sharbaraz nodded. "The Videssians have ceremonial usages of their own, as complicated as ours. Only an Avtokrator may wear boots all of red, without black stripes or something of the sort. Hosios is junior Emperor in his own right, in other words. I am treating with an equal, at least in theory."

Abivard didn't need that explained to him. In practice, Likinios made the decisions. Abivard said, "I'm glad Hosios speaks Makuraner. Otherwise I'd be as useful here as a fifth leg on a horse."

Sharbaraz waved him to silence; Hosios was drawing close enough to hear. He was about Abivard's age, with a narrow-chinned Videssian face made distinctive by a sword scar on one cheek and by eyes that gave the strong impression of having seen everything at least once. He wore a golden circlet that did not quite hide the fact that his hairline had begun to recede.

Because Sharbaraz had entered Videssos, he spoke first. "I, Sharbaraz, King of Kings, good and pacific, fortunate and pious, to whom the God has given great fortune and a great realm, a man formed in the image of the God, greet you, Hosios Avtokrator, my brother."

Hosios inclined his head; evidently he knew not only the Makuraner language but also the flowery rhetoric that flourished in Sharbaraz's realm. He said, "In the name of Likinios, Avtokrator of the Videssians, viceregent of Phos on earth, I, Hosios Avtokrator, greet you, Sharbaraz by right of birth King of Kings, my brother."

He held out his hand. Sharbaraz urged his horse forward a pace or two and clasped it, without hesitation but also without joy. Abivard understood that. The Videssians had flowery ceremonial language of their own, but he had caught the implications of *by right of birth King of Kings*. It sounded well, but promised nothing. If at some future time Likinios saw wisdom in recognizing Smerdis, he could do so with a clear conscience, for having the birthright of a King of Kings was not the same as actually being one.

Sharbaraz released Hosios' hand and introduced Abivard to him. Abivard bowed in the saddle, saying "Your Majesty—"

"I am styled 'young Majesty,' to distinguish me from my father," Hosios broke in.

"Your pardon, young Majesty. I was about to say, I never expected to have the honor of meeting a Videssian Avtokrator, save perhaps on the battlefield—and then the introduction would have been edged with iron, not words."

"Aye—sharper than the one of us or the other would have liked, that's certain." Hosios sized up Abivard with the knowing eyes that, along with his scar, said he had been on a few battlefields in his time: perhaps against the Kubratoi, whoever they were: to Abivard, at any rate, no more than a name.

Sharbaraz said, "You will understand, Hosios—" With his rank, he was entitled to use the junior Avtokrator's name unadorned. "—I would sooner meet you as foe and outright enemy myself. You would know I was lying if I said otherwise. But since fate compels me to come before you as a beggar, I own that is what I am." He bowed his proud head to Hosios.

The junior Avtokrator reached out to set a hand on his shoulder. "No harm will come to you and yours in Videssos,

Sharbaraz: may Phos the lord with the great and good mind
damn me to the eternal ice if I lie. Whatever else befalls, I
promise you a mansion in Videssos the city and estates in the
countryside, with appropriate lodging throughout the Empire for
the men who have followed you here."

"You are generous," Sharbaraz said, again with something
less than a whole heart. Again, Abivard had no trouble figuring
out why: Hosios proposed to dissolve the Makuraner army like
a small spoonful of salt poured into a great tun of water. After
a moment's pause to show he also grasped that point, Sharbaraz
resumed: "But I did not come here seeking a new home for me
and mine. I came to beseech your aid that I might return to
Makuran, where I already have a home."

"I know that," Hosios answered calmly. "Were it in my
power, you would have what you ask for on the instant. But my
power, though large, does not reach so far. You will have to wait
on my father's will."

Sharbaraz inclined his head once more. "Your father is well
served in you. The God grant he realize it."

"In such ways as you can in your distress, you are generous
to me," Hosios said, smiling. "One would have to be a very bold
man indeed to contemplate going against my father's will. As
with my power, my boldness is large, but does not extend so
far."

Beside him, Kalamos the *epoptes* nodded vigorously. He had
a good and healthy respect for the Avtokrator's power. Abivard
approved of that. He wished a certain mintmaster back in
Mashiz had shown similar respect for the power of the King of
Kings.

"May I ask a question, Majesty?" he murmured to Sharbaraz.
When his sovereign nodded, he turned to Hosios and said, "If
Likinios has such power and boldness as you describe, young
Majesty, what could keep him from coming to our aid?"

He didn't know what sort of answer he had expected, but it
was not the blunt reply Hosios gave him: "Two things spring to
mind, eminent sir. One, your principal there may not offer concessions substantial enough to make it worth our while to restore
him to the throne. And two, related to one, the war against the
Kubratoi has caused a hemorrhage in the treasury. Videssos may
simply lack the funds to do as you desire, however much we
might want to."

"We in Makuran speak of Videssos as a nation of merchants,"
Sharbaraz said. "I regret to say it seems to be so."

Hosios had his own kind of pride, not the haughty arrogance a Makuraner noble would have displayed, but a certainty all the more impressive for being understated. "If we were but a nation of merchants, Makuran would have conquered us long since. I would be impolite to remind you who seeks whose aid, and so I would never presume to do such a thing."

"Of course," Sharbaraz said sourly. Hosios' not-reminder could scarcely have hit any harder had the junior Avtokrator held up a sign.

"We are friends here, or at least not enemies," Hosios said. "I bid you to a feast this evening, to be held in the residence of the noble *epoptes* here. Bring a score of your chiefest captains with you, or even half again as many. And, since I am told you and your brother-in-law have your wives accompanying you, bring them, as well. Many of the leading citizens of Serrhes will have their ladies with them. My own wife is back in Videssos the city, or I would do the same."

"This is not our custom." Sharbaraz' voice was stiff. Abivard nodded.

Hosios ignored both of them. He said, "We have a proverb: 'When in Videssos the city, eat fish.' If you come to the Videssian Empire, should you not accommodate yourselves to our usages?"

Sharbaraz hesitated. As soon as he did, Abivard knew another fight was lost. This time, he resolved to get ahead of the rightful King of Kings. "Thank you for the invitation, young Majesty," he said to Hosios. "Roshnani will be honored to attend, especially since it's you who command it."

Hosios beamed and turned to Sharbaraz. The rightful King of Kings gave Abivard a so-you've-had-your-revenge look, then yielded with as much grace as he could muster: "Where Abivard's wife may go, how can his sister be left behind? Denak, too, will conform to your customs this evening."

"Excellent!" The junior Avtokrator carefully refrained from sounding smug or triumphant. "I shall see you at sunset this evening, then."

"At sunset." Sharbaraz carefully refrained from sounding enthusiastic.

"I'm so excited!" Roshnani squeaked as she walked through the streets of Serrhes toward the *epoptes'* residence. She stared at the golden dome atop a temple to Phos. "I never imagined I would see a Videssian city from the inside."

"I hoped I would, after taking it in war," Abivard said, "but not this way—never as guest to the Avtokrator's son."

A couple of paces ahead, Denak strode along beside Sharbaraz. By the casual glances she cast this way and that, she might have been born in Serrhes and come back to it after a few months' absence: she appeared interested but a long way from fascinated. Unlike her sister-in-law, she took the invitation to Hosios' supper as no more than her due.

The officers who trailed after Sharbaraz and Abivard imitated Denak in one respect: just as she did her best to seem unimpressed with the Videssian city, so they tried to pretend that she and Roshnani were not with their party. Their idea of society was rigidly masculine, and they aimed to keep it that way.

Kalamos' residence and Serrhes' main temple to Phos looked at each across the market square below the hillock in which the citadel stood. The temple was impressive, with a large dome surmounting on pendentives walls thick enough to make another citadel in time of need. By contrast, the *epoptes'* residence was severely plain: whitewashed walls, slit windows, a red tile roof. If such a meager home was a perquisite of office, Abivard wondered how the Videssians managed to lure anyone into the job.

His perspective changed when he went inside. Videssians confined the loveliness of their homes to the interior, where only those so bidden could observe it. Mosaics of herding and hunting scenes brightened the floors, while tapestries made the walls seem to come alive. The residence was built around a courtyard. A fountain splashed there, in the middle of a formal garden. Torches did their brave best to turn evening to noontime.

Hosios and Kalamos greeted the Makuraner leaders as they arrived. Beside the *epoptes* stood his wife, a plump, pleasant-faced woman who seemed pleased to greet Roshnani and Denak and a trifle puzzled—though politeness masked most of that—the rest of the guests had no women with them. Other officials, as Hosios had said, also had their wives—and sometimes, along with their sons, their young and pretty daughters—at the supper. They all took that utterly for granted, which bemused even Abivard, who thought of himself as a liberal in such matters.

"It's what you're used to, I suppose," Sharbaraz said after accepting greetings from yet another highborn Videssian lady. "But, by the God, I'll need a while to get used to this."

Not all the Videssians spoke Makuraner, nor did all the Makuraners know Videssian. Those who had both languages interpreted for those who did not. Some from each group hung back, resolutely unsociable, suspicious of their longtime foes, or both.

No one hung back from the wine. Servants circulated with trays of already-filled cups. Some of the wine had a strong taste of resin. A Makuraner-speaking Videssian explained to Abivard, "We use pitch to seal the wine jars and to keep the precious stuff inside from turning to vinegar. I hadn't noticed the flavor for years, till you reminded me of it."

"It's what you're used to," Abivard said, echoing his sovereign.

The main course for the banquet was a pair of roasted kids. As the second highest-ranking Makuraner, Abivard was seated by Kalamos. He turned to the *epoptes* and said, "I recognize garlic and cloves and the flavoring, but not the rest of the sauce."

"The oil is from the olive," Kalamos answered, "which I know is not common in Makuran. And the rest is garum, brought hither all the way from Videssos the city."

"Garum?" That was not a word Abivard knew. "What goes into it? It has a tang not quite like anything I've tasted." He smacked his lips, unsure whether he liked it or not.

"It's made from fish," the *epoptes* explained. If he had stopped there, everything would have been fine, but he went on, "They make it by salting down fish innards in pots open to the air. When the fish are fully ripe, a liquid forms above them, which is then drawn off and bottled. A great delicacy, don't you agree?"

Abivard needed a moment to realize that, when the helpful Videssian said *ripe*, he meant *putrid*. His stomach got the message before his head did. He gulped wine, hoping to quell the internal revolt before it was well begun. Then he shoved his plate away. "I find I'm full," he said.

"What was he saying about fish in the sauce?" asked Roshnani, who had been talking in very simple Makuraner with the *epoptes'* wife.

"Never mind," Abivard answered. "You don't want to know." He watched the Videssians downing their young goat with gusto, sauce and all. They really thought they were giving their guests the best they had. And in fact, the meal, while strange to his palate, hadn't tasted bad—but after he found out what garum was, he couldn't bring himself to eat another bite of kid.

Fruit candied in honey and cheese made safer choices. Minstrels played pipes and pandouras and sang songs that struck the ear pleasantly, even if Abivard couldn't understand the words. The sweets and wine helped drown the memory of fermented fish sauce.

Sharbaraz and Hosios had spent the banquet in earnest conversation, sometimes in the language of one, sometimes in that of the other. They seemed to get on well, which Abivard thought an advantage. It would have been a bigger one, though, had Hosios had authority to do anything much without Likinios' leave.

Sharbaraz bowed to his host as he stood to go. Abivard and the rest of the Makuraners imitated their sovereign. As they headed out of the *epoptes'* residence, a Videssian woman let out a short shriek and then exclaimed volubly in her own language.

"Oh, by the God!" Sharbaraz clapped a hand to his forehead. "She says Bardiya stuck his hand between her—well, felt of her where he shouldn't have. Get that fool out of here, the rest of you."

As some of the Makuraner officers manhandled Bardiya out into the night, he howled, "What is she complaining about? She must be a whore, or she wouldn't show herself to other men like that. She—" Somebody clapped a hand over his mouth, muffling whatever else he had to say.

"Forgive him, I beg you, kind lady, and you also, my generous hosts," Sharbaraz said rapidly. "He must have drunk too much wine, or he would not have been so rude and foolish." To Abivard, he muttered under his breath, "This is what comes of banquets run by customs other than our own."

Hosios said, "Perhaps it would be wiser if that man did not come into Serrhes again. One lapse is fairly easily forgiven. More than one—"

Sharbaraz bowed. "It shall be as you say, of course. Thank you for your gracious understanding."

Torchbearers lighted the Makuraners' way back to their encampment. Once they were out of earshot of the *epoptes'* residence, Abivard said, "That idiot might have ruined everything."

"Don't I know it," Sharbaraz answered. "Lucky Bardiya didn't try to drag her back among the flowers. That would have been a pretty picture, wouldn't it—a rape at a feast given us by our benefactors?"

"If he'd done that, he should have answered for it with his head," Denak said. "As it is, he ought to suffer more than just being hustled away in disgrace." Her voice had a brittle edge;

Abivard remembered what she had endured from Sharbaraz's guards back at Nalgis Crag stronghold.

"What do you suggest?" Sharbaraz asked, though his tone gave no assurance he would heed what she said.

"Stripes, well laid on," Denak answered at once. "Use him to teach the lesson and it won't have to be taught again."

"Too harsh." Sharbaraz sounded like a man dickering over figs in the market square. "Here's what I'll do: come morning, I'll have him apologize to that lady as if she were Likinios' wife, right down to knocking his head on the floor. That may even humiliate him worse than a flogging, and it won't cost me as much goodwill in the army."

"It's not enough," Denak said darkly.

"It's better than nothing, and more than I expected you'd get," Roshnani said. Having her sister-in-law speak up for what Sharbaraz had proposed made Denak nod, too, a sharp, abrupt motion that showed consent without enthusiasm.

"We think of the Videssians as devious double-dealers," Sharbaraz said. "Like a coin that has two sides. In their poems and chronicles, they look on us as fierce and bloodthirsty. Most times, that's a good reputation for us to have. Now, though, we have to seem civilized enough by their standards to be worth helping. A formal apology should do the job."

"It's not enough," Denak repeated, but then she let the argument go.

Hosios conveyed his recommendations, whatever they were, to a courier to take to his father in the distant northeast of the Empire of Videssos. Not long after he did so, he, too, departed from Serrhes: he had other things to do besides attending to a ragtag band of Makuraners. After he was gone, the town seemed to shrink in on Abivard, as if the world outside had altogether forgotten him and his companions.

Summer turned to fall. The local farmers harvested their meager crops. Without the wagonloads of grain that came into Serrhes every day, its Makuraner guests would have starved.

Fall brought rain. Herders—much like their Makuraner counterparts—drove their cattle and sheep to the fields that showed the most new green. Soon the winds from out of the west—from Makuran—would bring snow instead of rain. The climate might be somewhere close to as harsh as that round Vek Rud stronghold . . . and tents were worse suited than castles to riding out winter blizzards.

Rain turned roads to mud. Even had Sharbaraz and his host wished to pull up stakes and go somewhere new, they would have been hard-pressed to move far or fast through the gluey, clinging ooze. Only when the first freeze turned the mud hard did travel cautiously begin again.

About a month after that first freeze, a courier came into Serrhes to report that the Avtokrator Likinios was little more than a day outside of town. The *epoptes* went into a cleaning fit, like a village woman who sees from her window her fussy mother-in-law approaching. As if by sorcery—and Abivard wasn't altogether sure Kalamos hadn't resorted to magecraft—wreaths and bunting appeared on the streets that led from the gates to the square below the citadel: just the streets Likinios was likeliest to travel.

Sharbaraz also did his best to bring order and cleanliness to his camp outside the wall. Even after that best was done, the camp still struck Abivard as a sad, ragged place: as if a broken dream had been badly animated and brought halfway to life. But he held his peace, for Likinios, should he choose, had the power to revitalize Sharbaraz's cause in full. Anything that might prompt him to do so was worth trying.

When Likinios did reach Serrhes, the ceremonial ordained for his meeting with Sharbaraz was similar to that which Hosios had employed. With Abivard and his honor guard, Sharbaraz rode out from his camp to greet the Avtokrator, who came forth from the city walls.

Abivard had looked for an older version of Hosios, just as Peroz, in both looks and style, had been an older version of Sharbaraz. But Likinios, although by his face he had plainly sired his eldest son, as plainly came from a different mold.

His features were individually like those of Hosios, but taken as a whole gave Abivard the impression that the Avtokrator was totting up how much the ceremony cost—and not caring for the answer he got. Likinios wore gilded armor, but on him it seemed more a costume than something he would don naturally.

"I welcome you to Videssos, your Majesty," he said in fair Makuraner. His voice was tightly controlled, not, Abivard thought, because he was using a language foreign to him but because that was the sort of man he was. The word that ran through Abivard's mind was *calculator*.

"I thank you for your kindness and generosity to me and my people, your Majesty," Sharbaraz replied.

"You have already dealt with the *epoptes* here, so I need not introduce him to you." Likinios sounded relieved at not having to spend any unnecessary words.

"Your Majesty, I have the honor to present to you my brother-in-law the lord Abivard, *dihqan* of Vek Rud domain," Sharbaraz said. Abivard bowed in the saddle to the Avtokrator.

Likinios grudged him a nod in return. "You're a long way from home, sir," he observed. Abivard stared at him. Could he know where in Makuran Vek Rud domain lay? Abivard would not have bet against it.

Sharbaraz said, "All my men in this your realm are a long way from home, your Majesty. With your gracious assistance, we shall return there one day in the not too distant future."

The Avtokrator studied him for a while before replying. Likinios' eyes didn't see just surfaces; Abivard had the feeling they measured like a cloth merchant checking the exact length of a bolt—and reckoned up cost with the same impersonal precision. At last Likinios said, "If you can show me how helping you is worth my while, I'll do it. Otherwise—" He let the word hang in the air.

"Your son was more forthcoming on this, your Majesty," Sharbaraz said. He did not presume to call Likinios by name, as he had Hosios.

"My son, as yet, is young." The Avtokrator made a sharp chopping gesture with his right hand. "He has no trouble deciding what he wants, but he has not yet learned that everything has its price."

"Surely having a King of Kings in Mashiz who was grateful for your generosity would be worth a pretty price," Sharbaraz said.

"Gratitude is worth its weight in gold," Likinios said. Abivard thought the Videssian ruler was agreeing with Sharbaraz until he realized words had no weight.

Sharbaraz also needed a moment to catch that. When he did, he frowned and said, "Surely honor and justice are not words without meaning to a man who has held the imperial throne for more than twenty years."

"No indeed," Likinios answered. "But other words also have meaning to me: risk and cost and reward not least among them. Putting you back on your throne won't be easy or cheap. If I decide to do it, I expect to be rewarded with more than gratitude, your Majesty." The way he aimed the honorific at Sharbaraz only emphasized that the rightful King of Kings would not be truly entitled to it without Videssian aid.

"If you fail to help me now, and I reclaim the throne even so—" Sharbaraz began.

"I'll take that chance," Likinios said, his voice flat.

Abivard leaned over to whisper to Sharbaraz: "Bluff and bluster will get you nowhere with this one, Majesty. All that's real to him is what he can see and touch and count. His son may be sentimental—his son might not even make a bad Makuraner, if it comes to that—but he's the cold-hearted Videssian in all our tales come to life."

"I fear you may be right," Sharbaraz whispered back. He raised his voice to address Likinios once more: "What could be more valuable to Videssos than quiet along your western frontier?"

"We have that now," the Avtokrator answered. "We're likely to keep it as long as Smerdis rules, too."

Sharbaraz grunted, as if kicked in the belly. Also as if kicked in the belly, he needed time to find the breath for a reply. "I had not looked for your Majesty to be so ... blunt."

Likinios shrugged. "My father Hosios had me work in the treasury for a time before the throne came to me. Once you're around numbers for a while, you lose patience with twisting words around."

"That's not what Smerdis found," Sharbaraz said with a sour laugh. He pointed to Likinios. "You took the throne from your father, and you want your son to have it from you. But what if some treasury official not of your house takes courage from what Smerdis did in Mashiz and steals the throne that ought to belong to Hosios? If you encourage usurpers in Makuran, you encourage them in Videssos, too."

"There is the first argument of sense you've put forward," Likinios remarked. Abivard felt like hugging himself with glee. That wasn't Sharbaraz's argument, it was Roshnani's, at least in essence. How she would laugh—how she would brag!—when he told her what the Avtokrator of the Videssians had said about it.

"How much weight does it have?" Sharbaraz asked.

"By itself, not enough," Likinios said flatly. "Smerdis will give me peace in the west as well as you will. I need that peace for now, so I can properly deal with the Kubratoi once for all. Their horsemen raid all the way down to the suburbs of Videssos the city. A century and a half ago, the cursed savages forced their way south of the Istros River and set up their robbers' nest in land rightfully Videssian. I aim to take it back if it costs me every goldpiece in the treasury."

"This I understand, your Majesty," Abivard said. "We have our own trouble with nomads spilling south over the Degird." Videssos had subsidized those nomads, but he forbore to mention it. His sovereign needed Videssian aid.

Likinios' eyes swung away from Sharbaraz and onto him. They were red-tracked, pouchy, full of suspicion, but very wise—maybe dangerously wise. Had his father Godarz been filled with bitterness instead of calm, he might have had eyes like those. The Avtokrator said, "Then you will also understand why I say Videssos' aid has a price attached."

"And what price will you seek to extract from me?" Sharbaraz asked. "Whatever you ask of me, you may be fairly sure I will tell you aye. But you may also be sure I shall remember."

"And you, your Majesty, may be sure I am sure of both those things." Likinios' smile stretched his mouth wide but did not reach those disconcerting eyes. "A nice calculation, don't you think?—how much to demand so that I show a profit from the arrangement and yet keep from enraging you afterward." He shrugged. "We need not decide the matter now. After all, we have the whole winter ahead of us."

"You look forward to the dicker," Abivard blurted. Imagining a Videssian Avtokrator as devious was easy. Imagining him as a merchant in the bazaar was something else again.

But Likinios nodded. "Of course I do."

Snow swirled through the streets as Sharbaraz and Abivard rode toward the *epoptes'* residence. Abivard was beginning to pick up some Videssian. He laughed after he and the rightful King of Kings went past a couple of locals chatting with each other. Sharbaraz gave him a curious look. "What's so funny?"

"Didn't I understand them?" Abivard said. "Weren't they complaining about what a hard winter this is?"

"Oh, I see." His sovereign managed a smile, but a thin one. "I would have said the same thing till I saw what you endured every year."

In front of Kalamos' home, a servitor took charge of the Makuraners' horses. Another servitor, bowing deeply, admitted them to the residence, then made haste to shut the door behind them. Abivard heartily approved of that; ducts under the floor carried heat from a central fire to keep the *epoptes'* residence if not warm, then at least not cold.

That second servant led them to the chamber where Likinios awaited. They could have found the room without his help; they had been here a good many times before. The servant turned to Abivard. "Shall I bring hot spiced wine, eminent sir?" he asked in Videssian—he knew Abivard was trying to learn his tongue.

"Yes, please, that be good," Abivard said. He wouldn't be writing Videssian poetry any time soon, but he was starting to be able to say things other people could follow.

Likinios bowed to Sharbaraz, then nodded to Abivard. When the formalities were done, the Avtokrator said, "Shall we go back to the map?"

He spoke of the square of parchment as Abivard might have of a fine horse, or Ganzak the smith of a well-made sword: it was his passion, the place where his interest centered. In most circumstances, Abivard would have judged that a spiritless thing to have as a controlling interest. But not now. In the duel Likinios waged with his Makuraner guests, maps were tools of war no less than horses and swords.

As he always did, Abivard admired the Videssians' lucid cartography. His own people didn't worry so much about portraying every inch of ground, perhaps because so much of the ground in Makuran held little worth portraying. But Likinios had detailed pictures of land Videssos didn't even own—yet.

"I knew we would come down to haggling over valleys in Vaspurakan," Sharbaraz said gloomily.

"You'd not have the wit to be King of Kings if you didn't know it," the Avtokrator retorted. He pointed to the map again. The mountain valleys of Vaspurakan ran east and west between Videssos and Makuran, up to the north of Serrhes. They offered the best trade routes—which also meant the best invasion routes—between the two lands. These days most of those routes lay in Makuraner hands.

Sharbaraz said, "Along with the lay of the land, Vaspurakan grows good fighting men. I hate even to think of giving them up."

"Caught between your realm and mine, they have to be good fighting men," Likinios said, which drew a startled chuckle from Abivard; he hadn't thought the Avtokrator a man to crack any jokes, even small ones. Likinios continued, "The Vaspurakaners also worship Phos. Videssos grieves to see them under the dominion of those who will spend eternity in Skotos' ice for their misbelief."

"I think Videssos grieves more over that than the Vaspurakaners do," Sharbaraz answered. "They think you worship your god the wrong way, and complain that you try to make them follow your errors."

"Our usages are not errors," Likinios said stiffly, "and no matter what they are, you, your Majesty, are in a poor position to point them out to me."

Sharbaraz sighed. "That's true, I fear." Reluctantly, he walked over to the map. "Show me again what you propose to wring from me in exchange for your aid."

Likinios ran his finger down a zigzagging line from north to south. He was not modest in his demands. At the moment, Makuran held about four fifths of Vaspurakan. Were Sharbaraz to accept what Likinios wanted, that holding would shrink to less than half the disputed country.

Abivard said, "Tell him no, your Majesty. What he asks is robbery, no other word for it."

"That is not true," Likinios said. "It is a price for a service rendered. If you do not wish the service, your Majesty, you need not pay the price."

"It is still too high a price," Sharbaraz said. "As I warned you when we first met, did I pay it, I should feel honor-bound to try to recover it when my strength allowed. I tell you this again, your Majesty, so you may be forewarned."

"You'd start that war of revenge for this, eh?" Likinios frowned and paced back and forth. "It could be so."

"It *is* so," Sharbaraz answered. "I pledge my word on it, and the word of a Makuraner noble—unless he be Smerdis—is to be trusted. If you insist, I will pay this price, but we shall have war afterward."

"I cannot afford more war now," Likinios said irritably, spitting out *afford* as if it were a curse. "However much I should like a friendly King of Kings in Mashiz, you tempt me to think an ineffectual one will serve as well."

Abivard studied the map once more. He also listened again in his mind to the way Likinios had spoken. He pointed to a symbol in one of the valleys Likinios sought to claim. "These crossed picks represent a mine, not so?" Likinios nodded. Abivard continued, "What would your Majesty say to a boundary that marched more like this?" He drew his own zigzag line, this one taking in several valleys with mines but not the great stretch of territory to which the Avtokrator wanted to lay claim.

"It still gives away too much," Sharbaraz said.

At the same time Likinios said, "This is not enough."

The two men of royal blood looked at each other. Abivard took advantage of their hesitation: "Your Majesties, isn't a plan that leaves both of you less than happy better than one that satisfies Videssos too well and Makuran not at all, or the other way round?"

"Ah, but if I am not satisfied, I have only to withhold aid and my life goes on anyway, much as it would have without these talks," Likinios said.

"While that's true, your Majesty, if you don't give me aid, you lose the chance to put a King of Kings beholden to you on the throne in Mashiz, and you leave a usurper there as a temptation to every ambitious man in Videssos," Sharbaraz said. "And if you think Smerdis will be grateful to you for not backing me, remember how he treated me."

Likinios scowled and studied the map again. Encouraged because he did not reject the proposal out of hand, Abivard said, "If the precise border I suggested fails to please you, your Majesty, perhaps you will propose one along similar lines. Or perhaps my master the King of Kings, may his years be many and his realm increase, might offer one of his own?"

"How do you speak of the realm's increasing in one breath and ask me to take away a great slice of Vaspurakan in the next?" Sharbaraz asked. But, to Abivard's relief, he did not sound angry. Instead, he walked over and gave the map a long, hard look himself.

Abivard thought serious talk, as opposed to posturing, began then between the King of Kings of Makuran and the Avtokrator of the Videssians. The next time he tried to suggest something to move the talks along, both men stared at him as if he were a drooling idiot. He felt humiliated, but not for long: two days later, they reached an agreement not very far from the one he had outlined on the map with his finger.

Tanshar bowed low to Abivard. "May it please you, lord," the fortune-teller said, "you are being spoken of—complimented, to make myself clear—by our people and the Videssians alike." He bowed. "Always an honor to serve you, and doubly now. What is your wish?"

"Were I to suggest what I propose to you in aid of a King of

Kings rather than an Avtokrator, I should be guilty of treason," Abivard answered.

The fortune-teller nodded, unsurprised. "You want me to learn what I can of the Videssian royal house?"

"Just so," Abivard said. "I want you to scry out, if you can, how long Likinios will remain on the throne and how long Hosios will rule after him."

"I shall try, lord, but I make no guarantees as to the results," Tanshar answered. "As you say, you would be committing treason if you sought to learn these things about the royal house of Makuran. Not only that, you would have a hard time learning them even if you had no fear of treason: the King of Kings will normally surround himself with spells that make divining his future as difficult as possible, in my judgment a sensible measure of self-preservation. I would be most surprised if the Avtokrator did not similarly ward himself."

"I hadn't thought of that," Abivard said unhappily, "but yes, you're likely to be right. Do your best all the same. Perhaps you will have better luck than a Videssian mage might, for I'd guess the Avtokrator would be best protected against the kind of sorcery usual in his own country."

"No doubt that's so, lord," Tanshar agreed, "but we, plainly, are the next greatest magical threat to the Avtokrator's well-being, so his future may be shielded against our magecraft, as well."

"I understand," Abivard said. "If you fail, we're no worse off than we would be otherwise. But if you succeed, we'll have learned something important about how far we can rely on the Videssians. Do the best you can; that's all I can say."

"Fair enough," Tanshar said. "I appreciate your not expecting the impossible of me. What I can do, I shall do. When do you want me to make the attempt?"

"As soon as may be."

"Of course, lord," Tanshar said, "although you may not find it exciting to watch. The charms involved have little drama to them, I confess, and I may have to go through several of them to find one that works—if, indeed, any of them succeeds. As I said, I have no assurance of success in this undertaking. But if you like, I will begin trying this evening after you return from the latest talks between his Majesty and the Avtokrator Likinios."

"That will be fine," Abivard said. Having haggled over what Sharbaraz would yield in exchange for aid, the two men were now dickering over how much aid he would get; Likinios would indeed have made a marvelous rug seller. In the end, Abivard suspected Sharbaraz would make most of the concessions once more. Having the royal blood without ruling Makuran ate at him.

When Abivard went back to Tanshar's tent, he found the fortune-teller waiting for him. "I have assembled a number of means for looking into what may be," Tanshar said. "The God willing, one will pierce not only the veil of future time, but whatever the Videssians may have thrown up around their Avtokrator."

He tried scrying with water, as he had when Abivard brought him Ardini's curse tablet. Since Abivard had touched and dealt with Likinios, Tanshar reckoned him an appropriate link to the Avtokrator of the Videssians. But no matter how still the water in the scrying bowl became, it never gave the fortune-teller and Abivard any picture of what Likinios was doing or how long he might go on doing it.

"I might have known," Tanshar said. "Scrying with water is the simplest way of looking into the future. If the Videssians warded against any of our styles of divination, that would be the one."

He tried again with a clear, faceted crystal in place of the bowl of water. The crystal turned foggy. Abivard did not need to ask anything of the fortune-teller to realize that meant his magical efforts were being blocked. Tanshar replaced the clear crystal with one of chalcedony. "This is a Videssian-style divination," he said. "Perhaps it will have more success."

But it didn't. As he had guessed, the Videssians warded the Avtokrator against their own methods of seeing what lay ahead, too. Next he tried a divination that was in large measure an invocation of the God. Abivard had high hopes for that one: surely the God was stronger than the false deities of good and evil in whom the Videssians believed.

The invocation, though, failed as utterly as had the earlier divinations. "How can that be?" Abivard demanded. "I will not imagine for a moment that the Videssians worship correctly and we do not."

"Nor need you imagine that," Tanshar answered. "The truth is more simple and less dismaying: while the God of course outstrips Phos and Skotos in power, so, also, must the Videssian wizards charged with protecting their ruler surpass me. Together, they and their gods—" He curled his lip in scorn, "—suffice to block my efforts. Had we a stronger Makuraner mage here—"

"Like the one who tried to slay Sharbaraz?" Abivard broke in. "Thank you, but no. I'm sure you will use whatever you find in the service of the rightful King of Kings, not against him."

Tanshar bowed. "You are kind to an old man who never looked to be drawn into the quarrels of the great." His clouded eye but made the smile he donned more rueful. "I wish I could live up to the confidence you place in me."

"You shall. I have no doubt of it," Abivard declared.

"I wish I didn't." Tanshar rummaged in a leather pouch he wore on his belt and came up with a lump of coal that left black smears on his hands. "Perhaps divination by opposites will evade the Videssians' wards," he said. "Few things are more opaque than coal; Likinios' future, however, seems at the moment to be one of them."

He poured the water out of the scrying bowl and set the coal in its place. The dialect of Makuraner in which he murmured his summons to the God was so archaic, Abivard could hardly understand it. He wondered what would happen if the scrying succeeded. Would the lump of coal become transparent, as his clear crystal had grown murky?

With a *snap!* almost like a small bolt of lightning, the coal burst into flame. Tanshar jerked his head away just in time to keep his mustache and bushy eyebrows from getting singed. A pillar of greasy black smoke rose to the roof of his tent.

"Does that tell you anything?" Abivard asked.

"One thing, and that most clearly," Tanshar answered in a shaken voice. "I am not likely to learn how long Likinios will remain Avtokrator, not with any sorcery I have under my control."

Abivard bowed his head, accepting that. But he was the sort who, when thwarted in one direction, would turn to another to gain his ends. "All right, then," he said. "Let's see how long Hosios will reign once he succeeds his father."

Tanshar waited till the coal had burned out, then swept the ashes from the scrying bowl. He swung a small censer full of bitterly aromatic myrrh over the bowl. "I want to purify it before my next attempt," he explained. "No trace of that previous magic may remain."

He began anew with the simplest scrying tool: plain water in the bowl. Together he and Abivard waited for stillness, then touched the bowl and waited again.

Abivard had not placed much faith in this try. He gasped when the water roiled and bubbled, then gasped again when, instead of showing him a scene that would answer his question, it turned thick and red. "Blood!" he said, choking a little.

"You see that, too?" Tanshar said.

"Yes. What does it mean?"

"Unless I'm much mistaken," Tanshar said, sounding sure he was not, "it means Hosios shall not live to wear the Avtokrator's crown and red boots, for, by that conjuration, the blood was surely his."

X

Spring came to Serrhes a couple of weeks earlier than it would have in Vek Rud domain. By the time rain replaced snow and closed the roads for a spell, though, Likinios had brought in a good-sized force of cavalry to join Sharbaraz' men against Smerdis.

At the head of the cavalry regiments was a general who reminded Abivard of a fatter version of Zal: a tough fellow in his fifties, not long on polish but liable to be very good in the field. His name was Maniakes. In spite of that, he didn't look like a Videssian; he was blocky, square-featured, with a truly impressive fleshy promontory of a nose and a tangled gray beard that hung halfway down the front of his mail shirt.

"I'm Videssian enough, thanks," he answered when Abivard asked him about it, "even if all four of my grandparents came out of Vaspurakan."

"But—" Abivard scratched his head. "Don't you worship differently from the Videssians?"

"I do, aye, but my son was raised in Videssos' faith," the officer answered. "From what my grandfathers said, that's a smaller change to make than worshiping the God whom you Makuraners were trying to ram down the throat of Vaspurakan."

"Oh." Abivard wondered if the Makuraner overlords of Vaspurakan still behaved as they had in the days of Maniakes' grandfather. He hoped not. If they did, the folk of that land might be more ready to welcome Videssos than Sharbaraz thought.

With the cavalry came a regiment of engineers with wagons full of carefully sawn timbers and lengths of thick rope and fit-

246

tings of iron and bronze. The men seemed more like mechanics than soldiers. They practiced assembling engines and putting together bridges much more than they went out with bow and spear. In his campaign against Smerdis the year before, Sharbaraz had enjoyed no such aid. That had cost him in the maneuverings between the Tutub and the Tib. It would not cost him this time.

"When do we move out?" Abivard asked the rightful King of Kings after a morning of mock cavalry charges.

"We're ready. The Videssians are ready—and so is their Vaspurakaner general." Sharbaraz made a sour face. He had found out about Maniakes, then. "The trouble is, the Tutub and the Tib aren't ready. This is their flood time. The engineers don't want everything swept away if the flood proves worse than usual—and there's no way to gauge that till it happens."

"The Vek Rud and the Degird wouldn't come into flood so soon," Abivard said. After a moment he went on musingly, "Of course, the snow wouldn't be melting so early in the season up in my part of the world, either." He shrugged, prepared to make the best of it. "More time to spend with Roshnani."

Sharbaraz laughed at him. "Having but one wife along has turned you uxorious. What will the rest of your women think when you go back to your stronghold?"

"They knew she was my favorite before she set out on campaign with us," Abivard said. "I do begin to understand now, as I didn't before, how the Videssians, even the grandees among 'em, make do with but one wife each."

"Some truth to that," Sharbaraz agreed. "Having the wife in question be as clever and lovely as the lady your sister does add to the compensation, I must say."

"You are gracious, Majesty."

"I'm yearning to return to my country," Sharbaraz said. "I wonder what Smerdis is expecting. He'll know we fled to Videssos, of course, and he'll know some of what's been going on here from caravans and single traders. But whether he knows we'll have an imperial army with us when we head west again—that we'll have to find out."

"If he does, he'll be using it to whip up hatred against you," Abivard said. "He'll be calling you things like traitor and renegade."

"All he can call himself is thief and usurper," Sharbaraz answered. "Next to that, he can't do much of a job with the tar brush on me. But you're right—he'll try. Let him." The rightful

King of Kings folded his hands into fists. "I'm looking forward to renewing our acquaintance."

Abivard had always reckoned his own folk pious. He believed in the God and the Prophets Four, he invoked them frequently, and he would not have thought of undertaking anything major without first praying; the same held true for any Makuraner.

But the Videssians were not merely pious, they were ostentatiously pious in a way that was new to him. When their army prepared to sally forth with that of Sharbaraz, the chief prelate of Serrhes came out to bless them in a robe of cloth-of-gold and seed pearls with a blue velvet circle over his heart. Behind him marched a couple of younger men, almost as gorgeously robed, who swung golden censers that distributed puffs of incense widely enough for even Abivard's heathen nostrils to twitch. And behind them came a double line of priests in plain blue robes with cloth-of-gold circles on their breasts. They sang a hymn of praise to Phos. Abivard could not understand all of it, but the music was strong and stirring, a good tune with which to march into battle.

Among all the holy men, the farewell from Kalamos almost got lost in the shuffle. The *epoptes* made his little speech, the Videssian cavalrymen near enough to hear it clapped their hands a couple of times, and he went back to his residence to sign parchments, stamp seals, and probably do his best to forget that the Makuraners had ever disturbed his nearly vegetative peace.

Sharbaraz made his own speech. Pointing to the gold sunburst on blue that fluttered at the head of the Videssian ranks, he said, "Today the lion of Makuran and Videssos' sun go forth together for justice. The God grant we find it soon."

His men cheered, a roar that dwarfed the spatter of applause the Videssians had deigned to dole out to Kalamos. One thing Sharbaraz knew was how to play to a crowd. He waved, made his horse rear, and then turned it toward the west, toward Makuran and home.

His lancers followed. After them came his baggage train, refurbished and supplemented by the Videssians. Their army did not ride directly behind Sharbaraz's, but on a parallel track. That was not just to keep from having to swallow their new allies' dust—it also served to remind Sharbaraz and those who traveled with him that the Videssians were a force in their own right.

Before long, they rubbed that in even more unmistakably. Videssian scouts trotted up to ride alongside the lead detachments of Sharbaraz's force. That did not sit well with Abivard; he pointed to them as they went past and said, "Don't they trust us to keep a proper watch on what lies ahead?"

Sharbaraz sighed. For the first time since he had learned Likinios would aid him, even if at a price, he seemed almost like the hopeless, despairing self he had shown when things went wrong the summer before. He said, "The short answer is, no. The Videssians will do as they please, and we're in no position to call them on any of it."

"You're in overall command of this army," Abivard insisted. "Likinios agreed to that without a murmur, as he was in honor bound to do."

Now Sharbaraz smiled, but the expression seemed more one of pity than amusement. "Every so often, brother-in-law of mine, you remind me that the world of a *dihqan* along the Vek Rud differs from that of Mashiz—or of Videssos the city." He held up a hand before Abivard could get angry. "No, I mean no offense. Your way is surely simpler and more honest. But let me ask you one question: If Maniakes declines to obey an order I give, how am I to compel him?"

Abivard bit down on that like a man breaking a tooth on a pebble in his bowl of mutton stew. As many Videssians were riding west as Makuraners, maybe more. Maniakes could more easily force Sharbaraz to do his bidding than the other way round. If he withdrew, Sharbaraz's Makuraners could not beat Smerdis by themselves. They had proved that the year before.

"I begin to think running a realm may be a deeper sorcery than many over which the mages crow," Abivard said at last. "You have to keep so many things in mind to hope to do it properly—and you have to see them to be able to keep them in mind. That one never occurred to me; maybe I am the innocent you say I am."

Sharbaraz leaned over and set a hand on his arm. "You do fine. Better not to have to look for serpents under every cushion before you sit down."

"If they're there, you'd better look for them," Abivard said.

"Oh, indeed, but I wish they weren't there," Sharbaraz replied. "By the God, when I take Mashiz and the throne, I'll kill every one I find."

"That would be splendid, Majesty; may the day come soon." Abivard rode along for a while in silence. Then he said, "In a way, though, I am sorry to be leaving Videssos so soon."

"What? Why?" Sharbaraz asked sharply. "Has your own realm lost its savor after half a year in another?"

"No, of course not." Abivard's fingers twitched in a gesture of rejection. He went on, "It's just that, because Videssos has around it so many seas, I thought Tanshar's prophecy of something shining across a narrow one might come to pass here. I've already seen fulfilled the other two he gave me."

"If that's your reason, I forgive you," Sharbaraz said, nodding. "But prophecy is a risky business."

"That's so." Abivard remembered he hadn't told his sovereign of the scrying he had had Tanshar do of Hosios' future. He described how the water in the scrying bowl had taken on the semblance of blood.

"Now that's . . . intriguing," Sharbaraz said slowly. "Had Likinios refused me aid, I might have used it against him to claim he, like my father, ran the risk of being the last of his line. But since the Videssians do ride with us, I don't know quite what to make of it or how to employ it. Best simply to bear it in mind, I suppose, till the time comes when it proves of value to me." He paused. "I wonder if Likinios' wizards made similar inquiries into my future, and what they learned if they did."

That was something else that hadn't occurred to Abivard. He bowed in the saddle to the rightful King of Kings. "Majesty, henceforward I leave all the searches for serpents and scorpions to your sharp eyes."

"I'd be more flattered at that if I'd spotted Smerdis," Sharbaraz said. Abivard spread his hands, conceding the point. Every pace their horses took moved them farther west.

Roshnani said, "I'm sorry we're leaving Videssos."

"That's odd." Abivard sat up in her little cubicle in the wagon she shared with Denak. The sudden motion stirred the air and made the lamp's flame flicker. "I said the same thing to the King of Kings earlier today. What are your reasons?"

"Can't you guess?" she asked. "Women there live as your sister and I would."

"Oh." Abivard chewed on that for a little while, then said, "And they also suffer outrages they never would in Makuran. Look what happened to that Videssian lady when Bardiya took her for a woman of no virtue."

"But Bardiya is from Makuran," Roshnani said. "I dare hope, at least, that Videssian men, used to the freedom of their women and not thinking it wrong or sinful, would never behave so."

"I didn't see them doing so, or hear tales of it," Abivard admitted. "But, being a man, I know somewhat of men. If men find themselves around such free women all the time, a good number of them will surely become smooth, practiced seducers of a sort we also do not know in Makuran."

Roshnani bit her lip. "I suppose that is possible," she said. Abivard admired her honesty for admitting it. She went on, "On the other hand, I doubt the Videssians are troubled by problems like the one Ardini caused in your women's quarters last year."

"You're probably right there," he said.

Now she smiled. He did, too, understanding her well. Neither of them was one to deny the other could have a point. Lowering her voice to a whisper, Roshnani said, "Unlike your sister, I don't claim giving women freedom from their quarters will solve all their old problems without causing any new ones. That's not how the world works. But I do think the problems that come will be smaller than the ones that go."

Abivard said, "Do you suppose some women, once freed as you say, might turn into seducers themselves?"

Denak would have got angry at such a suggestion. Roshnani considered it with her usual care. "Very likely some would," she said. "As with men, some are more lecherous than others, and some also less happy with their husbands than they might be." She ran a hand down along his bare chest and belly. "There I proved very lucky."

"And I." He stroked her cheek. He thought of what he had said to Sharbaraz earlier in the day. "With you, I think I'd have no trouble holding to the Videssian custom of having but one wife. My father would laugh at that, I'm sure, but after all, we've been together on this campaign for most of a year, and I've never felt the need for variety." He sighed. "Somehow I doubt, though, that all men are so fortunate."

"Or all women," Roshnani said.

He took her hand in his and guided it a little lower yet. "And what shall we do about that?"

"Again? So soon?" But she was not complaining.

Even the badlands that lay between Videssos' western outposts and the Land of the Thousand Cities donned a ragged cloak of green in springtime. Bees buzzed among flowers that would soon wilt and crumble, not to be seen again till the following year. Horses pulled plants from the sandy ground as they trotted west, saving some of the fodder the army had brought with it.

Maniakes rode up to Sharbaraz and Abivard. With him came a young man, hardly more than a youth, who was his image but for a beard that showed no sign of gray and features thinner and less scarred. He said, "The worst thing Smerdis could do to us would be to poison the wells along the way. We'd have Skotos' own time making it to the Tutub without stopping for water along the way, even at this time of year when the stream beds may yet hold some."

"He won't," Sharbaraz said confidently.

Maniakes raised a bushy eyebrow. "What makes you so sure?" he wondered. Abivard wondered the same thing, but couldn't have been so blunt about asking it.

Sharbaraz said, "The first thing Smerdis thinks of is money. If he poisons the wells, caravans can't cross between Videssos and Makuran, and he can't tax them. Sooner than that, he'll try to find some other way to deal with us."

"It could be so. You know Smerdis better than I do; nobody in Videssos knows much of him at all." Maniakes kept his voice neutral. He turned to the young man who looked like him and asked, "What do you think?"

In slow Makuraner, the young man replied, "I would not give away a soldierly advantage, sir, to gain money later. But some might. As Smerdis was mintmaster, money may matter much to him."

"Well reasoned," Sharbaraz said.

"Indeed," Abivard said. To Videssians, who loved logic-chopping, that was higher praise than it would have been for a Makuraner; he wondered if the same held true for Vaspurakaners who had adopted Videssian ways. In case it didn't, he nodded to the younger man—who was a few years younger than he—and asked Maniakes, "Your son?"

Maniakes bowed in the saddle—Abivard *had* pleased him. He said, "Aye, my eldest. Eminent sir," he said, rendering the Videssian title literally into Makuraner, "and your Majesty, allow me to present to you Maniakes the younger."

"Unfair," Sharbaraz said. "Makuran and Videssos are usually foes, not friends, and one of you on Videssos' side is trouble enough for us. Two seems excessive."

The elder Maniakes chuckled. The younger one murmured, "Your Majesty does me too much credit, to rank me with my father so soon."

Abivard noted the qualification of his modesty. He said, "May I ask a question?" After waiting for the two Maniakai to nod, he went on, "How is it that you both share a name? In Makuran, it's against custom to name a child after a living relative; we fear death may get confused and take the wrong one by mistake."

"The Videssians share that rule with us, I think," Sharbaraz put in.

The elder Maniakes rumbled laughter. "Just goes to show that, even if my line follows Videssian orthodoxy, we're still Vaspurakaners under the skin. Phos made us first of all peoples, and we trust him to know one of us from another, no matter what name we bear. Isn't that so, son?"

"Aye," the younger Maniakes answered, but he said no more and looked uncomfortable at having said so much. Abivard suspected he was less Vaspurakaner under the skin than his father thought. After a while, if a family lived among people different from them, wouldn't that family take on more and more of its neighbors' ways?

Spurred by that thought, he asked the elder Maniakes, "Have you any grandchildren, eminent sir?" He used the same non-Makuraner honorific the general had applied to him.

"No, none yet," Maniakes answered, "though a couple of my boys have wed, as will my namesake here if the girl's father ever stops pretending she's made of gold and pearls rather than flesh and blood."

Even though his own father hadn't so much as named the lady to whom he would—or rather, might—be married, the younger Maniakes got a soft, dreamy look in his eyes. Abivard recognized that look; he wore it whenever he thought of Roshnani. From that he concluded that the younger Maniakes not only knew but had already fallen in love with his not-quite-betrothed. That was yet another way the Videssians differed from his own people, among whom bride and groom seldom set eyes on each other before their wedding day.

Or so things worked among the nobility, at any rate. Rules for the common folk were looser, though arranged marriages were most common among them, too. Abivard wondered how lax things were for Videssian commoners, and if they had any rules at all.

The elder Maniakes turned the conversation back toward the business at hand: "Your Majesty, what do we do if the wells are fouled?"

"Either fall back into Videssos or press on toward the Tutub," Sharbaraz answered, "depending on how far we've come and how much water we have with us. I won't lead us across the waste to die of thirst, if that's what you're asking."

"If you try, I won't follow you," the elder Maniakes answered bluntly. "But aye, you talked straight with me, and you'll seldom hear a Vaspurakaner prince—which means any Vaspurakaner, just so you know—complain about that." He snorted. "Sometimes you can go for days before you get a Videssian to come out and tell you what he means."

Again, Abivard glanced toward the general's son. The younger Maniakes didn't say anything but didn't look as if he fully agreed with his father. Abivard chuckled to himself. Aye, Videssos had its hooks deeper in the son than in the father. Knowing that might prove useful one day, though he couldn't guess how.

Sharbaraz pointed ahead. "There's the first oasis, unless my eyes are playing tricks on me. We'll soon find out what Smerdis has been up to here."

Smerdis had not poisoned the wells. Both armies had their wizards and healers test the water at each stop on the journey west toward Makuran, and used a few horses to drink several hours before the men and the rest of the animals refreshed themselves, just in case the wizards and healers were wrong.

With the last oasis past, nothing but scrub—now rapidly going from green to its more usual brown—lay between the armies and the Tutub. But before they reached the river that marked the eastern boundary of the land of the Thousand Cities, Smerdis sent forth an embassy not to Sharbaraz but to the elder Maniakes.

Abivard had feared that. Smerdis' best hope now was to split the Videssians away from the rightful King of Kings. He had a way to do that, too: by offering more concessions to Likinios than Sharbaraz had. The Videssians were a devious people. For all Abivard knew, Maniakes might have accompanied Sharbaraz precisely to extort those concessions from Smerdis. If he got them, would he turn on Sharbaraz? Or would he simply order his horsemen to turn around and ride for home? That would be disastrous enough by itself.

Scouts had reported to Sharbaraz the arrival of the embassy. Had Sharbaraz been dismounted, he would have paced back and forth. Abivard understood that. When Zal's men had in essence seized his stronghold to force Smerdis' tax levy from him, his fate was taken out of his hands. Now Sharbaraz had to wait for others to decide his destiny.

"If he sells us out, I'll kill him," Sharbaraz snarled, one slow word at a time. "I don't care what happens to me afterward. Better I should fall slaying Videssians than at Smerdis' hands."

"I'll be beside you, Majesty," Abivard answered. Sharbaraz nodded, pleased at the pledge, but his face stayed grim.

Then the elder Maniakes, accompanied by his son, rode toward the rightful King of Kings. Trailing the two Videssian officers came a handful of unhappy-looking Makuraners. The elder Maniakes jerked a thumb back toward them. "They were inquiring into the price of having us switch sides," he remarked.

"Were they?" Sharbaraz fixed Smerdis' envoys with a smile that might have belonged on the face of a wolf. "The God give you good day, Paktyes. So you serve the traitor now, do you?"

One of the envoys—presumably Paktyes—looked even more uncomfortable than he had before. "S-son of Peroz, I serve the authorities in Mashiz," he said.

"By which he means he'll lick any arse that's shoved in his face," Abivard said, his voice greasy with scorn. "I never thought I'd see anything worse than a traitor, but now I have: a man who just doesn't care."

"He is disgusting, isn't he?" Sharbaraz remarked. Talking about Paktyes as if he weren't there was nicely calculated to make the ambassador all the more miserable. Ignoring him again, the rightful King of Kings turned to the elder Maniakes and asked, "Well, my friend, how much is the Pimp of Pimps offering?"

The Videssian general blinked, then guffawed till he coughed. When the coughs subsided to wheezes, he answered, "Oh, these fellows here say he'll give up the whole of Vaspurakan, along with enough silver for a man to walk dryshod from the westlands across to Videssos the city if he poured it into the Cattle Crossing—that's the strait between 'em."

A narrow sea, Abivard thought. Maybe that was what Tanshar had meant. But how likely was he to cross all the wide westlands and come in sight of Videssos' fabled capital?

Thinking of his personal concerns made him miss for a moment the way Sharbaraz stiffened. "That is a considerable offer, and one more, ah, generous than I would care to make," Sharbaraz said carefully. "How have you replied?"

"I haven't, till now," the elder Maniakes answered. "I wanted you to hear it first."

"Why? To make me match it? If Likinios needs silver so badly—"

"Likinios always needs silver," Maniakes interrupted. "And even if he didn't, he'd think he did. I'm sorry, your Majesty—you were saying?"

"If he needs silver, I can pay him some once I regain the throne," Sharbaraz said. "If he must have all of Vaspurakan—" The rightful King of Kings bent his head back, exposing his throat. "Strike now. He shall not have it from me."

"There, do you see?" Paktyes cried. "My master offers you better terms!"

"But *my* master doesn't care," the elder Maniakes said. "He doesn't like the idea of people stealing thrones that don't belong to them. He'd sooner have an honest man ruling Makuran than a thief, you see. Can you blame him? Whoever's on the throne in Mashiz, Likinios is going to have to live with him, and honest men make better neighbors."

"Very well, then," Paktyes said. He did his best to seem fierce but succeeded only in sounding liverish. Still snapping, he went on, "The brave armies of the King of Kings, may his years be long and his realm increase, have routed the renunciate once. They can surely do it again, even if he has treacherously gained aid from our ancient foes in Videssos."

He and his delegation rode back toward the west. The elder Maniakes turned to Sharbaraz and said, "If he's the best your rival can send out, this campaign will be a walkover. That would be nice, wouldn't it?"

"Aye, it would," the rightful King of Kings answered. "But I thought my campaign last spring would be a walkover, too. And so it was—for a while. The longer it went on, though, the tougher Smerdis' men got."

Maniakes chuckled. "I know how to fix that: beat him good early so he doesn't have time to get better late." Sketching a salute, he kicked his horse in the ribs and went off to his own army.

"There's a relief," Abivard said. "The Videssians could easily have sold us out, and they didn't."

He thought Sharbaraz would also be pleased, but the rightful King of Kings replied, "So far as we know they didn't. Paktyes and Maniakes could have said anything at all before they came to us. I have no idea how good a mime Maniakes is, but any general needs some of that if he's to adapt himself to the things that can go wrong in war. As for Paktyes, I know for a fact that deceit's in his blood. How could it be otherwise, when he swings this way or that like a bronze weathervane on a farmer's roof, always turning whichever way the wind of influence blows."

"Your Majesty, you are right." Abivard looked over his right shoulder at the elder Maniakes, who had almost rejoined his men. For a few minutes, he had been elated at the idea of the Videssians' probity being assured. Now he saw it was not so. The world remained full of ambiguity.

Sharbaraz said, "The only way to be certain the Videssians stay on our side is to have them actually fight against Smerdis. Even then we won't be absolutely sure until after the last fight is won: any sooner than that and they could be dissembling, building our confidence and trust so as to make betrayal the more devastating when it comes."

Abivard sighed. With every day that passed, he was gladder his brother-in-law was the rightful King of Kings and not himself. Sharbaraz saw and took precautions against treachery in places where Abivard didn't even see the places. He had let down his guard for one moment against his elderly cousin, and that lapse might yet forever cost him his throne. Abivard wondered if Sharbaraz would ever let down his guard for anyone again.

He said, "If the Videssians do betray us, what can we do about it?"

Sharbaraz gave him a very bleak look. "Nothing."

Even so early in the season, mirages danced and sparkled across the badlands that lay between Serrhes and the land of the Thousand Cities. Abivard had grown used to them, and as used to ignoring them. When he saw water ahead, then, he discounted it as just another illusion.

But this water did not seem to stay the same unchanging, tantalizing distance ahead of him no matter how far he traveled. The farther west he rode, the closer it looked. Before long he could make out the greenery it supported. A murmur ran through the army: "The Tutub. We've come back to the Tutub."

How many of them, when they had left the easternmost river of Makuran and struck out across the desert for Videssos, had really believed they would return—and return with a good chance of restoring Sharbaraz to the throne? Not many was Abivard's guess. He had had doubts himself, and the move had been his own wife's idea. What must the rank-and-file soldiers—those who hadn't deserted the rightful King of Kings—have thought?

The murmur grew to a great roar: "The river! The river!" Men cheered and wept and pounded one another on the back. Makuran lay ahead of them. No, so many had never expected to see this day. Abivard's eyes filled with tears. No matter how little the land of the Thousand Cities resembled Vek Rud domain, he, too, was coming home.

As he drew nearer, he saw horsemen waiting on the far side of the Tutub. They probably had not looked for Sharbaraz's return, either, and had to be less than delighted to see it now. Some held their places; others rode off to the west, no doubt to warn of Sharbaraz' arrival.

Green and growing things covered both banks of the river. So soon after the spring flood, the greenery extended a long way out from the Tutub. Canals guided every precious drop to plants that would perish without the lifegiving water.

Sharbaraz sent riders up and down the Tutub, a couple of farsangs north and south, to see if Smerdis' men had left behind a bridge of boats on which they could cross. Abivard was unsurprised when they found none.

He had watched the engineers of Peroz King of Kings throw a bridge across the Degird River. That had taken days. Now he saw the Videssian engineers in action. The structure they put together was a lot less impressive than the bridge the Makuraners had run up, but they built it a lot faster. They anchored thick, heavily greased chains to the shore at one end and to a wooden pontoon at the other. Then they rowed out to the pontoon in a tiny boat, anchored a new set of chains to its far side, and hitched them to another pontoon farther out in the Tutub.

They had long planks to reach from pontoon to pontoon and, incidentally, to reduce the distance each newly placed pontoon could drift downstream from its predecessor. They had shorter planks to lay across the long ones. And, in an amazingly short time, they had themselves a bridge.

At first, Smerdis' men on the west bank of the Tutub didn't seem to realize the Videssian engineers were creating a structure on which Sharbaraz's army could cross to attack them. Only when the western end of the bridge was well within bowshot did they send a few arrows toward the laboring engineers. The

Khamorth on the north bank of the Degird had harassed Peroz's artisans much more effectively.

As Peroz's men had, the Videssians used soldiers with big shields to hold off most of the arrows. They also brought archers of their own forward along the growing bridge to shoot back at their foes. Before long the bridge was anchored to the west bank of the Tutub as well as the east. Riders began to cross—first Videssians, for the elder Maniakes made his own men use the bridge before he risked Makuraners on it, then Sharbaraz's lancers, and last of all the wagons of the Videssian engineers and the rest of the baggage train.

As soon as the last wagon rolled onto the west bank of the Tutub, the engineers began disassembling the pontoon bridge. Watching, Abivard thought they might have used a magic to aid them in the deconstruction; just as the bridge had grown from the east bank of the Tutub to the west, so now it shrank in the same direction. The engineers rolled up the last heavy, greasy chain, stowed it in the wagon from which it had come, and shouted in Videssian that they were ready to move on.

The elder Maniakes rode up to Abivard and Sharbaraz. Coughing a little, he said, "You understand, I hope, it won't be this easy all the time."

"Oh, indeed," Sharbaraz said. "We caught them by surprise. They'll be more ready to fight back, next crossing we have to force. But being back in Makuran, in my own realm, feels so fine in and of itself that I won't worry about the future till I bump into it."

"The Land of the Thousand Cities isn't much like Vek Rud domain," Abivard said. "I was thinking that a little while ago. Serrhes reminded me a lot more of home: dust and heat—aye, and cold through the winter—and a healthy fear for enemies from over the border."

"You mean us," Sharbaraz said, grinning.

"So I do." Abivard smiled, too. "But I got to thinking what I would have done if an important Khamorth chief crossed the Degird with his clan and came to my stronghold asking for Makuraner help to get him back his grazing lands. What should I do there? Probably about what Kalamos did: act as friendly as I could while I sent a messenger hotfooting it to the capital to find out how I was really supposed to act."

"You couldn't go far wrong doing something like that," Sharbaraz agreed. "Such things have happened now and again, too. Sometimes we'd aid the nomads, sometimes we wouldn't, depending on what looked advantageous."

Abivard thought of Likinios and his beloved map. Yes, the Avtokrator had settled for fewer concessions from Sharbaraz than he had demanded at first, but he had taken a bite out of Makuran just the same. Suppose Sharbaraz had refused to yield that bite. Where would he and his followers be now?

Abivard saw two answers. The first was the one Hosios had promised: the army broken up, with each man getting land according to his rank. In that case, Abivard's grandchildren would likely have ended up as Videssian as the younger Maniakes. Not the worst of fates, but not the best, either.

Given the way Likinios looked at the world, though, the second picture that sprang into being in Abivard's mind struck him as much more likely. What better use for the Avtokrator of the Videssians to get out of a host of Makuraner refugees than to take them to the northeast and hurl them against the Kubratoi? Every nomad horseman they killed would help Videssos, while they did the Emperor no harm even if they died.

The scheme was devious, underhanded, and economical . . . Likinios to the core. Abivard was glad the Avtokrator had not had the chance to think of it.

Sharbaraz said, "This whole realm is mine, the land of the Thousand Cities no less than any other part of it. Perhaps it helps that I grew up looking out on it from Mashiz and that I visited some of the cities down here on the flood plain. It's not alien to me, though I admit I prefer the highlands. I am a true Makuraner by blood, after all."

"Of that, Majesty, no one had any doubt." Abivard waved to the flat, green landscape ahead. "Where I have doubts is wondering how we're to move here in any direction save the ones Smerdis dictates. Are the Videssian engineers good enough to let us do that?"

"My father always had the greatest respect for them," Sharbaraz said, invoking Peroz as Abivard was wont to invoke Godarz. "Never having fought against them nor seen them in action, I cannot speak from firsthand knowledge. I will say this, though: they'd better be."

As they had before, the cities of the land of the Thousand Cities closed themselves to Sharbaraz' army. As he had before, the rightful King of Kings bypassed them and kept moving. If he beat Smerdis, they would fall to him. If he didn't ... Abivard saw no point in worrying about that.

Smerdis did not have a large force between the valleys of the Tutub and the Tib. His men shadowed Sharbaraz's host and the accompanying Videssian army but made no effort to attack. "Cowardice." Sharbaraz snorted. "He thinks he'll stay on the throne if he can outwait me."

"Strategy," the elder Maniakes insisted. "He's holding back to hurt as much as he can, at a time of his choosing."

Being the two men of highest rank in the army, they had trouble finding an arbiter to choose between them, but before long they settled on Abivard. He said, "May it please your Majesty, I think the eminent sir is right. Smerdis isn't quite the fool you made him out to be; if he were, we'd never have needed aid from Videssos."

"He's a thief and a liar," Sharbaraz said.

"No doubt he is, your Majesty," the elder Maniakes agreed politely. "However wicked those qualities are in most walks of life, though, they often come in very handy in war."

Two days later Smerdis' men broke down the eastern bank of one of the larger canals that stitched together the Land of the Thousand Cities. The Videssian engineers quickly repaired the breach and ended the flood, but that did nothing to deal with the furlongs of black, smelly mud the waters left in their wake.

"Now we see if they earn their silver," Abivard declared.

The engineers earned not only Makuraner silver but also Videssian gold. They used the same planks that had paved the pontoon bridge over the Tutub to lay down a roadway that let the army advance through the flooded zone and up to the canal. They also recovered the planks—except for a few that had been trampled deep into the mud—so they could use them again in either bridge or roadway.

"Now I understand," Sharbaraz said as the engineers matter-of-factly went about bridging the canal. "They let the Videssian army go wherever it wants to. You can't just make a flood or build field fortifications and think you're safe from the imperials: they'll be inside your tent before you even know they're around."

"They are good," Abivard admitted grudgingly. "I haven't had a lot to do with them, but just watching them go about their business, seeing them talking and gambling around campfires of evenings, makes them seem more like ordinary men than they ever did before. Our tales always make Videssians out to be either wicked or ferocious or underhanded or—I don't know what all, but none of it good. And they're just . . . people. It's very strange."

"You take any one man from anywhere and he's apt to be a pretty good fellow," Abivard said. "Even a Khamorth will probably love his children—"

"Or his sheep," Abivard put in.

The rightful King of Kings snorted. "It's rude to interrupt your sovereign when he's waxing philosophical. I don't do it much; maybe it comes from being around Videssians, since they're finer logic-choppers than anyone else. As I was saying, your plainsman will love his children, he won't beat his wife more than she deserves, and he'll care for his horses as well as any groom in Makuran. Put him in the company of a couple of hundred of his clansmates and let him overrun a Makuraner village, though, and he'll do things that will give you nightmares for years afterward."

"But we have a lot more than a couple of hundred Videssians here, and they're still behaving well," Abivard said. "That's what surprises me."

"Part of that, I suppose, is that they're aligned with us: if they act like a pack of demons, they'll make the people here hate them and us both, and so hurt our cause," Sharbaraz said. "And they're more like us than the Khamorth are. When they aren't soldiering, they're farmers or millers or artisans. They don't destroy canals for the fun of watching other farmers starve."

Abivard plucked at his beard. "That makes sense, Majesty. Maybe you should—what did you call it?—wax philosophic more often."

"No, thank you," Sharbaraz answered. "There's also one other thing I didn't tell you: I asked the elder Maniakes to make sure his priests stuck to their own and didn't go about trying to get honest Makuraners to worship their false god. The blue-robes who follow Phos are better organized than our servants of the God, and they go after converts like flies diving into honey."

"They have been quiet," Abivard said. "I didn't realize this isn't the way they usually behave."

"It isn't," Sharbaraz assured him. "They're as certain of the truth of their Phos as we are about the God. And since they think they have the only true god, they're sure anyone who doesn't worship him—or who doesn't worship him the right way—will spend eternity in ice, just as we know misbelievers vanish into the Void and are gone forever. They think they have a duty to get people to worship as they do. Getting Maniakes to muzzle them hasn't been easy."

"Why not?" Abivard asked, puzzled. "If a noble gives an order, those who serve under him had better obey."

Sharbaraz laughed raucously. Abivard looked offended. The rightful King of Kings said, "Brother-in-law of mine, you're not used to dealing with Videssians. From all I've seen, from all I've heard, those blue-robed priests are so drunk with their god, they don't care to take orders from any mere noble. Even the Avtokrator sometimes has trouble getting them to do his bidding."

"We don't do things so untidily in Makuran," Abivard said. "Northerwesterner though I am, I know that much. If the Mobedhan-mobhed ever presumed to displease the King of Kings in any way—"

"—there'd be a new Mobedhan-mobhed inside the hour," Sharbaraz finished for him. "After all, the King of Kings is the sovereign. No one has any business displeasing him." He laughed again, this time at himself. "I've been nothing but displeased since the throne came—or should have come—into my hands. When it's truly mine at last, that won't happen any more."

His voice held great certainty. At first, that pleased Abivard: Sharbaraz needed confidence that he would be restored. Then Abivard wondered if the rightful King of Kings simply meant he would refuse to listen to anything distasteful once he ruled in Mashiz. That worried him. Even a King of Kings might need to be reminded from time to time of how the world worked.

Something had changed. Abivard knew it as soon as he climbed up into the wagon Roshnani and Denak shared, even before he set eyes on his wife. The serving woman who bowed to him said not a word out of the ordinary, but her voice had a timbre to it he hadn't heard before.

"My husband," Roshnani said as he stepped into her small cubicle. Again, the words were everyday but the tone was not. Then she added, "Close the curtain. It helps keep out some of the mosquitoes that plague this land." That sounded like her.

Abivard obeyed. As he did, he studied Roshnani. She looked—like herself, if a little more tired than usual. He scratched his head, wondering if his imagination was running away with him. "Is anything wrong?" he asked as she tilted her face up for a kiss.

"Wrong? Whatever makes you think that?" She laughed at him, then went on, "Unless I'm very much mistaken, though, I am going to have a baby."

"I'm glad everything's all ri—" Abivard said before what Roshnani had told him got from his ears to his mind. His mouth fell open. When he shut it again, he said, "How did that happen?"

If Roshnani had laughed before, now she chortled, great ringing peals of mirth that left her hiccuping when she finally brought herself back under control. "Unless I'm very much mistaken," she said, deliberately echoing herself, "it happened in the usual way. We've been wed for going on two years now. I was beginning to wonder if I was barren."

Abivard's fingers twisted in a sign to turn aside words of evil omen. "The God prevent it," he said. Then he blinked. "The God has prevented it, hasn't he?"

"Yes, she has," Roshnani said. They both smiled; when a man and a woman talked about the God in back-to-back sentences, the effect could be odd on the ear. Roshnani went on, "May I give you a son."

"May it be so." Abivard sobered. "I wish my father were here, so I could set his first grandchild in his arms. If that child were heir to Vek Rud domain, all the better." He thought of something else, lowered his voice. "I might even wish it weren't Father's first grandchild. Have you told Denak you're with child?"

Roshnani nodded. "I told her this morning; this is the first day I've been sure enough to speak to anyone. She hugged me. I understand what you mean, though: how wonderful it would be if a first grandchild were also heir to the throne of the King of Kings."

"Of course, if Father were alive, Peroz King of Kings would likely also still live, and Denak wouldn't be wed to Sharbaraz King of Kings," Abivard mused. "The more you look at things, the more complicated they get." He spoke quietly again. "I'm glad she's not jealous you've conceived when she hasn't."

"I think perhaps she is, a little," Roshnani said, almost whispering herself. "But then, she's also a little jealous that you visit me more often than the King of Kings comes to see her."

"Is she? Do I?" Abivard knew he wasn't altogether coherent, but he had never before been told he was going to be a father. None of the serving women and occasional courtesans he had bedded had made that claim on him, and they would have with even the slightest suspicion he had put a child in them: as a *dihqan*'s son, he would have been obligated to make sure their babes were well cared for. And none of his other wives had quickened before he left with Sharbaraz. Perhaps he should have fretted over the strength of his seed.

"Yes and yes," Roshnani answered. Everything he said this evening seemed to amuse her. She called to the serving woman for a jar of wine and two cups. The jar was a squat one from the land of the Thousand Cities; when she tilted it to pour, the wine slithered out slowly. She made a wry face. "Not only is it made from dates, the people here seem to think they ought to be able to poke a knife in it and bring it to their mouths that way."

"It doesn't matter, not for this." Abivard took one of the cups from her and raised it in salute. "To our child. May the God grant him—and you—long years, health, and happiness." He drank. So did Roshnani. Not only was the wine thick as molasses, it was nearly as sweet, too. He almost felt the need to chew to get it down.

It did what wine was supposed to do, though. By the time he had finished the cup, the world seemed a more cheerful place. Roshnani poured it full again. As he sipped, the words of his toast came back, and so did worry. Women could die giving birth, or of childbed fever afterwards. The possibility loomed too large to be ignored, but the idea of commending young and vital Roshnani to the God because her span was cruelly cut short sent fear through him.

To keep from thinking about it, he gulped down the second cup of sweet date wine. When he had finished it, he said, "May Denak and Sharbaraz soon know this same happiness." He *was* happy, despite the worry. He would worry about his sister, too, but he would also be glad for her and her husband.

Roshnani nodded. "Not only will it be good for them, it will be good for the realm as well, especially if it proves to be a boy. Having an heir to the throne can only help settle the realm."

"It should help settle the realm, you mean," Abivard said. "Peroz King of Kings had an heir, too, if you'll recall."

"I recall it perfectly well," Roshnani said. "If Smerdis had recalled it, too, we'd all be better off—except for Smerdis, which, I daresay, was all he thought about."

"Too true." Abivard sighed. "When I was growing up at Vek Rud stronghold, I thought about seeing the land of the Thousand Cities and Videssos, aye, but I expected to go to war against Videssos for the King of Kings, not with Videssian allies against a man who calls himself the King of Kings. Civil war is a strange business."

"When I was growing up, I never thought about seeing anything except the stretch of road between my father's stronghold and yours," Roshnani answered. "I'd known only the stronghold and later only the women's quarters in it. Next to that, my bridal journey seemed travel enough to last me a lifetime." She laughed. "We can't always guess what's to come, can we?"

"No," Abivard said, thinking of Tanshar. "And even if we do learn what's to come, we don't know when or where or how."

"The only thing left for us is to go on as best we can," Roshnani said. "Come to think of it, that's what we'd be doing even if we knew just what all the prophecies meant."

"So it is." Abivard looked at her sidelong. "The best way to go on after finding out you've a child in your belly that I can think of is—"

Roshnani might have had the same thought at the same time. The date wine made Abivard's fingers a little clumsy as he unfastened the wooden toggles at the back of her dress, but after that everything went fine.

Smerdis' men did their best to delay and misdirect Sharbaraz's army and his Videssian allies by opening canals between the Tib and the Tutub, but their best was not good enough, not when the Videssian engineers could repair holes in the canal banks and plank roads as fast as the enemy damaged them.

"When we cross the Tib, they're ours," Sharbaraz said.

"Aye, Majesty," Abivard answered, though he could not help thinking that Sharbaraz had shown the same confidence the summer before, only to have it prove to be overconfidence.

But perhaps Smerdis came to the same conclusion as his rival. As Sharbaraz's men neared the Tib, their foes drew up in battle array to try to stop them from crossing a major canal. Prominent in the ranks of Smerdis' men were the dismounted archers who had brought such grief to Sharbaraz's forces as they had advanced from the south against Mashiz the previous year.

The elder Maniakes looked down his formidable nose at the bowmen. "If we ever close with them, their souls will be falling down to Skotos' ice quick enough after that," he said.

"Oh, indeed," Sharbaraz answered. "The same holds true for my lancers. But I don't relish trying to force a crossing in the face of all the archery they can bring to bear on us."

He's learning, Abivard thought with something approaching

joy. The summer before, Sharbaraz would have chosen the most straightforward way to cross the canal and get at his foes, and would have worried about casualties later, if at all.

"Your Majesty, may I make a suggestion?" the elder Maniakes asked.

"I wish you would," Sharbaraz said. The Videssian commander spoke for several minutes. When he was through, Sharbaraz whistled softly. "You must have a demon lurking in you, to come up with a scheme like that. No wonder Makuran seldom profits as much as it should in its wars against Videssos."

"You're too kind to an old man," the elder Maniakes said, considerably exaggerating his decrepitude. "You would have seen it yourself in a moment, had you but noticed the little hill that town there rests on."

"You'll want us to sit tight through the night and start the attack in the morning, then, won't you, eminent sir?" Abivard said.

"We'll have better hope for success that way, surely," the Videssian general answered. He beamed at Abivard. "You do see what needs doing, eminent sir, and that's a fact. Can't complain about that, and I wouldn't think of trying." He plucked at his gray beard. "Hmm, now that I think on it, 'eminent sir' is probably too low a title for you, what with you being brother to his Majesty's wife, but I mean no harm by it, I promise you."

"I took no offense," Abivard said, "and even if I had, I wouldn't have shown it, not after that lovely plan you came up with."

The elder Maniakes beamed. "The only reason I thought of it was to give my son some glory. I'll have him lead the interesting half."

Sharbaraz turned to Abivard. "The time to trust Videssians least is when they're being modest. Of course, that isn't something you'll run into often enough to have to worry about it much."

"Your Majesty, I am wounded to the quick!" The elder Maniakes clapped both hands over his heart, as if hit by an arrow. "You do me a great injustice."

"The biggest injustice I could do you would be to underestimate you," the rightful King of Kings answered. "You will forgive me, I pray—you're not so young, you're plump, you're droll when you want to be. And you're as dangerous a man as I've ever seen, not least because you don't seem so."

"What do I say about that?" the elder Maniakes wondered aloud. "Only that if you've seen through the act, it isn't as good as it should be, and I'll have to put more work into it." He sounded genuinely chagrined.

The next morning dawned clear and hot, as did almost every morning in late spring, summer, and early fall in the land of the Thousand Cities. The Videssian engineers had enough pontoons and chains and planks to bridge the Tib and Tutub—plenty to bridge an irrigation canal many times over. As soon as it was light, they started throwing a good many bridges across the canal that held them apart from Smerdis' men.

To Abivard's dismay, scouts from Smerdis' army were alert. No sooner had the bridges started to snake across the oily-looking water than the unmounted archers came rushing up from their camp and began shooting at the engineers. As at the crossing of the Tutub, some of the Videssians held big shields to protect the rest from the rain of arrows. As the bridges moved forward, Videssian horse archers rode out onto them and started shooting back at Smerdis' men.

They were badly outnumbered, but did damage to the foe all the same: few of Smerdis' bowmen wore any sort of armor. The heavy cavalry with the foot soldiers gathered in knots in front of the growing bridges to fight off any of Sharbaraz' men who managed to cross.

Sharbaraz's own armored lancers assembled near their end of a bridge that grew ever nearer the west bank of the canal. Abivard sat his horse at their head, wondering how, if the men he led charged over the bridge in one direction while Smerdis' followers charged in the other, the Videssian engineers would keep from getting squashed between them.

He found out: as soon as the engineers got the last planks in place, they dove into the canal and started swimming through the turbid water back toward the eastern bank. No sooner had they splashed down into the water than Abivard cried, "Sharbaraz!" and booted his horse forward.

The bridge swayed, as if in an earthquake, under the galloping hooves of dozens of horses. Abivard met his first foe not quite two thirds of the way toward the west bank of the canal—he might have started a heartbeat sooner than Smerdis' man, and perhaps he was better mounted, too.

He twisted his body away from the questing point of the foe's lance. At the same time, he struck with his own. The blow caught Smerdis' soldier in the chest and pitched him off over his horse's tail. Abivard's mount, a trained warhorse, lashed out at the fallen lancer with iron-shod hooves. Abivard spurred the horse ahead toward the next enemy.

The bridge was not wide. More splashes, some of them big ones, marked men and horses falling or getting pushed into the canal. In their heavy iron armor, most of them did not come up again.

"Sharbaraz!" Abivard cried again. He and the backers of the rightful King of Kings slowly pushed Smerdis' men toward their own end of the bridge. Not one of Sharbaraz's followers, though, had yet set foot on the muddy western bank of the canal. Smerdis' troopers yelled the name of their candidate for the throne as loudly as Sharbaraz's warriors extolled him.

Then, from the north, a new cry rang out along the canal's western bank: "Sarbaraz!" Abivard whooped gleefully. Even if the Videssians couldn't pronounce the *sh* sound, they were not only good soldiers but subtle planners. The elder Maniakes had predicted Smerdis' soldiers would be so busy fighting the warriors they saw that they would pay no attention to anything else. Some of his engineers had taken advantage of the cover offered by the hillock the Videssian general had mentioned to run one more floating bridge across the canal. A large force of Videssian mounted archers proceeded to cross with no opposition whatever.

They shot up Smerdis' unarmored foot soldiers, then, crying "Sarbaraz!" once more, they charged them, swinging sabers and thrusting with light spears. They weren't quite so deadly as Makuraner lancers would have been, but they were more than enough to rout the dismounted archers, who were useful when they could ply a foe with arrows without being directly assailed in return, but whose clubs and knives offered next to no defense in close quarters.

Smerdis' heavy cavalry had to break off the fight at the bridgeheads to swing back against the Videssians and keep themselves from being surrounded and altogether destroyed. But that let Abivard and his men reach the west bank of the canal, just as the flight of the bowmen let the Videssian engineers finish more bridges so more of Sharbaraz's lancers could cross.

The officer who led the Videssian flanking force had a nice sense of what was essential. He let the archers run and concentrated on Smerdis' horsemen. His own troopers were more heavily armed than nonnoble Makuraner warriors, though they didn't wear iron from head to toe and their horses bore only quilted cloth protection. They could hurt Smerdis' men if those men didn't assail them with everything they had, and could stand up well enough against an all-out charge to ensure that Smerdis' lancers couldn't smash through them and escape from Sharbaraz's men.

Smerdis' lancers were quick to realize that. They began throwing down their long spears and swords. Some cried, "Mercy!" Others shouted Sharbaraz' name. Some fought on. Most of those went down, but a few managed to break away and run.

The Videssian commander—it was the younger Maniakes, Abivard remembered—was not content with victory, but sent his own horsemen after Smerdis' fleeing lancers. They brought down quite a few more before returning to their comrades.

"A cheer for the Maniakai, father and son," Abivard shouted. "The one planned the victory, the other made it real." The Makuraners he had led yelled themselves hoarse. Any of them who happened to be near Videssians pounded their allies on the back, bawled in their ears, and offered them wine from the skins they wore on their belts. For that moment, at least, the ancient enemies could not have been closer friends.

Abivard rode toward the younger Maniakes. "Well done," he said. "You're younger than I am; I envy you your cool head."

The younger man smiled. He had a small cut on his left cheek and a dent and a sparkling line on the bar nasal of his helmet; without the nasal, he would have taken a bad wound. He said, "You did well yourself, eminent sir; if you hadn't pressed them so hard, they might have punched through us and got away in a body."

"That's what I was trying to stop, all right," Abivard said, nodding. "There'll be a great wailing and gnashing of teeth in Mashiz when word of this fight gets back to Smerdis Pimp of Pimps."

"Good," the younger Maniakes said, grinning. "That was the idea, after all. And there'll be a great wailing and gnashing of teeth in the land of the Thousand Cities, too. We used those unmounted archers hard, and anyone with an eye in his head to see with can figure out that we would have used them harder if we hadn't had more important things to do. The folk hereabouts may want to think twice before they back Smerdis over Sar—*Shar*baraz." He pumped his fist in the air in triumph at correctly pronouncing the Makuraner sound.

"We beat those archers once and fought them again, but it

didn't make the Thousand Cities change their mind," Abivard said. "Maybe this time it will, though. I hope so."

"This fight happened in the middle of the Land of the Thousand Cities, not off in the southern desert," the younger Maniakes said. "And Smerdis' army looks to have broken up, to boot. Every man who gets away alive will go home, and every man who gets home will spread the tale of how we smashed Smerdis' general. That can't do Smerdis' cause any good."

"So it can't." Abivard eyed the Videssian commander's son with new respect. "Not just a fighter, eh? You like to think about the way things work, too; I can see that."

The younger Maniakes had an impressively luxuriant beard for a man of his few years, a trait that, Abivard had learned, testified to his Vaspurakaner blood. In spite of that beard, which reached up almost to his eyes, Abivard saw him flush. He said, "You are generous to a man who, after all, is more likely to be your enemy than your friend."

"I hadn't forgotten that," Abivard assured him. "But maybe, just maybe, the help Likinios Avtokrator is giving to Sharbaraz will bring our two realms a long peace. The God knows we both could use it."

"Phos grant that it be so," the younger Maniakes said. Impulsively, he stuck out his hand. Abivard took it. They squeezed with all their strength and let go, smarting, after a draw.

"All I truly want to do is get back to my domain in the northwest and make sure the Khamorth haven't ravaged my lands too badly—or punish the plainsmen if they have," Abivard said. "Peace with Videssos will ensure that I can do that."

"Peace with Makuran will let the Avtokrator Likinios finish punishing the Kubratoi, too," the younger Maniakes said. "A peace both sides can use is more likely to last than any other kind I can think of."

"Aye." Abivard had agreed before he remembered that Videssian gold had stirred up the Khamorth tribes north of the Degird River against Makuran in the first place. Without that incitement, Peroz King of Kings might never have campaigned against the nomads, which meant Smerdis wouldn't have stolen the throne from Sharbaraz, which meant in turn that Videssos and Makuran wouldn't have joined together against the usurper. Abivard shook his head. Indeed, the more you looked at the world, the more complex it got.

Something else crossed his mind: the more you looked at the world, the more you could learn. Videssos would never directly threaten his domain; the Empire's reach wasn't long enough. But the Khamorth were causing endless trouble in the northwest of Makuran, and that worked to Videssos' advantage. If Makuran ever needed to put similar pressure on Videssos, who could guess what a subsidy to Kubrat might yield?

Abivard stuck the idea away in the back of his mind. Neither he nor any Makuraner could use it now. Makuran had to put its own house in order before worrying about upsetting those of its neighbors. But one of these days . . .

He glanced toward the younger Maniakes. For all his obvious cleverness, the Videssian officer hadn't noticed Abivard was thinking about enmity rather than friendship. *Good,* Abivard thought. As he had said, he wouldn't mind a spell of peace, even a long one, with Videssos. But certain debts would remain outstanding no matter how long the peace lasted.

The younger Maniakes said, "Do you think they'll try to stop us again this side of the Tib?"

"I doubt it," Abivard answered. "We smashed Smerdis' cavalry, and you were the one who noted that those unmounted bowmen are likelier to make for home than to come back together again. What does that leave?"

"Not bloody much, eminent sir," the younger Maniakes said cheerfully. "That's how I read things, too, but this isn't my realm, and I wondered if I was overlooking something."

"If you are, I'm overlooking it, too," Abivard said. "No, as I see it, we have one fight left to win: the one in front of Mashiz." He had thought as much the summer before, too, but Sharbaraz hadn't won that fight.

After the victory, Sharbaraz's forces and their Videssian allies pushed hard toward the Tib. Smerdis' men broke the banks of canals on their route; the Videssian engineers repaired the damage and the armies kept moving. Smerdis' troops did attempt one stand, along the western bank of a canal wider than the one they had used as a barrier before the battle. Abivard worried when he saw how strong the enemy's position was. So, loudly, did Sharbaraz.

The elder Maniakes remained unperturbed. As the sun was setting on the day the army came up against Smerdis' force, he ostentatiously sent a detachment of engineers and a good many of his horse archers north along the east bank of the canal. Inky darkness fell before they had gone a quarter of a farsang.

When morning came, Smerdis' soldiers were gone.

"You are a demon, eminent sir," Sharbaraz exclaimed, slapping the Videssian general on the back.

"We'd hurt 'em once with that trick," the elder Maniakes replied. "They weren't going to give us a chance to do it again." He chuckled wheezily. "So, by threatening that trick, we won with a different one." The army crossed the canal unopposed and resumed its advance.

After that, city governors from the land of the Thousand Cities began trickling in to Sharbaraz's camp, something they had never done the summer before. They prostrated themselves before him, eating dirt to proclaim their loyalty to him as rightful King of Kings. Not yet in a position where he could avenge himself on them for having stayed loyal to Smerdis so long, he accepted them as if they had never backed his rival. But Abivard watched his eyes. He remembered every slight, sure enough.

Abivard wondered if Smerdis' men would contest the crossing of the Tib. Though the flood season had passed, the river was still wide and swift-flowing. Determined opposition could have made getting across anything but easy. But the west bank was bare of troops when Sharbaraz and his allies reached it. The engineers extended their bridge, one pontoon at a time. The army crossed and moved west again.

XI

Abivard eyed the approaches to Mashiz with suspicion. Sharbaraz's troops had come to grief there once before, and the army the rightful King of Kings commanded now was smaller than the one he had led the previous summer. One more victory, though, would redeem usurpation and defeat and exile. The Makuraners who had suffered so much for Sharbaraz's cause were grimly determined to achieve that victory.

The Videssians who had accompanied them and made victory possible had no such personal stake in the war. Abivard wondered how they could fight so well without that kind of stake. He asked the younger Maniakes, with whom he had become more and more friendly after the battle in the land of the Thousand Cities.

The Videssian commander's son rolled his eyes. "From what my father says, you've met Likinios Avtokrator. How would you like to go home and explain to him that you hadn't done quite all you could?"

At first, the prospect didn't seem too daunting. Likinios hadn't struck Abivard as a man who flew into a murderous rage without warning, as some memorable Kings of Kings of Makuran had been in the habit of doing. Then he thought of the Videssian Emperor's coldly calculating mind. Likinios wouldn't kill you because he was angry; he would quietly order you slain because he judged you deserved it. But you would end up just as dead either way.

"I take your point," he told the younger Maniakes. The Videssian ruler's style might be coldblooded and alien to the

Makuraner way of doing things, but it had its own kind of effectiveness.

Sharbaraz's force advanced through the wreckage of the failed campaign of the year before: skeletons of horses and mules, some with mummified skin still clinging here and there; the burned-out remains of overturned supply wagons; and unburied human bones, as well. The rightful King of Kings surveyed the near ruin of his hopes with an expression thoroughly grim. "Not this time," he declared. "Not this time."

But taking the capital of the realm would not be easy. Where before Smerdis' men had built a temporary barricade across most of the one wide way into Mashiz, now permanent fortifications protected the city from attack. Getting past them looked like a formidable undertaking.

"Don't worry about it," the elder Maniakes said when Abivard did just that. "We'll manage, never you fear."

Promises, even from one who had shown he delivered on them, left Abivard cold. When the Videssian engineers began taking wood and ropes and specialized parts of bronze and iron from their wagons and assembling them into large, complicated contraptions, however, he felt oddly reassured. What they did with such things wasn't magic in any true sense of the word, but it struck him as every bit as marvelous as a lot of the things sorcerers achieved.

"They're very good," Sharbaraz agreed when he said that aloud. "I think the ones who went north over the Degird with my father could have matched them, though. But most of my father's engineers are dead with the rest of his army, and I don't think Smerdis has many of those who are left alive working for him, either. Were things different, the lack could hurt Makuran badly; we'll have to train up a new team of such folk as soon as may be. But for now having engineers, when our foes don't, works for us."

The timbers the Videssians had used to make the flooring for their pontoon bridges and to corduroy roads through the muck left by flooded canals also proved to be the right size for constructing the frames of the engines they were erecting. At first, Abivard thought that an amazing coincidence. Then he realized it wasn't a coincidence at all. The sophisticated planning inherent in that deeply impressed him.

The engines went up at the front and on the right of the northern flank—the one on which Smerdis' men had gained success the summer before—well out of range of archers sheltered by the works the usurper had thrown up. Sharbaraz asked, "Will they be enough to let us pass by the fortress without losing so many men as to ruin us?"

"Provided we beat the men they have outside the walls, the engines will keep those within too busy to do much to us," the elder Maniakes replied.

Abivard said, "What about men issuing forth from one of the narrow ways into Mashiz? That flank attack ruined us last year, and we don't have the men to plug all those routes, not if we want to do real fighting, too."

"The trick of the trade is getting what you want with as little fighting—especially the messy, expensive hand-to-hand you mean—as you can," the Videssian general said. He pointed over to the bank of dart-throwers going up on the northern flank. "Skotos hold my soul in the ice forever if those don't make any charging lancer ever born the most thoughtful man you know."

"May it be so," Sharbaraz said. "My men are eager for the attack. When will all this hammering and spiking be done?"

"We'll be through by evening," the elder Maniakes replied. "Smerdis' men could have given us a deal of grief if they'd come sneaking around trying to wreck the engines or burn 'em down, but they didn't. Maybe they didn't think of it, or maybe they just didn't think it'd work." He shook his head to show his opinion of that. "You always try. Every once in a while, you end up surprising yourself with what you can do."

"I agree," Sharbaraz said. "If I didn't, I never would have fled into Videssos last year."

If Roshnani hadn't thought of it, you'd never have fled into Videssos, Abivard thought. That brought a surge of pride in his wife. It also brought the realization that Denak had been right all along: women's counsel could be as valuable on campaign as back in the women's quarters of the stronghold. Abivard wondered if Sharbaraz had figured that out yet.

He didn't get long to contemplate the notion. The elder Maniakes said, "True enough, your Majesty, but we're on the point of bringing you back home now."

Dawn brought the promise of a day to steam a man in armor. Abivard was sweating even before he donned the leather-lined shirt of mail and splints, the mail skirt, and the trousers of iron rings. By the time he had affixed his ring-mail veil and aventail and settled his helmet on his head, he felt ready to go into the oven and come forth as cooked meat.

Perhaps, in spite of everything, Smerdis still had spies in Sharbaraz's camp, or perhaps his officers were just good at piecing together what they saw from the works he had built in front of Mashiz. In any case, his soldiers came forth from their camps behind those works and filled the gaps between their walls and the nearly impassable badlands to either side. No, getting into Mashiz was not going to be the triumphal parade Abivard and Sharbaraz had imagined when they set out from Vek Rud stronghold.

The elder Maniakes took charge of proceedings at the outset. Collaring Abivard, he said, "I want you and your best men in front of the siege engines to protect them."

"What?" Abivard said indignantly. "You'd ask me and our best lancers to forgo the charge?"

If the Videssian general noticed his ire, he ignored it. "That's just what I'd ask, for the beginning of the fight, anyhow," he answered. "If we're to win this battle, that's what we need to do. You'll get enough fighting to satisfy the most picky honor later on, I promise you."

He spoke as if honor were something worth only a couple of coppers. *You make war like a merchant, and your son is twice the man you'll ever be,* Abivard thought. But he could not insult an ally by saying such things to his face. If he took the question to Sharbaraz . . . He shook his head. He couldn't do that. If he did, the elder Maniakes would lose prestige, or else he would lose some himself. Either way, the alliance would suffer.

That left him only one choice. "Very well, eminent sir," he said icily. "I shall rely on your promise."

The elder Maniakes paid no more attention to ice than he had to indignation. "Good, good," he said, as if he had taken Abivard's compliance for granted. "Now do get moving, if you'd be so kind. We can't put on our little show until you do."

Still fuming, Abivard rounded up Zal's regiment of lancers. Zal and many of his riders grumbled when Abivard told them they weren't going to sweep gloriously down on the enemy. He said, "You'll do real fighting later in the day. By the God I swear it." He had to hope he wasn't giving them a false oath.

Grumbling still, the lancers took their places in front of the siege engines the Videssians had built. Made with muddy timbers, the engines looked like frameworks for houses abandoned after a flood. The engineers loaded heavy stones into some and large, stoppered jars with greasy rags sticking out of the stoppers into others.

Abivard twisted in the saddle so he could watch the Videssians touch torches to those greasy rags. At the command of their captains, the engineers discharged the creations. The engines jumped and kicked, as if they were wild asses like those that had given Sharbaraz's followers such a fright the autumn before.

The stones and jars described graceful arcs through the air. As their captains cursed them to ever greater efforts, the Videssians turned windlasses to rewind the engines' ropes and ready them to shoot again. Abivard paid scant heed to that. He watched the stones smash into Smerdis' works. Some fell short, some crashed against the wall, some flew over it to land within. He wouldn't have wanted to be under one of those stones when it came down, any more than he would have cared to be a cockroach stepped on by a lancer's armored boot.

The jars trailed smoke as they flew. Even from a couple of furlongs, even through the shouts of Smerdis' soldiers inside their fortress, he heard pottery smashing. Columns of black, greasy smoke started rising from within the fortifications.

Abivard turned in the saddle again. "Any of you speak my language?" he asked the engineers behind him. When one of them nodded, he went on, "What's in that stuff you're flinging there?"

The Videssian grunted. "Rock oil, sir, and sulfur," he said in fair Makuraner, "and some other things I don't want to tell you what it is. Burns good, don't it?"

"Yes," Abivard said. One of the pillars of smoke was growing rapidly; he guessed the inflammable liquid had splattered over wood or canvas. The engines bucked again, this time in a more ragged salvo. Ragged or not, though, it sent another round of stones and jars flying against the fortress.

"By the God," Zal said, "I'd not like to have to go out in that kind of rain." His gaze sharpened. "And if that kind of rain keeps falling on the fortress for very long, the folk there won't be worth much. They'll be too squashed or toasted to do anything to speak of in the way of fighting."

"That's the idea," Abivard said, also suddenly figuring out why the elder Maniakes had said defending the engines would be a crucial role to play. Sooner or later, Smerdis' generals would realize they had to stop the Videssians from rendering their fort useless. They couldn't do it with archers; the engines were out of range of any bowman. They would have to charge down on them instead.

Sure enough, the charge came, but not from the warriors gathered directly in front of Mashiz. Instead, Smerdis' generals loosed a flanking force of the sort that had brought Sharbaraz such grief in his last attack on the capital. Shouting Smerdis' name, the horsemen thundered down out of the narrow way to the north, as they had the year before.

They got a different reception from the one they had had then, though. The engines on the army's right flank went into action. Some of them threw stones that smashed men and horses alike. No armor could stop the yard-long darts others shot. They pinned soldiers to their mounts and sent them crashing to the ground to foul the troops behind them.

Smerdis' men were brave enough. They kept coming in spite of the toll the engines took. Videssian horsemen rode out to keep them away from those engines and from the main body of Sharbaraz's force.

That was the sideshow, the distraction. The chief action remained at the front. The Videssian engines there kept on pounding the fortress Smerdis had erected. Its wall, which could have stood forever against mere lancers, began to look like a man with bad teeth as it got knocked to pieces. Behind the wall, flames leapt high. Smoke rose higher. It made Abivard cough, and must have been twenty, a hundred times worse for Smerdis' soldiers in the fort, those lucky enough not to have been cooked.

The Videssian captain of engineers shouted more orders in his own language. His men swung the engines slightly off to one side. Then they started shooting again, this time at Smerdis' lancers gathered by the fortress.

Zal grinned a wicked, carnivorous grin. "What a nasty choice that leaves them," he said. "Withdraw out of range and open the way for us or come out and fight and open it anyhow if they lose."

Horns rang out in Smerdis' battered army. Lanceheads glittered in the sun as riders couched their weapons. "Here they come," Abivard said. Smerdis might have been a treacherous usurper, but the troops who had stuck by him had courage enough and to spare.

Abivard swung down his own lance till it pointed straight at the onrushing horsemen. "Sharbaraz!" he cried, and booted his horse in its armored sides to get it going. It sprang forward, seemingly glad to run. Zal echoed his war cry. So did the rest of the soldiers. They had waited far too long to suit them. Now they would have the straight-up fight they had craved.

Someone screeching "Smerdis!" spurred straight for Abivard. Above the fellow's chainmail veil, he caught a brief glimpse of hard, intent eyes. His foe was as glad to be fighting at last as he was. Smerdis' men hadn't just had to wait. They had also watched their comrades in the fortress bombarded and then taken a bombardment themselves.

By the way he sat his horse, the fellow boring in on Abivard knew exactly what he was doing. Instead of aiming for the larger target of Abivard's torso, at the last moment he flicked the point of his lance up at his face.

Fear turned the inside of Abivard's mouth dry and rough. He barely turned the stroke with his shield. His own went wide. He didn't care. He was just glad to be alive to fight someone else who wouldn't unfurl quite so many lethal tricks.

As cavalry battles have a way of doing once the initial impetus of the charge is lost, this one turned into a melee, with men milling about and cursing at the top of their lungs when they weren't shouting their chosen sovereign's name to keep their friends from trying to kill them. They thrust with lances and slashed with swords; their horses, many of them stallions, joined in the fight with bared teeth and flailing hooves that could dash the brains out of a man on the ground.

Somehow one of Smerdis' men had got turned around so he faced back toward the burning fortress. Abivard thought him an ally till he yelled the usurper's name. Then he speared the fellow in the back, thrusting with all his strength to force the lance point through the warrior's armor.

The fellow screamed and threw his arms wide; his sword went spinning through the air. The soldier screamed again. He crumpled, blood pouring from a hole somewhere between his left kidney and his spine. He hadn't known Abivard was there till the lance went into him. Abivard felt more like a murderer than a warrior until someone tried to blindside him. After that, he bore in mind that in battle there was precious little difference between the two.

Little by little, Sharbaraz's men forced their foes back toward the fortress. Videssian horsemen and light-armed Makuraner cavalry, more nimble than either side's lancers, tried to nip in behind Smerdis' horse and cut them off, clearing the way for Sharbaraz's lancers to burst through and storm for Mashiz.

A few archers up on the battered walls of the fortress shot at them. Hundreds would have been up there but for the pounding the siege engines had given the place. But many now were dead, many more hurt, and others fighting the fires the pots of oil had started.

"Onward!" That voice, some yards ahead of him, made Abivard jerk his head up. Sure enough, there was Sharbaraz, laying about him with his sword and spurring his horse on toward the gap that led to Mashiz.

Abivard couldn't imagine how the rightful King of Kings had pushed so far forward in the fighting, but Sharbaraz would have been a dangerous warrior no matter what his station. The only trouble was that, if he fell now, everyone else's exertions would be for nothing.

"Onward!" Abivard cried, and pointed to his sovereign. Now he did not call out Sharbaraz's name, for fear of drawing the enemy's notice to the rightful King of Kings. He pointed to him, though, and waved his arm to urge on his own followers. Not all of them understood his gestures, but enough did to give Sharbaraz a respectable force of protectors in a few minutes.

But Sharbaraz did not want protectors—he seemed to want to be the first man into Mashiz. He plunged into the press once more. His ferocity made those of Smerdis' men who were not in deadly earnest draw back from him. His own men pushed forward to fill the gap and to guard him from the foes who remained full of fight.

A tiny lull in the battle gave Abivard a moment to look around at more than sword's length from him. He realized with surprise and sudden and growing triumph that Smerdis' fortress was no longer in front of him and the rest of the leaders of Sharbaraz's forces—instead, it lay to their right. Sharbaraz had lost this fight the summer before, but he was winning it now.

"Come on!" Abivard yelled, waving again. "One more push and we have them. Once we get past the walls here, the way opens out again, and drop me into the Void if Smerdis' lancers can hold us out of Mashiz then."

Smerdis' soldiers saw that as clearly as he did. They rallied, fighting desperately. But Sharbaraz' men were desperate, too, knowing what another defeat in front of the capital would mean. And their Videssian allies, even without personal stake in the battle, fought as bravely as anyone. They plied Smerdis' men with arrows and pressed the fight at close quarters with sabers and spears. Sharbaraz had worried about betrayal, but the men from the east stayed not only loyal but ferocious.

The counterattack from Smerdis' lancers faltered. Yard by yard, they began giving ground once more. Then, all at once, the way the fortifications had narrowed grew wide again. "To Mashiz!" shouted Sharbaraz, still at the van.

Not only the capital of Makuran loomed ahead. Closer and perhaps more tempting were the tents that marked the encampment of Smerdis' men. "I'll castrate anybody who thinks of loot before victory," Abivard said. "First we win, then we plunder."

As far as he was concerned, the prospect of entering Mashiz was worth more than any booty he could pull from the camp. Other, poorer men, though, were liable to think of silver before victory.

Smerdis' army, the last army that could hold Sharbaraz out of his capital, began to break up. Here and there knots of determined men still fought on, although they had to know victory was hopeless. But others fled, some back toward Mashiz, others over the badlands, hoping their foes would be too busy to pursue them. And still others, as they had between the Tib and the Tutub, threw away their weapons and gave up the fight.

Abivard shouted for some Videssians to take charge of the prisoners. "That's well done," Sharbaraz said, recognizing his voice.

"Thank you, Majesty," he answered. "My thought was that they won't be as hot for revenge as our men." He rode closer to the rightful King of Kings before quietly adding, "And the fewer of them who go into Mashiz with our men, the better."

"Aye, that's just right," Sharbaraz agreed. "They've been all we could ask for as allies—more than I looked for them to be, the God knows. But Mashiz is *ours*; we can reclaim it on our own." Bitterness crossed his face for a moment. "The Videssians have sacked Mashiz a couple of times, while we've never made our way into Videssos the city. What I wouldn't give to be the King of Kings who changed *that*."

"Oh, indeed," Abivard said, quietly still. "Not tomorrow, though."

"No." Sharbaraz nodded at that. "But I'm willing to bet Videssos will give us the chance before too many years go by, however well we work with father and son of the Maniakes clan. As you say, first things first." He booted his horse in the ribs, wanting to lead his army into Mashiz. The capital lay less than a quarter of a farsang—a quarter hour's ride—to the west.

Abivard kicked his own mount up to a fast trot to keep pace with his sovereign. "Will we have more fighting to do inside the city?" he asked.

"I hope not," Sharbaraz said. "With any sort of luck, his army will have gone to pieces. But the palace is a formidable place. If he has men willing to fight for him, he could hold out a long time there."

"The Videssians and their siege engines—" Abivard began.

Sharbaraz shook his head. "No, by the God," he said harshly. "If they pound the usurper's men or the works he threw up against me, well and good. But the palace doesn't belong to Smerdis—it's mine, just as Mashiz is ours. I don't want it wrecked if I can find any way around that; I want to live in it after I take Mashiz, as I did before Smerdis stole the throne."

"Very well, Majesty," Abivard said, humbled. To him, the palace was just another military target. To Sharbaraz, it was home.

On they rode. The closer they got, the bigger Mashiz looked to Abivard. It dwarfed Serrhes, which was the only city into which he had ever gone. The towns of the land of the Thousand Cities might well have been as crowded, but they weren't large, not with each one sitting atop a mound made from generations of its own rubble. Mashiz sprawled over the foothills of the Dilbat Mountains. At the eastern edge of the city was a marketplace big enough all by itself to swallow Serrhes. Now it boiled like an anthill knocked down by a small boy. All the merchants who had never imagined Sharbaraz's troopers could enter the capital—and there seemed to be quite a few of them—now were trying to hide their goods, and often themselves, too.

"Too late for that," Sharbaraz said, pointing ahead. "I wonder how big an indemnity to set on them for doing business as usual under my thief of a cousin." His laugh held a predatory note. "They're wondering the same thing, too."

"We can worry about that later, though, surely, Majesty," Abivard said. "First we need to take the palace and lay hold of Smerdis Pimp of Pimps."

"Aye," Sharbaraz said, predatory still.

He knew the way through Mashiz's maze of streets. Though the palace was an imposing structure of gray stone, other, lesser buildings kept blocking it from view, so Abivard might have taken hours to find his way to it down streets that twisted back on themselves like snakes, as if in a deliberate effort to keep newcomers from going anywhere on them.

The palace had an outwall formidable enough to make Abivard think once more of having to batter it down, but no soldiers paced upon it or shouted defiance down at the rightful King of Kings. All the gates, their timbers shod in iron, looked formidable, but they all stood open.

"He's yielded," Sharbaraz said in tones of mixed wonder and suspicion. He urged his horse across the open area in front of the wall. Abivard went ahead with him. So did the soldiers who had accompanied them through the city.

Abivard was about halfway across the open area when everything went black.

It did not feel as if he had been stricken blind. Rather, night—moonless, starless, lightless—seemed to have fallen on Mashiz. His horse snorted and stopped dead. In an odd way, that reassured him: if the animal was dumbfounded, too, the trouble did not lie inside his own eyes.

"Majesty?" he called to Sharbaraz a few feet away.

"Abivard?" the rightful King of Kings replied. "Is that you? I can hear your voice, but I can't see you."

"I can't see anything," Abivard said. "Can you?"

"Now that you mention it, no." Sharbaraz raised his voice to call to his soldiers. "Can anyone see anything?"

Several people said no. Several others were shouting things that weren't answers but that also meant no. Abivard stared through the darkness that filled his eyes, seeking without success to find light. He also stared with his ears, trying to have them serve for the sense that had failed him. With them he had better luck. Shouts and screams came not only from near but also from as far as he could hear.

"The whole city's gone black," he exclaimed.

"You're right, I think," Sharbaraz said a few moments later, as if he had first paused to listen and to weigh what he was hearing. "Smerdis must have made the court magicians cast this gloom down upon us for his own purposes."

"Battle magic—" Abivard began, but then stopped—it wasn't battle magic, not really, for it seemed to have fallen on all of Mashiz's inhabitants—even on the animals—and not just on combatants. In battle, magic rarely bit on a man; his passions were too likely to be inflamed for it to be effective. Now, though, Sharbaraz's soldiers, victory already in their hands, had eased away from the peak of life-or-death excitement, and so . . .

"I pray the gloom does extend over the whole of Mashiz," Sharbaraz said. "If Smerdis' men can see while our eyes stay swaddled in darkness—" Abivard admired him for laughing, but he did not sound amused. "In that case, Smerdis Pimp of Pimps will enjoy a longer reign than I'd thought."

There was a thought to put fear in a man. Abivard wondered what he would do—what he could do—if horns suddenly blared and horses clattered across the cobbles at him. Swing his sword wildly in all directions until a lance he never saw skewered him? Better to yank off his helm and draw that sword across his own throat. That, at least, would be quick.

But no horns belled out a blast of triumph. All he heard around him was chaos. Slowly the fear of sudden attack faded. But fear did not flee—it merely changed its shape. Smiths at their forges, tavernkeepers with torches to light up their taprooms, cooks at hearths and braziers . . . how long before one of them started a fire impossible to fight?

If that happened, he didn't know what he could do about it, save to bake like a round of pocket bread in the oven. You couldn't flee fire any more than foe, not if you couldn't see which way to run.

"What do we do?" Sharbaraz asked. By his voice, thoughts like Abivard's had been running through his mind.

"Majesty, I don't know," Abivard answered. "What *can* we do? All I can think of is to stay as calm as we can and hope the light returns."

"Believe me, brother-in-law of mine, I have no better ideas." Sharbaraz raised his voice, called out his name and Abivard's suggestion, and added, "Pass my words on to those too far away to hear them straight from my lips. Say also that our sorcerers will soon overcome the darkness Smerdis Pimp of Pimps has raised against us." In a muttered aside to Abivard, he said, "They'd better."

"Aye," Abivard said. "I wonder how far out from the palace—or out from Mashiz—this blackness reaches." As soon as he spoke the words, he wished he hadn't. They made him imagine not just the magicians groping in darkness but the whole world so afflicted.

From the noise wrenched out of Sharbaraz, the rightful King of Kings—the veritable King of Kings, if light ever returned—didn't care to think about that, either. After a moment, he found words: "I'm going to ride forward very slowly until I fetch up against the wall. Then I'll know exactly where I am—and I'll have something at my back."

"I'm with you, Majesty," Abivard said at once; having something at his back suddenly seemed precious as emeralds. Foes might still come at him then, but from only one direction.

Sharbaraz' horse clip-clopped across the cobbles, one cautious step after another. Abivard didn't know how—or if—his own mount would respond when he urged it ahead. But it obeyed, as if relieved to find that the human atop it knew what he was doing after all. Abivard hoped the animal wasn't paying him too great a compliment.

He heard a faint thump from ahead, followed a moment later by an indignant snort. "Ah—I've found the wall," Sharbaraz said.

"Found it the hard way, unless I'm wrong," Abivard said, and Sharbaraz did not tell him he was. He eased back on the reins, slowing his horse even more in an effort to keep from imitating his sovereign. He didn't succeed, though; his horse fetched up against the wall before he knew it was there. In the absence of eyes, the other senses hadn't given either him or the animal warning enough to stop in time.

The horse let out the same sort of irritated snort Sharbaraz's beast had used. It turned its body till it was parallel to the wall, in the process scraping Abivard's leg against the stones. It snorted again, this time in satisfaction, as if assured it had taken its revenge. For his part, he was glad of the armor he wore.

"Is that you, brother-in-law of mine?" Sharbaraz asked.

"Yes, Majesty," Abivard said. "I wonder how long we'll have to wait till the light returns." What he really wondered, but would not say, was whether the light would ever return. When he got thirsty and hungry, how would he find his way out of Mashiz if he couldn't see where he was going?

"Those are all fascinating questions," Sharbaraz said when he posed them aloud. "I'm sure they're occurring to other people about now, too. I wish I could truthfully say I had so little concern that they'd never occurred to me, but I can't." He sighed. "I wish I had answers for them, too."

Time stretched. Since Abivard could see neither sun nor moon nor stars, he couldn't tell how much of it was passing. To give him some sense of duration, he sang and hummed and hummed and sang. That helped, but not enough. His ears told him other men were doing the same, and doubtless for the same reason.

Eventually he had to make water. When he dismounted, he was careful to hold onto the horse's reins, for fear of getting turned around and never finding the animal again if he let go of them. That meant he had to take down his armored breeches little better than one-handed and, worse, pull them up again the same way. "Amazing what you can do when you try," he remarked to the blackness around him.

Out of the blackness, Sharbaraz answered, "So it must be. I'm going to have to try to imitate you before too long. If I manage to lose myself, call my name and I'll come to the sound of your voice."

"As you say, Majesty. If I'd dropped the reins there, I would have asked the same of you."

"I wonder what happened to Smerdis' men," Sharbaraz said. "It's as if the God scooped us all into the Void."

Abivard drew in a sharp, frightened breath at that. The comparison was only too apt—Abivard wondered if it wasn't literal truth rather than comparison. Why the God should choose to do such a thing at a moment when righteousness was about to triumph, he could not imagine—but the God did not have to justify himself to a mere mortal, either.

Through the confused and often panic-stricken hubbub, through the ragged snatches of song that calmer men used to keep themselves enspirited, came a more purposeful chant, sung by many men at once. At first Abivard just noted the strong, calm music of it, which lifted his own spirit. Then he realized it was not in his own tongue, but in Videssian.

The chanters came closer. As they approached, he made out more and more words. He had heard the hymn before, back in Serrhes; it was a song of praise to Phos, the Videssian god of good—and, Abivard remembered, of light. Whether he believed in Phos or not, light was what he and all of Mashiz needed most at the moment.

His ears said the Videssians were entering the square around the palace. Their joyous song rang out, glorifying not only their god but also the sun, Phos' chiefest symbol, marked by the golden domes atop the spires of their temples and by the cloth-of-gold circles Videssian priests wore on the breasts of their blue robes, just above their hearts.

Then he saw the Videssian priests. For a moment, they were all he did see, striding through the blackness all around them as if unaware of its existence. After that moment, his sight cleared altogether, and he saw the whole square. When it blurred in his sight, alarm ran through him, but he did not need long to realize tears of relief accounted for that.

Sharbaraz gave the Videssians one of their own salutes, his right fist over his heart. "My friends, I am very glad to see you," he said in Videssian, then dropped into his own language to add, "and you may take that however you wish."

One of the Videssian priests bowed in return. The late-afternoon sun gleamed from his shaven pate as if it were one of the gilded domes that topped his faith's temples. Seeing how close to the mountain peaks the sun had slid gave Abivard an idea of how long he had been without sight—quite a while longer than he had thought.

In fair Makuraner, the priest said, "Your Majesty, we are sorry we did not come sooner to your aid. This was a strong magic, and needed all our strength to overcome. Also, you Makuraners have a way of working wizardry different from ours, so we had trouble devising counterspells to deal with what had been done."

"However you did what you did, I'm glad you did it," Sharbaraz said. "Now we can enter the palace and cast down Smerdis once for all."

"Happy to be of service, your Majesty," the priest said, and bowed again.

With light restored, servitors began straggling out of the palace compound. Some of them recognized Sharbaraz. They went to their bellies, eating dirt before the King of Kings. "Now you come into your own, Majesty," Abivard said softly.

"Not quite yet," Sharbaraz said. "Not until the usurper is in my hands."

But none of the palace functionaries, for all their loud protestations of loyalty to Sharbaraz, admitted to knowing where Smerdis was. Sharbaraz sent soldiers through the palace. He sent eunuchs into the women's quarters, where soldiers could not go. No one found a trace of his elderly cousin.

Before long, though, some of the soldiers brought him three men whom he recognized. "Ah, the royal wizards," he said, while the Videssians and his own men bristled. "I take it you worthies are to blame for the recent events?"

Abivard admired his sangfroid. The wizards knocked their heads on the cobblestones. "Majesty, forgive!" one of them wailed. "Your rival compelled us to do his bidding, holding our families hostage to ensure that we did as he demanded. Forgive!" he repeated, and the other two echoed him.

"Perhaps I shall. Then again, perhaps I shan't," Sharbaraz said. "Tell me more, Khuranzim—tell me the purpose of a magic that darkened everyone's sight, for instance."

"Why, to allow Smerdis to escape unseen, of course," answered the wizard who had spoken before—presumably Khuranzim. "Over him the spell held no power. He tried to make us extend that over his soldiers, as well, but we told him truthfully that such was impossible: attempt to employ this cantrip as battle magic and you throw it away, for the spleen of men assailed by unseen foes would be so roused that in moments it would hold no sway over them."

Beside Sharbaraz, Abivard let out a long sigh of relief. The nightmare he and the King of Kings had feared could not have come true—although no small number of men would have died before the rest awoke from that nightmare.

He thought of something else. "Wizard, you say Smerdis had you cast this large and complicated spell just to let him get away?"

"Yes, uh, lord," Khuranzim answered cautiously. Sharbaraz he knew. He had never seen Abivard before and could not gauge how high in the affection of the King of Kings he stood. High enough to merit a soft answer, at any rate.

Abivard said, "By the God, why didn't he simply have you change his face, so he could sneak out of Mashiz with no one the wiser?"

"Lord, your words make it evident you are a man of sense," Khuranzim said, bowing. His lip curled. "The same cannot be said of Smerdis. To him, how large and showy a magic was counted for more than its mere effectiveness. When I suggested to him the very plan you named, he said he would cut the throat of my eldest son, give my principal wife over to his guardsmen ... I am a potent mage, lord, given time to prepare my charms. Edged iron can be too quick for me."

"Can you track him now, to learn where he's fled?" Sharbaraz asked.

"Possibly, your Majesty," Khuranzim said, cautious again. "But some of the shielding spells laid on a King of Kings do not require frequent renewal, so detecting him by such means will not be easy."

Sharbaraz made a sour face, but then his expression lightened. "Never mind. Search your best, but whether you find him or not, my men will." His voice flamed with anticipation.

"Lord Abivard?" One of the serving women who had accompanied Roshnani and Denak from Vek Rud stronghold waited for Abivard to notice her, then went on, "The lady your sister would speak with you, if you have the time."

"Denak? Of course I'll see her," he said, though he suspected he sounded surprised. She had sometimes come to talk with him when he visited Roshnani, but he couldn't remember the last time she had asked him to come herself. "Lead me to her."

The wagon that had taken his sister and his principal wife

through so much remained with the rest of the baggage train just outside of Mashiz. The serving woman went up and into it ahead of Abivard. After a moment, she beckoned at the entrance for him to follow.

Denak waited in her little cubicle, which was on the other side of the wagon from Roshnani's and fitted out in mirror image to hers, which made it familiar and disconcerting at the same time for Abivard. After he hugged his sister, he sat down crosslegged on the carpet and said, "What is it? How can I help you?"

"You probably can't," Denak answered bleakly. She sat down, too, leaning against the outer wall of the wagon with her hands on her belly. "I'm with child, and I'm going into the royal women's quarters tomorrow."

"You're going to have a baby, with luck an heir to the throne? That's wonderful!" Abivard exclaimed. Then he really heard the rest of what Denak had said. "Where else would you stay but in the women's quarters?"

"Staying there is one thing," Denak said. "Whether I ever come out again before they bury me is something else again." Her eyes flicked back and forth, like those of an animal caught in a trap. "I might have borne it before, when I knew no better. But I've been free—well, freer—awhile now, and the thought of being caged up again . . . I don't think I can."

"Why should you be? Trapped, I mean?" Abivard said. "The King of Kings let you travel with him, we all dined in Serrhes together . . . He's been good about keeping the promise he made back at our stronghold."

"Not as good as he might have been, but on the whole, yes, you're right." All the same, Denak looked at Abivard as if he had proved himself a blockhead. As if teaching a small boy his letters, she went on, "I am going into the women's quarters tomorrow. My husband will ride out in pursuit of Smerdis the same day. Until he gets back, do you think I shall be able to poke so much as the tip of my nose outside the women's quarters?"

"Oh," Abivard said, and tasted the emptiness of the word. He did his best to look on the bright side: "He's already sent riders after the usurper. The God willing, he'll be back in Mashiz very soon."

"The God willing, yes, but what if he's gone for months? Even if I'm resigned to spending some time in the women's quarters here, will he remember his promise—will he honor it?—when he gets back after he's gone for a long time?"

"I don't know," Abivard admitted. "I will say, though, that he strikes me as careful in matters that touch his honor. From the little I saw of Peroz King of Kings, his father was the same way."

"May you be right," Denak said. "The other thing I worry about is what will become of *me* in the women's quarters. I'll be a white crow there, not just because I'm the daughter of a frontier *dihqan* and not a princess from one of the Seven Clans, but also because I've been out in the world and seen things and done things. What will they think of me?"

"If they have any sense, they'll be jealous," Abivard said. "When Sharbaraz does come back, why don't you try to get him to give his other wives the same privileges he's granted you? If that works, how can they help but be grateful to you?"

"Knowing what goes on in women's quarters, I suspect they'd find a way," Denak said. But she leaned forward and kissed Abivard on the cheek, just above the line where his beard stopped. "It *is* a good idea. I'll try it; the worst he can tell me is no." She seemed to change the subject. "You'll be riding with Sharbaraz, won't you?"

"Yes, of course," Abivard answered.

Denak sighed, then lowered her voice. "And you'll be taking Roshnani with you, naturally—even though Smerdis fled south, away from Vek Rud domain, that's still the way around the mountains and back toward home." She sighed again. "How I envy her those extra weeks of freedom."

"It will be all right, Denak." Abivard summoned up courage of a kind different from what he had needed to face foes lance to lance on the field and said, "Surely it will be better than what you would have known at Nalgis Crag domain, even had Sharbaraz never ended up there."

Denak stared at him. Since she and Sharbaraz had escaped from Nalgis Crag stronghold, Abivard had hardly ever mentioned it. That he did so now, deliberately, made her stop and think. "Aye, it will be better than that," she said, but her voice was grudging. "Better, though, is not good."

"I didn't say it was," Abivard answered at once. "But nothing happens all at once, no matter how we wish it would. And if you work to make 'better' better still, your daughter—or her daughter—may think her life is . . . good."

"Maybe." At first Denak did not seem convinced, but after a moment she slowly nodded.

* * *

The pursuit of Smerdis went south, as Denak had said. Every day Abivard expected the hard-riding scouts at the head of Sharbaraz' pack to run his cousin to earth like an exhausted antelope. Every day, though, the hunt went on. The Dilbat Mountains were dwindling into desert foothills. Soon, if he so desired, Smerdis would be able to swing north and west.

"I wonder what Likinios would have done if he'd fled to Videssos," Abivard said as they encamped east of those foothills.

Sharbaraz looked at him like a man staring at a cockroach cooked into his bowl of lentils. "Now there's an . . . interesting . . . thought," he said after a pause in which he seemed to discard several more pungent descriptions. "I don't suppose he'd put him at the head of a new Videssian army—that would be too raw. More likely, he'd keep him in luxury at Videssos the city for as long as he lived, just to remind me I'd better behave myself unless I wanted trouble from the east. That's what I'd do in his boots, anyway."

Abivard nodded. "That's about what I was thinking, Majesty. Now I want us to be able to do something to Smerdis."

"So do I," Sharbaraz said. "If he'd yield himself up, I'd be grateful enough that I'd strike off his head and have done. I wouldn't even bother hauling him back to Mashiz to see how ingenious the executioners could be."

"Fair enough," Abivard said, then kicked at the dirt in frustration. "Where has he gone to, anyway?"

"Drop me into the Void if I know," the King of Kings answered. "When I set out on this chase, I thought it would be over soon. Now—" He stamped his foot, too. Abivard thought of what Denak had said. Before he could speak, though, the King of Kings went on, "I'm glad we brought the regiment of Videssian engineers with us after all. If he's managed to hide himself in a stronghold somewhere, they'll help us winkle him out."

"What with their baggage train, they slow us down," Abivard said in oblique disagreement. "Even the scouts can't get too far ahead of our main body, for Smerdis has scraped up enough followers to treat a small band roughly."

"I'm not worried about that. We'll run him to earth pretty soon, come what may," Sharbaraz said. "He's an old man, after all, and he was a mintmaster, not a horseman. He'll wilt in the saddle like greens in the stewpot."

He stood tall and proud and young and confident, every inch

a proper King of Kings of Makuran. Seeing that kingly arrogance—all of it deserved, no doubt—Abivard had to remind himself that Sharbaraz had underestimated Smerdis before.

"I don't believe it," Sharbaraz said in disgust.

"I don't believe it," Abivard said in sympathy.

"I don't believe it," the commander of the Videssian engineers said in awe. Ypsilantes was a lean, dour, sun-baked man who would have been on the quiet side even for a Makuraner; for a Videssian, he was astonishingly taciturn. But when he stared up and up at the stronghold atop Nalgis Crag, he was as impressed as any Makuraner would have been.

Sharbaraz treated him with respect, perhaps more than he might have given to a Makuraner in the same position. He said, "Having seen what your men accomplished between the Tutub and the Tib, I refuse to believe anything beyond your powers. Surely you'll devise some ingenious way to force Smerdis to come down."

"Damn me to the ice if I know what, your Majesty," Ypsilantes answered. His quiet had nothing to do with the way he spoke Makuraner; he was quite fluent. He was simply one of those uncommon people who say only what's necessary and not a word more.

The King of Kings scowled. "Starving Nalgis Crag stronghold into submission would take years." Ypsilantes just nodded, which did nothing to improve Sharbaraz's temper. He clenched his fists. Abivard knew he would have liked nothing better than to see Nalgis Crag stronghold torn down stone by stone. But getting up to the stronghold, let alone tearing it down, would be the next thing to impossible.

Abivard said, "Majesty, it strikes me that the stronghold does have one weakness after all."

Ypsilantes grunted and shook his head; he got more meaning into that than some men would have with an oration. Sharbaraz freighted his voice with sarcasm: "Enlighten us, O sage of the military art. The distinguished engineer sees a perfect fortification. I must confess I see a perfect fortification. How gratifying, then, that you've found a weakness which evades us. And that weakness is?"

"Pradtak son of Artapan," Abivard answered at once. "The fortress itself could be all of adamant, not just stone and iron. With Pradtak leading it, it might yet fall. You've had some dealing with him, Majesty. Am I right or am I wrong?"

Sharbaraz did not reply at once. His eyes got a faraway look that had nothing to do with staring up and up to the fortress that crowned Nalgis Crag. Till that moment, he had been considering only the fortress, not the men inside it. He made small clicking noises as he thought. At last he said, "Brother-in-law of mine, it could be so."

"Knowing the man you fight is better than knowing the fort he fights from," Ypsilantes said—a very Videssian notion, when you got down to it. He turned to Abivard. "What of this Pradtak, eminent sir?"

Now Abivard hesitated. How to characterize his former brother-in-law? "He's . . . weak," he said after a moment. "He's not a coward, nothing like that, but he has a crust of bluster, if you know what I mean. Crack that and he's soft underneath."

"Like an oyster," Ypsilantes said. Abivard knew the word, though he had never tasted one. He nodded. The engineer rubbed his chin. "How to crack the shell, then?"

"Tell him what will happen to him when Nalgis Crag stronghold does fall at last—and fall it shall," Sharbaraz said, anticipation in his voice. "Not only do I owe him for giving Smerdis refuge, but also for the delightful accommodations he granted me year before last. Put enough fear in him and he'll do what we want. He must know what the executioners back in Mashiz can make him suffer before they finally let him die."

But Abivard shook his head. "Forgive me, Majesty, but I don't think you can put him in fear for himself, not that way. Even if we do take Nalgis Crag stronghold—" He was too polite to contradict the King of Kings directly, but he still doubted it could be done. "—how do you propose to take Pradtak himself? A step off the wall and he's cheated the executioners." He shivered a little. From the walls of Nalgis Crag stronghold, it was a *long* way down. What would you think about, the wind whipping at you, till the moment of blackness?

Sharbaraz glared at him. But Ypsilantes said, "Good sense," in a way that would have made Sharbaraz seem petulant, even to himself, if he disagreed.

"What then?" the King of Kings snapped. "If we can't even reach Pradtak, how are we to put him in fear enough to make him want to hand over Smerdis?" He meant it as a rhetorical question, and it was certainly one for which Abivard had no good answer. Clenching his fists, Sharbaraz went on, "Outrageous that a single *dihqan* should be able to defy the entire realm."

Had Abivard not defied the entire realm, Sharbaraz rather than Smerdis would have been mured up in Nalgis Crag stronghold. He thought it impolitic to mention that. But the complaint from the King of Kings sparked a thought in him. "Majesty, you're right: all the realm is yours, while Pradtak holds but the one domain here. If you were to begin to wreck it, most methodically, leaving him with the prospect of holding nothing but the stronghold once you were through—"

With an engineer's practicality, Ypsilantes said, "He is up high. He can see a long, long way. Every village that burned—"

Sharbaraz didn't answer right away. Abivard had learned better than to push him too hard, especially now that he was coming into full awareness of his power. He waited to hear what the King of Kings would say. "We'll try it," Sharbaraz declared at last. "First, though, we shall warn Pradtak of exactly what we intend. If he chooses to sacrifice his domain for Smerdis Pimp of Pimps, let the blame rest on his head."

"As you say, Majesty." Abivard nodded. "The God willing, he'll yield to the threat alone and not make us carry it out."

"He will if he cares a fig for his domain," Sharbaraz said. "And I know the perfect envoy from this force to put our terms to him, too."

"Who's that, Majesty?" After getting his idea, Abivard hadn't taken it any farther.

Sharbaraz clicked his tongue between his teeth, as if to say Abivard had disappointed him. He stabbed out a forefinger. "You."

Abivard held the truce shield high as he rode the narrow, winding track up toward Nalgis Crag stronghold. He wished he had a surefooted mule or donkey under him rather than his horse. Prestige forbade it, of course. If his horse slipped and he fell, he would die of prestige. That was far from the most common cause of death in Makuran, but it was also far from unknown.

He felt very much alone. If Pradtak wanted to seize him, too, and hold him as a hostage to try to twist Sharbaraz's will, he could. Abivard didn't think that would have any effect on the King of Kings, and didn't care to think about the effect it would have on him.

He had already passed several of the garrisons on the lower, less steep parts of Nalgis Crag. Sharbaraz's army could conceivably have driven them out of their positions, though it would have hurt itself badly in the driving. As for the barrier ahead and the men who stood guard beyond it . . .

A warrior scrambled over the stones. "What would you?"

Abivard flourished the shield of truce. "I come with a warning from Sharbaraz King of Kings, may his years be many and his realm increase, as to what will befall Nalgis Crag domain if the *dihqan* Pradtak fails to yield up the rebel Smerdis to him. I am ordered to deliver this warning to Pradtak personally."

"You wait here," the man said. "Who are you, that I may give your name to my lord the *dihqan*?"

"Abivard son of Godarz, once his brother-in-law," Abivard answered.

Pradtak's man stiffened, as if unexpectedly stung by a wasp. Abivard stiffened, too. He had dreaded that question. Pradtak was liable to have left orders that he be killed out of hand. But evidently not; the warrior said, "I shall take the *dihqan* your words. Wait." Rather jerkily, he climbed back over the stones that could rain down on attackers and hurried toward the stronghold.

Abivard dismounted, fed his horse some dates, and brushed down the animal. He did his best to ignore the men watching him from behind the heaped stones—and the ones he had already passed, the ones who could block him from returning to friends and safety. It wasn't easy, and grew harder as time crawled by.

He looked up the ever steeper slope toward the stronghold. His patience was at last rewarded when he caught sight of two men riding slowly in his direction. After a few minutes, he knew one of them was the officer who had gone up to tell Pradtak he would come. Then he recognized Pradtak, too.

His former brother-in-law scrambled over the stony barrier between them and approached. Behind the barrier, Pradtak's men waited with drawn bows. If Abivard thought to try anything, he would be pincushioned before he could. Since he didn't, he bowed to Pradtak and said, "The God give you good day. You're moving very well; I'm glad the ankle has healed as it should."

"It doesn't trouble me much any more, not so far as moving goes," Pradtak answered. "But when rain or bad weather is coming, I always know it a day before anyone else in the stronghold." He fixed Abivard with a suspicious stare. "You didn't ride up here to talk about the state of my leg."

"That's true," Abivard said. "I came up here to demand in the name of Sharbaraz King of Kings, may his years be many and his realm increase, who is my brother-in-law through my sister Denak whom you will no doubt recall, the person of the usurper Smerdis."

"I don't give a moldy date for what Sharbaraz demands," Pradtak said, snapping his fingers in contempt. "He's nothing but a renunciate, and Smerdis the proper King of Kings. And I don't give a moldy date about *you*, either. The sooner you drop into the Void, the happier I'll be. Have you forgotten it's war to the knife between us? Only your truce shield and my generosity keep me from ordering you slain this instant."

He puffed out his chest, obviously sure he had made Abivard afraid. Having seen him bluster before, though, Abivard was less than impressed. He said, "Sharbaraz King of Kings will spare you even though you imprisoned him, providing you yield up the usurper. If you don't, your domain will pay the price for it— and so will you, once he starves you out."

Pradtak snapped his fingers again. "That for Sharbaraz and his threats, and you may tell him I said so. If he proposes to take Nalgis Crag stronghold, I wish him joy of the attempt."

"But Nalgis Crag stronghold is not all of Nalgis Crag domain," Abivard answered. He told Pradtak what he and Sharbaraz had worked out, adding, "By the time we're through with your lands, a crow that flies across them will have to carry its own provisions. I warn you, heed what I say."

Pradtak's face darkened with fury. Now Abivard knew fear, fear that Pradtak would be enraged enough to forget the shield of truce and the generosity he had averred only moments before. "I shall not give Smerdis up," Pradtak said thickly. "He has my oath of loyalty, which I honor yet."

"He lied as to the terms under which you swore it," Abivard said, "for Sharbaraz King of Kings did not give up the throne of his own free will. Thus the oath has no true hold on you."

"You might as well be a Videssian, like the ones to whom Sharbaraz sold his soul for a chance to steal the realm," Pradtak said. "I don't care what you claim—I shall not surrender Smerdis to you."

"Your domain will pay the price for your stubbornness, and so will you, when eventually you yield to the King of Kings," Abivard warned. "Think twice, think three times, on what you do today, Pradtak."

He didn't want to push his former brother-in-law too far, lest he push Pradtak into a place from which he could not extricate himself. Thus he spoke as softly as he could, within the limits Sharbaraz had set him. But it was not soft enough. Pradtak shouted, "Go down to your master and tell him I'll never wear his livery."

Abivard could not resist a parting shot. "Why should that worry you, when you wore his seeming for a couple of days?" He wheeled his horse and rode down Nalgis Crag, away from the curses Pradtak hurled after him.

Sharbaraz looked gloomy when Abivard returned emptyhanded. He said, "If that pompous fool thinks I'm bluffing, I'll have to show him how wrong he is. I hate it—his subjects are my subjects, too—but I will have Smerdis from him, come what may."

Abivard rode with the party that fired the village at the base of Nalgis Crag. The people there had been warned of what was coming; most of them were already on the road, carrying such belongings and treasures as they could, when the soldiers came into their village. A few stragglers still remained behind, though. One of them, an old woman, shook her fist at the jingling horsemen. "The God and the Four curse you for harming us who never harmed you," she cried, her voice mushy because she had no teeth.

"Go on, grandmother, take yourself out of here," Abivard said. His left hand twisted to turn aside the curse. "Blame your lord, for not giving Sharbaraz King of Kings the fugitive who is his by rights."

"If you blame Lord Pradtak, burn Lord Pradtak," the old woman retorted. But Sharbaraz's army could not do that, not with the *dihqan* impregnable inside Nalgis Crag stronghold, so Pradtak's subjects would have to suffer in his stead. Still cursing and bemoaning her fate, the woman shouldered a blanket wrapped around her few meager possessions and trudged after the rest of the villagers.

"I don't envy these folk," Abivard said. "If Pradtak holds to his purpose, we may have to burn them out again and again."

One of the horsemen passed out torches. Another got a fire going in the center of the market square. When flames crackled there, Abivard thrust the head of his torch into them, then waved it in the air to bring it to full life. He touched it to the thatched roof of a nearby house. The dry straw caught almost at once. Flames ran toward the crown of the roof; burning straw fell down into the building to ignite whatever was inside.

A couple of dogs sat in the square, not far from the fire the trooper had set. They howled disconsolately, breaking off only to sneeze and snort now and again as the smoke grew thicker. Abivard watched the soldiers torch the village. Some of them went at it with real enjoyment, ducking into houses to emerge with jars of wine or with trinkets for camp followers, then burning with whoops of glee the places they had just looted. Others simply set a fire, went on to another building, and did it again.

In the end, Abivard couldn't see that it mattered much one way or the other. The village burned.

Coughing, his eyes streaming from the smoke, he rode with the rest of the incendiary party back to camp. The black column of smoke that rose from the village's funeral pyre climbed higher than the summit of Nalgis Crag. The wind whipped it and frayed it and eventually dissipated it, but the smell of the burning must surely have reached the stronghold.

Pradtak, though, made no move to surrender Smerdis.

When morning came, Sharbaraz sent Abivard out with another troop of horsemen to burn down the village next nearest to Nalgis Crag—about a farsang off to the north. A shower of arrows greeted them when they arrived. A couple of men and a horse were wounded. "Forward!" Abivard cried. The troopers rode into town full of grim determination. More arrows fell among them, wounding another horse. In this kind of fight, horses were not much use. Armored men were. Once they knocked down a few doors and killed the defenders inside, the fight went out of the rest of the people in the village.

Abivard barely kept his soldiers from slaughtering them just the same. "They had a right to fight," he insisted. "No one warned them there'd be a massacre afterward if they did. Next time, though—"

He drove the villagers out of their homes with only the clothes on their backs and a chunk of pocket bread and a wine jar each. After that, the smoke rose into the air again, a pillar even thicker and darker than the one that had gone up the day before. The troopers went about their business with a single-mindedness they hadn't shown in the other village; they wasted no time on horseplay here.

Sharbaraz nodded when Abivard told him what he had done. "That was just right, brother-in-law of mine. Tomorrow, if we need to go out tomorrow, we'll tell them they may leave with what they can carry if they offer no resistance. Otherwise, we'll treat it as war in all ways." He looked up toward Nalgis Crag stronghold. "With any luck at all, Pradtak will see he'll have no domain left if he keeps the usurper much longer."

But a village to the south went up in smoke the next day. The people there left sullenly but without fighting the King of Kings' lancers, who went out in greater force. The day after that, villagers in a fourth hamlet had to be overcome in battle—and were.

Along with the houses, vines and pistachio trees also burned. Sharbaraz had meant what he said: Pradtak might keep Nalgis Crag stronghold for a long time, but nothing in the domain except for the stronghold would be worth having once the soldiers and their torches were done.

On the fifth day, the village of Gayy, the one Sharbaraz had known of and exploited during his escape from the stronghold, was given over to the flames. Sighing, he said, "Whatever I learned about the town will have to be rewritten."

His incendiaries were about to ride out for their sixth day of devastation when a man bearing a shield of truce came down from Nalgis Crag and prostrated himself before him. After the ritual eating of dirt, the fellow said, "Majesty, may your years be many and your realm increase. If Lord Pradtak surrenders to you the person of your cousin Smerdis, will you forgive him whatever transgressions he may in your mind have committed, leave off destroying his domain, and confirm not only his safety but his tenure as *dihqan* here?"

"I hate to give him so much," Sharbaraz said. But when he glanced at Abivard, Abivard nodded. Sharbaraz frowned, irresolute, but finally said, "Very well. For the sake of ending this civil war, I will. Let the usurper be brought to me before noon today and all shall be as Pradtak says." The *dihqan*'s envoy rode back toward Nalgis Crag at a gallop. Sharbaraz turned back to Abivard and said, "I may forgive, but drop me into the Void if I forget."

Abivard took that to mean Pradtak would be wise to stay up in Nalgis Crag stronghold the rest of his mortal days unless he wanted those days abruptly curtailed. The thought slid out of his mind almost as soon as it formed, overwhelmed by surging relief that the long struggle which had torn Makuran apart soon would at last be over.

He was also consumed with curiosity to learn—finally—what the man who had taken Sharbaraz' throne looked like. Long before the sun reached its high point in the sky, three men rode down from Nalgis Crag: two warriors leading a graybeard who had been tied onto a mule. Once Smerdis was in Sharbaraz's hands, the soldiers didn't wait around to learn what sort of reception they would get from the King of Kings. Like Pradtak's earlier spokesman, they galloped back toward safety.

Though Smerdis was unkempt and wearing only a dirty caftan, the family link among him, Peroz, and Sharbaraz was easy to see. He did his best to hide the fear he had to feel.

"Well, cousin, what have you to say for yourself?" Sharbaraz asked him.

"Only that I should have taken your head along with your throne," Smerdis answered. His voice was almost as mushy as that of the old woman in the village; he had lost a good many teeth.

"A mistake I will not imitate," Sharbaraz said. "But you have more spirit than I credited to you. I'll just shorten you and have done."

Smerdis nodded. Sharbaraz's officers gathered round to witness the execution. One of his men cut Smerdis' bonds and helped him off the mule. He got down on all fours and stretched out his neck for the sword. It bit. His body convulsed briefly. Had he lived as well as he died, he might have made a worthy King of Kings.

"It's over," Sharbaraz said.

XII

ALONG WITH THE WAGON THAT CARRIED ROSHNANI, THE SURVIV-ing horsemen who had come from Vek Rud domain, and Tanshar the fortune-teller, Abivard rode back toward his home with a company of troops from the army that had besieged Nalgis Crag stronghold. "Call them my parting gift," Sharbaraz said as he took his leave. "You may run into plainsmen along the road to your domain."

"That's so." Abivard clasped the hand of the King of Kings. The rest of Sharbaraz's army was breaking camp, too, some of the northwestern contingents to return to their home domains, some to go south to Mashiz with the King of Kings, and Ypsilantes' Videssian engineers to fare back to their native land. Abivard went on, "Majesty, I'll miss you more than I can say. After so long—"

Sharbaraz snorted. "I named these men here a parting gift, brother-in-law of mine, not a farewell gift. You have to make sure your own house is in order; I understand that. But before too long I'll want you at my side again. You know what my plans are."

Abivard glanced over toward the Videssians. None of them was in earshot. Even so, he lowered his voice: "We owe them a debt, Majesty." That was as close as he felt like coming to re-proving the King of Kings.

"I know," Sharbaraz answered calmly. "A debt is exactly what it is, as if I'd had to borrow ten thousand arkets from a moneylender. I'll pay it back as I can. And once I have, do you think such a stickler as Likinios will give me no excuse to get back Makuran's own?"

"Put that way, no," Abivard said. Likinios was a very able ruler; he had seen that. But Sharbaraz was right: in trying to calculate everything beforehand, the Videssian Avtokrator left scant room for anything outside his calculations. And no man, however wise, was wise enough to foresee everything. That was for the God alone.

Sharbaraz clapped him on the back. "The God grant that all's well with your domain and your family."

"Thank you, Majesty." Abivard hesitated, then said, "Majesty, if you see your way clear to giving my sister some freedom from the women's quarters, it would mean a great deal to her."

"I know that, too," Sharbaraz said. "You need not worry there. I owe Denak far more than I owe Likinios. I shall attend to it." He laughed. "I may even make it the fashion for men to be seen with their wives. What a scandal that will be for the graybeards!" He sounded as if he relished the prospect.

"Majesty, I thank you," Abivard said.

"Go on home, tend to your business—and, in a while, it will be time to tend to mine," Sharbaraz said.

The last time Abivard had traveled from Nalgis Crag stronghold back to Vek Rud domain, he had made the trip as fast as he could without killing the horses he, Sharbaraz, Tanshar, and Denak were riding. Till he got back onto his own land, he had feared Pradtak's warriors were one ridge behind him, riding hard to recapture the fugitive King of Kings.

Now he could make the journey at an easier pace. Not only did he no longer fear enemies at his back, he had enough men with him to overawe almost any band of Khamorth. Turning to Tanshar, who rode beside him, he said, "The nomads missed their chance to take big chunks of the northwest and turn them into an extension of the Pardrayan steppe."

"So they did," the fortune-teller said, nodding. "They all joined together against us when Peroz King of Kings crossed the Degird in arms, but they're clans, not a nation. If they started squabbling among themselves once their victory was won, they wouldn't have had the chance to do as you said. I don't know that's what happened, mind you, but it could have been."

Abivard laughed. "Odd to hear a fortune-teller say he doesn't know what happened. You're supposed to know such things."

"Lord, when as many years pile onto you as weigh my shoulders down, you'll find out that one of the biggest things you know is just how little you know," Tanshar answered. "Oh, if I was ordered and if I could get past the tribal shamans' magic, I might be able to learn why the Khamorth didn't swarm over the Degird as we feared, but who cares about the why after the fact? That they didn't is what matters."

"Mmm." Abivard chewed on that; he found a hard core of sense there. "I see what you're saying. But don't go parading your own ignorance. You accomplished more on that campaign than—than—" He stopped, not sure how to go on without insulting Tanshar, which was the last thing he wanted to do.

"More than you'd expected from a village fortune-teller, do you mean?" Tanshar asked gently. Abivard felt his ears heat but had to nod. Smiling, Tanshar went on, "I've lived in the village under Vek Rud stronghold all my days, and what came to me were village-size concerns. I do not complain, mind; I was as content as a man without a good wife can be. There must be many men like me, in all walks of life, through the whole of Makuran. Most of them stay in their villages their whole lives long and never have the chance to show what they might do on a larger stage. Thanks to you, I had that chance, and I took it."

The fortune-teller's quiet words gave Abivard a good deal to think about. Was what Tanshar said true? Could any man, if opportunity came his way, do more than he had ever dreamed of? If so, how many common folk were wasting lives of potential excellence just in the round of making a daily living on farms and in villages throughout the realm? If Tanshar was right, would it pay the King of Kings to seek them out? How would he find them, without some crisis in which they could display their talents? Abivard didn't know the answers, but thought the questions worth sending on to Sharbaraz.

He also found another question to put to Tanshar: "When darkness came on Mashiz, the Videssian priests were the ones who raised it. What happened to you and the rest of the Makuraner wizards Sharbaraz King of Kings had with him?"

"What happened to us, lord?" The fortune-teller's laugh was full of self-deprecation. "What happened shows the limits of what I said before, for against that magic we were all helpless as children; we had neither the training nor the skill to raise it. Till this past year I never heard anything good about Videssos, but I thank the God the Videssians were there. Without them, Mashiz might be dark yet."

"Now there's a thought—a nasty one," Abivard said. The idea of blundering through the streets trying to escape the spell, of being essentially blind, sent cold chills through him even though the possibility had evaporated weeks before.

The party rattled on toward Vek Rud domain. High summer lay heavy on the land, burning spring greenery yellow-brown and the ground itself gray. Without the fodder and the jars of water in the supply wagons, Abivard wouldn't have cared to make the trip through the desert at that season.

Little spiral winds kicked up dust and danced across the flat, baked ground. Abivard took them for granted. Some of the soldiers in the company Sharbaraz had given him, though, claimed the little whirlwinds were the outward manifestation of mischievous demons. One of the men shot an arrow through a whirlwind, which promptly collapsed. He turned in triumph to Abivard. "You see, lord?"

"Hmm," was all Abivard said, though he wondered if the fellow might not have been right.

The next day, strong winds threw sand and grit at the travelers from sunup to sundown. It wasn't one of the disastrous sandstorms that could change the whole look of the landscape and bury a caravan in blowing dust, but it was quite bad enough. When, toward evening, the wind eased at last, Abivard issued a stern decree: "No more shooting at whirlwinds." He didn't know whether the archery could have had anything to do with the storm, and he didn't care to repeat the experiment.

That evening, when he went into the wagon to see Roshnani, he found her green around the gills. "Morning sickness," the serving woman said. "I wish lemons were in season; sucking on one would help ease it."

"Given the choice between those two, I think I'd sooner have morning sickness," Abivard said.

Roshnani wanly shook her head. "You don't know what you're talking about," she said. Since that was literally true, he spread his hands and yielded the point. She said, "At my father's stronghold, some of the women would be sick all the way through their time, while others would have no trouble at all. I seem to be in the middle. Some days I'm fine, but others—" She made a horrible gagging noise. "Today was one of those."

"I hope tomorrow will be a good day for you." Abivard patted her hand. "Just a few days more and we'll be home again at last."

From outside Roshnani's cubicle, the serving woman asked, "My lady, would you care for some mutton broth and flatbread? That should sit well in your stomach."

"Maybe later," Roshnani said, gulping.

"You should eat," Abivard said reprovingly.

"I know I should," she answered. "But if I ate anything now, I'd just give it back, and that wouldn't do me any good." She hugged herself, carefully. "My insides are sore enough as is."

"Very well," Abivard said. Since he knew next to nothing about how pregnancy worked—not that a man could know much anyhow—he was willing to trust his wife's estimate of the state of her stomach. From what he had seen of Roshnani these past couple of years, her estimates of most matters deserved trust.

She laughed a little. He raised a questioning eyebrow. She said, "Forgive me, but I still have trouble thinking of Vek Rud stronghold as 'home.' I've spent more time in this wagon than I did in your women's quarters, and we've been gone for more than a year, so it hardly seems real to me."

"I can understand that," Abivard said. "I've seen more of the world since we set out on campaign than I ever imagined I would."

"You!" Roshnani exclaimed. "What of me? I don't have quite the same fear Denak did of being caged forever, but staying in one place, seeing only rooms and walls and always the same landscape out the windows, will seem very strange."

She stopped there, but sent Abivard an anxious look. He knew what it meant: now that he was coming home in triumph, would he forget the promise he had made to let her out of the women's quarters now and again? He said, "Don't worry. You'll be able to go round the stronghold and see things from all sides."

"Thank you," she said quietly. "After so much travel, even that will seem little enough, but thank you."

Abivard thought of the conversation he'd had with Tanshar. If men in large numbers never got to do all they might because they stayed on farms or in villages and never met the wider world, what of women confined to their own quarters from the onset of womanhood to death? If his fellow *dihqans* didn't ostracize him for the scandalous favoritism he had shown Roshnani, he might quietly accomplish more for the realm simply by his example than by most things he had done during the civil war.

When he musingly said as much aloud, Roshnani cocked her head to one side and studied him for a few seconds, as she had a way of doing. "Well, of course," she said.

Traveling with a large force and the supply wagons needed to keep it fed and watered meant a slow journey back to Vek Rud domain. To compensate for that, it gave Abivard the luxury of posting van- and rear guards, as well as scouting parties out to either side of the track that ran through the wasteland. He availed himself of that luxury. Had Peroz King of Kings done the same, Sharbaraz might still have been a prince back in Mashiz and Smerdis mintmaster there. Now the one was King of Kings and the other, no doubt, would serve as an object lesson of execration to minstrels and chroniclers for generations to come.

A couple of days before Abivard expected to enter his own territory once more, a rider from the vanguard came pelting back toward the main body of the force, which traveled with the wagons. "Lord, there's plainsmen and their flocks up ahead," he said. "Don't know how many of them and how many of their beasts, but enough to stir up a deal of dust, that's certain."

Abivard ran a hand down the front of his caftan. In the summer heat, without expectation of a fight, neither he nor his horse wore armor. The same held true for his entire band. *No help for it now,* he thought. He and his followers could quickly don helmets and grab shields, at any rate. That would be plenty to put them on a par with the Khamorth.

Before he started talking, he spent a little while in thought. Though nearly two years had passed since the disastrous battle on the Pardrayan steppe, he could still hear his father as if Godarz stood beside him: "Your brains are smarter than your mouth, son, if you give them the chance to be."

When he gave his orders, they came in crisp succession. He sent riders galloping out to recall the scouting parties on either wing. He sent another man back down the road they had just traveled to bring up the rear guard to protect the wagons. Meanwhile, like him, the soldiers of the main body were grabbing helms and targets and checking to make sure their bowstrings were sound and their quivers full. When everyone had come in and prepared, he waved his arm and shouted, "Forward!"

Crying his name and that of Sharbaraz, his men rode forward. But he kept a wide line of scouts out a couple of furlongs ahead of the main band. He had no reason to expect the Khamorth might have set a trap. As far as he could tell, this was but a chance encounter. But he had no interest in repeating the tragedy of Peroz on a smaller scale.

A man nearby pointed ahead. Abivard saw not only the cloud of dust the nomads and their animals kicked up but also the animals themselves: sheep. He clucked thoughtfully. Maybe sheep could find enough forage to get through summer in the badlands, but he wouldn't have wanted to try it. Cattle would already have starved.

Instead of giving him the fight for which he had nerved himself, the nomads fled in wild disorder. They numbered somewhere between a double handful and a score; when they saw more than a hundred Makuraners bearing down on them, they did the only thing that might have saved their lives. In their stirrups, Abivard would have acted the same way.

Some of his men pursued the Khamorth and knocked a couple of them out of the saddle with good archery. The nomads shot back over their shoulders as they fled, and scored one or two hits on troopers from the company Sharbaraz had lent to Abivard. The Khamorth steppe ponies were little and ugly, but they could run. After perhaps half a farsang's chase, the Makuraners gave up and went back to rejoin their comrades.

Abivard set the men to work rounding up the sheep, which had done their best to scatter in the confusion. "Fresh mutton tonight!" he shouted, which raised cheers—everyone was tired of smoked meat, yogurt, pocket bread, and other travelers' foods. He added, "The sheep we don't butcher, we'll bring home to my domain. Here's a fight against the nomads where we turn a profit."

That brought fresh cheers from the soldiers. Only after he had said it did he stop to think that he sounded more like a Videssian than a proper Makuraner noble. *Too bad,* he thought. Winning fights was better than losing them, no matter how you phrased it.

The Khamorth had let their flock range wide over the desert floor so the sheep could take advantage of whatever dry grass and water they happened to find. The nomads let the animals set their direction, and they followed. Unlike them, Abivard was going somewhere in particular and bringing the sheep along. If the forage happened to be bad alongside the track that led to his domain, he preferred losing a few beasts to turning aside to let them fatten up.

When he and his followers approached the most southeasterly village in his domain, the villagers saw the flock and began to flee, thinking the sheep heralded the arrival of a band of plainsmen. On discovering they were wrong, they returned to their homes with glad cries, greeting Abivard as warmly as if he were King of Kings himself.

News was slow trickling into the northwest of the realm; the villagers had yet to hear that Sharbaraz had vanquished Smerdis. The report sent them into fresh transports of delight, although Abivard had trouble seeing how it would change their lives much one way or the other.

By way of experiment, he brought Roshnani down from the wagon in which she had traveled so far and announced his hope that she was carrying the heir to the domain. Some of the people in the village—the older ones, mostly, and a couple of well-off merchants who probably kept their own wives secluded in imitation of the nobility—seemed startled to see her out in public, but most cheered that as one more bit of good news for the day.

Emboldened by those cheers, Roshnani leaned over and kissed Abivard on the cheek. That startled him with its boldness, but the raucous yells of approval it drew from the crowd declared the people weren't shocked. Beaming, Roshnani said, "There, you see—no one really cares if a noble's wife turns out to be a human being like any other."

"Most people don't seem to," he admitted. "I must say, I expected it to cause a bigger stir. But I can tell you one person who will care very much: my mother."

Roshnani's face fell; she had been away from the formidable presence of Burzoe for more than a year, and flourished like a flower transplanted from shady ground into bright sun. After a moment's pause to collect her thoughts—and perhaps to hold back something biting—she said, "If living her life in the women's quarters suits her, I would never be so rude as to try to make her do anything different. Why can't she extend me the same privilege?"

"Because her way of life has been customary for so long, she thinks the God ordained it," Abivard said, only half joking. "But you have one weapon in the fight that I don't think she'll be able to resist."

"What?" Roshnani suddenly giggled. "Oh." She interlaced her fingers and put both hands over the child growing, as yet invisibly, in her belly.

"That's right." Abivard nodded. "Not many mothers, from all I've heard, can resist the idea of becoming grandmothers." He paused thoughtfully. "Of course, we've been traveling long enough that Frada may have taken care of that already. He's fond of a pretty face; no reason he couldn't have sired a bastard or two in all this time. But that's not the same as fathering—or carrying—the heir to the domain . . . if it's a boy, of course."

"If it's a boy," Roshnani echoed. "Just how much that would

matter never struck me till now." She gave Abivard a worried look. "Will you be very angry at me if it turns out to be a girl?"

"Me? Of course not. I'd just want to try again as soon as we could. Eventually, I expect, we'd get it right. But Mother might be upset. I've heard that she apologized to Father when Denak was born because she was a daughter, not a son."

"No wonder Denak wants so much to be free of the women's quarters," Roshnani exclaimed.

"I hadn't thought of it that way, but you're probably right," Abivard said.

"Of course you hadn't thought about it that way—you're a man," Roshnani said. "Men don't have to worry about such things. Women do."

Abivard spread his hands, not having any reply he thought adequate. When Denak had said things like that, she sounded angry. Roshnani just said them, as if remarking that the mutton wasn't cooked with enough mint. Somehow, that made coming up with an answer even harder.

Sensibly, he changed the subject. "If it is a boy, we ought to know that, so we can tell my mother right away." He snapped his fingers. "Tanshar should be able to tell us."

"Are you that curious?" she asked. When he nodded, her face lit up. "Good. I am, too. Let's go find him."

The village boasted a couple of taverns, but the fortune-teller wasn't in either of them. Nor was he still feasting with the soldiers and villagers. They finally came upon him rubbing down his horse. When Abivard had explained what they wanted of him, he smiled. "Aye, I believe I can do that, lord, lady. The village women ask it of me often enough. Only—"

"There, you see?" Abivard said triumphantly. Then he noticed he had interrupted the fortune-teller. "Only what?"

Tanshar coughed delicately. "The magic requires a single hair plucked from, ah, the private place of the woman who is with child. As soon as the spell is complete, the hair is burned, but if the noble lady objects to providing it, of course I shall understand." He seemed a little uneasy in Roshnani's presence.

Again, though for a very different reason this time, Abivard didn't know how to respond. His face warmer than summer alone could be blamed for, he looked to Roshnani. She said, "If the women in the village can do this, I can, too. I see you have your saddlebags there, Tanshar. Do you have what you'll need for the spell in them?"

"Let me think, lady," the fortune-teller said. After a few seconds, he nodded. "Yes, I'm sure I do. Are you certain that . . . ?"

Before he could answer the question, she turned her back and walked off toward her wagon. When she came back, she was holding something—presumably the hair—between thumb and forefinger. She made a wry face. "That stung," she said.

"Er—yes." Tanshar didn't quite know what to make of such cooperation. "If you will just keep that for a bit while I ready the spell—"

He fumbled through one of the saddlebags until he found his scrying bowl. Instead of filling it with water, though, he kept on rummaging until at last he turned up a small, shapely glass jar with a cork stopper. He held it up with a grunt of satisfaction.

"That looks like Videssian work," Abivard said.

"It is," Tanshar answered. "It's full of olive oil. Often a wizard will attempt this spell with melted fat. Then, if he's not most careful, the sex of the animal that provided the medium will affect the magic. Choosing a vegetable oil should reduce the chances of that."

"Rock oil would be even better," Roshnani said.

"In that particular way, yes, but not in others: Since it comes from the ground rather than from a living creature, it is not the medium to be preferred for detecting new life," the fortune-teller said.

"You know best, I'm sure," Roshnani said.

"Yes," Tanshar agreed absently. He poured oil into the bowl, then held it out to her. "If you would be so kind as to put in the hair, my lady . . ." When she had done so, he turned to Abivard and said, "You see, lord, that I have not and shall not touch the hair myself."

"So you haven't," Abivard said. From the fuss the fortune-teller made, it was as if he was assuring Abivard he hadn't and wouldn't touch the place whence that hair had come. Abivard suddenly sobered. Magic dealt with just such equivalences. Perhaps the assurance was more than polite formality after all.

Tanshar set the bowl on the ground, then squatted by it. "Lord, lady, I daresay you will want to observe this for yourselves," he remarked, so Abivard and Roshnani squatted, too. Tanshar began a slow, nasal chant that frequently invoked Fraortish eldest of all and the lady Shivini, using two of the Prophets Four, one of each gender, to seek from the God the information he desired.

The short, curly black hair quivered in the bowl of olive oil, then all at once stretched out perfectly straight. "What does that mean?" Roshnani asked.

"My lady, it means you have a boy child growing inside you," Tanshar answered. "May he prove as brave and clever and handsome as his father."

Roshnani and Abivard stood up and hugged each other. "That's splendid news," Abivard said. He dug in the pouch at his belt, took out a jingling handful of silver arkets, and gave them to Tanshar. When the fortune-teller tried to protest, he ignored him. Then curiosity got the better of him, and he asked, "Were it a girl, what would the sign have been?"

"Instead of straightening so, the hair would have twisted into the form of a circle," Tanshar said. He pulled flint and steel from the saddlebag, then a clay lamp, which he filled from the jar of olive oil. He also took out a small leather pouch filled with crushed dry leaves, dry grass, and small twigs. He made a small pile of the tinder, striking flint and steel over it till it caught. When he had a small fire going, he lit a twig at it and used the twig to set the lamp alight. Pointing at the scrying bowl, he told Roshnani, "Take out the hair and burn it in the lamp's flame. Since it's been used once for magic, it becomes more vulnerable to being used so again unless consumed."

She did as he bade her. The oil that coated the hair made the flame flare hot and bright for a moment. Roshnani had got her fingers oily, too; she jerked them away to keep from being burned.

"A boy," Abivard said softly after he and Roshnani made their good-byes to Tanshar. "You're going to have a boy." It seemed real to him for the first time. Women know intimately what it is to be with child. Men have trouble taking it in until their wives' bellies swell, or sometimes until they hold the babes in their arms.

"Your mother will be pleased," Roshnani said.

"I wasn't thinking about that, not in the slightest," he replied. They smiled at each other and, ignoring centuries of encrusted custom, walked back to her wagon hand in hand.

After Nalgis Crag, the rocky knob on which Vek Rud stronghold sat seemed to Abivard hardly more than a pimple on the face of the earth. But the familiar bulk of the almost triangular fortress raised a lump in his throat. So much had changed for him in the year and more he had been away, but the stronghold, his home, remained the same. *As it should,* he thought.

Actually, that wasn't quite true. Banners flew from the walls. As he drew closer, he saw they bore the red lion of Makuran. Considering why he had set out on campaign, that felt fitting and proper.

The village below the fortress was also decked out in festival garb, bright with banners and garlands and with everyone dressed in holiday finery. Abivard turned to the commander of the company Sharbaraz had lent him. "You're welcome to revel with us for as long as you like, but feel free to make for your own homes whenever you care to."

"Thank you, lord," the captain said, grinning. "By your gracious leave, I'll take you up on both halves of that."

Tanshar rode up to Abivard. "Lord, with your kind consent, I'll go start cleaning out my house. The women here will have taken care of it for me, no doubt, but no one's hand is ever as right as your own."

Abivard pointed up toward the stronghold. "You're welcome to come and stay with me, you know. You're not just a village fortune-teller any more; as you yourself said, you've shown your talents are greater than that."

"That may be, but my place is here," Tanshar answered. He sounded so determined, Abivard did not try to argue with him. The fortune-teller headed for his neat little home by the marketplace.

The gates to the stronghold were open. Frada stood there waiting for Abivard. The two brothers waved to each other, one on horseback, the other afoot. "By the God, it's good to see you," Frada called.

"By the God, it's good to see everyone and everything here," Abivard answered, which raised a cheer from all who stood close enough to hear him. He went on, "Roshnani's back there—" He pointed to the wagon. "—and carrying, Tanshar says, a boy. And Denak, back in Mashiz, will bear the child of the King of Kings."

That news also brought cheers, though not quite so many as he had expected. He rode past Frada into the courtyard and looked toward the doorway of the living quarters, wondering if his brother had arranged a procession of his mother and wives and half sisters. The occasion was surely solemn enough. But no women came forth from that iron-shod door; he supposed Frada hadn't cared to usurp a prerogative he might have reckoned exclusively his own, and concluded that Frada had more delicacy than he had suspected.

He got another cheer, a loud one, when he swung down off his horse and set foot on the cobbles of Vek Rud stronghold once more. Roshnani's wagon rattled through the gates and into the fortress. He walked over to it and called to her to come forth. She did, to loud applause. No one thought he was violating custom by showing her off now, not when he and she were returning in triumph.

"I give my last command before turning the domain back to Abivard my brother," Frada shouted. "Let everyone feast and drink and make merry!" The yell that went up after that dwarfed any Abivard had got, but he didn't care. Had Frada not given that command, he would have.

He hugged his brother. "It is *so* good to be home," he said.

"As may be, but here I am jealous of you again," Frada said. "You get all the glory, and I stay behind."

"I told you two years ago, there's less glory to war than you think," Abivard answered. "Whatever there is, though, you'll get your share. With Sharbaraz on the throne, may his years be many and his realm increase, there's not doubt of that."

"May you be right," Frada said. "I'm glad you're home, too, though." His face clouded. As if continuing the same sentence, he went on, "Mother wants to see you as soon as you can spare even a moment."

"I want to see her too, of course," Abivard said.

"I really think you should do it as soon as you can," Frada said, still sounding unhappy. "Maybe even now—what with the feasting, no one will particularly notice if you're away from the middle of things for a bit."

Roshnani caught what Abivard was missing. "Something's gone wrong in the women's quarters, hasn't it?"

Frada seemed uneasy at the prospect of speaking to his brother's wife, but he nodded. Abivard clapped a hand to his forehead. Battle was clean and simple; you could tell at a glance who had won and who had lost, and often have a good idea about why. None of that held true for disputes in the women's quarters. Having but one wife with him, he had been free of such tangles the past year and more, an advantage of monogamy he hadn't considered till now. He said, "All right, I'll see her this instant."

Relief blossomed on Frada's face. "Come with me, then." He gestured to include Roshnani in the invitation but still did not say anything directly to her.

As Abivard walked toward the doorway into the inhabited

part of the stronghold, eyes watched from the windows of the women's quarters. What were his wives, or perhaps his half sisters, thinking in there? What had gone wrong past the power of his mother and brother to fix?

Inside the entranceway, the savory smells of fresh pocket bread and roasting mutton, the bouquet of sweet wine, made his nose twitch and his stomach rumble. No less than anyone else, he wanted to feast and drink and rejoice. But he turned away from the kitchens and went with Frada and Roshnani down the hall that led to the *dihqan*'s bedchamber. Frada stopped at the door. "I've gone into this room, brother, to meet with our mother. By the God, I swear I have not gone past it and into the women's quarters proper since you set out with Sharbaraz to reclaim his throne."

"Just telling me would suffice," Abivard said. "You needn't take on about such a matter as that. If I didn't trust you, would I have left you in charge of the stronghold?"

Frada didn't answer, nor did he seem eager even to enter the bedchamber now that Abivard was back at Vek Rud stronghold. His scruples seemed excessive, but Abivard shrugged and went into the chamber with Roshnani alone. As he closed and barred the door, Frada's footfalls rapidly receded down the corridor. Abivard shrugged again.

He had carried a key to the door of the women's quarters all the way to Videssos and back. Now he used it to open that door. He was anything but surprised to find his mother waiting for him on the other side. He took her in his arms, kissing her cheek. "It's so good to be back," he told her, as he had Frada.

Burzoe accepted his affection as her due, as she did Roshnani's more formal greeting. To Roshnani she said, "If you think I approve of your breaking our ancient customs, you are mistaken. If you think I am not delighted to learn you are carrying a son and heir, you are even more mistaken. I welcome you back to the domain and your proper place in it, principal wife of my son."

"I may not always stay in what you think my proper place, mother of my husband," Roshnani answered. Abivard would have had trouble imagining her impolite, but that did not mean she would abandon the greater freedom she sought.

"We shall speak of this again," Burzoe said, retreating not a barleycorn's width from her position, "but now is not the proper moment." She turned to Abivard. "Come with me to my chamber—the two of you may as well come, now that I think on it. The decision here, though, must be yours, my son."

"What *is* this in aid of, Mother?" Abivard asked as they walked down the hall. "Frada told me something was amiss, but would say no more than that."

"He acted properly," Burzoe said. She stood aside to let Abivard precede her into the chamber, then went in ahead of Roshnani. A serving woman appeared at the doorway, as if conjured up by magic. Burzoe fixed her with a baleful glare. "Bring Kishmar and Onnophre here. They know what they need to bring."

"Yes, mistress." The woman hurried away. Her face was pale and frightened.

Wives, not half sisters, at any rate, Abivard thought. In a way, that was a relief. He had bedded both the women a few times for form's sake, but that was about all. They were pretty enough, but no great spark had flared in him, nor, he thought, in either of them.

The serving woman returned. Behind her came Kishmar and Onnophre. Their appearance startled Abivard: both were heavier, softer, than he remembered, and both had dark, tired circles under their eyes. The reason for that was easy enough to understand, though—each of them carried a baby wrapped in a soft wool blanket. Abivard did not know a great deal about babies, but someone who knew much less than he would have known these two were far too small to have been conceived while he was at Vek Rud stronghold.

He stared at his mother. She nodded grimly. "Oh, dear," he said.

She rounded on his junior wives, her voice fierce. "The *dihqan* has returned to his domain. What have you to say for yourselves, whores?"

Onnophre and Kishmar both began to wail, producing a hideous discord that grated on Abivard's ears. "Forgive!" Onnophre cried, a heartbeat before Kishmar bawled out the same word. They started telling their stories at the same time, too, so he sometimes had trouble figuring out which one he was listening to. It didn't matter. Both stories were about the same. They had been bored, they had been lonely, they had feared he was never coming back from wherever he had gone—neither woman seemed quite clear on that—and so they had managed to find a way to amuse themselves . . . and paid an all too common price for that amusement.

He looked at them. "By the way things seem, you didn't wait any too long before you found yourselves, ah, friends." That set his wives wailing again. Ignoring the racket, he turned back to Burzoe. "Are there any others with bulging bellies?"

She shook her head. "There should not have been these two. The blame for them is mine; I failed to keep proper watch on the women's quarters. But the fate of these two sluts and their worthless brats lies in your hands."

"Oh, dear," Abivard said again. If he felt like slaughtering the women and the babies, he would have been within his rights. Many a *dihqan* would have whipped out his sword without a second thought. Many a *dihqan* wouldn't have waited to hear what the miscreant wives had to say; he would have slain them as soon as he saw the babes in their arms.

"What will you do with those who have brought cuckoo's eggs into your nest?" Burzoe demanded. Her eyes expected blood.

Roshnani stood silent. This choice was Abivard's, not hers. All the same, he looked at her. He could not read her face. He sighed. "I make a decent soldier," he said wearily, "but I find I haven't it in me to be a butcher. I shall find black pebbles and divorce them and send them far away. Too many in Makuran have died this past year. Four more will not help."

"It is not enough!" Burzoe cried, and Abivard was reminded overwhelmingly of Denak's dismay at anything that smacked of half measures. *Father and son, mother and daughter,* he thought.

Kishmar and Onnophre babbled out thanks and blessings. Onnophre took a step forward, as if to embrace him, then checked herself, which was one of the wiser things she had done. Abivard said, "If I didn't put Ardini to the sword, how can I kill these two? They weren't so much wicked as foolish. They can sew; they can spin. They'll make their way in the world."

"Cast them out at once then," Burzoe said. "Every day they stay in the women's quarters adds to their shame—and to my own."

Abivard suspected the latter concern weighed more heavily in his mother's mind than the former. He said, "Since the scandal has been here for months, one more day to settle it won't matter. I've been away for more than a year. Today I aim to enjoy my return."

Burzoe's upraised eyebrows spoke eloquently of disagreement, but all she said was, "You are the *dihqan* of Vek Rud domain and the master of the women's quarters. It shall be as you ordain."

Abivard's soon-to-be-former wives showered him with benedictions. They could have faced the sword like Smerdis, with their babes left out on the hillside for dogs and ravens, and well they knew it. No doubt it hadn't seemed real to them while he was away on campaign. He might not have come back at all, in which case their adulteries stood a chance of going unpunished. Having him before them suddenly put matters in a different light.

"Be still," he said, in a voice he might have used to order his lancers to charge. Onnophre and Kishmar stared at him. No one, plainly, had ever spoken to them so. If someone had, perhaps they might not have found themselves in their present predicament. He went on, "I do not forgive you. I merely spare you. If the God grant that you find other husbands, use them better than you did me." The women started to talk. He overrode them: "You've said too much, you've done too much already. Take your bastard babes and get out of my sight. Tomorrow I will find the black pebbles and send you forth."

They fled out of Burzoe's chamber. Burzoe looked at him with a small, grudging hint of approval. "That was well done," she said.

"Was it?" Abivard felt weak and sick inside, as if he had just been through a battle in which he almost died. "Tomorrow it will be over. They can go off and be stupid at someone else's expense, not mine."

"It won't be easy for them, even so," Roshnani said. "Yes, they can earn their bread, but they'll have hard lessons in living outside the women's quarters. How to deal with butchers and merchants, how to speak to men—"

"That they know already," Burzoe said savagely.

"What would you have had me do?" Abivard asked Roshnani. She sighed. "What you could do, you did. As you said, this should be a day of joy. I'm glad you chose not to stain your hands with blood here."

Burzoe shook her head. "He was soft. Mercy now will only encourage others to act as those sluts did."

"Mother of my husband, we do not agree." Roshnani's voice was quiet. She did not offer Burzoe argument, but she did not back away from her own view, either.

Burzoe did not seem to know what to make of that. Roshnani had been properly deferential, as a daughter-in-law should have, but had not yielded, as most daughters-in-law would have. The combination was disconcerting. She took refuge in a common complaint: "You young people have no respect for the way things should be done. If I'd gone gallivanting off to the ends of the world the way you and Denak did, I don't know—and I don't want to think about—what would have happened to my reputation."

"Nothing happened to Denak's reputation," Roshnani said with the same quiet determination to get her point across that she had shown before, "save that she got to bear a child who, with luck, will be King of Kings far earlier than she could have if she'd stayed behind here till the war was won."

"If Roshnani hadn't come with us, the war likely would have been lost, not won," Abivard told his mother, and explained how it had been his principal wife who had the idea to take refuge in Videssos. He added, "If they'd stayed, you probably never would have had a grandchild with a chance to be King of Kings."

"Custom—" Burzoe said, but she let it go as that. The prospect of a King of Kings or royal princess as a grandchild did have considerable allure.

Abivard said, "Nor will the world end if Roshnani, who after all has already traveled far, sometimes comes out of the women's quarters to see the rest of the stronghold. Sharbaraz King of Kings has promised to allow Denak the same liberty in the palace at Mashiz, and how can following what the King of Kings does be wrong?"

"I don't know the answer to that—you'd have to ask Smerdis," his mother replied tartly. Abivard felt his ears heat. Roshnani sucked in her breath with a sudden sharp sound—Burzoe could still be formidable. But she went on, "You will do as you will do and take no special notice of me in the doing. So life goes, however the old try to make it otherwise. But if you think you will make me love the changes you work, please think again."

Greatly daring, Abivard went over to her and put an arm around her shoulder. She had always been the one to console him, never the other way round—till now. He said, "By the God, Mother, I shall let no dishonor come to Vek Rud stronghold, nor to any who dwell here."

"I thought the same," Burzoe said, "and look what came of it."

"It will be all right," Abivard said with the confidence of youth. Roshnani nodded vigorously.

Now it was Burzoe who did not agree but forbore to argue. She said, "It will be as it is, however that may prove. But I know, son, that you would sooner be feasting than dealing with the troubles of the women's quarters—or with me. Go on, then. Perhaps the lady your wife will spend a little while here and regale us with tales of the far-off lands she's seen."

"Of course I will," Roshnani said at once. Abivard could read her thoughts: the more women heard of the outside world, the less content they would be with separation from it.

Maybe Burzoe saw that, maybe she didn't. In either case, having made the invitation, she could scarcely withdraw it. Abivard took leave of them both. He locked the door to the women's quarters behind him—not that that had mattered much to Onnophre and Kishmar. He wondered who had fathered their children. If he ever found out, Vek Rud stronghold would have a couple of more folk leaving it.

Frada still waited in the hallway not far from the *dihqan's* bedchamber. "You heard?" he demanded. Abivard nodded. His brother went on, "What will you do?"

"I'll divorce them both tomorrow and send them out of here," Abivard answered. "That will do. I've seen too much blood spilled this past year to want more on my hands."

His brother's shoulders slumped with relief. "I told Mother your answer would be something like that. She was all for taking their heads the minute their bellies started bulging." He rolled his eyes. "We went round and round on that one like peasant women in a ring dance. Finally I got her to wait for your word."

"What was it Father would say? 'Easier to do something now than undo it later if it happens to be wrong.' Something like that, anyhow. I'd have been upset if I got home to find two of my wives had gone on the chopping block like a couple of pullets."

"That's what I thought," Frada answered. "You're more tenderhearted than Father was, or you put up with more nonsense, anyway. Women promenading all over the landscape—" His snort showed what he thought of that. "But you're the *dihqan* now, and the stronghold runs by how you think we ought to do things."

"Am I?" Abivard said. "More tenderhearted, I mean." He wondered what Godarz would have done had a wife of his borne a child he could not have sired. Something interesting and memorable, he had no doubt. "Well, maybe I am. Every now and then, the world does change."

"Maybe so." Almost like Roshnani, Frada acknowledged without necessarily agreeing. Then he clapped his brother on the back. "However that may be, there's a feast waiting for us down the hall. If you'd stayed closeted much longer, my nose and my belly would have dragged me off to it."

"I expect I'd have forgiven you," Abivard said. "Let's go."

Somehow, word of what he had decided in the women's quarters got out to the rest of the stronghold faster than he did. Some people praised his mercy; others plainly thought he had been too soft. But everyone knew what the verdict had been. He drank two quick cups of wine to try to dull the edge of his bemusement.

In the kitchen, a cook gave him a plate of lamb and herbs and chickpeas all mashed together, and a bowl of lamb broth with toasted chunks of pocket bread floating in it as an accompaniment. He dug in with a silver spoon. "That's good," he said blissfully. "Now in truth I start to feel at home."

"Didn't they make it at Mashiz?" Frada asked.

"They did, yes, but with different spices—too much garlic and not enough mint, if you ask me," Abivard answered. "This is the way it's supposed to taste, the way it's tasted ever since I was a boy."

"The way it's tasted as long as Abalish has commanded in the kitchens, you mean," Frada said, and Abivard nodded. His brother went on, "And what did they eat in Videssos? That must have been interesting."

"They generally bake their bread in loaves, not in pockets," Abivard said, thinking back. "They eat lamb and kid and beef, much as we do; they're even more fond of garlic than the folk around Mashiz. And—" He broke off suddenly, remembering the fermented fish sauce.

"What is it?" Frada asked eagerly. Abivard told him. He looked revolted, though not as revolted as Abivard had felt. "You're making that up." Abivard shook his head. Frada said, "I hope you didn't eat any of the horrible stuff."

"I did till they told me what it was." Abivard spooned up some broth to drive away the memory. When that didn't work, he drank some wine.

"What . . . did it taste like?" Frada asked, like one small boy querying another who had just swallowed a bug.

Abivard had trouble recalling. After he had learned the sauce was made from rotten fish, horror overwhelmed whatever flavor it might have had. At last he said, "It wasn't as bad as it might have been—more cheesy than anything else."

"Better you than me, brother of mine, that's all I have to say." Frada waved to a halt a woman with a tray of boiled mutton tongues, sweetbreads, and eyes. He filled the plate he had emptied of mashed lamb. "Now here's proper fare."

"You're right, of course," Abivard said. "Here, Mandane, let me have some of those, too." When his plate was full, he took out his belt knife and attacked the savory spread with gusto.

Presently, full to the point of bursting and drunk to the point where he seemed to float a hand's breadth above the stones of the floor, he made his way back toward the bedchamber. Only then did it occur to him that he ought to summon one of his wives to bed with him, and one other than Roshnani. She had had him all to herself for a year and more, which had to have stirred up savage jealousy in the women's quarters. He hoped that jealousy wouldn't manifest itself as it had with Ardini.

But whom should he choose? Whichever wife he first bedded on his return would also be an object of jealousy. The other relevant issue was that he was so laden with food and drink that he did not want a woman and had doubts he could do one justice. Such fine points spun slowly through his mind as he went into the bedchamber and, after a couple of fumbles, let down the bar.

He took off his sandals. Trying to work the buckles was harder than barring the door had been. At last he managed. With a sigh of relief, he lay down to think about which wife he should call. The next thing he knew, it was morning.

For the first time since he had become *dihqan*, Abivard had the chance to run his domain in something approaching peace. From time to time, small bands of Khamorth would cross the Degird and trickle south to his lands, sometimes with their flocks, sometimes as mere raiders, but he and his horsemen always managed to drive them off. The great eruption of plainsmen into Makuran everyone had feared after the disaster on the Pardrayan steppe did not come.

"Much as I hate to say it, maybe the tribute Smerdis paid the nomads did some good," Abivard remarked.

Frada spat on the walkway of the stronghold wall they paced together. "That for Smerdis and his tribute both. Stinking

usurper. How could you speak any good of a man against whom
you spent most of two years at war? If it weren't for you, he'd
likely still be King of Kings. Aren't you glad he's gone?"

"That I am. As you say, I went through too much getting rid
of him to wish he were still here." A little voice inside Abivard,
though, asked how much difference having Sharbaraz on the
throne rather than Smerdis would mean for Makuran in the long
run. Was changing the ruler worth all the blood and treasure
spilled to accomplish the job?

Fiercely, he told the little voice to shut up. In any case, whatever the civil war had done for Makuran as a whole, it had
surely made his fortune—and his clan's. Without it, he would
never have become brother-in-law to the King of Kings, nor
possibly uncle to Sharbaraz's successor. He would have stayed
just a frontier *dihqan*, rarely worrying about what happened outside his domain.

Would that have been so bad? the little voice asked. He ignored it.

Roshnani came out of the door to the living quarters and
strolled across the courtyard. She saw him up on the wall and
waved to him. He waved back. The stablemen and smith's help-
ers and serving women in the courtyard took no special notice
of her, which Abivard reckoned progress. The first few times
she had ventured out of the women's quarters, people had either
stared popeyed or turned their backs and pretended she wasn't
there, which struck Abivard as even worse.

From the women's quarters, eyes avidly followed Roshnani as
she walked about. Because of what Kishmar and Onnophre had
done, Abivard hesitated to give his other wives and half sisters
the freedom Roshnani enjoyed. He would willingly have granted
it to his mother, but Burzoe did not want it. If one of the faces
behind the narrow windows was hers, he was sure her mouth
was set in a thin line of disapproval.

Frada nodded down to Roshnani and said, "That hasn't
worked out as badly as I expected."

"There's the most praise I've yet heard from you about the
idea," Abivard said.

"It's not meant as praise," Frada answered. "It's meant as
something less than complete hatred of the notion, which is the
place from which I began."

"Anything less than complete hatred is the most praise I've
heard from you," Abivard insisted.

Frada made a horrible face at him and mimed throwing a

punch in his direction. Then, hesitantly, he said, "I hope you don't mind my telling you that I've talked to the lady Roshnani a few times."

Abivard understood his hesitation; if by Makuraner custom a noble was the only man who with propriety could look at his wife, he was even more emphatically the only man who could with propriety speak to her. Abivard said, "Don't fret yourself about it. I knew such things would happen when I gave her leave to come out of the women's quarters. I didn't see how it could be otherwise: if she came out and no one would speak to her, that might be even worse in her mind than staying confined in there."

"Doesn't it bother you?" Frada demanded. "You've stood more customs on their heads—"

"I'm not the only one," Abivard reminded him. "Sharbaraz King of Kings is doing with our sister what I'm doing with my wife. And a lot of customs got overthrown summer before last, along with our army. I've tried to keep the changes small and sensible. Really, I don't think Father would have disapproved."

Frada pondered that. At last, he gave a grudging nod. "You may be right. Father . . . I won't say he often broke custom, but he never seemed to take it as seriously as, say, Mother does."

"Well put." Abivard nodded in turn. "He'd work within custom whenever he could, but I don't think he'd let it bind him if he needed to accomplish something."

"Hmm. If you put it that way, brother of mine, what do you *accomplish* by letting Roshnani out of the women's quarters?" Frada looked smug, as if sure he had come up with a question Abivard couldn't answer.

But Abivard did answer: "I get the benefit of her advice more readily, which served me—and Makuran—well on campaign. And her advice is apt to be better if she sees things for herself than if she hears about them secondhand. And, on top of all that, I make her happy, which, as you'll discover when you marry, is not the least important thing in the world." He sent Frada a challenging stare.

His brother said, "If it's not the least important thing in the world, why did you set it at the foot of your list of arguments, not at their head? No, don't answer. I know why: to make the others seem bigger."

"Well, what if I did?" Abivard said, laughing. He set a hand on his brother's shoulder. "You've grown up, this past year.

When I went off to war, you'd never have noticed the way an argument was made."

"I've heard enough of them since, wearing your sandals while you were away." Frada rolled his eyes. "By the God, I've had more people try to sneak lies past me than I ever imagined. Some folk have no shame whatever; they'll say anything if they think they see an arket in it."

"I won't say you're wrong, because I don't think you are. What made Smerdis do what he did, except that he thought he saw an arket in it?"

"Rather more than one," Frada said.

"Well, yes," Abivard said. "But the idea behind his greed and everyone else's is the same." He gave Frada a sidelong look. "And how many lies got past you?"

"Drop me in the Void if I know—I couldn't very well notice the ones that got past me, now could I?" Frada answered. He paused for a moment, then resumed. "Fewer and few as the months went by, I do hope."

"Yes, that's something worth aiming at," Abivard agreed.

He looked out over the battlements toward the Vek Rud River to the north. Ripening crops watered by *qanats* made the land close to the river a carpet of gold and green; herds grazed on the scrub farther away. He let out a long sigh.

"What is it?" Frada asked.

"I was standing just here, near enough, and peering out toward the river two years ago, when Father came up on the wall and told me the Videssians had been spreading gold around among the Khamorth to make them want to fight us," Abivard said. "Everything that followed sprang from that."

"It's a different world now," Frada said.

"It certainly is. I didn't expect to be *dihqan* for another twenty years—the same for Okhos and for Pradtak, too, I suppose," Abivard said. "Sharbaraz didn't expect to be King of Kings for a long time, either—and Smerdis, I daresay, never expected to be King of Kings at all."

Frada looked out at the domain, too. "Lords come and lords go," he said. "The land goes on forever."

"Truth again," Abivard said. "I give thanks to the God that the nomads contented themselves with going after our flocks and herds and didn't seriously try to wreck our croplands. Repairing *qanats* once they're broken isn't a matter for a season; it takes years."

"We fought a couple of skirmishes with them last year near

the edge of the irrigated land; they wanted to pasture their flocks in the wheat and the beans," Frada said. "But when they found out we had enough warriors left to keep that from being an easy job, they gave it up—the God and the Four be praised." He wiped his forehead. "I'd be lying if I said I wasn't worried; for a while, I feared you'd hardly have a domain to come home to."

"That's all right," Abivard said. "For a while, I didn't think I was coming home, anyway. Smerdis had us by the neck—pushed out across the Tutub, away from the land of the Thousand Cities, with the desert at our backs ... If it hadn't been for Roshnani, I expect we'd have perished there."

Frada glanced down at Roshnani, who was talking with a leatherworker. He still hesitated to look directly at her for more than a moment, but let his eyes slide across her and then back. Even so he said, "Well, considering what she did, maybe she does deserve to be out and about."

Since that was as close to a concession as he would get from his brother, Abivard clapped Frada on the back. "I thank you," he said. "Do remember, this is new for me, too. I expect it will grow easier for both of us—and maybe for Roshnani, as well—as time goes by. The Videssians let their women out freely, and so do our common folk. I don't think we'll fall into the Void if we do the same."

"I notice you haven't turned your other wives loose," Frada said.

"I would have, if Kishmar and Onnophre had kept their legs closed while I was away," Abivard answered irritably. "You'll notice they both got themselves with child while they were supposed to be locked away in the women's quarters, too; they could hardly have done more if they were selling themselves in the market square down in the village. But rewarding the others right after that would have been too much."

"What about our half sisters?" Frada asked.

"You're full of impossible questions today, aren't you?" Abivard said. He thought that one over, then sighed. "I probably won't let them out, not right away, anyhow. Having them known for wandering about outside the women's quarters wouldn't do their chances for a proper marriage match any good."

"That makes good sense," Frada allowed. "I give you credit for seeing the potholes and ruts in the road you're traveling."

"I'm glad of that," Abivard said. "Sometimes I don't think you see the road in the potholes and ruts I'm traveling." Both brothers laughed. Abivard said, "By the God, I did miss you.

Sharbaraz King of Kings is a fine man and a good friend, but he's not an easy fellow to be foolish with."

"Nice to know I'm good for something," Frada said. "If all's well up here, as it looks to be, shall we go down and find out how Ganzak is doing with the latest armor? If he stays as busy as he has been, we'll be able to outfit a formidable band of lancers before long." His grin turned predatory. "All the neighboring *dihqans* will fear us."

"There are worse things," Abivard said. "Aye, let's go." Together, they descended from the wall and hurried across the courtyard to Ganzak's smithy. In winter, the smithy had been a welcome refuge against the cold. With fall still some ways away, sweat started on Abivard's brow as soon as he went into the fire-filled chamber.

Ganzak labored naked to the waist; his forehead and broad, hairy chest gleamed with sweat. Its odor filled the smith, along with woodsmoke and the almost-blood smell of hot iron. When Abivard and Frada came in, Ganzak was working not on armor but on a sword blade. His muscles rippled as he brought a hammer down on the iron bar he held to the anvil with a pair of tongs. Metal clashed against metal; sparks flew.

The smith plunged the blade-to-be into a barrel by the anvil. The hiss that rose might have come from the throat of a great venomous snake. Ganzak lifted the blade out of the quenching bath, examined it with a critical eye, and set it aside. He laid the tongs down on the anvil with a clank. "The God give you good day, lord," he said, nodding to Abivard.

"And to you," Abivard answered. Then he blurted, "How do you stand the heat in here?"

Ganzak threw back his head and laughed, loudly and gustily. "'Lord, this chamber is my home. When I come out of it, I sometimes think I'm about to start shivering, I'm so used to it here."

Abivard and Frada exchanged glances. Frada said, "What I think is that you ought to go down into the village and have Tanshar or one of the old wives brew you up a potion, for it's plain you're not a well man."

The smith laughed again. He was always good-natured, which, given his size and strength, was fortunate. Now he stretched, and the molten motion of the muscles under his sweat-shiny skin was like those under a lion's pelt. "Do I look infirm to you?" he demanded.

"No, no," Frada said hastily. However good-natured Ganzak was, only a foolish man would undertake to argue with him.

Abivard said, "We came to see how you were faring with the armors the domain needs."

"I should finish the eighth suit before the moon is new again," the smith answered. "That's gear for man and horse both, you understand, and puts us two equipages ahead of where we were before Peroz King of Kings led the army up into Pardraya. We're also ahead in helms and shields both, and I've had men ask for mail shirts, too: they're a long way from full armor, I'll not deny, but better than leather dipped in boiling wax."

"I know where they got the idea, unless I'm much mistaken," Abivard said. "Are they men who rode with Sharbaraz King of Kings?"

Ganzak's brow furrowed. "Now that you mention it, lord, they are. How did you know that?" Before Abivard could answer, the smith snapped his fingers. "Wait! I have it. You think they filched the notion from the Videssians, don't you?"

"I certainly do," Abivard said. "The Videssians wore armor enough to dominate our light-armed horse archers and even to confront our lancers, but they were a lot more mobile than heavy cavalry. Their way of doing things had merit, I thought, and from what you say, I wasn't the only one."

"Mm—I wouldn't quarrel with you," Ganzak said. "They turned out to be men of more parts than I'd expected, I will say that for 'em. I figured they'd be all gold and sneakery and no guts, and they weren't like that at all." His jaw worked, as if he were chewing on something whose flavor he didn't quite fancy. "I don't know but what I'd sooner have had 'em be more like the tales tell. They'd be less dangerous, I think."

"I think you're right," Abivard said. Ganzak showed clear understanding. He was a good smith, no doubt about that. Abivard wondered what sort of *dihqan* he would have made, had he been born to the nobility. A good one, was his guess. The realm needed smiths, yes, but it also needed good leaders. As Tanshar had asked, what was it losing because so many men never got to display the things of which they were capable?

Frada looked frustrated to the point of bursting. "Everyone chatters on about the Videssians and how they're this and how they're not that," he cried, "and here I've never been within a thousand farsangs of one."

"Don't let it bother you, brother of mine," Abivard said. "You'll have your chance against them, too."

"When?" Frada asked. "When I'm old and gray like Smerdis? I won't be able to do any good against them then. What with Sharbaraz King of Kings all friendly with Likinios Avtokrator, we're liable to have peace for the next generation." He spoke as if that were one of the worst things that could happen, but then, he had never been to war.

"I don't think you'll have to wait so long," Abivard said. "Sharbaraz King of Kings is a man of honor; he wouldn't pick a fight with Likinios without good reason. But Likinios is liable to give him reason. He took a chunk of Vaspurakan from us, remember, as the price for his aid. He's the kind who's always reaching out for his own advantage. One day he may well overreach himself, and then you'll have your wish."

Frada bent his arm, as if to couch a lance in the crook of his elbow. "It can't come soon enough."

Abivard laughed at him. "I said one day, brother of mine, not tomorrow or even next year."

"I heard what you said," Frada answered. "I just didn't listen to you."

XIII

THE WINTER BEFORE, ABIVARD HAD PASSED HIS TIME IN CHILLY EX-ile at Serrhes in the Empire of Videssos. The winter before that had been filled with excitement and frantic preparations for revolt, with Sharbaraz a fugitive and Smerdis holding most of Makuran in the hollow of his hand.

This winter was different. It wasn't the near hibernation Abivard had known in his younger days. He was *dihqan* now, not Godarz, and on his shoulders rested responsibility for solving the squabbles in his domain and for making sure supplies would stretch till spring. But the harvest had been good—better than he had expected—and the storehouses held enough wheat and nuts and fruit to ensure that the domain would not go hungry before warmth returned.

He got the chance to relax a little, the first time he'd had that chance for two and a half years. He made the most of it, sleeping through long winter nights, drinking hot spiced wine to fight the chill of snowstorms and icy breezes, taking advantage of the good harvest to eat until he had to fasten his sword belt one notch closer to the end than he had before.

Some crops grew despite the beastly weather. Roshnani's belly swelled, which she regarded with a mixture of pride and wry amusement. As her pregnancy advanced, her ankles also swelled when she was on her feet for any length of time. That limited her trips outside the women's quarters, much to her annoyance.

Abivard kept calling her to his bed even after she had grown quite round. That irked his other wives; one of them complained,

"Why don't you summon me more often? Aren't I prettier than she is?"

"If you have to ask the question, the answer is always no," Abivard answered, "because just letting it cross your lips makes you ugly."

The woman stared at him in bafflement. "I don't understand," she said.

"I know," he answered, sighing. "That's part of the problem."

Little by little, he began to let his other wives make excursions outside the women's quarters. He remained unconvinced that was a good idea but found no way around it. Before he let any of his wives out to explore the rest of the stronghold, he offered such freedom to his mother. Burzoe rejected it, as she had before. He had expected as much, but it still saddened him. Others were moving in new directions, but her path through life remained fixed.

"What are we going to do with her?" he asked Roshnani one chilly night when the two of them huddled together in the bed in the *dihqan*'s bedchamber as much for warmth as from affection. "If those others go out and see things and do things she doesn't, how will she keep the lead in the women's quarters?"

"She probably won't," Roshnani answered. "It will pass to someone else." Since she was the present *dihqan*'s principal wife, when she said "someone else" she undoubtedly meant herself, but she was characteristically self-effacing.

She was also sure to be right. Abivard realized that change would have to come anyway, sooner or later: Burzoe was, after all, only the widow of the former *dihqan*. But she had been undisputed mistress of the feminine side of the stronghold for longer than he had been alive; the idea of that power slipping out of her hands was as upsetting as an earthquake. He shook his head in bemusement.

Roshnani felt the motion and asked, "What is it?"

He explained, then said, "I was thinking of all the changes that have happened lately, but here's one I hadn't looked for: maybe that's what makes it so upsetting."

"As you said, though, it's a change that's coming because she refuses to change," Roshnani reminded him. "And more changes are yet to come." She took his hand and set it on her belly. The skin there was stretched tight over her growing womb.

The baby inside her kicked and squirmed, then pushed something hard and round against Abivard's palm. "That's the head," he said in delight. "That has to be his head."

Her hand joined his. "I think you're right," she said, just before, like some magical island that could rise out of the water and then vanish once more, it sank away from them as the baby shifted position.

Abivard hugged Roshnani to him. As he did so, the baby kicked vigorously. They both laughed. "Someone's doing his best to come between us," he said.

Roshnani turned serious. "That will happen for a while, you know," she said. "I'll need some time to recover after the baby's born, and he'll need me for a while, too, in spite of servants and wet nurses."

"I do know that," Abivard said. "I expect it will be all right. I'm just waiting to see which of us he favors. If he looks like your brother Okhos, he'll have all the maidens sighing for him."

"I've no reason to complain of the looks on your side of the family," Roshnani said, which made Abivard hug her again and also made the baby wiggle in her belly—or perhaps the baby would have wiggled anyhow. Roshnani went on, "And what shall we call him, once he comes out?"

"I'd like to name him Varaz, after my brother who perished up on the Pardrayan plain," Abivard answered. "Do you mind? You lost your father and brothers on the steppe, as well."

"He'll be of Vek Rud domain, and heir to it, so he should have a name that goes with it," Roshnani said after a little thought. "We'll have others to remember my kin—and your father, too. I'd thought you might want to name the boy Godarz, in fact. Why don't you?"

"Because my father's memory will stay green for years to come in the hearts and minds of everyone who knew him," Abivard said; he had thought about that, too. "He was *dihqan*, and a good one; he touched people's lives. That's a better monument than a baby's name. But Varaz was cut down before he had the chance to show everything he could do in life. He deserves to be remembered, too, and for him I think this is a good way."

"Ah." Roshnani nodded against his chest. "Every so often, you've accused me of being sensible. Husband of mine, I have to say I'm not the only one here with that affliction."

"Accused? Affliction?" Abivard snorted. "You make it sound as if something's wrong with common sense. The only thing wrong with it I can think of is that not enough people have any of it . . . Some of my former wives spring to mind," he added with a touch of malice.

Roshnani refused to let the last gibe distract her. "What could be more wrong with it than that?" she asked, and, as she had a way of doing, left Abivard groping for an answer.

Winter solstice came and went. The year before, in Serrhes, the Videssians had celebrated the day with raucous, sometimes rowdy rites. Here it passed quietly, almost unnoticed. In a way, that felt good and normal. In another way, Abivard missed the excitement of the Videssian festival.

Snowstorms rolled down from the north one after another: invaders from the steppe as dangerous as the Khamorth and, unlike the nomads, impossible to repel. The storms killed beasts and occasionally herdsmen; like everyone in the stronghold and the village below, Abivard worried that the fuel carefully gathered during the warm season would not last through the cold. Every icy blast that shook the shutters on the window to his bedchamber made him fret more.

Then, one day when the year's reckoning said the equinox was approaching but the snow-covered ground seemed certain winter would last forever, such mere pragmatic concerns as fuel vanished from his mind, for a maidservant came out of the women's quarters and, wrapped in thick sheepskins, hurried down to the village. She soon returned with the midwife, a gray-haired woman named Farigis.

Abivard met the midwife in the courtyard, just inside the main gate. She bowed politely, then said, "Your pardon, lord, but I would sooner not stand about here making polite chitchat. Your wife has more need of me than you do right now."

"Of course," Abivard said, stepping aside to let her pass. She swept by him without a backward glance, her long coat trailing in the snow. Far from being offended, Abivard was relieved: to his way of thinking, anyone who put business ahead of conversation was likely to know that business.

He did not follow Farigis into the women's quarters. For one thing, he suspected she would have thrown him out, and in such matters her word, not his, was law. And for another, childbirth was a women's mystery that frightened him worse than any of the armored lancers he had faced during the civil war: this was a battlefield on which he could not contend.

As he paced the hall outside his bedchamber, he murmured, "Lady Shivini, if you'll hear the prayer of a mere man, help bring my lady through her ordeal." That done, he went back to pacing. He wanted to send the prayer up again and again but refrained, fearing he would anger the prophet if he seemed to nag.

After a while Frada took him by the arm, led him into the kitchens, sat him down, and set a mug of wine in front of him. He drank mechanically, hardly aware of what he was doing.

"This is taking a very long time," he said presently.

"It can do that, you know," Frada answered, although he knew less about the matter than Abivard did, which, given the level of Abivard's ignorance, was not easy. He picked up Abivard's empty mug and carried it away, returning a moment later with it full and a matching one for himself in his other hand.

Every time a serving woman came into the kitchens, Abivard jumped, thinking either that she was Farigis or that she brought word from the midwife. But the sun had set and darkness settled over the stronghold like a cloak before Farigis came forth. Abivard sprang to his feet. The smile on the midwife's face told him everything he needed to know, but he stammered out his questions anyhow. "Is she . . . ? Is the baby . . . ?"

"Both well, and you have a son, as I gather Tanshar told you that you would," Farigis answered. "A good-size lad, and he cries as loud as any I've heard, which is good, though your lady won't think so when he wakes up howling a few weeks from now. She says you'll name him for your brother. The God grant him a long and healthy life."

"May I see her?" Abivard asked, and then, correcting himself, "May I see them?"

"Aye, though she's very tired," the midwife said. "I don't know how long she'll want to see you, and this once, lord, you'd do well to let your wife's wishes prevail, not your own."

"My wife's wishes prevail more often than you think," Abivard told her. She didn't seem much impressed; Abivard got the feeling she was anything but easy to impress. The sweet jingle of the silver arkets with which he paid her fee, though, definitely gained her complete, undivided, and approving attention.

"Congratulations, lord!" The call followed Abivard through the stronghold to the door of his bedchamber, then picked up again, higher-pitched, in the women's quarters.

Roshnani looked up when he came into her room. Farigis had warned him she was weary, but the exhaustion she showed shocked him. Beneath her naturally swarthy cast of skin, she was dead pale. The room smelled of stale sweat, as if she had labored in the fields rather than in childbed.

"Are you all right?" he asked, alarmed.

The corners of her mouth turned upward in what would have looked more like a smile had it come with less obvious effort. She said, "If I could sleep for the next week, I might be well enough after that, but I doubt Varaz here will give me the chance." She shifted the blanket-covered bundle she held in the crook of her left elbow.

"Let me see him," Abivard said, and Roshnani lifted the soft lamb's wool from his son's face.

Again he was shocked, and again did his best not to show it. Varaz looked like nothing so much as a wizened little red monkey with an absurd fringe of hair like a bald old man's. His eyes were shut tight enough to pull his whole face into a grimace. He breathed in little snorting grunts and occasionally twitched for no reason at all.

"He's a handsome boy," Abivard declared, the most sincere lie he had ever told.

"Isn't he?" Roshnani said proudly. Either she was lying, too, or mother love—or possibly the rigors of childbirth—had left her blind.

Abivard would have bet on the latter—the longer he stared at Varaz, the better the baby looked. "May I hold him?" he asked, gulping a little. He knew how to hold newborn pups, but babies—especially this baby, his own baby—were something else again.

"Here." Roshnani held the wrapped bundle out to him. "Keep one hand under his head, mind you—he can't hold it up for himself."

"I don't blame him, poor chap," Abivard answered. "It's much the biggest part of him." Varaz squirmed as the transfer was made and threw out his arms and legs without waking up. Abivard carefully supported his head. "Once I was this small, with my father holding me. Could it be possible?"

"If you'd been born the size you are now, your poor mother would have been . . . upset is hardly the word," Roshnani returned. "Bringing forth even a baby is quite hard enough, thank you."

Abivard blinked, then laughed. "If you can joke, you'll get over it sooner than you think."

"May you be right." Roshnani yawned and said, "Set him in the cradle, would you? I'd like to sleep as long as he'll let me."

As if Varaz were made of parchment-thin glass, Abivard laid him down. When the corner of the baby's mouth brushed the blanket that lined the cradle, he made little sucking noises. Abivard kissed Roshnani and said, "Do rest. I hope he gives you plenty of chances."

"So do I," Roshnani said, "but that's in his hands, not mine." She yawned again. "Whatever chances he gives me, I'll take."

When Abivard had walked to his bedchamber the night he had come back to Vek Rud stronghold, too much wine had made him feel his feet were floating above the ground. He had drunk some wine waiting nervously while Roshnani delivered Varaz, but was for all practical purposes sober. Nevertheless, he floated much higher now than he had then.

Winter yielded to spring in its usual grudging, curmodgeonly way. Varaz thrived as if he were an early spring flower himself. Everyone exclaimed at his size, at his looks, at how enthusiastically he nursed. He quickly learned to smile. He had had Abivard's heart before, but with that he captured his father all over again.

The first crops were beginning to sprout when a dusty, muddy horseman made his way up the knob to Vek Rud stronghold, asking after Abivard. Men hurried to fetch the *dihqan*, for the rider bore word from Sharbaraz King of Kings.

He bowed when Abivard came before him and said, "Lord, I am bidden to deliver two messages to you. First is that your sister, the lady Denak, was before I departed for this domain delivered of a daughter, the princess Jarireh. She and the little one were both well when I left Mashiz."

"This for your good news," Abivard said, giving him a couple of arkets. He hoped Denak hadn't apologized to Sharbaraz for bearing a girl. He would have reckoned the news better still if she had had a boy, but as long as she had come through birth all right, she would have more chances for that later. He asked the horseman, "What is the King of Kings' other message?"

"Lord, it may not please you." The rider nervously licked his lips. "Sharbaraz King of Kings orders you to come to Mashiz as fast as you may."

"What?" Abivard said. "Does he say why?"

"He does not," the messenger said. "But there you are bidden. Would you presume to disobey the King of Kings?"

"Of course not," Abivard replied at once. He suddenly realized that being Sharbaraz' brother-in-law could bring him danger as well as privilege. If he didn't obey the King of Kings, even in the smallest particular, he ran the risk of being suspected of treachery or undue ambition—not that the two would look much different from Sharbaraz's point of view. If an obscure cousin could aspire to the throne, what of a less obscure brother-in-law?

Abivard had no more desire to become King of Kings than he did to climb up on the stronghold wall and jump off. He also had the feeling that the more he tried to convince Sharbaraz of that, the less Sharbaraz would believe him. He asked the messenger, "Does his Majesty want me to leave for Mashiz today?"

"Indeed he does, lord," the fellow answered. "I am to accompany you on the journey, and to make it as quick as may be." He pulled a pair of parchments from a message tube on his belt. "Here is his written order, which I have just delivered. And here is a command enabling us to draw on the stables of all the domains on the way back to the capital, thus speeding us on our way."

"He's in earnest, then," Abivard said, nodding. Only half in jest he added, "Have I your leave to make farewells before we set out?"

"Lord, I am your servant," the messenger said. "But we are both servants of Sharbaraz King of Kings, may his days be long and his realm increase."

"Well said," Abivard answered. "Here, come to the kitchens, take food and drink. I shall attend you as soon as I can." He called to one of his men to take the rider into the living quarters of the stronghold, then went looking for Frada.

His brothers' eyes snapped with excitement when Abivard gave him the news. "What do you suppose it means?" Frada asked. "Do you think we're at war with Videssos already?"

"I don't see how we could be," Abivard said. "Sharbaraz wouldn't attack Likinios without good reason, and Likinios went to too much trouble too recently to put Sharbaraz on the throne to give him a good reason so soon."

Frada made a clucking noise. "I'd argue with you, but I don't see how I can. But off you go again, and leave me behind to watch over the stronghold. It hardly seems fair." He laughed at Abivard's expression. "No, no, don't look like that. I'm just giving you a rough time. Whatever Sharbaraz wants, I expect I'll find out if there's a place in it for me. Maybe it's something to do with Denak."

"There's a thought," Abivard agreed. "You could be right— that might account for his not telling the messenger much." Now he knew he looked worried. "I hope it's nothing bad. But no, it could hardly be, not with the other word the fellow brought."

"You'll know fairly soon," Frada said. "Mashiz is a long way from here, but you won't have to fight any battles to get there, not this year."

"I'd better not!" Abivard exclaimed, laughing. He quickly grew serious once more. "That leaves you in charge of the domain again, brother of mine. I know you can run it—you've had more chance to show that than I have. Only one place where I'll tell you anything at all—"

"The women's quarters, I hope," Frada said.

"Why did I guess you were going to say that?" Abivard's chuckle was rueful. "As a matter of fact, though, you're right. Let my wives keep the privileges I've given them, but grant no new ones. If you need advice, you could do far worse than going to either Mother or Roshnani, or to both of them. If they agree, they're almost sure to be right. If they don't, you'll have to use your own judgment. Myself, I'm more inclined to think along with Roshnani."

Frada nodded. "I'll bear all that in mind. But it's not what I'm really worried about. That's simple: what do I do if one of your wives has a belly that starts to bulge?"

"I'll take care of *that*, by the God," Abivard said grimly. He hunted in the dirt of the courtyard till he found three black pebbles, then rounded up three witnesses. He chose men of unquestioned probity, among them Ganzak the smith, whom no one would have thought of doubting. With the witnesses watching, Abivard passed Frada the pebbles, saying, "To my brother I commit these, and give him my proxy to use them to divorce any wife of mine who adulterously gets herself with child while I am gone from the stronghold."

"I shall keep these pebbles safe against a day I hope never comes," Frada said, his voice solemn.

"We have seen your purpose, lord, and will speak of it should there be need," Ganzak said. "I also hope that day does not come." The heads of the other witnesses bobbed up and down.

"So do I," Abivard said. "But what I hope and what will be . . ." He let that hang. His brother and the witnesses all knew whereof he spoke.

By the time he went into the women's quarters, the messenger's news had already got there. He did not warn his wives he had left the pebbles with Frada; he doubted threats of that sort would keep them on the straight and narrow path if they were inclined to stray. And if they could not figure out that he might do such a thing, they were too foolish to belong in the women's quarters even as ornaments.

Roshnani said, "You won't have me nagging you to come along this time, husband of mine, not with Varaz still so small. I'll pray to the God that she bring you home quick and safe."

"I'll offer him the same prayer," Abivard answered.

Roshnani started to say something, closed her mouth on it, then cautiously tried again: "Will your other wives and I be confined to the women's quarters while you're away from the stronghold?"

"No," Abivard answered. "I've told Frada that your privileges are to remain the same."

That got him a hug fervent enough to squeeze the breath from him and to make him wish Sharbaraz's messenger wasn't waiting impatiently in the kitchens. Roshnani said, "Truly the God has been kind enough to grant me the most generous, most forbearing husband in all the world. I bless her for it and love him for it."

Abivard had intended to go on with something commonplace and fatuous about not abusing the privileges that would continue. Instead he stopped and stared. He and Roshnani had been man and wife for close to three years now; in all that time, he didn't think either of them had mentioned love. Marriages were made to bind families together. If you were lucky, you got on well with your wife, you could rely on her, and she gave good advice—to say nothing of an heir. All those things he had had with Roshnani. Anything more . . .

She was watching him warily, perhaps wondering if she had said too much. After a moment, he observed thoughtfully, "Do you know, wife of mine, until you named the name I didn't realize we had the thing it describes. That's a magic worthy of Tanshar at his best. And do you know what else? I'm angry at you because of it."

"You are? Why?" Roshnani asked, puzzled.

"Because now I'll be even sorrier to go away from you, and even more begrudging of every day till I'm home again." He squeezed her as hard as she had him.

"Those days will be empty for me, too," Roshnani said. But then, because she was a practical person, she laughed at her poetic pretension and said, "Well, not quite empty, not with Varaz filling them so. But I'll miss you more than I know how to say."

"I understand, because I feel the same way," he said, and then, cautiously: "I love you, too." He hugged her again. "And now I have to leave." He kissed her, then made his way quickly toward the door to the women's quarters. Because those steps were so hard to take, he made himself hurry them, lest he find he could not.

Sharbaraz's man was finishing his wine when Abivard walked into the kitchens. He got up from the bench on which he sat. "Let us be off, lord," he said. "If you will be so kind as to show me to the stables—"

"Certainly, although I would like the chance to ready a pack-horse before we set out," Abivard answered. "Strongholds, even villages, are few and far between up here in the northwest, and the land from one to the next often bad. If anything should go wrong, which the God prevent, I'd sooner not be stuck in the desert without any supplies at all. That's how vultures grow fat."

The messenger muttered under his breath but had to nod. Servants carried sacks of pocket bread and lamb sausage rich with garlic and mint and cardamom and skins of rough-edged red wine out to the stables, where grooms lashed them aboard a big gelding with good endurance.

A couple of hours before sunset, Sharbaraz's man swung up onto his horse with very visible relief. Abivard mounted, too, and put the packhorse on a long leather lead. With the messenger, he rode out of Vek Rud stronghold, down the knob on which it sat, and away toward the southeast.

As Abivard had predicted, the journey to Mashiz went far more smoothly than it had when he had set out for the capital with Sharbaraz two years before. Not only did no one take up arms against him as he traveled, but lesser nobles went out of their way to offer hospitality as extravagant as they could afford. Being brother-in-law to the King of Kings had its advantages.

So did the warrant Sharbaraz's man flourished whenever occasion arose. Not only did it entitle him and Abivard to fresh horses at their stops, but to victuals on demand. The bread and meat and wine Abivard had packed back at Vek Rud stronghold stayed all but untouched.

"I don't care," he said when the messenger remarked on that. "Who knows what might have happened if we didn't have them with us?"

"Something to that," the fellow admitted. "Things you get ready for have a way of not going wrong. It's the ones you don't look for that give you trouble."

Sharbaraz's rebellious army had swung south around the

Dilbat Mountains and then up through the desert toward Mashiz. Because the realm was at peace and the season approaching summer, Abivard and Sharbaraz's man traversed the passes through the mountains instead.

Abivard had thought he was used to high country. He had grown up atop a knob, after all, and he had scaled Nalgis Crag, which was a most impressive piece of stone all by itself. But looking up to steep mountains on either side of him reminded him of his insignificance in the grand scheme of things more forcefully even than the immense emptiness of the Pardrayan plain.

Fortresses in the passes could have held up an army indefinitely, both by their own strength and with the avalanches they could have unleashed against hostile troops. Seeing the gray stone piles and the heaped boulders, Abivard understood why Sharbaraz had never once considered forcing his way through the shorter route. He would not have reached Mashiz.

As things were, though, the officers who commanded the forts vied with one another to honor the brother-in-law of the King of Kings. The men struck him as being as much courtiers as soldiers, but the garrisons they commanded looked like good troops.

And then, early one morning, he and the messenger came round a last bend in the road and there, laid out before them as if through some great artist's brush, sat Mashiz, with the river valleys of the land of the Thousand Cities serving as distant backdrop. Abivard studied the scene for a long time. He had seen and even entered Mashiz from the east, but the capital of the realm took on a whole new aspect when viewed from the other direction.

"This is how it must have looked to our ancestors the God only knows how many years ago, when they first came off the high plateau of Makuran and saw the land they would make their own," he said.

The messenger shrugged. "I don't know anything about that, lord. I'm glad to see Mashiz again because I'm coming home to my wife and son."

"You took me away from mine," Abivard said, although not in real reproof: the man was but obeying the command of Sharbaraz King of Kings. "Lead me to the palace now, so I can learn the King of Kings' wishes and go back to my home once more."

In many ways, this was the first good look he had had at Mashiz. When he had entered it with Sharbaraz, he had been too busy fighting for his life to pay much attention to his surroundings, and then, just as he reached the palace, sorcerous darkness had swallowed the city. Now he took it all in: merchants and whores, servants of the God and horse traders, drunkards and servitors, farmers selling lettuces, farmers buying copper trinkets, singers, dancers, beggars, two men with picks stolidly knocking down a mud-brick wall, women hawking caged songbirds, and a thousand more besides. The noise was overwhelming, both in volume and variety.

Without the messenger to guide him, he would soon have been hopelessly lost. Streets writhed and twisted and doubled back on themselves, but Sharbaraz's man unerringly picked his way through the maze and toward the palace. At the gates, he turned Abivard over to a plump, beardless flunky and rode away.

At first Abivard thought the functionary was a man, although he had never seen a man without a beard. Then he thought the person was a woman, for the voice with which he was addressed seemed too high and smooth to belong to a man. But he had trouble imagining a woman in such a prominent position at the court of the King of Kings.

Then he realized he was dealing with a eunuch. He felt like a country bumpkin, unused to the sophisticated ways of the capital. As the courtier guided him to the throne room, though, he wondered what the fellow thought of his own state. Sophistication had its prices, too.

"Great and magnificent lord, I shall be beside you as you are presented to Sharbaraz King of Kings, may his years be many and his realm increase," the eunuch said. "At my signal, thus—" He touched Abivard on the arm. "—you are to prostrate yourself before him."

"As you say," Abivard agreed. Being brother-in-law to the King of Kings did not excuse him from any of the formalities of court ceremonial. If anything, it made his punctiliousness in observing those formalities more important than it would have been for someone of less exalted rank.

His feet glided soundlessly over thick wool carpets beautifully dyed and elaborately woven: carpets too fine to be walked upon anywhere save in the palace of the King of Kings. The torches that lit the hallways were of sandalwood; their sweet smoke filled the air. He had put on his best caftan to enter Mashiz, but felt woefully underdressed all the same.

"We approach the throne room," the eunuch murmured in his

strange, sexually ambiguous voice. "Walk beside me, as I told you, and be ready for my signal."

Courtiers, ministers, generals, and high nobles from the Seven Clans filled the throne room. Abivard felt their eyes on him and did his best to bear up under the scrutiny. He looked straight ahead and tried not to notice the grandees staring at him, studying him, taking his measure. They had to be wondering, *What is this backwoods noble like?*

Holding his own eyes on the throne helped him keep his composure. It was not, he saw, a single seat, but two. There sat Sharbaraz, unmistakable in his gorgeous robes and crown, but who was that beside him? The throne room was very long. Abivard had advanced halfway toward the high seats when he suddenly grinned an enormous grin and felt all his nervousness fall away—Denak sat next to her husband.

Now he looked around at the important personages who packed the throne room, to see how they liked the idea of having a woman—and not just any woman, but his sister!—in the company of the King of Kings. If they didn't like it, they didn't let on. That was as he had expected.

No one but Sharbaraz's guards stood closer than about five paces from the throne. The eunuch halted there. Like a well-trained horse, Abivard halted, too. The eunuch unobtrusively tapped him on the arm. He prostrated himself before the monarch of Makuran.

The carpet had stopped a few paces before. The stone to which Abivard pressed his forehead was worn smooth and shiny. He wondered how many prostrations had been performed just there over the centuries. He also noticed a thin, tiny seam that separated the stone on which he crouched from the one just ahead, and tried without any luck to figure out what it might mean.

"Rise, brother-in-law of mine, and advance to receive my favor," Sharbaraz said.

Abivard got to his feet and walked up to the throne. The guards stood aside to let him pass, but did not leave off watching him. Sharbaraz also rose, took two steps toward him, embraced him, and offered him a cheek to kiss, suggesting the two of them differed only slightly in rank. Tiny murmurs ran through the throne room as the courtiers, used to reading such subtle signs, drew their own conclusions. Denak beamed proudly.

"I have come to Mashiz in obedience to your command, Majesty," Abivard said, hoping Sharbaraz would give him some clue as to why he had been summoned.

But the King of Kings merely said, "That is as it should be. We have much to discuss, you and I, of great import to the realm." Again Abivard's ear caught those little ripples of whispering, this time, he thought, with an excited undertone to them. The assembled grandees knew what Sharbaraz was talking about, even if Abivard didn't. But, he thought proudly, the King of Kings wanted to confer with him, not with them.

After that formal greeting, Sharbaraz gave him back into the keeping of the eunuch, who led him into a little chamber of such perfect elegance that he guessed it had to be a waiting room for the King of Kings. A servant brought in roasted pistachios, little cakes savory with almond paste, and a wine sweet as honey, smooth as silk, and warming as the sun on a fine spring day.

Abivard refreshed himself, then piled some cushions high and leaned back against them to await his sovereign. Sure enough, Sharbaraz came in after a little while, Denak a pace behind him. When Abivard rose and began another prostration, Sharbaraz waved him to a halt. "You've finished the ceremony," he said. "Now we do business."

"May I see my niece first, Majesty?" Abivard asked.

"I'll go fetch her," Denak said, and hurried away.

"I have someone else I want you to meet, but I'll introduce him to you presently," Sharbaraz said. He took a pistachio, cracked the thin shell between thumb and forefinger, and popped the nut into his mouth.

Denak came back. She pressed a tiny bundle into Abivard's arms and smiled when he automatically held the baby so as to support her head. "That's right, you have a son of your own," she said, as if reminding herself. Was that jealousy in her voice? Maybe a little, he judged. She went on, "Hard to remember I'm an aunt, just as you're an uncle."

"She's a pretty baby," he said, looking down at Jarireh. Not only was she pretty, she was, for the moment, being quiet; that, as he had learned, was a virtue of considerable magnitude. "I'm trying to decide which of you she favors."

"She looks like a baby," Denak said, as if that explained everything.

Sharbaraz impatiently shifted from foot to foot. "I thought you were eager to hear why I summoned you across the length and breadth of the realm."

"I am, Majesty. It's only—" Abivard held up Jarireh. "May I use your daughter as my excuse?"

"You'd have trouble finding a better one," Sharbaraz said with a laugh. "But hear me all the same: Likinios Avtokrator is dead."

Ice ran through Abivard. "How did it happen?" he whispered. "Are you on decent terms with Hosios his son, or does the war begin now?"

"Hosios is dead, too, as Tanshar foretold," Sharbaraz said. Abivard could only gape at the King of Kings, who went on, "Hear the tale, as it came to me with the beginning of spring. You know Likinios Avtokrator was a pinchpenny; we saw that when we were in Serrhes. And you know also that the Empire of Videssos was at war with the nomads of Kubrat, up north and east of Videssos the city."

Abivard held his niece out to the King of Kings to show how confused he was. "What you say is true, Majesty, but what has one of these things to do with the other?"

"As it turns out, everything," Sharbaraz answered. "Likinios won a string of victories against the Kubratoi last year and hoped to ruin them for good and all, maybe even conquer them altogether. He didn't care to pull his army back into his own country and have to start over again this spring, so he ordered them to winter north of the Istros River, out on the edge of the steppe, and to support themselves by foraging. That way he wouldn't have to pay for feeding them through the winter, you see. He was already behind with their silver; no, I take it back, Videssians pay—or, in his case, don't pay—in gold."

"By the God," Abivard said softly. He tried to imagine a Makuraner army ordered to winter north of the Degird. Troops would, to put it mildly, not be happy about that. He had to ask the next question: "What happened then?"

"Just what you'd expect," Sharbaraz answered. "I can see that in your eyes. Aye, they mutinied, killed a couple of generals—"

"Not the Maniakai, I hope," Abivard exclaimed, and then remembered whom he had interrupted. "Forgive me, Majesty."

"It's all right," the King of Kings said. "This news is enough to make anyone jumpy. No, the Maniakai, father and son, had nothing to do with it. When they got back to Videssos, Likinios named the elder one governor of some island on the edge of nowhere and sent the younger there, too, to command the garrison. It was supposed to be a reward for a job well done, but I think the Avtokrator was just putting someone who might be a rival out of the way. Now, where was I with the main story?"

"The mutiny," Abivard and Denak said together.

"Ah, that's right. Likinios' army rebelled, as I say, killed some high-ranking officers, and named a fellow called Genesios as Avtokrator. The God only knows why; he was nothing more than a cavalry captain, a commander of a hundred. But they made some red boots, put 'em on him, and marched for Videssos the city."

"With that kind of leader against him, you'd think Likinios would have won easily," Abivard said.

"If they fought wars on parchment, you'd be right," Sharbaraz said, "but as soon as Likinios had a rival, any sort of rival, everyone stopped paying attention to him. This wasn't the first time he'd fallen behind with soldiers' pay, and everybody just got sick of him. He ordered troops out against Genesios. They left Videssos the city, sure enough, but then they went over to the rebel. That city could stand siege forever, I think, but the men at the gates opened them for Genesios' soldiers."

"Likinios should have fled," Abivard said. "He must have known you'd have received him well here, just for what he did for us in Serrhes."

"None of the sailors would take him and his sons across the little strait to the westlands," Sharbaraz said; the words tolled like doom through the little private chamber. Abivard picked up a pistachio, then put it back in its silver bowl—he had lost his appetite. The King of Kings went on, "In the end, he tried to get across in a boat he and his sons would row themselves. Too late: Genesios' men were already in the city. They caught him."

"And killed him, and Hosios, as you already told me," Abivard said.

"They did worse than that," Denak said; she had heard this tale of horror before. "They slew each of Likinios' sons before his eyes, Hosios his eldest last of all, and then they slew Likinios, too, a little bit at a time." She shuddered. "Filthy." Maybe because she had just had a baby herself, she seemed to find the idea of slaying anyone's child, particularly in front of him, especially dreadful.

"And that is how Genesios Avtokrator took the throne in Videssos," Sharbaraz said. "Part of it I've pieced together through the tales of travelers and merchants, and the rest from the embassy Genesios sent me to announce his accession as Avtokrator of the Videssians. Once he'd murdered his way into the palace, he decided he would start observing the forms, you see."

"What did you tell the envoys?" Abivard asked.

"I told them to leave the realm and be thankful I didn't clap them into the dungeons under the palace here," Sharbaraz answered. "I said I would not treat with men who served a ruler who had murdered my benefactor." His eyes flashed; thinking of Likinios' terrible end infuriated him. But he shook his head before going on, "I might have served my purpose better if I'd kept my temper and given them a soft answer. As things stand, Genesios knows I am his foe and can prepare accordingly."

"Do the Videssians all recognize him as Avtokrator?"

Sharbaraz shook his head again. "Videssos writhes like a snake with a broken back, seethes like a soup pot left too long over the fire. Some in the Empire support the usurper, some proclaim they are still loyal to the house of Likinios even though that house has been destroyed to the foundations, and I've heard rumors that another general, or maybe other generals, have proclaimed themselves Avtokrator in opposition to Genesios." He rubbed his hands together. "It is indeed a lovely mess."

"Aye, it is," Abivard breathed. "We had our civil war over these past years. Now it's the Videssians' turn, and from what you say, they have the disease worse than we did. What will you do, Majesty?"

"Let them stew in their own juice this year, I think, unless they fall altogether to pieces," Sharbaraz replied. "But I will take back all the stretch of Vaspurakan Likinios made me cede to him, and I will do it in the name of avenging him." He rubbed his hands again, plainly savoring the irony there. His voice turned dreamy. "But I want more than that, much more. And I have a key to open the lock. I'll show it to you." He hurried out of the chamber.

"What does he mean?" Abivard asked Denak.

She smiled. "I know, but I won't tell you, not when you'll see in a moment. That would spoil the surprise."

The King of Kings returned then, in the company of a young man gorgeous in Videssian imperial robes and shod with scarlet boots. He had a Videssian cast of feature, too, narrow and more delicate through the lower part of the face than most Makuraners. To Abivard he said, "It is good to see you again, eminent sir." He spoke with a strong Videssian accent.

"Forgive me, sir, but I do not believe we've met," Abivard

told him. Then he turned to the King of Kings. "Majesty, who is this fellow? I've never set eyes on him in my life."

"What?" Sharbaraz played startled confusion too melodramatically to be quite convincing. "Can you tell me you've been so quick to forget the face of Hosios son of Likinios, legitimate Avtokrator of the Videssians?"

"He's not Hosios," Abivard blurted. "I've seen Hosios and talked with him. I know what he looks like, and he . . ." His voice trailed away. He stared from Sharbaraz to the man who was not Hosios and back again. "I know what Hosios looks like, and you, Majesty, you know what Hosios looks like, but how many Videssians really know what Hosios looks like?"

"You see my thought perfectly," Sharbaraz said in a tone of voice that suggested anything less would have disappointed him. "As our armies move into Videssos, how better than if we come to restore the murdered rightful Avtokrator's son and heir? If the God grant that we reach Videssos the city than to install Hosios here—" He spoke the name with a perfectly straight face, "—in the imperial palace there?"

"No better way," Abivard said. He looked over to the fellow in the Videssian imperial costume. "Who are you really?"

The man glanced nervously at Sharbaraz. "Eminent sir, I am only and have always been Hosios son of Likinios. If I am not he, who that walks the earth is?"

Abivard thought it over, then slowly nodded. "When you put it that way, I suppose no one has a better claim to the name than you do."

"Just so." With justice, Sharbaraz sounded proud of his own cleverness. "Here we'll have the King of Kings and the Avtokrator leagued together against the vile usurper, just as we did against Smerdis. How can anyone hope to stand against us?"

"I see no way," Abivard said loyally. He knew, though, that ways he did not see might exist. That was why you went to war: to find out how well the plans you had made meshed with the real world.

He let his eyes slip to "Hosios" once more. Whoever he was—most likely a trader who happened to have been in Mashiz when Sharbaraz learned of Likinios' murder, or perhaps a renegade Videssian soldier—he had to be anxious, though he hid it fairly well. He was disposable, and was a fool to boot if he didn't know it. The first time he made Sharbaraz unhappy with him, he was only too likely to suffer a tragic accident . . . or maybe he would just disappear, and someone else styled "Hosios" would end up wearing the imperial raiment.

Sharbaraz said, "We understand each other well, Hosios and I."

"That's as it should be, Majesty," Abivard said. He glanced at the man who was now the only Hosios there was. Taking Videssos the city would be splendid; no King of Kings had ever done it, not in all the years of warfare between Makuran and the Empire of Videssos. But if Sharbaraz succeeded in capturing the imperial capital and put "Hosios" here on the throne, how long before the fellow forgot he was a puppet and remembered he was a Videssian? *Not long enough* was Abivard's guess.

"It was a pleasure to renew my acquaintance with the eminent sir, Majesty, but now—" "Hosios" paused.

"I know you have urgent business of your own," Sharbaraz said, again without obvious irony. "I shan't keep you here any longer."

"Hosios" bowed to him as equal to equal, though that rang as false as the King of Kings' ostentatious politeness toward him. The pretender nodded to Abivard, one sovereign to another's close companion, then left the small private chamber. Sharbaraz poured himself another cup of wine and looked a question to Abivard, who nodded. Sharbaraz poured one for him, too, and one for Denak.

Abivard raised his cup—not plain clay, as it would have been back at Vek Rud stronghold, but milky alabaster, bored out so thin he could see the wine through it. "I salute you, Majesty," he said. "I can't think of a better way for us to take vengeance on Videssos." He drank.

So did Sharbaraz and Denak. The King of Kings said, "And do you know what the best of it is, brother-in-law of mine? Not only are the Videssians themselves up in arms against this Genesios, but, from the word that filters through Vaspurakan and across the wasteland, the man would make the late unlamented Smerdis seem a paragon of statesmanship beside him."

"Have a care, there," Abivard said. "You almost made me choke on my wine. How could anyone make Smerdis look like a statesman?"

"Genesios manages, or so it's said," Sharbaraz answered. "Smerdis had some notion of keeping his enemies quiet: the tribute he paid to the Khamorth, for instance. The only thing Genesios seems to know how to do is murder. Killing Likinios and his sons made sense enough—"

"Not the way he did it," Denak broke in. "That was brutal and cruel."

"By all accounts, Genesios *is* brutal and cruel," Sharbaraz said, "and terror the only tool he turns to in ruling. He's meted out torture, blindings, and mutilation to all of Likinios' cronies he could catch, and each new tale that comes in is more revolting than the last. Part of that may spring from the nature of tales, but when you smell something bad, you're probably riding past a dung heap."

Thoughtfully Abivard said, "He'll frighten some folk into following him with ways like those, but most of them will be men who would have favored him anyway. He won't cow the ones he really aims to terrify, the ones with true spirit. They'll just hate him more than they do already."

"Just so," Sharbaraz agreed. "The more he tries to break their spirits, the more they'll do battle against him. But he holds Videssos the city, and if ever there was one, it's Videssos' Nalgis Crag, all but impossible to take without treachery." His grin was quite broad. "Our best course, I think, is to let it be known we have 'Hosios' here, wait while Videssos falls farther into chaos—and, by all appearances, it will—and then move in. If Genesios is as bad as latest rumors paint him, we truly will be welcomed as liberators."

"Isn't that a lovely thought?" Abivard said dreamily. "You said the two Maniakai were sent off to some distant island?"

"Aye. Likinios did that, not Genesios," Sharbaraz said.

"Either way, it's just as well. They'll be safe off at the edge of the world, where Genesios' eye can't fall on them. They're good men, the father and the son, and they did quite a lot for us. I don't want to see them come to harm."

"No?" Sharbaraz said. "I'd send up a loud, long prayer of thanks to the God and the Prophets Four if I heard Genesios had ordered both their heads to go up on the Milestone in Videssos the city. They'd be in good company, by all accounts; the Milestone's supposed to be a crowded place these days."

"Majesty!" Abivard said, as reproachfully as one could speak to the King of Kings. Denak nodded, agreeing with her brother rather than her husband.

Sharbaraz refused to apologize. "I meant what I said. Brother-in-law of mine, you said the Maniakai were good men, and you were right. But that's not the point—no, it is, but only a small part of it. The true rub is that the father and son are both of them *able* men. The more like that Genesios murders, the weaker Videssos will be when we move against her."

Abivard pondered his sovereign's words. At last, he bowed. "Spoken like a King of Kings."

Sharbaraz preened, ever so slightly. But Abivard hadn't altogether meant it as a compliment. A King of Kings had to do things for reasons of state and to look at them from his realm's viewpoint rather than his own. Thus far, well and good. When you began to forget your viewpoint as a man, though, and were willing, even eager, to celebrate the deaths of loyal friends, you became something rather frightening. That, to Abivard's way of thinking, was different from, and much worse than, recognizing that those deaths would be to your advantage while mourning them nonetheless.

He opened his mouth to try to explain that to Sharbaraz, then shut it again with the words unspoken. As he had discovered, what even a brother-in-law could tell the King of Kings had limits. The office Sharbaraz held, the robes he wore, worked toward stifling criticism of any sort. Oh, Abivard's head wouldn't answer for such an indiscretion; Sharbaraz would even listen politely—he owed Abivard that much, and did not think him a potential enemy . . . or Abivard hoped he didn't, at any rate. But while he would listen, he would not *hear*.

Sharbaraz said, "Your brother or his designee will be running Vek Rud domain for some time to come, brother-in-law of mine. I'll want you here at my right hand, readying our forces for the move against Videssos. We'll begin next year, I expect, and not just as raiders. What I take, I intend to keep."

"May it be so, Majesty," Abivard said. "I think I'll have to write to Frada to give him leave to appoint a designee and join the campaign himself. Otherwise, my guess is that he'd appoint one without my leave and come just the same. He's missed two chances already; he won't stand it a third time. Sometimes you need to know when to yield."

"A point," Sharbaraz said, though the only time he had yielded, so far as Abivard knew, was when Smerdis' minions held a knife to his throat. Abivard shook his head. No, the King of Kings had also given in when Likinios demanded territory in exchange for aid. In the face of necessity that dire, he could retreat.

"A good point," Denak said, and Abivard remembered that Sharbaraz had also yielded to her in a variety of ways, from letting her accompany him on campaign to allowing her to show herself in public here in the palace. No, he had done more than merely allow that: he had adjusted court ceremonial to accommodate it. Abivard revised his previous opinion—Sharbaraz could make concessions, after all.

Turning to his sister, Abivard asked, "How does it feel, living in the palace here at the capital instead of back at our domain?"

She considered that with almost the care Roshnani might have given it before answering. "There are good things here I could never have had in the stronghold." She glanced down at the sleeping Jarireh—remembering Kishmar and Onnophre, Abivard knew Denak could have had a baby in the women's quarters, but he kept quiet—then over to Sharbaraz. The King of Kings smiled as his eyes met hers; the two of them seemed well enough content with each other.

Denak went on, "But, at times, it's harder here. I often feel very much a stranger, which of course would never have happened back home. Some of the women in the women's quarters openly resent me for being principal wife when my blood's not of the highest."

"I've told them they'd better not," Sharbaraz said sharply. "When they've rendered a hundredth part of the service you have, then they may begin to complain."

"Oh, I don't much mind that," Denak said. "If I were in their slippers, I should probably resent me, too. The ones who frighten me, though, are those who spread on sweetness as if it were mutton fat on a chunk of pocket bread, when in their eyes I see them wishing I'd tread on a viper. You'd not see that sort of dissembling back at Vek Rud stronghold."

"No?" Abivard said. "You were already at Nalgis Crag when Ardini tried to bespell me, but you must have heard about it when you came home again."

"That's true; I did," Denak said in a small voice. "I'd forgotten." She laughed, perhaps in embarrassment, perhaps nervously. "Memory always makes the things you've left behind seem better than they really were, doesn't it?"

"Sometimes it can make bad things seem better than they were," Sharbaraz said. "Then it's a blessing from the God."

"And other times, when you sit and brood . . ." Denak didn't go on. She shook her head, angry at herself. "I try to forget, I truly do. But sometimes things swim up, all unbidden. It doesn't happen as often now as it did before."

"Good," Sharbaraz said. "If the God is kind, we have many years ahead of us in this world. Before the time your span is done, my principal wife, I pray your troubles will have vanished altogether from your mind."

"May it be so," Denak said. Abivard echoed her.

Sharbaraz turned to him. "Now you know part of why I summoned you here. As I told you, I'll want you to stay in Mashiz. You showed in the battles of the past two years that you're fit to be one of my great captains. You've hoped to lead an army against Videssos; now that hope comes true."

Abivard bowed. "Majesty, you could do me no greater honor."

Sharbaraz laughed. "That's not honor, brother-in-law of mine: That's because I need you. The other part of the reason I ordered you here to Mashiz was to do you honor. I shall lay on a great feast tonight, and summon courtiers and soldiers to see what sort of man has a sister fit for the King of Kings."

Now Abivard laughed nervously. "One with a northwestern accent and rustic ways, one from the lesser nobility rather than the Seven Clans—"

"One who makes too little of himself," Sharbaraz interrupted. "Remember, the purpose of the feast is to honor you, and I delight in doing so. Everyone there, no matter how high his blood, will be hoping you offer him a cheek to kiss; and for all of them, the choice will be yours."

"The prospect is . . . dizzying, Majesty," Abivard said. "That grandees from all over Makuran will be noting what I do, what I say . . . almost I wouldn't mind going back to obscurity, just for the sake of escaping that."

"If you hadn't said 'almost,' I would be angry with you," Sharbaraz answered. "I know you traveled here quickly, I know you're worn, and I know you'll want to be properly decked out to meet the court: clothes are armor of a sort. Sleep for a bit, if you care to; when you wake, or when we wake you, we'll see to it that you're properly bathed and groomed and dressed."

Sharbaraz and Denak left the little room. Abivard stretched out among the pillows on the floor and did fall asleep. A eunuch presently woke him and led him to a steaming chamber where he soaked in deliciously warm water, then rubbed scented oil on himself and scraped it off with a strigil, Videssian-style. A barber curled his hair and beard with hot irons, then waxed the tip of that beard and his mustachios to disciplined stiffness. He had to admire the image he made in a polished bronze mirror the barber handed him.

The caftan the eunuch brought him was of saffron silk shot

through with silver threads. He knew it must have come from the closet of the King of Kings and tried to protest, but the eunuch was gently implacable. Along with the caftan came a bucket-shaped *pilos*, also covered in saffron silk, for Abivard's head and a pair of sandals with heavy silver buckles. The sandals fit perfectly, which impressed him all over again, for his feet were smaller than Sharbaraz's.

When he was properly turned out, the eunuch conducted him to the dining hall. He hoped a servitor would conduct him back when the feast was done; he had doubts about finding his way around the immense palace without help.

A man with a big, deep voice called out his name when he entered the dining hall. Immediately he found himself under siege, for the courtiers and generals of Makuran converged on him to introduce themselves, to put forward their schemes, and to take his measure.

From what they said, every word that fell from his lips was a perfect pearl of wisdom. Until that evening, he had thought he knew what flattery meant. Listening to such fulsome praise was seductive, like having a sloe-eyed dancer sway before you while the tambours and pandouras poured forth a passionate tune. But, just as the dancer might take you to bed more in hope of a gold bracelet than for yourself, so the courtiers' fulsome words were also plainly self-seeking.

At last Abivard said, "Gentlemen, were I as wise as you make me out to be, which for a mortal man not of the Four seems scarcely possible, would I not see that you are interested in me as brother-in-law to Sharbaraz King of Kings, may his years be many and his realm increase, rather than as Abivard son of Godarz, who otherwise would scarcely draw your notice?"

That produced a sudden, thoughtful silence. The crush around him drew back a little. He hoped he hadn't offended the grandees of Makuran—but if he had, he would bear up under it.

Sharbaraz came in just then, with Denak on his arm. The arrival of the King of Kings cast all lesser luminaries, Abivard included, into the shade. The eunuchs presently began moving people to their proper places. Abivard was surprised to note that a couple of men had, like Sharbaraz, brought their wives with them to the feast. There as in other matters, the royal pleasure counted for a great deal.

Abivard took his place at Sharbaraz's right hand. Servitors fetched in wine, a sherbet of quinces and lemon juice, and another of rhubarb sweetened with honey. For the opening toast, everyone filled his cup with wine. Sharbaraz proclaimed, "Let us drink to Abivard, whom the King of Kings delights to honor!"

In return, Abivard rose and said, "Let us drink to the King of Kings, to the Makuran he rules, and to vengeance for Likinios Avtokrator!"

A storm of applause washed over him. "Hosios," who sat at the same table, clapped loud and long. Abivard wondered if his ambitions were for Sharbaraz and Makuran or for himself.

Then the waiters brought in tureens of soup, and Abivard stopped worrying about anything but his appetite. The soup was a simple one—yogurt thinned with water, finely chopped cucumber, and ground onions, with raisins sprinkled over the top. Salt was the only spice Abivard could taste. A peasant might have served the dish's like. Of its kind, though, it was as good as any Abivard had ever had.

After the soup came bowls of buttered rice topped with slices of mutton spiced with cloves, cinnamon, cardamom, and ground rosebuds. More yogurt and raw eggs accompanied the dish. Abivard spooned yogurt into his bowl, then broke two raw eggs and stirred them into the rice, too.

He didn't remember eating raw eggs in Videssos, and glanced over at "Hosios." The man who would take the place of Likinios' murdered son mixed eggs into his rice without a qualm. Abivard caught his eye and said, "You have a taste for Makuraner food, I see."

"So I do, eminent sir," "Hosios" answered. "I've eaten it a great many times, and find it tasty." Maybe he had been a merchant, then, and in the habit of going back and forth between Videssos and Makuran.

The servants cleared away the bowls after the feasters had emptied them. This time they set plates before the grandees: gleaming copper for those tables farthest from the King of Kings, silver for those closer, and gold for his table. Abivard stared at his platter. With such wealth as this at his command, Smerdis had chosen to squeeze his nobles to find money to pay the Khamorth! Truly the man had been a fool!

On the plates the servitors set pieces of braised duck cooked in a sweet-and-sour sauce of onions fired in sesame oil, pomegranate syrup, lemon juice, honey, pepper, and pistachios ground to powder. More pistachios, these chopped coarsely, were sprinkled over the duck. Abivard worried meat from the bones with knife and fingers, then dipped his hands into a bowl of rose-scented water and dried them on a square of pure white linen.

Talk and wine and sherbets occupied the meal. By the time he got down the last bite of fat-rich duck, Abivard was convinced, as he had been on the day he returned to Vek Rud stronghold, he would never need to eat again. He had been wrong then; he supposed he might be wrong now.

He soon found he was. From the kitchen came goblets filled with a compote of melon balls and peach slices in a syrup of honey, lime juice, and rose water. As a special treat, they were topped with snow brought down from the peaks of the Dilbat Mountains.

Abivard got to his feet. "Behold the power of the King of Kings, who brings snow to Mashiz in summer!" he called.

Again the nobles cheered—this time, he reckoned, for him and Sharbaraz both. Sharbaraz beamed. Abivard sat quickly down to enjoy the wonder; not all the power of the King of Kings could long keep snow from melting here at this season.

The snow glittered in the light of lamps and torches. That gleam called to mind Tanshar's last prophecy: a silver shield shining across a narrow sea. The sea, Abivard was suddenly certain, would be the strip of salt water that separated the Videssian westlands from Videssos the city, the great imperial capital. But who would make the shield shine, and why?

Abivard dug his spoon into the compote. When Sharbaraz moved against Videssos, he would find out.

HARRY TURTLEDOVE

Published by Del Rey Books.

DEL REY ONLINE!

The Del Rey Internet Newsletter...
A monthly electronic publication, posted on the Internet, GEnie, CompuServe, BIX, various BBSs, and the Panix gopher (gopher.panix.com). It features hype-free descriptions of books that are new in the stores, a list of our upcoming books, special announcements, a signing/reading/convention-attendance schedule for Del Rey authors, "In Depth" essays in which professionals in the field (authors, artists, designers, sales people, etc.) talk about their jobs in science fiction, a question-and-answer section, behind-the-scenes looks at sf publishing, and more!

Online editorial presence: Many of the Del Rey editors are online, on the Internet, GEnie, CompuServe, America Online, and Delphi. There is a Del Rey topic on GEnie and a Del Rey folder on America Online.

Our official e-mail address for Del Rey Books is delrey@randomhouse.com

Internet information source!
A lot of Del Rey material is available to the Internet on a gopher server: all back issues and the current issue of the Del Rey Internet Newsletter, a description of the DRIN and summaries of all the issues' contents, sample chapters of upcoming or current books (readable or downloadable for free), submission requirements, mail-order information, and much more. We will be adding more items of all sorts (mostly new DRINs and sample chapters) regularly. The address of the gopher is gopher.panix.com

Why? We at Del Rey realize that the networks are the medium of the future. That's where you'll find us promoting our books, socializing with others in the sf field, and—most importantly—making contact and sharing information with sf readers.

**For more information, e-mail ekh@panix.com